Fair Play

"Martin depicts the worlds of both professional hockey and ethnic Brooklyn with deftness and smart detail. She has an unerring eye for humorous family dynamics [and] sweet buoyancy." —*Publishers Weekly*

"Fast-paced, wisecracking, and an enjoyable story . . . Makes you feel like you're flying." —*Rendezvous*

"A fun and witty story . . . The depth of characterizations and the unexpectedly moving passages make this an exceptional romance and a must-read for all fans of the genre." —*Booklist*

"A fine sports romance that will score big-time . . . Martin has provided a winner." —*Midwest Book Review*

"Sure to delight both fans of professional ice hockey and those who enjoy a good romance." —*Affaire de Coeur*

continued . . .

Body Check

"Heartwarming."
—Booklist

"Combines sports and romance in a way that reminded me of Susan Elizabeth Phillips's *It Had To Be You*, but Deirdre Martin has her own style and voice. *Body Check* is one of the best first novels I have read in a long time."
—All About Romance
(Desert Island Keeper)

"Deirdre Martin aims for the net and scores with *Body Check*."
—The Romance Reader
(Four Hearts)

"You don't have to be a hockey fan to cheer for *Body Check*. Deirdre Martin brings readers a story that scores."
—The Word On Romance

"Fun, fast-paced, and sexy, *Body Check* is a dazzling debut."
—Millie Criswell, USA Today bestselling author of Mad About Mia

"Fun, delightful, emotional, and sexy, *Body Check* is an utterly enthralling, fast-paced novel. This is one author I eagerly look forward to reading more from."
—Romance Reviews Today

"An engaging romance that scores a hat trick [with] a fine supporting cast."
—The Best Reviews

TOTAL RUSH

Deirdre Martin

B

BERKLEY SENSATION, NEW YORK

THE BERKLEY PUBLISHING GROUP
Published by the Penguin Group
Penguin Group (USA) Inc.
375 Hudson Street, New York, New York 10014, USA
Penguin Group (Canada), 10 Alcorn Avenue, Toronto, Ontario M4V 3B2, Canada
(a division of Pearson Penguin Canada Inc.)
Penguin Books Ltd., 80 Strand, London WC2R 0RL, England
Penguin Group Ireland, 25 St. Stephen's Green, Dublin 2, Ireland (a division of Penguin Books Ltd.)
Penguin Group (Australia), 250 Camberwell Road, Camberwell, Victoria 3124, Australia
(a division of Pearson Australia Group Pty. Ltd.)
Penguin Books India Pvt. Ltd., 11 Community Centre, Panchsheel Park, New Delhi—110 017, India
Penguin Group (NZ), Cnr. Airborne and Rosedale Roads, Albany, Auckland 1310, New Zealand
(a division of Pearson New Zealand Ltd.)
Penguin Books (South Africa) (Pty.) Ltd., 24 Sturdee Avenue, Rosebank, Johannesburg 2196,
South Africa

Penguin Books Ltd., Registered Offices: 80 Strand, London WC2R 0RL, England

This is a work of fiction. Names, characters, places, and incidents either are the product of the author's imagination or are used fictitiously, and any resemblance to actual persons, living or dead, business establishments, events, or locales is entirely coincidental.

TOTAL RUSH

A Berkley Sensation Book / published by arrangement with the author

PRINTING HISTORY
Berkley Sensation edition / March 2005

Copyright © 2005 by Deirdre Martin.
Cover art by Monica Lind.
Cover design by Lesley Worrell.

ISBN: 0-425-20152-X

BERKLEY® SENSATION
Berkley Sensation Books are published by The Berkley Publishing Group,
a division of Penguin Group (USA) Inc.,
375 Hudson Street, New York, New York 10014.
BERKLEY SENSATION and the "B" design are trademarks belonging to Penguin Group (USA) Inc.

PRINTED IN THE UNITED STATES OF AMERICA

10   9   8   7   6   5   4   3   2   1

For my sister Allison,
with gratitude for her love and friendship

Special thanks to

Lt. Dave Burbank and Lt. Gillian Sharp of the Ithaca Fire Department, whose willingness to take me inside their world helped make this book possible. Also firefighter Rob Covert, my CISD source.

Lt. John Miles of Ladder 35/Engine 40 in Manhattan, for allowing me to see how it's done in the big city and answering my endless questions without complaint.

Assistant Fire Chief Mike Schnurle, Mark Spadolini, Wade Bardo, Dan Zajak, and anyone else I might have missed from IFD's "D" shift. Your hospitality and friendliness made all the difference in the world to me.

The firefighters of Ladder 35/Engine 40 in Manhattan.

Thanks also to

My husband, Mark Levine, for his incredible patience.

Roberta Caploe, for allowing me to put her gorgeous
apartment in three books.

Ken Dashow, for putting me in touch with
Lt. John Miles.

Maggie Shayne.

Rachel Dickinson.

Dr. Brian Carpenter.

Elaine English and Allison McCabe.

And last but not least, Mom, Dad, Bill, Allison, Beth,
Jane, Dave, and Tom, who, along with Mark and
"the lads," make everything worthwhile.

CHAPTER

01

"I need your help."

Looking up, Gemma Dante smiled as her cousin Michael came bounding to the counter of the Golden Bough. As usual, the cozy, welcoming bookstore in Greenwich Village was filled with customers, some browsing among the bookshelves, others lounging in one of the plump armchairs Gemma provided. Soft Celtic music played, while the faint scent of lavender incense filled the air. The sense of serenity had no effect on Michael Dante, however. Right winger for the New York Blades, he was a man always in a hurry, both on the ice and off.

Gemma stepped out from behind the counter to give her cousin an affectionate hug. "'I need your help,'" she repeated. "I think I'll have that carved on my tombstone." People instinctively came to her for aid and advice—not that she minded. She enjoyed playing the part of an offbeat Ann Landers to friends and family.

"Tombstone?" Michael feigned surprise. "I always figured when you went, you'd have some kind of moonlight ceremony where you'd be transformed into fairy dust and returned to the cosmos."

"Remember that old Squeeze song that begins, 'If I didn't love you, I'd hate you'? I think of you every time I hear it, Mikey."

"And I think of you every time I hear Donovan's 'Season of the Witch.'" He glanced around the store. "Not too many freaks today."

Gemma ignored the crack, returning to her post behind the cash register. "What can I do for you?"

"There's this new guy on the team, Ron Crabnutt. He was just called up from Rochester and he doesn't know a soul in the city apart from us guys. He's dying to go out with a 'real New York woman.' So I thought maybe—if you had time—you could break bread with him one night this week."

Gemma looked dubious. "Are you trying to set me up on a date?"

"No, no, no," Michael swore. "Well—yeah. It's an act of kindness, you know? For someone who's new to town."

"I thought I was too 'weird' for your teammates."

Michael snorted. "You're too good for them! If you saw some of the skanks these guys hung out with . . ." He shuddered.

"Good to know I'm one up on the skanks, Mikey."

He rounded the counter and gave her a bone-crushing squeeze. "Will you do it? He's a really nice guy, Gem, cross my heart. And who knows? Maybe you two will hit it off." He winked.

Gemma chuckled. "I'm not looking for a boyfriend."

"A relationship would be good for you."

Gemma changed the subject. "Speaking of relationships, how's Theresa? The baby?"

Michael smiled giddily. "Both doing great. The christening invitations just went out in the mail. You're coming, right?"

"Are you kidding? I wouldn't miss it for the world."

"Good. And Crabnutt? You'll have dinner with him?"

Gemma shrugged. "Okay. What have I got to lose? It might be fun."

"I knew I could count on you!"

"That'll be the second line on my tombstone."

Goddess, why did I let Mikey talk me into this? Gemma thought, struggling to keep her eyes from glazing over. She had agreed to do this as a favor, and because it might fun. Little did she know she'd be listening to someone drone on ecstatically about his screwdriver collection.

"Now, your clutchhead tips have four points of contact—"

"Excuse me," she interrupted Ron Crabnutt politely. "Could we talk about something other than screwdrivers?"

"Sure." Ron looked wounded. "What would you like to talk about?"

"How about politics?"

"Well, I gotta be honest with you . . ." A mild grimace tugged at Crabnutt's lower lip. "I don't really give a monkey's hinder about politics."

Gemma blinked. *Monkey's hinder?* "How about music, then?"

Ron's face lit up. "You like Skid Row?"

"Skid Row?"

"Don't tell me you've never heard of Skid Row!" Ron exclaimed, smacking the table in disbelief. "They're only the greatest band EVER."

Maybe talking about screwdrivers wasn't so bad after all. "I'm more into Celtic music myself. Solas, Loreena McKennitt . . ."

"Never heard of 'em," Ron grumbled. "If it doesn't make your teeth rattle, I don't want to know."

Gemma deflated. "Right." She decided to give it one

more try. Perhaps a conversational push in the right direction would reveal unimagined depth to his personality. "Do you have any hobbies besides the screwdrivers?" she asked.

"Other hobbies." Ron peered hard at his fork. "Hhmm."

The longer he took to answer, the more Gemma knew the only depth she'd be exploring would be that of her own despair.

"I like gum," Ron offered hopefully.

Gum, Gemma thought desperately. *I can work with that.*

"Collecting it or chewing it?"

"Chewing." Ron bobbed his head thoughtfully. "Definitely chewing."

"Me, too."

She would have called it a night right then, but she didn't have the heart. Ron looked so happy. And in the grand scheme of things, what was one night of her life? Sighing, she asked if he was a Bazooka or Juicy Fruit man. Another half hour passed. Crabnutt talked about Teaberry, curling, and then worked his way right back to Phillips cross slot screwdrivers. Not once did he ask Gemma what she did for a living or inquire what her hobbies were. Finally Gemma stifled a yawn. "It's getting late. I really should be going." She rose from the table.

Ron followed suit. "This was really fun," he confessed shyly. Gemma's heart went out to him. He was boring, but still. Uncomfortable, she peered down at her feet.

"Can I call you?"

Gemma lifted her head and saw Ron nervously pull at his collar. "Sure," she returned softly, completely against her better judgment. She couldn't stand the thought of hurting him. Besides, how many guys actually called after taking your number? She gave it to him.

Fastening the front of her cape, she was careful to lift the back of her hair out from under it. Ron paid the bill, and together they walked outside, where Gemma hailed a cab.

"Talk to you soon," Ron said cheerily as he closed the door of the cab for her.

Once inside, Gemma was glad the turbaned cabbie was blasting the Jets game on the FAN. She'd had enough conversation for one evening.

Early the next morning, Gemma went to meet her closest friend, Francis "Frankie" Hoffmann, for breakfast. New Yorkers knew Frankie as "Lady Midnight," a deejay whose sexy, deep-throated voice filled the airwaves between midnight and 6 A.M. every Monday through Friday on WROX, the city's top-rated classic rock station. Gemma often met Frankie for an early-morning cup of coffee. Afterward, Gemma would head to her store in the Village, and Frankie would go home to crash.

Their favorite meeting place was the Happy Fork Diner on Thirty-fourth and Eighth, a twenty-four-hour greasy spoon run by two burly Greek brothers. Pushing through the heavy glass door, Gemma was greeted by the familiar smell of fresh coffee brewing. Sliding onto a booth's narrow Naugahyde bench, she waited for Stavros to take her order.

"Ah, Miss Gemma." Despite girth a pro wrestler might envy, Stavros always appeared out of nowhere, the steaming coffeepot in his gigantic, hairy hand dangerously full. "One taste. C'mon. One sip and you will never want to drink that peeswater tea again."

Gemma clucked with mock disapproval. "You know I don't do caffeine, Stavros."

"So?" He jutted his chin out. "I bring you decaf. Best decaf in New York."

Gemma batted her eyes at him, enjoying their little ritual. "Chamomile tea will be fine, thank you."

"Bah," he muttered, turning from the table. "An old lady's drink."

He's right, it is an old lady drink.

Stavros returned with her tea, muttering under his breath in Greek as he served her. Just then Frankie pushed through the door of the diner. On the air, Frankie sounded like a wet dream, her low, husky radio voice and teasing, kittenish laugh the perfect vocal accompaniment for the overnight hours. All the male listeners who called during her air shift begging for a date assumed she was a major babe. In truth, she was tall and painfully thin, with wispy blond hair she had a hard time styling and a spray of freckles across the bridge of her tiny stub nose.

"Sorry I'm late," Frankie said in her real voice, pure Brooklynese. She slipped into the booth opposite Gemma. "The Rock showed up late." The Rock, whose real name was Marshall Finklestein, was the jock on the air right after Frankie. He had a chronic problem telling the big hand from the little one.

Gemma squeezed her steeping tea bag before tipping a smidgen of soy milk into her mug. "I listened a bit between two and three. You sounded good."

"I screwed up the lead-in to 'Layla,' but oh well. Win some, lose some." Her gaze turned quizzical as Gemma's words sank in. "What were you doing up between two and three?"

"Not sleeping."

"Because—?"

"This and that." She proceeded to tell Frankie all about her riveting evening with her blind date, Big Red. Frankie kept a straight face as long as she could. But when Gemma got to the part where Crabnutt expounded on the virtues of chewing gum as opposed to collecting it, she lost it. She burst out laughing, and so did Gemma. There were tears rolling down their faces by the time Gemma was done.

"Oh, Lordy," said Frankie, swiping at her eyes. "I needed that."

"So did I."

"So, why the insomnia?" Frankie still wanted to know.

"I don't know." Gemma looked genuinely baffled. "I guess the date just got me thinking. Suppose I never find anyone?"

"I'm insulted you would even think that."

Gemma laughed. When she and Frankie were teenagers, they'd vowed that if they were both alone when they were old, they'd move in together. They'd rent male strippers, sunbathe nude, and ride motorcycles.

"You know what I mean."

"You're not going to be alone forever," Frankie consoled.

The sympathetic tone acted as a tonic to Gemma. It always did. She and Frankie were as close as sisters. Then Frankie took a deep breath and said, "Okay, let me ask you something." Gemma stiffened. "Okay, let me ask you something" was Frankie's standard windup to hitting Gemma between the eyes with the brutal truth.

"What?"

"Can't you cast a love spell for yourself?"

Gemma squirmed uncomfortably in her seat. Of course she could. But to her, witchcraft was a path centered around the reverence for nature she'd carried deep within her since she was a child. It was not about trying to bend nature to your will.

"Well?" Frankie prodded.

"I suppose I could."

"What's the point of being a witch if you don't use it to help yourself?"

"Maybe I'll do a spell tonight."

"Can I watch?"

"Sure. As long as you don't interrupt."

"I won't, I swear!" The look of excitement in Frankie's eyes faded, replaced by one of unmistakable distraction.

"What's wrong?"

"Nothing," Frankie murmured dismissively.

"Tell me."

"I've been feeling kind of confused lately. Plus, I have this." She pushed up her shirt sleeve, revealing a blister on her left forearm.

"So?"

"Necrotizing fasciitis. Flesh-eating disease. I have it, Gemma."

Gemma sighed deeply. To say Frankie was a hypochondriac was an understatement. Over the past year alone, Frankie had diagnosed herself with a brain tumor, West Nile virus, Crohn's disease, and a host of other ailments, all of which mysteriously faded in their own in time. Gemma rued the day she'd bought Frankie *The Merck Manual* as a joke.

"You do not have flesh-eating disease," Gemma said patiently.

"Oh, no? Two of the symptoms are mental confusion and blisters, both of which I have!"

"Are you sure you didn't burn your arm taking something out of the oven?"

"I'm sure."

"Then call up Dr. Bollard and make an appointment."

"I'm going to."

Gemma knew Frankie wouldn't call. She never did. Instead, she'd walk around convinced she had flesh-eating disease—until new symptoms appeared and then she'd move on to her next self-diagnosed ailment.

Frankie leaned toward Gemma eagerly. "So, do I get to be your assistant tonight? Hand you your eye of newt or whatever?"

"I'm a witch, not a magician! I don't need an assistant. All I need from you," she added under her breath just as Stavros approached to take their breakfast order, "is to send positive thoughts my way while I work the spell. Think you can do that?"

"If you promise to make me black bean tostadas for dinner."

Gemma extended a hand across the table for a shake. "Done."

Gemma got home from work itching to cast her spell.

"Just let me get changed," she told Frankie, who'd been waiting for her in the lobby of her building, eager to begin.

Frankie nodded, following Gemma into her bedroom as she changed into sweats.

"I still can't believe how gorgeous this place is," Frankie marveled.

"I know." Gemma loved this apartment now just as much as she did the day she moved in. Rather than selling, her cousin Michael's wife Theresa decided to rent her beautiful two-bedroom apartment on the Upper East Side. It had shining parquet floors, high ceilings, and a wall of windows looking out on the Fifty-ninth Street Bridge. It was by far the best place Gemma had ever lived in.

"Now what?" Frankie asked excitedly as Gemma headed back out to the living room.

"Follow me."

She led Frankie into the spare room, which had built in floor-to-ceiling bookcases lining three walls that Gemma had already filled to overflowing. French doors led out to a small terrace where she grew her herbs. In the center of the room were three standing candelabrums, each with four tapers, and a low round table draped in purple velvet cloth. The table held a small vase of fresh flowers and an old cracked pentacle. To the left of the vase were a gold candle, a ritual knife, a censer for incense, and a bowl of salt. To the right were a white candle, a silver chalice, and a bowl of water. A small silver plate held a few pins, matches, and various cones of incense.

"Now what?" Frankie asked again, eyes fixed on Gemma's altar.

"I'm going to light the candles. You sit over there." She pointed to one of two meditation cushions on the floor. Were she alone, she would probably cast a more elaborate, intense spell. But since Frankie had the attention span of a three-year-old on Christmas morning, she decided some simple candle magick would suffice.

Frankie did as she was told, slipping off her shoes before twisting her gangly legs into a modified pretzel position. Gemma lit the standing tapers. The room blazed to life around them.

"Now what?" Frankie whispered.

"Now you stop asking, 'Now what?'" Gemma whispered back, amused. She settled down on her meditation cushion opposite Frankie, large red candle in hand. She lit it, placing it on the floor before her. Closing her eyes, she struggled to concentrate. The sound of snarled traffic drifted up to her ears, but she blocked it out. She waited until she felt absolutely centered before opening her eyes and speaking softly.

"Okay, here's what we're going to do. We're both going to stare into the flame of that candle. In my mind, I'm going to think about the man I want to be with. You can do the same if you want."

Frankie wrinkled her nose. "Think about the man I want to be with, or the man you want to be with?"

"Either."

"Can it be someone famous? Like Russell Crowe?"

"It can be anyone. Russell Crowe. Russell Stover. Just concentrate."

"Okay." Brows furrowed, Frankie stared hard into the candle while Gemma did the same.

Describe the man you want to be with, Gemma.

It took a few seconds, but then the words came to her: I want someone confident, smart, honest, hardworking, and strong. Someone who loves nature the way I do. Someone loyal and sensitive, who'll respect who I am and what I do. Someone who'll love me just as I am.

She poured herself into these thoughts until she ran out of words to describe her dream man. The next step was to picture him.

"Picture him," she whispered to Frankie.

"Who?" Frankie whispered back.

"Russell Stover," Gemma replied impatiently.

This was harder. In her mind's eye, Gemma saw the hazy outline of someone tall, but when she tried to fill in the details of his face, she couldn't. The only thing she saw were his eyes. They were green . . . no, blue. Blue and wise and full of compassion. She still couldn't see his face, but now she could hear his laugh—deep, hearty—and delight swept through her. She wanted someone who laughed often. Someone unafraid to feel.

"Gemma?"

"Mmm?"

"I keep trying to picture Russell Crowe, but the only man who keeps coming to mind is Damian."

Gemma shuddered. Damian was Frankie's ex-husband. "Concentrate harder."

"I can't," Frankie said helplessly.

"Then concentrate on someone for me."

"Okay."

They sat a few minutes more in silence. Gemma kept trying to picture more details of her dream man, but none were forthcoming. She glanced at Frankie hopefully.

"See anything?"

"I see . . . I see . . . a big, steaming tostada on a plate."

Gemma sighed.

"What about you?" Frankie wanted to know. "Anyone?"

"Someone tall, with kind blue eyes and a really good laugh."

"Sounds promising."

Gemma reached forward and gently snuffed out the red candle.

Frankie looked disappointed. "That's it? No incantations? No flying monkeys? Nothing?"

"Feel free to say an incantation if you want."

"That's your realm, Glinda, not mine."

"Then I guess the spell is complete." Gemma hugged her knees to her chest. "Let's just hope it worked."

CHAPTER

02

Riding her bike to work the next morning, Gemma was upbeat. With any luck, Mr. Right could walk into her life today.

Her friends and family thought she was nuts to bike in the city, but for Gemma, nothing could beat watching the world pull past as she pedaled along, cutting her own, slow swath through the breeze. It was magic to be in motion, especially now that summer's stifling humidity was finally beginning to fade into fall. Her attention was drawn to every attractive man she pedaled past—could the cute guy in the weathered bomber jacket be the future father of her children? What about that sandy-haired fellow with the cell phone glued to his ear? Maybe he had gorgeous blue eyes . . .

Man watching made her reckless: Twice she nearly crashed into parked cars.

Arriving at her store, she whipped off her helmet, shaking out her hair before unlocking the door and carefully wheeling her bike to the small storage room in the back.

She had just lit a cone of juniper tree incense and put on a Brigit's Kiss CD when the front door bell tinkled. Anticipation shot through her. Smoothing the front of her long, peasant skirt, Gemma perched as delicately as she could on the stool behind the counter, anxiously hoping she'd catch sight of her dream man.

"Hi."

The man standing before her was pale and weedy. His sunken chest was lost inside a wrinkled black T-shirt with BLESSED BE in large white letters across the front. Hanging limply from his chin was a long, straggling blond beard. Yes, he had blue eyes—but they were the color of washed-out denim, not a Caribbean ocean. Gemma's heart sank. Sometimes, what you wanted and what the universe decided to send you were two very different things. Still, she managed to come up with a smile. "Hello. May I help you?"

The man reached into his pocket, handing her a crumpled newspaper clipping. It was the ad she'd placed in the *Village Voice* offering tarot classes. It was a way to help offset the costs of her ever-spiraling store rent.

"You're interested in learning tarot?"

The man nodded.

"What's your name?"

"Uther."

Gemma bit her lip. In her opinion, telling strangers your name was Uther or Gwyddion or Raven only gave the public more ammunition for not taking witchcraft seriously. She knew it was a person's right to use their Craft name publicly, but *still.*

"Uther what?" she prompted.

"Abramowitz."

"Uther Abramowitz," Gemma repeated thoughtfully. Was it possible the universe had sent her someone named Uther Abramowitz to love? If so, she was going straight home and dismantling her altar. She extended a polite hand across the counter. "I'm Gemma Dante."

Uther's grasp was limp, like a wet sock. The urge to bundle him up and hustle him to the deli for some minestrone soup was strong. "What do you do?" Gemma prodded.

"I write computer code."

Gemma smiled. Lots of Pagans held high-tech jobs. She wasn't sure why. "Well," she said, sliding off her stool, "let me explain how I work. I give private lessons. I also give a group lesson on Thursday nights—"

"I'd prefer private," Uther cut in immediately.

"Okay." Gemma pulled out her Palm Pilot from beneath the counter. "I have an opening at eight o'clock on Tuesday nights. Does that work for you?"

Uther shook his head. "Not really. Can you do any during the day? When the curtain of night falls, I'm pretty busy."

Doing what? Gemma wondered. *Watching* Lord of the Rings *for the 500th time?* Actually, she didn't want to know. "Well, if you'd be willing to come in during your lunch hour, say between noon and one, I could squeeze you in on Tuesdays."

"At your humble abode?" he asked eagerly.

"No, here in the store." Gemma fought to ignore the overt way he was checking her out. Did she really want to be alone with this odd duck for an hour every week? As subtly as she could, she read his aura, something she'd been able to do ever since she was a child. It was gray. He was confused, not evil. She could handle that.

"I charge sixty dollars an hour."

"'Tis a fair fee," Uther replied.

"I should have told you seventy-five," Gemma joked, hoping to pierce his solemn demeanor. But Uther just blinked. "That was a joke," Gemma clarified.

"Oh," said Uther.

"You'll need your own Rider-Waite deck," she continued. "If you don't already have one, you can buy one here."

"I don't have one," he mumbled, shoving his hands deep in his pockets.

Slipping out from behind the counter, Gemma led him to the locked glass case where she kept the tarot cards. Some, like those she'd recommended to him, were very basic and reasonably priced. But she also carried unique, more expensive decks, like the Dali Universal Tarot as well as one set of the much-sought-after, now-out-of-print Shakespearean Tarot.

"What deck do you use?" Uther asked shyly.

"Rider-Waite." Gemma pulled out a set for him that came with an accompanying booklet. "I still use the set I bought when I was twelve."

"How old are you now?" he blurted.

Gemma felt a blush go up to the roots of her hair. "That, kind sir, is classified information." Cards in hand, she walked back to the counter to ring them up. Strange as he was, there was something about Uther's utter lack of social skills that touched her.

"You don't need to buy any books right now," she noted. "The book that comes with the set is pretty good. Plus, I use handouts. But a lot of people like to put their cards in a box or bag to protect them from negative energy when they're not in use." She pulled out her own cards, which she kept in a small, purple velvet bag. "Would you like to buy a bag?"

Uther cleared his throat nervously. "Not now."

"That's fine," Gemma assured him, ringing up his order. "That comes to twenty-one sixty-five."

Pulling out two twenties, he guided them shyly into her palm. Making change, Gemma continued, "What I'd like you to do before next week is get used to handling the cards. Spend a few minutes each day shuffling them, touching them, and laying them out. Look at the images. See if any trigger images or visions. Go wherever your mind leads you. It may feel strange at first, but what you're doing is enlivening your imagination and building a rapport with the cards."

"What if I have to miss a class?" Uther asked.

Gemma handed him one of her business cards she kept in a seashell beside the cash register. "Just call and leave a message here at the store." She smiled as she passed him his purchase in a plain white bag. "Anything else?"

Uther shook his head no.

"See you next Tuesday, then," Gemma concluded brightly.

Uther dipped his head shyly. "Many thanks," he said, holding the bag aloft. "I'll make sure to do my homework."

"Don't think of it that way," Gemma urged. "Think of it as fun."

"Fun," he repeated to himself as if the concept were foreign. Looking befuddled, Uther Abramowitz made his way out of the store.

Gemma watched him leave. *What if . . . ?*

She couldn't bear to finish the thought.

PLEASE STOP STINKING UP THE BUILDING.

After a hard day at work, Gemma longed to meditate before dinner, but last week, someone had slipped a note under her door. Taking a box of matches from the mantelpiece, she hesitated before lighting her favorite Indian incense. It was probably Mrs. Croppy, the old woman across the hall, who had written it. She lived to make other tenants' lives miserable. Gemma lit the incense. If Mrs. Croppy had something to say, she should say it face-to-face.

The incense and a few well-placed candles created instant serenity. Dragging one of her meditation cushions out to the center of the living room, Gemma sat down in full lotus position. Eyes closed, breathing slowly, her body felt almost weightless as she floated in a dreamy, fragrant white cloud. She was calm. She was well.

Until someone started pounding fiercely on her door.

"Fire department!" a voice shouted. "If anyone's in there, open up!"

Fire department?

Gemma unfolded her legs and headed quickly to the front door. Peering through the spy hole, she saw three New York City firefighters staring back at her. Dressed in full firefighting regalia, each was holding a tool that looked like it could pry her door off its hinges in three seconds flat.

She fumbled to open the door. "Can I help you?"

"Evening, ma'am," said a firefighter with the bluest eyes Gemma had ever seen. "We received a report of smoke coming from your apartment."

Peering past the handsome firefighter, Gemma saw the door to the apartment directly across the hall open a crack, then abruptly shut. *Mrs. Croppy.*

Gemma smiled politely. "I'm sorry, but there's been a mistake."

But Blue Eyes wasn't listening. He was craning his neck to see into the apartment. He brushed past her, the other two firefighters following suit. Speechless, Gemma trailed them, then realized what pulled them in: ribbons of thick white smoke curling in the air and hanging like smog.

"Ma'am?" asked a short and stocky firefighter. He had a graying handlebar mustache that made him look turn-of-the-century.

"It's incense," Gemma explained. The third firefighter, exotic as an Aztec with huge black eyes and smooth caramel skin, began coughing violently.

"Jesus H. Christ," he wheezed. "It smells like a funeral parlor in here."

"It's incense," Gemma repeated.

"Yeah, well, it stinks," Mustache said harshly.

"It's supposed to."

Aztec looked dubious.

Meanwhile, Blue Eyes—who, Gemma noticed, had the word BIRDMAN painted in bright yellow on the back of his heavy black rubber jacket—snuffed out the joss sticks.

Gemma couldn't believe his lack of manners. "Do you mind?"

"Do *I* mind?" Blue Eyes echoed, incredulity in his voice. "Excuse me a moment." He got on his two-way radio, announcing the call was a false alarm. Hearing those two words, Gemma felt terrible. His expression was serious as he turned his attention back to her.

"I can see it's incense, but your neighbors had no way of knowing that. They were right to call the fire department, especially if this stuff was seeping out under the doorway."

"It wasn't," Gemma insisted lamely. *Was it?*

Blue Eyes folded his arms across his chest. "Then why are we here?"

Gemma studied the floor.

"No offense, ma'am, but this incense is too strong." He removed his helmet. Thick, black curls sprang to life as those gorgeous eyes scoured the ceiling. Gemma felt a small flutter in the pit of her stomach. He was movie star handsome, with a strong jawline. And those eyes . . .

"Do you have a working smoke detector?"

Gemma turned pink. "I guess."

"You guess?"

She didn't want to tell him she'd deliberately removed the batteries from it precisely so she could burn this particular sweet, smoky incense. Blue Eyes was shaking his head. She caught the glance he exchanged with the other two firefighters and her blush deepened. *They think I'm a strange, eccentric idiot who burns repulsive, stinky incense and wastes the fire department's time.*

"Where is the smoke detector?" Blue Eyes asked.

"In the bedroom."

"Mind if we check it?"

"I take it that's a rhetorical question."

"Why, yes, ma'am, it is."

Gemma sighed her capitulation, and pointed the way then followed, praying she hadn't left the room in a mess. Blue Eyes flicked on the light switch inside the doorway. Her bed was indeed made; but one of her black silk teddies was flung against her carefully arranged pillows. It looked provocative, an invitation without words. She tried to ignore it as each of the firefighters' eyes darted to the item in question. Aztec sniggered audibly and Blue Eyes cracked "Nice jammies" under his breath, thinking she wouldn't hear.

"Thank you," Gemma said pointedly, and he looked distinctly uncomfortable. *Good,* Gemma thought. *That's what you get.*

Mustache unscrewed the top of the smoke detector. Gemma tensed, knowing what he would find.

"Ma'am?" he inquired politely, removing his helmet to scratch his head. Mustache was bald as a newborn. With the handlebar mustache, gleaming pate, and firefighter garb, he could moonlight as a member of the Village People. "There's no battery in this smoke detector."

Gemma feigned surprise. "Oh?"

"It's also older than God," Mustache continued. "You could use a new one."

"I'll get one first thing tomorrow."

Meanwhile, Blue Eyes's attention was drawn to the walls, decorated with photos of animals: whales, elephants, dolphins, and monkeys. Gemma caught his eyes darting to the picture of Michael and Theresa she kept on her dresser, along with other family photos. His gaze seemed to linger there before returning to the walls. He studied her wildlife photos quietly but seriously—so seriously that Aztec followed suit.

"You cut those out of *National Geographic*?" Aztec asked.

"No, I took them myself."

Blue Eyes's gaze locked on her. "Really?"

"Yes. I love animals. I like to vacation where there's wildlife."

"Interesting," Blue Eyes murmured.

Mustache rolled his eyes. "We done here, Marlin Perkins?"

Blue Eyes gave Mustache a scowl, and Gemma was glad not to be on the receiving end of it. His expression remained grave as he addressed her. "You realize if there'd been an actual fire in here, it could have been quite serious, ma'am?"

"Please. My name is Gemma." *When did I go from a "miss" to a "ma'am"?*

"Gemma," Blue Eyes repeated, trying it out. "Interesting name."

"Thank you." Gemma's smile was genuine.

"Please get some fresh batteries and a new detector," he continued. "If not for your own safety, then for the safety of others in the building."

"I will," she promised. "I'm sorry about this."

"You should be. This could have been quite serious."

But it wasn't, Gemma thought. Talk about beating a dead horse! Were they taught to do that? "Are we done here?" she asked.

Aztec nodded.

Turning off the light, Gemma led them back into her living room. Was there a protocol here? Was she supposed to offer them coffee or something, especially since this was a false alarm? Was she supposed to make a donation to the FDNY?

Blue Eyes turned to Gemma. "Would it be possible for you to burn a less smoky brand of incense, miss, um—"

"Dante," Gemma supplied.

"Dante," he echoed thoughtfully. "Could you do that? Please?"

"I suppose." She'd been using this brand of incense for years. Now, thanks to Mrs. Croppy, she was going to have to find something else.

"A less smoky brand wouldn't trip a smoke detector," Blue Eyes continued.

Gemma bit her lip. "What if I took the batteries out whenever I burned the incense?"

It was a bad question.

"Do you know how many people take the batteries out of detectors when they're cooking and forget to put them back?" Blue Eyes said wearily. "Look, just buy a new smoke detector, put the batteries in, and leave them there. In the meantime, try to find a less pungent brand of incense"—he sounded amused, which bugged Gemma—"burn it for a shorter period of time, and keep a window cracked. That should take care of the problem."

Then he smiled at her, his blue eyes so alive and full of life that Gemma thought, *Old soul, Good heart,* and goose bumps rose up on her arms. Ushering them to the front door, she apologized again for wasting their time.

"*Yo, Birdman, whaddaya* think? A wacko or what?"

Hanging up his turnout coat back at the station, Sean Kennealy turned to answer the question posed to him by Sal Ojeda, who, along with Mike Leary, had just helped him perpetrate a minor fraud on his neighbor.

"Could be." Sean shrugged. "I just hope she stops burning that crap."

"Oh, she will," Leary predicted, sliding out of his boots. "You were very professional."

Sean chuckled. For over a month, the smell coming out of Theresa Falconetti's old apartment had been driving him crazy. He'd come home from his shift, desperate for sleep, but he couldn't. The stinky smell wafting its way to his apartment was so strong it was suffocating. Opening all of his windows didn't help. The stink clung to the air, tormenting him. One morning, sleep deprived and pissed off, he slipped a note under the apartment's door, hoping that would do the trick.

Then two nights later the stench returned.

That bugged him.

Years earlier, someone down the hall had complained that Pete and Roger squawked their heads off whenever he wasn't home. He'd tracked down a vet who was able to prescribe some antianxiety meds. Presto! Problem solved. If he could respond to a neighbor's request, why couldn't the incense burner? Was his note too nasty? True, he'd scribbled it in haste. Maybe he should have knocked on the door and asked The Stinker to stop? But he was in no mood to get into it with someone who might be a wacko. What kind of person *wants* their apartment to smell like that?

Instead, Sean asked two of his buddies from the firehouse to help him take care of the problem once and for all. They waited until their shift was over, then bunkered up and walked over to his building on Fifty-ninth and First, feeling like three naughty schoolboys. Seeing where he lived, Leary and Ojeda razzed him about being Yuppie scum, but Sean offered no apologies. Years back, he'd worked hard on Wall Street to buy his apartment. Now he owned it outright and was proud of it.

"You catch that teddy on the bed?" Leary drawled. "I bet she was waiting for her guru to come over and take her to a higher plane, if you know what I mean."

Ojeda laughed. "All the way to nirvana, baby."

Sean laughed, too. He had expected The Stinker to be

some kind of urban ascetic, gaunt and unsmiling. Instead,
the door was opened by a tiny, curvaceous woman with
wild, tumbling red hair and the kindest eyes he had ever
seen. Her poise impressed him; so had the photos on her
bedroom walls. Leary's "Marlin Perkins" crack had annoyed him, because it kept him from finding out more
about Gemma Dante, who was obviously related to the
hockey player, Michael Dante, Theresa's husband. The
photo on the dresser was a dead giveaway. Was Gemma his
sister?

On the other hand, Leary's ribbing was a good thing.
Yeah, they rode him hard about being "Birdman," but teasing the shit out of the guys at the house was a firefighter's
favorite pastime. Since he'd come from Wall Street, it had
taken them a long time to accept him. The wisecracks
meant he was one of them.

Down the hall, the current shift at Engine 31/Ladder 29
was sitting down to dinner. Sean could smell the enticing
aroma of Al Dugan's famous "Help! My butt's on fire!"
chili as it wafted onto the apparatus floor, making his
stomach rumble.

"You guys up for a burger and a beer?" he asked.

"Depends," Ojeda said. "You paying?"

"What, in return for services rendered?"

"Shit, you make us sound like hookers," Leary said. He
turned to Ojeda. "Don't make the man pay for a favor, you
cheap little bastard."

"What?" Ojeda whined. "It's burgers and beers, for
Chrissakes, not filet mignon and Dom."

Leary thought a moment then turned back to Sean. "The
little bastard's got a point."

Sean grinned. "Geez, if I'd known you two were such
cheap dates, I'd have asked you out sooner. Shall we?"

Together, the three men left the firehouse and headed
down the street.

                    •   •   •

The first thing Gemma did when she saw her cousin Michael in the green room at Met Gar the next night was playfully punch him in the arm.

"Ouch!" Michael recoiled, rubbing the spot where her fist had landed. "What was *that* for?"

"That blind date you set me up on! All he talked about was screwdrivers and *gum!*"

"He's a nice guy!" Michael retorted.

"There's a difference between nice and boring."

Michael shrugged philosophically. "So it didn't work out. What matters is you did a nice thing, right?"

"True."

"C'mere, give cousin Mikey a hug, you do-gooder, you."

Gemma stepped into her cousin's embrace. It always amazed her how solid he felt. He'd been a scrawny little thing when they were kids, all pointy elbows and knobby knees and lack of coordination. And now look at him, Gemma marveled. Mr. NHL Bigshot.

And happily married, too, to the woman of his dreams, with a new baby girl. Pride burgeoned within Gemma as she recalled the pivotal role she'd played in getting Michael and Theresa together. It hadn't been easy; both were stubborn as mules, not to mention melodramatic. But with a little help from some tarot cards and a big, heaping dose of Dante family–style meddling, she'd helped them past their foolish pride and into each other's arms.

"So, who are you playing tonight?" she asked as they gently broke their embrace.

Utter disbelief flitted across Michael's face. "Do you ever bother to crack open a newspaper? Or are you too busy stirring your cauldron?"

"You're hilarious."

"I try."

"Seriously, Michael, who are you playing?" Gemma repeated, pushing back the hair from her forehead. Sometimes she just wanted to cut it all off, it was so wavy and unruly. "I've been really, really busy, I didn't have time—"

"Sshh." He put his index finger to her lips. "Relax. It's okay." Removing his hand, he said, "We're playing an exhibition game against the FDNY hockey team. The proceeds will benefit the Uniformed Firefighters Association Scholarship Fund. It's for kids whose dads got badly burned, or, you know . . ."

Died, Gemma supplied in her head. *Kids whose dads died.* Though it had been over four years since 9/11, it was still hard for New Yorkers to talk about it. Gemma nodded her understanding.

"I had a little adventure with the fire department myself," she said, trying to lighten the mood. She told Michael about the incense and the false alarm.

His response was typical. "Well, if it was the same stuff you burn in the store, I'm not surprised someone called the fire department. You could clear the block with that crap."

Gemma clucked her tongue. "You're an idiot, you know that?"

"Yeah, but you love me, anyway." His eyes shot to the clock on the wall. "I gotta go get dressed. You know where to sit, right?"

"Of course." Gemma glanced around the green room. She recognized some of the players there. The rest, she assumed, were members of the players' families, just like her. But why was she the only Dante present? "Theresa is coming, right?"

"Yeah, she's just running behind. She'll be here."

"And Anthony?"

Anthony was Michael's older brother, as well as the head chef and half owner of the family restaurant they owned in Brooklyn, Dante's. Hearing Gemma's question, Michael guffawed.

"Yeah, right. Like I could get him to leave his battle station at the stove on a Saturday night." He launched into an imitation of his brother. "'I run a business, Mikey. I can't just drop my freakin' ladle and run every time you shoot a puck down the friggin' ice for some *ubatz* charity.'"

The impersonation was so accurate Gemma erupted into appreciative laughter. "I guess that answers the question." Rising up on tiptoes, she gave Michael a kiss on the cheek. "I'm kind of beat, so I don't know if I'll see you after the game. But good luck."

"Thanks." He went to leave, then turned back, eyes gleaming with mischief. "Oh, and Gem?"

"Yeah?"

"We're the guys in blue and white with BLADES written on the front of our jerseys. Just so you know."

CHAPTER

03

Met Gar was packed. Gazing at the sea of exuberant faces as she took her seat behind the Blades' bench, Gemma noticed most of the people were families, many wearing T-shirts and baseball caps bearing the FDNY logo. Watching a father ruffle his young daughter's hair before rising to order a hot dog for each of them, Gemma ached with envy and longing. Though she adored her family, she was considered somewhat of a "black sheep." Her eyes continued surveying the buzzing crowd, her attention drawn to the many children there. How many were fatherless? How many had lost cousins, uncles, sons, brothers? Like most New Yorkers, she'd pretty much taken firefighters and what they did for granted. That is, until over three hundred of them died trying to save others on a bright, clear morning in September. Ever since then, they'd been lauded as heroes and christened sex symbols. Gemma hadn't thought about them being sexy until Blue Eyes and his cohorts came pounding on her door.

Blue Eyes. Just picturing his handsome, rugged face

made her run hot and cold all over. She wondered if he was here to cheer his buddies on, and if so, if their paths might cross.

"There you are!"

At the sound of Theresa's voice, Gemma turned. Silly though it was, she was feeling semiconspicuous sitting there alone, wondering if the surrounding families thought she was a puck bunny. She certainly didn't dress like a hockey groupie; that much she knew for sure. Unless bunnies had taken to wearing chunky, silver earrings, flowing floral scarfs, and maroon velvet trousers.

"Hey, you." Theresa's smile was warm as she maneuvered herself into a seat. "Know how I knew you were already here?"

"How?"

Theresa lifted her nose in the air and sniffed. "Your perfume. Very distinctive."

Gemma chuckled. "Is that good or bad?"

"It's good. Kind of tangerine-y." Theresa took in the crowd. "*Madonn',* the place is packed."

"They'll raise a lot of money."

"Hope so."

Reaching into her purse, Theresa took out a scrunchie and pulled her black, wavy hair into a loose ponytail. Gemma detected a few strands of gray in the mix; not that it mattered. If anything, it made the beautiful Theresa look even more exotic. Though she did look tired in that way many new mothers do.

"So, how's the baby?" Gemma wanted to know, squeezing Theresa's arm.

Theresa's smile was weary but happy. "Great."

"Have you named her yet?" Though their daughter was a month old, Theresa and Michael had yet to agree on a name. Michael wanted Philomena, after his mother. Theresa's reaction had been concise: "Over my dead body." Theresa was pushing hard for Galen. Michael said that sounded like an antacid.

"The way we're going, she's going to wind up being called 'Miss X.' "

Gemma smiled sympathetically. "Don't worry, you'll come up with something." Taking the jumbo-sized bottle of Evian from Theresa's hand, she helped herself to a sip. "I'm surprised you're here. I thought for sure you'd be home with Miss X."

"The first baby ever born in the history of the world is with my mother, God save her tiny, unnamed soul. No, I'm here because one of the Blades is a client and he's slated to do an interview after the game. I want to make sure he doesn't say anything stupid." She took the water back from Gemma. "And I wanted to support Michael, of course."

"Of course."

Gemma opened her mouth to say something else but was drowned out by the blaring horn signaling the game was about to begin. Since it was a charity game, they'd be playing only two periods. Though she enjoyed watching her cousin play, Gemma wasn't a big sports fan in general. She traced it back to elementary school phys ed, when she was always chosen last for basketball because of her height and teased unmercifully for her inability to hit a softball.

Since Met Gar was the Blades' home ice, they skated out first. A rousing cheer rose up from the crowd as each player skated out into the spotlight. Gemma noticed that Michael, especially, got a thundering reception, proof of his status as hometown favorite. He loved it, too, waving and smiling as he made a circuit round the ice before gliding to the players' bench.

"Your husband is such a ham," she remarked to Theresa, who heartily agreed.

As loud as the cheers were for the Blades, the decibel level went sky high when the FDNY hockey team appeared, their bright red jerseys dazzling against the white ice. Unlike the Blades, the players for the fire department hockey team came in all shapes and sizes. There were neckless little runts who would be pulverized by one modest hit from a Blades defenseman, refrigerator-sized brutes, and tall, sleek geeks Gemma could envision being blown over by the passing breeze created by a fast-skating teammate.

And there was Blue Eyes.

She turned to Theresa. "Do you have a program?"

"Sure."

Gemma eagerly flipped through the pages until she came to the FDNY players. There he was, Number 45, Sean Kennealy of Ladder 29 Company. Kennealy. Of course. Blue eyes, dark hair . . . he was "Black Irish."

Sean Kennealy. He was playing defense, probably because of his size. He was huge. Strapping. A strapping Irishman.

The puck dropped, and then both sides were in motion, one of the Blades carrying the puck, of course.

Since it was a charity game, the Blades weren't playing as hard or fast as usual. None of them really checked any of the firefighters, and the tempo of the skating was turned down a notch. That is, until the FDNY team scored a goal seven minutes in. After that, the Blades decided to be a little less kind.

None of it mattered to Gemma. Her eyes were glued to Sean Kennealy, whether he was on the ice or off it. She was no hockey expert, true, but he seemed fearless when he played, his expression as menacing as that of any NHL defensemen. Nor did he seem to shy from physical contact; unless Gemma was mistaken, he was one of the few FDNY players actually daring to fully check members of the Blades' offense. The game ended in a tie—"Rigged," Theresa whispered to Gemma—and people began the slow, shuffling departure from Met Gar.

"So," Theresa said to Gemma, "will I see you at Miss X's christening next weekend?"

"Of course." Gemma's eyes were still on the ice, picturing Sean as he confidently checked her own cousin.

Theresa leaned over to whisper in her ear. "Earth to Gemma, game's over."

Gemma turned to Theresa, smiling apologetically. "Sorry."

Filing out of the arena, she discreetly tucked the evening's program into her bag.

"I'm surprised the altar didn't burst into flames when you walked into church."

Ignoring her cousin Anthony's comment, Gemma rose up on tiptoes to plant an affectionate kiss on his cheek. They were standing among family and friends outside St. Finbar's Church in Bensonhurst, where Michael and Theresa had just had their infant daughter christened. Gemma had blanched when she'd heard the name they settled on: Domenica. Domenica Dante. It sounded like a deranged Italian film director. But she understood why they'd chosen it: They were honoring Theresa's father, Dominic, who had passed away two and a half years earlier.

Gemma's gaze ranged over the noisy group assembled on the church steps. She watched as her relatives jostled each other for their turn to have their picture snapped holding the baby, who was serene as a doll in her antique ivory gown. Gemma knew Anthony's wisecrack wasn't malicious, but it still smarted.

Happy tears had flooded Gemma's eyes during the ceremony. She'd watched Michael and Theresa lovingly convey their daughter from the front pew up to the baptismal font, accompanied by the godparents: Anthony, and Theresa's best friend, Janna. Gemma had been able to say hi to Janna and her husband Ty before the ceremony, but hadn't had a chance to chat with Anthony and his wife until now.

In fact . . .

"Where's Angie?"

Anthony frowned. "On duty. Couldn't get off. She's gonna try and swing by the party later."

The party was being held at Dante's a few blocks away. Once a neighborhood secret, it had become outrageously trendy. Anthony claimed he hated the Manhattanites who now descended regularly, but Gemma never heard him complain about all the money the restaurant was generating.

The baby, whom Gemma was aching to hold, had just been passed to cousin Paul, who had come in from Long Island with his wife and kids. Gemma started to move toward them—it had been months since she'd seen Paul and his family—but stopped dead in her tracks. Her mother, Aunt Betty Anne, and Aunt Millie were marching down the church steps heading straight for her. Anthony, rather than sentimentally noting that his late mother, the fourth Grimaldi sister, was missing, nudged Gemma in the ribs. "Heads up. Here come Mo, Larry, and Curly."

Gemma moved tentatively in the direction of her mother, who had pointedly ignored her in church. *Please don't make a scene, Mom.*

"Hello, Mom." Gemma leaned in to kiss her mother's cheek; her mother flinched slightly. She also kissed her aunts. Millie covertly winked at her as if to say, "Don't mind your mother," but Betty Anne was cold as marble.

"You look good," Aunt Millie croaked, her gravelly voice betraying her lifelong, three-pack-a-day Winston habit.

"I can't believe you came to church," her mother snapped.

"I was invited, Mom." Gemma was determined not to take the bait. "I'm a member of this family, too."

"You should have just come to the party. To show up at the house of God . . ." She made the sign of the cross while emitting a heavy theatrical sigh.

"Don't start," Gemma implored quietly.

"I'm not starting anything," her mother insisted shrilly, eyeing her younger sisters for backup. "Am I?"

Betty Anne's eyes fell to the ground. Millie excused herself for a smoke. That said it all. God forbid anyone stand up to Constance Annamaria Grimaldi Dante.

"I'm going to go talk to Nonna," Gemma informed her mother politely. *I tried,* she told herself. *That's what matters.*

Still, she felt like she'd been punched in the stomach.

She found her grandmother still inside the church, talking to one of the priests. Nonna's tiny, gnarled hands were waving madly, while the rapid-fire patter of her voice told Gemma that this priest was not number one in Nonna's hit parade. Gemma approached carefully, not wanting to interrupt. But the minute her grandmother caught sight of her, the tirade halted and she broke into a wide, delighted smile.

"*Bella,* I've been waiting for you!" She smiled knowingly at the young priest. "This is my granddaughter, Gemma. Bet you wish priests could get married, eh?"

"Nonna!" Gemma turned to the priest. "Please, Father. She didn't mean it."

The priest coughed uncomfortably and hurried off, clearly relieved to be free of speaking to an old devil like Nonna.

"I can't believe you did that!"

"What, told the truth?" Nonna snorted, watching the priest hustle up the center aisle of the church. "Tight ass," she added disdainfully.

"Nonna!" Gemma exclaimed again. Depending on who you asked, Maria Grimaldi was either "a pip," "a character," "a loon," or "a royal pain in the ass." To Gemma, she was simply Nonna, the grandmother she adored, and who loved her unconditionally.

"Here, let me look at you."

Gemma dutifully held still beneath her grandmother's loving eye, Nonna's head bobbing in approval. "Beautiful."

"You always say that."

"Because it's always true." Her hand clasped Gemma's forearm for support. Gemma jumped.

"Nonna, your hands are freezing!"

"My blood's getting too tired to make the full round." She waved a hand in the air. "It happens."

That was Nonna: no nonsense, philosophical about the passing of time. She'd been a great beauty, and to Gemma was beautiful still, with her long, white braid and her big, green eyes that were always alert, always watchful. "Have you held the bambina yet?" Nonna asked.

"Not yet. There's quite a crowd around her."

"She's gorgeous. Perfect. Her name is Theresa."

"Theresa is her mother, Nonna," Gemma laughed. "The baby is Domenica."

"Right, right," Nonna replied hastily. "Domenica." Slowly, they made their way toward the open church doors to join the rest of the family.

"So, your mother," Nonna began, her steps small and careful.

Gemma's eyes darted down to meet her grandmother's. "What about her?"

"Is she still upset about *La Stregheria,* or—?"

"Still upset."

"She needs a swift kick in the ass, that one."

Gemma chuckled. "A swift kick in the ass" was one of her grandmother's favorite expressions. It was actually made endearing by the soft edges of her Italian accent, which had worn away over the years.

"There's more than one way to worship, *cara.*"

"I agree with you there."

She gave Gemma's arm a squeeze. "You and me, we're a lot alike. Now, how about you give me a ride over to the restaurant?"

Nonna had the knack of turning a simple ten-minute jaunt into an hour-long production.

First, they had to stop by the house of Mrs. Crochetti, one of the women in Nonna's prayer circle, so Nonna could check up on her. Apparently, Mrs. Crochetti was suffering with a goiter. Next, Nonna had to be driven to the bakery to pick up bread, since it would be closed by the time the christening party was over. Finally, they had to go to Nonna's house to drop off the bread and pick up baby Domenica's christening gift, which required wrapping. By the time Gemma's battered old Beetle rattled into the restaurant parking lot, they were forty minutes late and the party was in full swing.

Gemma guided Nonna through the door, where they were bombarded by the sound of happy conversation among friends and relatives. The place was packed. Some people were already seated; others stood in small groups with drinks in hand, talking. It seemed more like a wedding reception than a baptismal bash for a tiny baby. Then again, Theresa was a publicist and Michael was the New York Blades' hometown hero. No wonder the room was packed.

"Who do you want to sit with?" Gemma asked her grandmother.

Nonna took her time assessing the crowd, finally pointing to a small, round table near the kitchen doors where Gemma's mother and her two sisters sat.

Gemma peered at her grandmother. "You sure? You might have more fun if you sat with someone else. Mussolini, for instance."

Nonna chuckled. "What could be more fun than making my daughters hot under the collar?"

"Well, don't come crying to me when Mom cuts you off after one glass of grappa."

As carefully as she could, Gemma maneuvered her grandmother through the dense, upbeat crowd. The baby was nowhere in sight. Theresa had probably taken her off somewhere to nurse. Seeing Gemma and Nonna approach the table, Gemma's mother frowned.

"We only have room for one here, and we're savin' this seat for Robert DeNiro."

Aunt Betty Anne gasped. "Bobby D is *here?*"

"Bobby D!" Aunt Millie snorted. "Like you know him!"

Betty Anne looked insulted. "We *do* go to the same podiatrist," she sniffed. "Bunions," she added knowingly.

"He's a client of Theresa's," Gemma's mother said. "He could come. You never know."

"He can go sit with Al Pacino, then," Gemma said as she helped Nonna into the empty seat.

"There goes our fun," Gemma mother's grumbled.

"Take a pill, will ya?" Aunt Millie snapped, lighting up. She squeezed Gemma's hand.

"Thanks for bringing her over here, doll. We'll make sure she stays out of trouble." She craned her neck, anxiously looking around the room. "I don't see Al Pacino."

Content her grandmother was now settled, Gemma headed for the bar. If anyone deserved a drink right now, it was her. That's when she saw him. Blue Eyes, Sean Kennealy, firefighter/hockey player in all his heart-stopping glory. He was holding a pint of beer and talking to Michael like they were old friends.

What was he doing here?

She made her way toward him, hoping she wouldn't face another lecture on fire safety. Michael's timing couldn't have been better: He moved off to speak with another cluster of guests just as Sean scoured the crowd and happened to light on Gemma. Seeing the smile on his face as their eyes met, Gemma felt a joyful heat surging through her body, radiant and strong.

"Hi," she said shyly, reaching his side.

"Hey." He seemed genuinely pleased to see her. "Gemma Dante, right?"

She nodded. "You have a good memory."

"It's not an easy name to forget." He squinted slightly, studying her face. "Are you Michael's sister?"

"No, we're double cousins." Seeing his puzzled expression, she added, "Our fathers were brothers and our mothers were sisters." Then she changed the subject. "How do you know Michael?"

"Through, uh, the FDNY hockey team."

"I was at the game the other night. The charity game."

Sean looked curious. "So, what did you think?"

"I think it was fixed."

Sean chuckled appreciatively. "The Blades probably could have played a little harder, you're right." He took a quick sip of beer. Gemma watched the bob of his Adam's apple as he swallowed and thought it the sexiest thing in the world. "But it's all for a good cause."

"I agree."

"Can I get you a drink?"

"That would be great."

"What's your pleasure?"

Better not answer that, she thought. "A gin and tonic would be great."

He smiled then, and it was killer. "Be back in a minute."

She watched as he made his way to the bar. God, he was a looker. And his body—muscled thighs evident through his faded jeans, strong shoulders swathed in a blue-and-white-striped oxford shirt, sleeves casually rolled. *No wedding ring.*

Taking her drink from him, she took a small sip, grateful for something to do with her hands. "Are you ever going to tell me your name, 'Birdman'?" She knew, of course, but she wanted to hear him say it, wanted to hear his deep, sexy voice caress the syllables.

He ducked his head shyly. "It's Sean. Sean Kennealy."

"Irish?"

"Just a bit." He took a long pull off his beer, his eyes seeming to dance with mischief. "So, have you gotten a new smoke detector yet, Gemma?"

Gemma colored. "Not yet. But I'm going to, I swear."

"Maybe I'll buy you one. As a present," he teased.

"If that's your idea of a present a woman would enjoy, then I pity you." They both laughed. "What does 'Birdman' mean?"

He looked uncomfortable. Gemma hoped she hadn't just put her foot in it. Suppose it had to do with sex? She braced herself.

"It's my nickname at the firehouse. I rescued these two birds from a fire and wound up adopting them. Ever since then, they've called me 'Birdman.'"

"Are nicknames big with firemen?"

"Huge. But not all of them can be repeated in mixed company. And since you're clearly a lady, I'll spare you."

For some reason, his calling her "a lady" sent giddiness charging through Gemma. *Is he aware of how sexy he is?* Two big gulps of gin and tonic slid down her throat.

"I loved those photos in your bedroom," he continued. "Are you a professional photographer?"

"Only in my dreams. In real life I run a boutique in the Village called the Golden Bough."

His brow furrowed. "Interesting."

"Is it?"

"Yeah. I don't run into too many businesswomen in my line of work. Unless their business has burned down."

"What kind of women do you run into? If you don't mind me asking."

"Not at all." He took another sip of beer. "Most of the guys' wives and girlfriends are regular working people:

schoolteachers, housewives, nurses—nothing fancy like owning their own business." He winked at her.

"It's not fancy. It's just what I always wanted to do."

He raised his glass to her. "I hear you."

"You too? You always wanted to be a firefighter?"

"Hell, no. I fought that for years! I've only been with the department for three years. Before that, I was a stock-broker." He put his index finger to his lips. "Don't tell any-one. People hear that and all of a sudden they treat me like I'm Merrill Lynch."

Gemma laughed. "I promise, I will never ask you for fi-nancial advice."

Sean's eyes caressed her body. "You don't look like you need it."

Gemma blushed, the bold compliment catching her off guard. She scrambled to keep the conversation going. "What made you switch careers?"

"Destiny. My dad was a ladder man and my granddad was an engine man. You can't outrun what's in the blood, you know?"

"But wasn't it hard? I mean, you must have gone from making a tremendous amount of money to—" Her hand flew to her mouth. "I'm sorry. That's none of my business."

"No, it's okay." Sean patted her shoulder reassuringly. "I like the fact you say what most people think. And the answer is yes, I took a big cut in salary. But the money's not why we do it." He eyed her curiously. "Enough about me. I want to hear about your store. Where is it?"

"In the Village. Thompson Street."

"I don't know the Village that well," he confessed.

"Oh." Gemma was surprised. "Don't you live in New York?"

"Yeah," he said evasively. "But I'm from Long Beach, originally."

"New Jersey?"

"Long Island."

Gemma nodded. She'd heard of Long Beach, but had never been there. Her only experience with Long Island was with her cousin Paulie's house in Commack.

"One of the guys at 35 Engine has an apartment right on the boardwalk," Sean continued. "Sometimes we switch apartments for the weekend, especially in the winter. He gets to play in the city, and I get to wake up to the sound of the ocean for a few days."

Gemma could picture it: the insistent cries of the gulls coasting on invisible currents of wind; the soothing rhythm of the tides; the sun dancing playfully off the surface of the waves, creating a kaleidoscope of diamonds. It had to be wonderful in the spring and summer. But the winter? "Isn't it lonely in the winter?"

"Are you kidding? Winter is when the beach is best." His tone bordered on the rapturous. "There's no one there. It's glorious."

She asked more questions, and he answered them all, though she got the sense he didn't really like talking about himself. Still, she learned that he was from a big Irish family and that most of them lived on Long Island. He'd been playing hockey since he was small, and one of his brothers-in-law—also a firefighter—was trying to talk him into learning the bagpipes. Sean was reluctant. Hockey took up enough of his time; he didn't need another hobby. When it was time to sit down for dinner, she was thrilled when he asked to sit with her. He ordered veal, then must have seen the disappointment in her eyes.

"You don't eat meat?" he asked.

"My rule is to never eat anything with a face."

Sean shot her a look. "I'm not touching that one."

Dinner flew by. They talked about hockey, the beach, animals, and photography. After dessert Gemma excused herself to search for Domenica. Come hell or high water, she was going to cuddle that baby before the night was through. She found mother and child sitting on the battered old couch in the restaurant's business office.

"Someone needed her diaper changed," Theresa explained as Gemma came toward them. "And someone else needed a few moments of peace and quiet."

Gemma held out her arms. "Hand her over."

Theresa smiled proudly as she passed her daughter to Gemma.

"She's gorgeous." Gemma cradled the baby in her arms. Domenica's perfect, rosebud mouth was closed, but her big green eyes were wide open and curious, framed with the longest lashes Gemma had ever seen. "She's going to be a stunner."

"Don't let Michael hear that. He'll get on the Internet and order a chastity belt now." Both women laughed, and Theresa stifled a long yawn. "Sorry. I'm exhausted."

"You must be."

"Miss Thing here likes to sleep all day and stay awake all night."

"You should have named her Vampira."

"Can you suggest herbs or anything?" Theresa asked seriously.

"For you or for her?"

"Both. I'm tired, and she's gassy."

"She's a true Dante. Michael and Anthony used to have farting contests when they were small."

Theresa sucked in her cheeks, mildly appalled. "Thanks for sharing that, Gem."

"My pleasure. You should take ginseng for energy. As for Princess here"—she brushed her lips against the velvety soft perfection of Domenica's forehead, reveling in her gorgeous baby scent—"there's a tonic called Baby's Bliss Gripewater. You can find it in any good health food store. It's got fennel and ginger in it, which should relieve stomach pain."

Theresa looked grateful as her body slumped farther down the couch. "How can I ever repay you?"

Gemma's mouth turned up into a sly smile. "Tell me everything you can about Michael's adorable firefighter friend, Sean Kennealy."

Theresa snorted. "Michael's friend? I'm the one who invited Sean! I've known him for years."

Gemma blinked. "But he said he knew Mike through the fire department's hockey team."

"Well, maybe he does, but he knows me from the building. He's been living in the apartment above mine—now yours—for years." She looked baffled. "I thought for sure you guys already met. You've been chatting away all night like bosom buddies."

Gemma gingerly handed Domenica back to her mother and edged quietly toward the door. "Can you excuse me a minute? I just remembered something I was supposed to tell Anthony."

"Sure."

Leaving the office, Gemma's mind turned to Sean Kennealy. *That devil!* she thought, not without affection. Beginning to put two and two together, she went back out to join him at the party. Sean Kennealy didn't know it yet, but his feet were about to be put to the fire. Only this time, it wouldn't be in the line of duty.

CHAPTER
04

The Dante family reminded Sean of his own.

They were large, close knit, and obviously enjoyed each other's company. They also knew how to have a good time, if the free flow of wine and spontaneous bursts of song were any indication. But while any friction in his family was subterranean, with the Dantes it was right out in the open. Michael and Anthony were shouting at each other one minute, hugging the next. And despite pointing her out to him, Gemma hadn't spoken with her mother all evening.

Gemma. Gem-ma Dan-te.

Her name sounded musical to him. Lyrical. They'd spent almost the entire party together, and he was seriously attracted to her. She seemed gentle and sweet, a genuinely good person. A bit New Age-y—he was skeptical when she suggested some herb for the carbon monoxide headaches he got from eating smoke. Meditation, herbs, vegetarian-ism—they weren't his thing. He was a man who liked steak for dinner, aspirin for headaches, and when he

wanted to relax, he read Alan Furst or watched the History Channel. But she was just trying to help. He liked how she looked, too. She was petite. *Five foot three,* he thought. *If that.* Yet she wasn't small. She had curves in the right places. Soft, that's what she was. Soft.

Best of all, she'd never dated a firefighter, wasn't related to a firefighter, and seemed to know nothing about firefighter culture. She was different, new, interesting. How that would go down with his buddies, he wasn't sure. He could already imagine the comments he'd get for dating a woman who probably made three times what he did. But that was putting the cart before the horse. First he had to get her to go out with him. And then . . . Sean drained his beer and ordered another. Just thinking about making love to her made him throb. That long red hair, those plump, curvy hips . . . God she was sexy.

"There you are."

A thrill shot through him as Gemma sidled up to him. He'd been sitting at the bar listening to her cousin Anthony, who was expounding on ricotta while puffing on a fat cigar.

"I thought smoking was banned in restaurants," Gemma said.

"Not when you own the place and it's a private party," Anthony declared.

Gemma shook her head. "It's bad for you, Ant."

"Listen to Miss Incense over here. All of a sudden she's the Surgeon frickin' General," he cracked to Sean. He snuffed out the offending stogie nonetheless. "There. Happy?"

"Very. And so are your lungs."

"*Madonn',* you're worse than Angie, I swear to God." He wiped his hands on his apron. "I'm being a bad host. Sean, this is my cousin Gemma. Gemma—"

"We've met." She smiled at Sean sweetly. "Sean and

two of his buddies tricked me into thinking someone had called the fire department to complain about my incense."

Sean spit up beer. "Excuse me," he rasped, turning away to cough into a napkin. *Damn. Busted.* He had planned to come clean with her at the end of the evening, preferably while they were alone, driving back to the city together.

"I don't understand," Anthony said thickly.

"It's a long story," Sean muttered.

Gemma's eyes flashed wickedly. "Shall I tell it?"

Sean used *his* eyes to plead for clemency. "I don't think that's necessary, do you?"

"I don't know. You sent the note, too, didn't you?"

Before Sean could answer, Anthony swung off the bar stool, his discomfort obvious. "Okeydokey. You guys are communicating in some bizarro code. I'm going to say *adios.*" He leaned down for a quick kiss to Gemma's cheek. "I'm going to take Nonna home now. She seemed a little off today, no?"

Gemma nodded absently, amused eyes still fixed on Sean.

"Too much vino, I bet," Anthony surmised, then walked away.

Alone with Gemma now, Sean launched his plea. "Look—"

"Confession time. Did you send the note?"

Sean's shoulders slumped. "Yes."

Gemma chuckled. "Why not just knock on my door and tell me face-to-face to stop burning incense? Why send a nasty note?"

Sean looked sheepish. "Because I had a killer headache and was in no mood to get into it with a stranger. Besides, that sh—incense you burn is strong. Admit it."

"What's wrong with strong?"

"Nothing, if the smell is nice. Like your perfume, for example."

She blushed, and he knew he was home free. Or so he thought.

"You said you knew Michael from the FDNY hockey team."

"I do know Michael through the hockey team!"

"That's splitting hairs. You purposely didn't tell me you knew Theresa from the building."

"You're right. I'm sorry." Feeling bold, he let his knuckles brush her cheek. "Anything I can do to make it up to you?"

He could see from the red rushing once again into her face that she was thinking the same thing he was.

Gemma suddenly seemed to turn shy. "Let me think about it."

"Buy you a new smoke detector," he said enticingly.

She tipped her head up, smiling at him. Sean felt his heart reel in his chest. "You already promised that."

"Guess it's time to get more creative, huh? Tell you what." He slipped his arm around her shoulder. "How 'bout I come up with some great way to make my deception up to you, and in return you agree to have dinner with me one night?"

"I'll think about it," Gemma said lightly, ducking out of his embrace.

Sean grinned, shaking his head. "You're torturing me on purpose, aren't you?"

"Torture? *Moi?*"

"Then say yes to dinner with me."

"I'll think about it," Gemma promised. "After you surprise me."

The next morning, Gemma slid into her regular booth at the Happy Fork and waited for Stavros to come and harass her. She hadn't gotten any sleep; instead, she had lain awake thinking about Sean: Sean kissing her, Sean peeling off her clothing, Sean whispering in her ear all the things he wanted to do to her. She was glad when Frankie appeared. She was bursting with the need to talk about him.

Before she could get a word in, Stavros appeared, pouring Frankie's coffee and then depositing an empty coffee cup in front of Gemma. He passed the steaming pot back and forth beneath her nose.

"Smells good, no?"

"Smells great," Gemma concurred. "Pour me a cup."

Stavros and Frankie exchanged shocked glances as Stavros complied.

"Sugar?" he asked in a stunned voice. "Cream?"

Gemma nodded. "Both."

Looking as if he might pass out, Stavros ran to fetch them for her.

"If this isn't a sign of imminent apocalypse, I don't know what is," said Frankie.

"No apocalypse," Gemma rejoined gaily. "I'm just up for trying new things."

Frankie caught her drift and her arm shot across the table. "Don't start yet; here comes Stavros with your milk and cream."

His demeanor was now obsequious, as if Gemma were a queen whose pronouncement he awaited. She fixed her coffee and, with Stavros and Frankie both looking on intently, raised it to her lips.

"Well?" he asked.

"Best coffee I've ever tasted."

"Ha!" Stavros beamed down at her knowingly. "I knew that would be your answer! Hasn't Stavros been telling you this for years?"

"You have," Gemma admitted.

He waddled off looking as if he'd just won the lottery.

"What's going on?" Frankie demanded.

First she told Frankie about the firefighters coming to

her apartment. Then she told her about the hockey game. She finished with details of Domenica's christening party. Frankie practically lunged across the table.

"You've crossed paths with this guy three times?" she said excitedly. "And he has blue eyes?"

"Yes."

"Like in your vision?"

"Yup."

"You think—?"

"I don't know." For the first time, Gemma felt uncertain. "I want it to be. I think." She drank some coffee. "He asked me out to dinner," she added shyly.

Frankie's eyes bulged so far out she looked like a cartoon. "And you said no?"

"I said maybe."

"*Maybe?* Why? Because Venus isn't in the third house of Lexus or some crap like that?" Frankie eyed her critically. "Something else is going on here. Why don't you want to go out with this guy?"

Gemma peered at Frankie over the rim her coffee cup. "If I tell you, do you promise not to laugh?"

"No. Now tell me."

"I think I'm a little nervous about going out with him because he's a firefighter."

"What's that got to do with anything?"

"They're tribal."

"Excuse me? You come from an Italian family where two brothers married two sisters and you're worrying about tribal?"

"That's different," Gemma insisted. "Look, I know they're heroes, okay? I know what they do is dangerous. I respect that." She ran a thumb along her napkin. "But remember the neighborhood firehouse in Brooklyn? Remember how those guys used to sit outside and call out rude things to us when we'd walk by on the way home from school?"

Frankie cringed. "Remember that time they rated us like they were Olympic judges and held up number cards?"

"Yeah, and gave us both zeroes." The memory still stung. "Remember how drunk they'd all get on St. Patrick's Day, spilling out onto the streets singing 'Danny Boy' and 'A Nation Once Again'?" Gemma shuddered. "That's not a tribe I want to be part of."

"Just because he's a fireman doesn't mean he acts that way."

"You're right. Though he was pounding down the Guinness at the christening party."

Frankie frowned. "Pounding down or had a couple? Which is it?"

"Had a couple," Gemma mumbled.

"Oohh, what a sin, a man having a few beers at a party. Better drag his ass to AA right now."

Gemma smiled at her friend affectionately. "You're a bitch, you know that?"

"I'm your favorite bitch and don't you forget it. Give this guy a chance. Please. I think he's got real potential."

"We'll see, okay? We'll see." Gemma was eager to get off the topic of Sean. "How's your flesh-eating disease?"

"The mental fuzziness and blister seem to have disappeared on their own," Frankie admitted sheepishly. "But now I have this." She lifted the pale blond bangs off her forehead to reveal . . . nothing.

"What?"

"I'm going bald, Gemma." Frankie's voice was laced with despair. "Look at my hairline! It's receding."

"The only thing receding is your grip on reality. I swear to God, you have got to talk to someone about your hypochondria. It's not healthy."

"I'll talk to someone about my 'hypochondria' when you talk to someone about why you're hesitating over a gorgeous guy who's obviously been put in your path. Sound fair?"

Gemma squirmed. "Stavros! More coffee!"

"Croppy's having a shit fit."

Tony the doorman's usual greeting was, "Hey, Short-stuff, what's up?" The words "Croppy" and "shit fit" were not words Gemma wanted to hear at the end of a long day.

"What's going on?" she asked as she put down her grocery bags.

"She's complained to the super twice about the junk outside your door. Says it's blocking the hall. It's a fire hazard."

"I don't have any junk in the hall."

"Croppy says you do." His tone was exasperated. "Do me a favor, will you? Whatever it is, whether it's yours or not, could you get rid of it? She's a pain in the ass. That's the only way she'll ever shut up."

"Not a problem," Gemma assured him. According to Mrs. Croppy, Gemma was responsible when the hot water didn't work, when the kids in the apartment upstairs blasted the TV, and when the elevator was out of order. *She probably thinks I'm responsible for global warming, too.*

"Thanks, Gemma. Have a good night."

"You too."

Since the grocery bags were unwieldy, Gemma asked another woman boarding the elevator to please press the button for the fifth floor. The woman complied, pressing the buttons for both five and twelve.

The doors opened on the fifth floor, and Gemma stepped out into the hall. She hadn't taken three steps before the door to Mrs. Croppy's apartment flew open. The old woman was hurtling toward her like one of the Furies, her shrill voice loud enough for the entire floor to hear.

"You! I've been waiting for you all day! Your junk is littering the hallway! People can't walk! It's dangerous!"

"What are you talking about?" Gemma tried to make her way down the hall. Her bags were getting heavier with every step. If she didn't put them down soon, they'd slip from her hands.

"Look! " Mrs. Croppy squawked, pointing a crooked, bejeweled finger at the other end of the hall. "Just look!"

Gemma wearily lowered the bags and looked. There, in front of her doorway and extending the entire width of the hall, was a menagerie of stuffed animals large and small. Penguins, polar bears, orangutans, rhinos—every animal imaginable, their colors as vivid as a rainbow.

"Oh my God," Gemma whispered, transfixed. Mrs. Croppy was still screeching, but Gemma had stopped listening. Slowly, as if in a dream, she made her way toward her apartment. Tigers, elephants, woodchucks—she was ankle deep in faux wildlife, the soft synthetic fur of zebras and raccoons brushing her skin as she fumbled to open the door of her apartment.

"What are you going to do about this mess?" Mrs. Croppy squawked.

Gemma barely heard the poison in the old woman's voice. "Just give me a minute, okay?"

Mrs. Croppy grunted and slammed her door shut, leaving Gemma in blessed silence. She knew just what she'd do. First, she'd dump her groceries on the kitchen table. Then she'd move her furry friends inside. And then—dear God, how she wanted to shout out his name!—then she would go upstairs and pay a visit to Sean.

Sean smiled when the doorbell rang, knowing just who it was. The electronic chime made Pete and Roger hop excitedly on their perches and they began squawking. Not the most relaxing sound in the world, but he was used to it.

"Settle down, guys," he soothed as he opened the door to reveal Gemma.

"Hi," she said shyly.

"Hi," he returned, ushering her inside and closing the door.

Gemma's gaze covered every inch of his living room: the dusty bookshelves crammed with his history books and spy novels; his coffee table, which held the latest issue of *Firehouse* magazine.

His gaze, meanwhile, was riveted on her. Her curling red hair looked windswept, and she was wearing the same scent as at the christening, faintly floral, but with a hint of spice that stirred his blood. His mind kept flashing back to the teddy on her bed, then flashing forward to an image of her in it. No one had ever captivated him so thoroughly, so fast. He felt bewitched.

"Care to introduce me to your roommates?" she asked, her gaze coming to rest on his birds.

They crossed the room, approaching the twin cages. "This is Pete and this is Roger. Pete is a parakeet, and Roger is a cockatiel."

As if they sensed they were the subject of conversation, the birds squawked even louder. Gemma leaned in to get a closer look at them, especially Roger, who boasted a small patch of orange feathers on his chest.

"You rescued them?"

"Yeah, from a fire in a dry-cleaning store, of all places. After the fire the owner went back to Korea and I took them."

"His loss." She tilted her head this way and that, observing them from different angles. "They're pretty."

"Pretty neurotic. Sometimes the only way I can get Rog to calm down is to pace with him, like a baby."

"Interesting." She turned to him, her smile shy. "Thank you."

"For—?" he asked, pretending he didn't understand.

She jostled his arm playfully. "You know what for. I love them."

"I'm glad. You have no idea how hard it was finding a pink wildebeest." Outwardly he was cracking jokes, but inside, he felt pure relief. It had been a gamble: Either she'd love it, or she'd think he was a nut. Lucky for him, it was the former. "Does this mean I'm forgiven for my deception?"

"I don't know," Gemma teased. "One of my neighbors was pretty upset."

Sean frowned. "Croppy, right?"

"Yes! How did you know?"

"The woman's a professional ball buster. Take off those orthopedic shoes of hers and you'll find cloven hooves."

Gemma laughed.

"I like making you laugh. C'mere."

As smoothly as he could, he took her face in his hands and, with the care of an artist, brushed his lips over hers once, then twice. Teasing kisses, nothing too forceful, just a taste of what could come should Gemma desire more. "More?"

Gemma's smile was demure yet seductive. "Yes, please."

"FDNY at your service, miss," he breathed, crushing his mouth down on hers as his arms drew her in tight. Through the soft crush of her breasts against his chest, he could feel her heart beating as fast as his own. He pressed on, feasting on the sweetness of her mouth. What was it about this woman that bewitched him so?

"Stop."

Stunned, Sean lifted his burning lips from Gemma's, and cleared his throat. "Stop?"

"Yes." Gemma gazed up into his face sheepishly. "I can't do this with them"—her voice dropped down to a whisper as her eyes slid quickly to his birds—"watching."

"You're kidding."

"I'm not. Their little eyes are glued to us." She gave a small shudder. "It's avian voyeurism!"

"I'll cover their cages. Or"—his thumb traced the plump curve of her lower lip, shocking even himself—"We can go into the other room."

Gemma hesitated. She was attracted to this man—very attracted. But she wasn't the sort to sleep with someone on the first date. Then again, this wasn't really a date, right? And she was a grown woman. She closed her eyes for a moment, trying to fully take in all she was feeling. "Can we go downstairs to my place?" she murmured.

"Of course."

She opened her eyes to look up into his. There she saw the deep, perfect blue of a Caribbean sea in which she longed to drown. Life without risk was no life at all. And since she was the one who was always telling others to have faith, it was time to practice what she preached.

She took his hand.

"Follow me," she said.

Gemma led Sean into her apartment. Since they were at her place, at her suggestion, she was now the one responsible for seduction. She went to light the candles scattered around her living room, hoping she appeared nonchalant, even serene. Part of her wanted to be the one in control: to show him how beguiling she could be, how powerfully she could enchant using the untapped magic of the senses. But another part wanted to be the one who surrendered, to be guided by this man to the place where she could soar free of the confines of her body, experiencing the past, present, and future in the simplicity of a single kiss.

Candles lit, she turned back to Sean, expecting to find him where she'd left him, standing near the front door. But he wasn't there. Instead, he was standing in the doorway of her bedroom, right hand held out to hers in unmistakable invitation.

"What are you doing there?" Gemma asked coyly as she walked toward him, kicking off her shoes along the way. Sean did the same.

"Checking to see if you'd gotten that new smoke detector."

"I thought you were getting one for me."

"Only if you're a good girl."

"I'd much prefer being a bad one, Mr. Kennealy."

"Prove it. Put on that black teddy of yours."

"That can be arranged." She nudged him gently in the direction of the bedroom door. "Give me a minute."

"Certainly."

Alone, Gemma paused to catch her breath. His request excited her more than she thought possible; a total rush of anticipation was twisting its way through her, delectable yet maddening. Trembling, she quickly shucked her clothing and took the teddy out of her dresser. She slipped it on, reveling in the soft feeling of the silk upon her bare skin. Tousling her hair for good measure, she threw back her shoulders, pushed her cleavage forward, and flung open the bedroom door.

There was Sean, restless, waiting, desire for her shining in his eyes. Drinking her in, he smiled. Candlelight suited him: The handsome angles of his face were made more so by the soft glow warming the room. Twining her fingers lightly through his, Gemma began pulling him toward a sea of oversized silk pillows arranged on the floor.

"No bedroom?"

Gemma smiled, catlike, and shook her head. Making love in the bedroom was predictable, and predictable was the last thing she wanted this experience to be. She wanted him left speechless, the memory of their coming together seared into his brain. She wanted him to want more.

"Come," she whispered, bidding him to sink down on the pillows with her.

"This is interesting," Sean observed. Gemma's reply was a smoldering smile and a swift, lusty nip to his lower lip. Sean's head jerked back slightly, eyes swallowed up by surprise. Whatever he'd been expecting, it certainly wasn't that. But she could see he liked it. Surprise gave way to animal drive and he clutched her to him.

"You sure this is how you want it?" he growled, his breath hot as he teased her earlobe with the tip of his tongue.

"No." It was hard to think straight. "I mean yes. I mean—"

His mouth silenced her, pressing upon hers with such fire, such demand, that Gemma could feel her body sizzling away, taking the last remnants of rational thought with it. There was only this: complete and total surrender to the sensual, spurred on by the thirst for more. She heard a voice crooning *yes, yes!* and it was a few seconds before she realized it was her own. Sean rewarded her begging with roughness, his teeth nipping and scraping so expertly that Gemma found herself gasping as golden heat shattered her core. She would go mad if she didn't learn every inch of his body, feel his burning skin beneath the soft pads of her fingertips. One minute she was clutching him tight, the next she was caressing his hair, his soft black curls a gift in her hands. She ached for more than simply being with him; she wanted to become him, to not be able to detect where he left off and she began.

His mouth's fierce demands left her lips bruised and swollen. Suns exploded behind the closed lids of her eyes, pleasure sluicing its way through her body like a river. All he demanded she would willingly give, and more. The harder he kissed, the more fervently his fingers explored, the deeper she dug her nails into the muscled terrain of his back. She was an animal, an animal whose blood and bone and sex beat out only one thought: More. More. More.

Breath ragged, Sean lifted his head, his wild eyes meeting hers. There was no need for words. Every need was conveyed in a glance. He tugged at the thin straps of her teddy, desperate for the softness beneath. Gemma helped him and held her breath, back arching as Sean lowered his mouth to her heated flesh.

Sean's tongue flicked and teased. His hands roughly explored her body—squeezing, probing, kneading—each sensation provoking in her a new round of blind arousal. She wanted him soon. She wanted him now. She needed to wrest back control.

Forcing his head up, she began frantically unbuttoning his shirt. He pushed her back down among the pillows and tore her teddy away from her body, the sound of ripping silk the most seductive music on earth. Gemma felt her own wet heat between her legs.

"Which of us is in charge?" Sean demanded hoarsely.

"You," Gemma moaned, dizzily ceding control. "You."

Nodding, Sean hurried to free himself, his breath hitching as his eyes locked on hers. Naked, he climbed atop her, fingers grasping her hips, hard, as Gemma arched upward, opening herself to him. He paused over her a moment and then plunged hard and deep, Gemma catapulting over the edge as their bodies began moving together, her dream of melding into one coming true.

His thrusting was strong and sure. Gemma tightened herself around him as he drove into her again and again, each meeting of flesh upon flesh pushing her higher and higher into the stratosphere. One minute she was a sweet prisoner of her body, her shocked senses unable to catalog the firestorm of relentless sensations coming one after another after another; the next she was flying, her body just a memory as she bucked wildly beneath him. It was a sensation she never wanted to end.

Gemma smiled with pleasure as Sean's body tensed and began moving faster, slamming itself into hers with an abandon that left her breathless. His desire for release was so urgent the expression on his face resembled pain. His hands searched for hers, their fingers twining together tight. *Now! Now! Now!* she thought feverishly, delighted when the drumming between her own legs resumed, sharp and insistent. Together they rode the storm their bodies created. And when he came—when they both came—a happiness she had never thought possible surged through her.

Her spell had worked.

She had found her soul mate.

CHAPTER

05

"What does your tattoo mean?"

Adrift on a cloud of postcoital bliss, Gemma languidly turned to Sean, in whose arms she lay. His thick curls were tousled wildly and his body boasted a thin sheen of sweat that made his flesh glisten in the candlelight. He looked like a warrior back from battle, weary yet triumphant, and very sexy. She'd been wondering when he'd notice the delicate tattoo gracing the small of her back. A small purple full moon framed by two opposite facing crescent moons, it was a present she'd given herself for her thirtieth birthday.

"It's a symbol of the goddess," she answered softly. Was the conversation about being a witch going to happen here, now, when they were both naked and vulnerable? Why not?

If Sean was baffled or curious, it didn't show. He nodded slowly as if mulling it over. Then he slid down her body, kissed the tattoo, and slid back up, holding her tight in his arms.

"I think tattoos on women are sexy."

"I'm glad," Gemma purred, trailing her fingers along the strong muscles of his damp back.

He grimaced. "I also think if we don't get off the floor soon, you'll need to call EMS. My back is killing me. Can we shift to the bed?"

Gemma chuckled. She was feeling uncomfortable herself. During their fierce lovemaking, the pillows she had so artfully arranged had slid, leaving the two of them lying on the bare wooden floor. Bed, with its promise of clean sheets and body-hugging blankets, seemed a wonderful suggestion. They could curl up together, maybe even make love again. In the morning they could go out for breakfast.

Gemma kissed his shoulder. "Bed sounds like a great idea." She stretched, surprised when it generated a small, sharp pain in her left shoulder. "I'm stiff, too."

"I guess this is what happens after thirty."

"Yoga helps."

"I'll stick to Advil."

His affectionate smile made Gemma's heart dance. Kissing the top of her head, he rose to his feet, extending his hand. Gemma took it, marveling at how easy this all felt, how natural, sharing her body with this man and now being led to her own bed. Hand in hand, they walked past the parade of stuffed animals, Sean pausing to pat the stuffed wildebeest on the head as if it were a faithful pet.

"Can I stay the night?" he asked as they burrowed beneath the covers.

Gemma nodded yes, burying her head in his neck. If she had her way, he'd never leave.

Sean didn't believe in fate. Yet there was something magical in the way their bodies had so smoothly blended together, a sense that this was meant to be. How else to explain his need to seduce this woman so quickly?

And she had a tattoo!

"A symbol of the goddess," she'd said. He knew a lot of women nowadays were into goddess worship. Not only had he read about it, but one of the guys he used to work with on Wall Street, Darryl Armbruster, was married to a woman who'd started out Catholic, gone Buddhist for a couple of years, and eventually wound up in some kind of all-girl coven. Armbruster used to bitch about coming home on the full moon to find his McMansion in Sommerville filled with chanting women. He glanced down at Gemma, who was sleeping peacefully. Could he picture her doing that? His gut tightened a little as he realized the answer was yes.

He continued watching her, her breath coming in short little puffs, the tangled mop of red hair curling wildly around her face. He envied her ability to just drift off. His rumbling belly kept him awake. He decided to go make himself a snack.

He gingerly slid out from between the sheets and made his way to the kitchen. He switched on the light, blinking against the momentary harshness. The feel of cold tile shocked the soles of his feet. *Pretty weird standing naked in someone else's kitchen,* he thought. Gemma's fridge held lots of salad and yogurt. He hated yogurt. Disappointed, he shut the door, and got a drink of water. Then he started opening cabinets, delighted to find Irish Breakfast tea among the boxes of herbal tea. A peek into the tiny pantry revealed a half-empty box of chocolate graham crackers just begging to be liberated. He put on her electric kettle. The appliance interested him; the only other person he knew to have one was his mother.

Waiting for the water to boil, Sean took in his surroundings. Her kitchen was small, but clean. Bundles of dried herbs hung from the ceiling in a corner of the room, and on the kitchen table sat an unopened box from Amazon.com. Curiosity drove him to check out the other bedroom. Turning on the light, he saw the room was basically bare, apart from an odd little table at its center and a bunch of giant candlesticks. Drawing close to the table, he saw a goblet, a white-handled knife, and a small bowl filled with ashes. There were also fresh flowers, two candles, and an old cracked, five-pointed star. He picked it up and turned it over in his hands. He'd seen these stars before. They had to do with heavy metal music or Satanism, he thought to himself grimly. Mildly perturbed, he tossed the star back onto the small table. What was the deal with the white-handled knife? The kettle buzzed and he jumped.

"Sean?"

He'd woken her up.

"Just making some tea," he called out. He turned off the kettle and poured the hot water into the cup. His chest now felt tight with anxiety. Between the vegetarianism, the herbs, and now this, he was having a hard time picturing Gemma hanging out with his friends. She just didn't fit in. Not only that, but she owned her own business. Were he still a stockbroker, it wouldn't be a problem. But some of the guys at the firehouse could be real pricks about this stuff. He could hear it already: You pussy-whipped, Kennealy? Does she give you an allowance? She your sugar mama or what?

"Can you bring me some, too?" Gemma called.

"Sure," he replied, forcing himself to sound calm.

"Bengal spice, please."

"You got it."

He extracted another cup from the cupboard as well as the tea in question. Tea steeped and ready, he picked up both steaming mugs and started back to the bedroom, acutely aware of his nakedness. He felt like the butler in a porn film.

Propped up in bed, Gemma smiled as Sean came through the bedroom door nude bearing two cups of tea. "You should have woken me," she said, eyes following him as he sat down atop the covers beside her. "I could have fixed you something."

"What? Yogurt pie? All you've got is yogurt and graham crackers."

"I'm sorry. I wasn't expecting company. We could order in; the Indian place around the corner doesn't close until one A.M."

"If I eat Indian food at this hour, I'll be up all night with heartburn." He shook his head, biting into one of the graham crackers he'd brought with him. "This'll tide me over."

Gemma sipped her tea, the taste of cinnamon and cardamom making her mouth tingle. She turned to thank him; that's when she noticed the pensive look in his eyes.

"Sean? Are you okay?"

He peered at her as if he needed to make out more clearly whom he was speaking to. "Yeah. I just . . ."

"What?"

Sean drew a deep breath. "While the water was boiling, I looked around the apartment and found—"

"My altar," Gemma finished for him, leaning back against the wall of pillows.

"Yeah." His expression was troubled. "You don't put dresses on cats and sacrifice them, do you?"

"What?" Gemma broke into laughter. "No! I practice Wicca, Sean. I'm not into Voodoo or Satanism."

"Wicca," he repeated.

"It's an earth-based, Pagan religion," she began explaining.

"I know what it is," he cut in impatiently. "It means you're a witch. Should I call you Sabrina or Samantha?"

"Neither. I don't wiggle my nose and turn people into bunnies. I do not own a black cat, a broomstick, or a big black hat."

Sean rubbed his forehead. "And your store?"

"What about it?"

"What do you sell?"

"Books and occult supplies."

Sean groaned.

"What? What's wrong?"

"It's nothing. Just forget it."

Gemma hopped out of bed, putting on her kimono. "You're completely weirded out, aren't you?" she sighed, settling down next to him.

"I guess." Sean peered at her nervously. "Are you in a coven?"

"No. I like to worship on my own." She seemed somewhat bemused. "Anything else you want to know?"

"Anything else you want to tell me?"

"Hhmm, let me think." Gemma rested her head on his shoulder. "Well, my best friend is a DJ and I give tarot card lessons."

"Great," Sean muttered.

Gemma lifted her head slowly and looked at him. "I'm the same person I was an hour ago, Sean. Nothing's changed."

"Except you might turn me into a toad."

She elbowed him in the ribs affectionately. "Don't be an ass." Taking the teacup from his hand, she put it on the nightstand with her own. Then she wrapped her arms around him.

"Ask me anything," she murmured tenderly. "I'm not embarrassed or shy about anything in my life. In fact, I'm pretty proud of the life I lead."

Lightening up a little, Sean kissed her forehead. "At least we've got that in common."

Trying to recapture the magic he'd felt earlier in the evening, he lay down with her, plying her with questions. She told him about the Golden Bough, and how happy she was to be able to run a business that reflected her beliefs. About Frankie, and how they'd known each other since they were little girls. Finally she talked about her family, and how much she loved them. Time passed, and their tea grew cold. Eventually, to Sean's relief, Gemma fell asleep.

"Sean?" Gemma reached out to touch the body slumbering beside her. But there was only a tangle of sheets and an empty pillow. Concerned, she switched on the light. The clock on the nightstand read 4:00 A.M. Maybe he was in the bathroom?

She waited a few minutes, determined not to immediately assume the worst. Donning her kimono, she made her way out into the silent living room and turned on the light.

That's when she saw it.

A note in the mouth of the stuffed wildebeest.

Back killing me.
Went to sleep on my own rock hard mattress.

She stared at it for a long time, then crumpled the note and let it drop to the floor. Picking up the wildebeest, she trudged back to her bedroom. The two cups of tea were still sitting there on the nightstand. Clutching the stuffed animal to her, she lay atop the covers, curling up in a ball. There were lots of ways to keep pain at bay; holding on tightly to something was one of them. It wasn't what she'd imagined holding through the night, but Sean had left her with no choice.

CHAPTER
06

"Birdman, you gonna take that lasagna out or what? It's startin' to smell like that warehouse fire on Forty-third."

It was Sean's turn to cook and he was making lasagna, tossed salad, and garlic bread. But Leary was right: He'd totally spaced on the lasagna, which now smelled more than well-done. Grabbing a pair of oven mitts, he hustled to the oven and opened the door. A wall of heat smacked him in the face, along with acrid smoke. The top of the lasagna was charred.

"Way to go, Chef Boyardee. Your head up your ass tonight or what?"

"Shoulda stuck with crunching numbers, boyo."

"Up yours," Sean called over his shoulder good-naturedly. His head was up his ass, it was true. But right now, his primary concern was salvaging dinner. He peeled the top layer off the lasagna and brought the rest to the table.

"You expect us to eat this?" Lieutenant Peter Carrey asked. Carrey had been with the FDNY for twenty years and was highly respected.

"Yeah, really," Leary echoed. "It's dryer than an AA meeting."

"You'd know all about that, Mikey, wouldn't ya?" Sal Ojeda ribbed.

"Damn straight. I've been free of Irish handcuffs for years."

Bill Donnelly looked at him questioningly. "Irish handcuffs?"

"Beer in each hand."

Everyone laughed.

Sean sat down beside Leary, who was eating like a man breaking a fast. "Not bad considering you burnt it to shit," he commented.

"Thanks," Sean said, taking a mouthful. Carrey was right: The lasagna was dry, but it wasn't inedible.

"So what's up with you?" Leary asked curiously. "You've looked like a zombie since you got here."

"Ah, it's nothing."

"C'mon, Sean." Leary draped an arm around Sean's shoulder. "Tell Uncle Mikey all your problems."

Sean hesitated. If he spilled, he wouldn't just be telling "Uncle Mikey," he'd be telling everyone on his shift. But maybe the more opinions he got, the better. "I met this girl, right?" Wolf whistles started immediately. Sean rolled his eyes. Maybe he didn't need more opinions.

"Go on, my son," said Leary solemnly, folding his hands on his chest in imitation of a priest hearing confession.

"She's kind of unusual."

"'Unusual,'" Bill Donnelly snorted. "What the hell does that mean? She got three tits?"

Laughter erupted around the table.

"No, she's into herbs and stuff. She's a vegetarian." No way was he going to tell them she was a witch. Not now, at any rate.

"Lots of people are vegetarians these days," probie Ted Delaney said knowingly. "That's not so weird."

"She meditates." His eyes shot to Leary's. "She burns incense."

"Sweet mother o' God." Leary let out a whoop of disbelief. "It's The Stinker, isn't it?"

"The Stinker!" Joe Johnson, ladder truck chauffeur, looked shocked. "You mean, the loony who lives below you who was burning garbage?"

"She's not burning garbage," Sean clarified, sounding—and feeling—semimiserable. "It's incense."

"Incense that smells like Elizabeth, New Jersey, on a bad day," Leary added.

"You've been bitching about The Stinker for months, bro!" Ojeda pointed out.

Ted Delaney looked confused. "And now you like her?"

"Yeah. I mean—she's really nice. And sweet. But she's, you know, different."

"Different can be good," Joe Johnson opined. "My wife changed her hair color last week. She looks ten years younger."

"We're talking about a woman here, you moron, not the pros and cons of Clairol." Leary gave Sean a penetrating look. "You've talked to her since—?"

Sean gave a quick nod. "Yeah. And we get along really well. But she's quirky. I mean, I told her about eating smoke and getting headaches and she told me to chew on some kind of root."

"Bet you want her to chew on your root," Ojeda cracked.

Sean seared him with a look and Ojeda slumped in his seat. The innuendo served only to remind Sean of how ungallantly he'd behaved. He had woken up in a room that wasn't his own with the backache from hell, beside a woman with an altar and a ritual knife, and his reflex was to run. So he left. It wasn't until he was stretched out in his own bed that it crossed his mind how Gemma might feel, waking up to an empty bed and a hastily scribbled note.

"Here's some food for thought, Kennealy."

Sean turned to the far end of the table, where Chris "Socrates" Campbell sat. Socrates had earned his nickname because he felt compelled to add what he thought were insightful comments to any conversation. Sometimes they actually *were* insightful.

"If you like this woman, what do you care if she's different?"

Because if there's one thing I want, it's to continue fitting in. I want to be normal, Sean answered to himself. Hooking up with a witch who ran an occult shop was not a smooth fit for the company's summer barbecues. Still, Socrates had a point.

"*Am I doing* this right?"

Uther Abramowitz's reedy voice brought Gemma back to herself. They were in her store, nearly done with his first tarot lesson, and somewhere between explaining to him why he needed to learn the meaning of each card and showing him how to do a three-card spread, her mind had drifted back to her night with Sean. The neediness in Uther's voice made her feel guilty. Here he was paying her money to learn tarot, and what was she doing? Daydreaming. Gently removing the tarot deck from his grasp, Gemma showed him again what to do.

"You shuffle the deck, and then you ask the querent— remember, that's the person who wants the reading—to cut the deck into thirds with his left hand. Then have them turn over the top three cards, and put them in any order they want. The first card denotes the past, the second the present, the third the future. This reading is good for someone who wants a specific question answered. You can also do the one card read I showed you earlier."

Uther stroked his straggly beard. "Can we try it? I mean—can I ask a question and see what happens?"

"Of course."

Gemma handed him the deck, unprepared for the directness in his eyes as he shuffled the deck.

"Will I ever find my lady love?" he intoned solemnly, staring straight at her.

"You don't have to ask the question out loud."

"Oh."

Uther shuffled . . . and shuffled . . . and shuffled, giving Gemma time to process the fact that he obviously had a crush on her. This wasn't good.

"Done."

Excited as a child completing his first finger painting, Uther turned over the top card. It was the Nine of Swords. *Damn,* thought Gemma.

"Do you know what card it is?" she prompted.

Uther's scrawny chest puffed up. "Nine of swords, obviously."

Gemma nodded approvingly. "Any idea what it signifies?"

"You tell me." His gaze hinted at seduction. "I am but your humble pupil, Lady, and hope always to be."

"It's symbolic of suffering," Gemma explained, ignoring his lame, faux-Shakespearean attempt at flirting. "Patient suffering that has to be borne with courage."

Uther deflated. "Oh."

"It's not absolute, you know," Gemma reminded him. Much as his blatant staring was beginning to unnerve her, she still felt sorry for the guy. He was obviously lonely. She tried to think if she had any girlfriends she might hook him up with, but came up blank.

"We need to wrap up," she told him. "The hour's up and I need to reopen my store."

"Okay." Uther looked almost petulant. "What task hast thou set for me this week?"

"Memorize the meaning of any five cards you want."

"That's it? I can do more, you know. I have a photographic memory."

"Really? Then learn the meaning for all the cards."

"O-okay." He looked uncertain.

"That was a joke, Uther. Learn at least five, and if you want to do more, feel free."

"Will do, Lady Most Fair. Mind if I look around the store awhile after you reopen?"

"Be my guest." Gemma slid out from behind the counter. "Oh, and Uther?"

She was going to tell him to can the poesy or he'd find himself not with Lady Fair but Lady Macbeth, but stopped herself. "Enjoy the rest of your day."

It embarrassed Sean, but to find Gemma's store he had to look Thompson Street up on a map. Like the area surrounding Wall Street where he'd once worked, the Village was filled with narrow, twisting streets, so different from the rigid grid system upon which the rest of Manhattan was mapped. Bleecker, Houston, Broome, Canal—Sean was familiar with the names, but had never hung out there himself.

He came up out of the subway on West Fourth Street, map in hand, looking like a tourist. It took a while, but he finally found the Golden Bough, right off the intersection of Thompson and Grand. Part of him expected something dark and Dickensian, with a black cat sitting in the store window atop a pile of dusty books. Instead, he found a small but bright shop whose sign blazed in gold and purple. The window display was pleasantly busy with books, tarots cards, crystals, and candles. Doubt crept in as he gripped the door handle. *Do I really want to do this?*

He paused, recalling Socrates Campbell's words of wisdom. So what if Gemma was different? Wasn't that what had attracted him to her in the first place? To automatically assume she wouldn't fit in was narrow-minded and ignorant, two adjectives he didn't want applied to him. At the very least, he owed Gemma an apology. In the best of all possible worlds, she would forgive him and maybe, just maybe, agree to a real date with him. Assuming she didn't catch sight of him and tell him to go to hell immediately. *Or send me there herself.*

He opened the door and slipped inside, gratified to see there were other customers in the store. The presence of other shoppers ensured she wouldn't wing things at him, call him names, and tear him a new one. He hoped.

The inside of the store was brightly lit and well organized, with a soothing aroma in the air that reminded him of Christmas trees. He recognized the music playing: Enya. His sister Christine threw her on the CD player at every family gathering. *So we both like Celtic music. That's a good sign, isn't it?*

Some customers were scrutinizing the tall bookshelves, while others sat in overstuffed chairs, leisurely thumbing through books. There was a welcoming feeling to the place that he realized reflected the warmth of the woman who owned the store. A quick peek up the "Reincarnation and Past Lives" aisle revealed Gemma sitting behind the counter, talking quietly to some skinny, bearded man who looked like he could use a strong dose of sunlight. Grateful she hadn't noticed him yet, Sean hung back, waiting until she finished. Her back was turned to him as she said goodbye to the man, who threw Sean a dirty look as he crept past him on his way out of the store.

"Excuse me, miss, I need your help finding a book."

Gemma jerked around. Sean saw shock in her eyes that quickly turned to distrust. He could see how much damage he'd done.

"What kind of book are you looking for?" She smelled

sweetly of the same perfume she'd worn at the christening, but spoke politely, as if to a stranger.

"A primer on Wicca."

"I see." Her expression betrayed nothing. "Follow me." Slipping out from behind the counter, she walked briskly down one of the tall aisles. Sean followed at a slight distance. Was this how it was going to be, shopkeeper and customer? The next move, he realized, was his.

Within seconds Gemma pulled a book off the shelf, handing it to him. "This is good for beginners."

Sean skimmed the cover. *The Complete Idiot's Guide to Witchcraft.* "Complete idiot: That's me, all right. Thanks." He peered at her, hoping his joke might melt the ice.

"You're welcome." Turning heel, she walked back to the counter, barely looking at him when he handed her the book to ring up.

"That'll be ten ninety-five, plus tax."

Forget humor, proceed directly to shame, 'cause it's the only chance you've got. "Gemma, I came here to apologize."

She pointedly refused to look at him as she took his twenty dollars.

"It was a shitty thing to do," Sean said quietly.

Her eyes looked up at him sadly. "Yes, it was. It made me feel cheap. You think I do that all the time? Give myself away like that?"

"I'm sorry. That's not how I want you to feel. And it's not what I think, either."

"Well, that's a comfort. God knows I've spent the past week worrying about what you think."

Sean flinched at her sarcasm. "I deserved that. Hit me again."

"I don't want to hit you again." Her voice was shaky. "Look, we slept together, it was a mistake, now let's move on."

She moved to hand him his change. Sean's hand shot out, gripping hers.

"I don't think it was a mistake."

Gemma gently withdrew her hand. "Then why did you leave without saying a word?"

Sean glanced around to make sure none of the nearby patrons could hear him. "Because my back was killing me and I was scared. I meet someone really interesting and then she turns around and tells me she's a witch. Wouldn't you have been freaked out?"

"I wouldn't have gone snooping around in someone else's apartment."

"If I hadn't found your altar, you wouldn't have told me?"

Gemma looked dismayed. "Of course I would have told you. But in my own time, in my own way. I might even have waited until we both had clothes on."

Sean swallowed, embarrassed. "I'm sorry," he repeated after a long moment. "I'm sorry I was nosy. I'm sorry I put you on the spot at an awkward moment, and I'm sorry I crept out in the middle of the night like a slimeball."

"Apologies accepted," Gemma murmured reluctantly.

She'd forgiven him! He had to grab the opportunity to see her again. "I was thinking."

"That could be dangerous, but continue."

"You and I did things ass backwards." His voice dropped. "You know, having sex first and all that."

"And?"

"I thought maybe we could do things right, you know, spend some time together."

"And then have sex," Gemma added acidly.

"No." Sean was reeling. "Well—I mean—if you want." Gemma frowned. "You know, I don't usually hop into bed so quickly, either," Sean added.

"Oh, really." Gemma looked skeptical.

"Yeah, really. I'm not quite sure what happened between us. It felt magical. I know that's probably not a good word for me to use, but I don't know how else to describe it."

Gemma's face lit up with a little smile.

"What?"

"Nothing."

"So, you'll go out with me, then?"

"Depends what you have in mind." When Sean looked surprised, Gemma laughed. "What, did you just expect me to say 'Yes' without hesitation after what you did to me?"

Sean could feel his ears burning. "Uh . . ."

"You did, didn't you?"

"I did, yeah," he admitted, defending his title as Stupidest Man in the World.

Gemma folded her arms across her chest, chuckling. "That's pretty presumptuous, don't you think?"

"That's me, ole Mr. Presumption."

"Well, Mr. Presumption, tell me what you have in mind."

Sean thought quick. "How about we go out, grab a bite to eat, and listen to some Irish music? There's this great place called O'Toole's down by Met Gar."

Gemma nodded slowly. "Irish music . . . that could be fun."

Sean's heart leapt. "So is that a yes?"

"I guess," Gemma said, beginning to look like her old happy self.

As she prepared for her date with Sean, Gemma's imagination danced with all sorts of visions. She pictured them at one of the city's small, trendy bistros, murmuring intimately at a table for two. Afterward, they would walk hand in hand to O'Toole's, the night air invigorating and full of promise. Both would be moved to tears by the heartrending sound of the Irish penny whistle as it trilled mournfully behind a singer with streaming raven hair who sang of hurling herself into her lover's open grave. The evening would leave them feeling tender and emotional. They'd go back to Gemma's place and make slow, deliberate love.

Instead, Gemma found herself being led by the hand down narrow steps to a basement pub. Sean opened the door, and Gemma found herself up against a solid wall of human bodies. Gabbing loudly, many were well on the road to intoxication despite it being only 9 P.M. She glanced sideways at Sean to see if he found the scene as disconcerting as she did.

"The food here is fantastic," he shouted in her ear.

Apparently not.

Doing her best not to jostle pub patrons as she squeezed past, she let Sean lead her to the front of the room. The combination of tightly packed bodies and lack of ventilation had perspiration dripping down the black concrete walls. Gemma was glad she hadn't worn a long-sleeved blouse as planned. Ten minutes in this sweatbox and she'd be drenched.

"Wait until you hear the music," Sean said as he pulled out a chair for her at a small table for two marked RE-SERVED. She already heard music coming from the jukebox in the corner, its main melody muddied by the nonstop din of voices. She strained to make out the tune. Something by U2? Their table was situated right in front of the small stage. If Gemma pushed back too far in her chair, her back practically touched an amplifier. She touched Sean's arm.

"Do you think we could find a different table?" she asked loudly.

Sean surveyed the room. "I think this might be it."

Gemma did a quick circuit of the room. He was right. This was it.

Out of the whirlwind a waitress appeared, handing each of them a menu. "What can I get you to start?" she asked in an Irish brogue so thick Gemma thought she had to be putting it on.

"A Guinness," Sean replied easily. The waitress turned to Gemma expectantly.

"Gin and tonic, please."

"Made with Tanqueray," Sean added. The waitress nodded and disappeared into the crowd.

"How do you know this place?" Gemma asked.

"It's a popular FDNY hangout." He glanced around the room. "I'm surprised no one I know is here."

Gemma suspected as much. She felt like a fish out of water. The last time she'd been in a place like this . . . wait: Had she ever been in a place like this?

Sean smiled at her, and she flipped open the menu, skimming the selections. Corned beef and cabbage. Bangers and mash. Fish and chips. Meat pies. Burgers. Gemma closed the menu.

"Know what you want already?"

"There's a small problem."

Sean dragged his chair closer to hers. Obviously he was having as tough a time hearing as she was. "What's that?"

"I'm a vegetarian, remember?"

"Shit. I didn't even think . . ." He trolled the menu, his easygoing expression slowly giving way to mild embarrassment.

"It's okay," Gemma assured him, squeezing his hand. "I'm sure I can find something." She leaned over so their shoulders were touching, taking another look at the menu. "There: cheese and onion pie. I'll have that."

Sean closed the menu, looking miserable. "I'm so sorry, Gem. I should have remembered."

"Not a big deal."

The waitress returned, plonking their drinks down on the table. "Do you know what you want, then?"

"I'll have the cheese and onion pie," said Gemma.

"Sorry, love, we're all out."

"Oh."

"Do you have any salads?" Sean asked.

The waitress bit down on the tip of her pen impatiently. "What you see on the menu is what you get. Sorry."

"In that case," said Gemma, "I guess I'll just have a plate of chips."

The waitress looked testy. "That's it? Chips?"

"Yes." Gemma shot Sean a baffled look.

"I'm not sure you can do that, you know. Just have chips."

"Oh," Gemma repeated, confused. "Why not?"

"Because chips *go with* something." The waitress clucked her tongue in frustration. "Fish and chips. Sausage and chips. We've never had anyone ask for 'just chips' before. I'll have to ask the chef if it's okay."

Gemma looked at the waitress warmly. "I'm sure it'll be fine."

"It might not be."

"Let's just see how it goes," Sean intervened, a big, fake smile cruising its way onto his face. It made Gemma want to laugh.

The waitress, now in a snit, peered down at Sean. "And what would you like, *sir?*"

"Bangers and mash, please." Sean closed his menu and handed it back with a knowing wink. "You can also tell the chef it's a New York City firefighter who wants that plate of chips."

"Very good," she bit out. "Thank you."

With that she left.

"Guess she doesn't care about getting a tip," Gemma joked.

"Customer service doesn't seem to be her strong point," Sean agreed.

Gemma sipped her drink. It was watered down, more tonic than gin. The evening was not starting out on the most auspicious note. Still, all might not be lost. So what

if O'Toole's was the kind of place she would never choose
to go to in a million years? The music was supposed to be
good, right? And there was Sean.

"How's your drink?" he asked, taking a pull of his
Guinness.

"Great," Gemma fibbed. "Yours?"

"Lovely," Sean said blissfully in a fake brogue.

"I've never understood the appeal of beer," Gemma admitted. "It's like"—she paused, searching for the right
analogy—"potato soda."

Sean laughed. "Spoken like a true beer connoisseur."

"So," Gemma began, permitting herself the great pleasure of gazing at long length into his incredible eyes, "have
you started to read the book on Wicca yet?"

Sean dipped his head, cupping his ear. "What?"

"The. Book. On. Wicca," she repeated loud and slow.
"Have you started it yet?"

"Yeah."

Gemma took this as a positive sign. "And—?"

"It's interesting."

She waited for him to elaborate, but he didn't. Gemma
could rattle off a slew of questions she was dying to ask
him about it, but she didn't want to make him feel pressured, or worse, that he was somehow being quizzed. Of
course, there was the possibility that he thought it was
bizarro mumbo jumbo and didn't want to hurt her feelings.
She was determined not to focus on that, not right now.
"How's work?" she asked brightly, practically shouting.

"Okay."

"Just okay? Any interesting fires?"

"They're all interesting. That's the problem." He
paused thoughtfully, then shrugged. "Things are fine.
Nothing exciting."

"I see."

"It's hard for me to talk about what I do, Gemma. If I
told you half the stuff that went down, you'd never want

me to leave my apartment, and the other stuff—the technical stuff—would probably bore you to tears."

"Try me," Gemma urged playfully. "What do you guys talk about? What do you do for fun?"

"Abuse each other." He took a sip of beer. "Wait, here's a good one: Some drunken teenager out on Long Island got stuck in the chimney of his frat house. By the time the fire department arrived, he was dead, unfortunately. Know what he died of?"

Gemma's hand flew to her throat. "What?"

"The flue." Sean laughed.

"Sean! That's not funny! That's awful!"

"Firehouse humor, babe. Sometimes it's the only thing that gets you through."

"I guess I can understand that," Gemma said. But deep down, she wondered.

The waitress returned with a smarmy look on her face and only one plate in her hand. She dropped the sausage and potatoes in front of Sean. "The chef said to tell ya, and I quote, that he doesn't give a flying feck if you're Mr. Jesus H. Christ himself, we only do what's on the menu."

"Bring us an order of sausage and chips, then," Sean said, slumping in his seat mortified. He turned to Gemma. "I'll take the sausages off the plate. So much for firefighters having some pull in this city," he added with a frown.

"We could go," Gemma suggested tentatively.

"But we haven't heard any music yet."

What does it matter? We'll be deaf by the time the band gets on, thought Gemma. The decibel level of the crowd was earthshaking. Still, Sean was right. They hadn't heard any live music yet. A few haunting Celtic ballads, a few foot-tapping ceilis, and the night would be back on track.

"Here, have some of these potatoes while we're waiting," Sean said, pushing his plate between them.

As delicately as she could, Gemma wiped away the perspiration she could feel beading on her upper lip. It was so

hot in O'Toole's she thought she might pass out. She tried
to see the place through Sean's eyes. Why had he had
brought her here? It had to be the music. The waitress
made a brief and unsmiling reappearance to drop the plate
of sausage and chips. Gemma and Sean tried to chat over
the raucous din; then just as they were finishing up their
meal, the lights dimmed and the crowd erupted into spontaneous hoots as the band hit the stage.

Gemma was expecting a quartet: fiddle, tin whistle, gui-
tar, and bodhran drum. Instead, eight musicians lumbered
onto the tiny stage. Two had fiddles and one had a tin whistle, but there was also a drummer, an organist, and much to
Gemma's dismay, a bass player and two electric guitarists,
one of whom plugged in to the amp at her back.

"Evenin'," the lead singer bellowed into the mike, a
pipe cleaner of a man with a buzz cut and black wrap-
around sunglasses. "We're deValera's Playground and
we'd like to start tonight with a little song you all know:
'Flogging Davy.'"

The nearest guitarist launched into a brain-searing riff
and the band were off. This was Irish music done a way
Gemma'd never heard, with screaming guitars vying with
mad fiddles and a lead singer who twitched and jerked like
Ichabod Crane being poked with a cattle prod. The crowd
was going nuts, pogoing in unison while their fists pumped
high in the air, shouting out the chorus in Gaelic along with
the band.

Gemma turned to Sean. He was clapping enthusiasti-
cally along with the music, which amazed her. Catching
her gaze, Sean broke into wide grin.

"AREN'T THEY GREAT?" he shouted.

"Great," Gemma mouthed, knowing he couldn't hear
her. As best she could, she averted her face from him so he
wouldn't detect her dismay. She'd been wrong: The music
wouldn't salvage this evening. Instead, it was the icing on
the cake. Time to face facts: Sean's idea of a fun night out

was radically different from hers. All she could do now was sit back and ride it out. She prayed the band did only one set and were either too drunk or tired to stand for encores. She wondered if Ron Crabnutt was somewhere in the crowd, chewing gum and waving a torx head in unison to the music.

And she wondered who Sean really was.

"Can I come in?"

The seductive undercurrent in Sean's voice as he teased Gemma's lips outside the door of her apartment almost caused her to give in. Almost. But then she remembered: This was the man to whom she'd given a second chance and he'd used it to take her to a rowdy Irish bar to see a band who played head-banging Celtic music. Now, to top it all off, he seemed to be hinting at sleeping with her again.

Gemma had been so sure that in agreeing to a proper date, she was sending a clear signal to him that she was interested in a relationship that existed beyond the boundaries of the bedroom. But now she wondered. Who did he think she was, that she would enjoy an evening like the one they'd just shared? Surprising her with all those stuffed animals had been wonderful, and his coming down to the Golden Bough to apologize to her in person spoke to his being a man of character. But if this was a firefighter's idea of a good date, then what she'd said to Frankie at the Happy Fork was right on target: This wasn't a tribe she wanted to join.

Maybe she was at fault, too. Just a little. When he'd asked her if she thought the band was great, she should have been honest and asked him to take her home. But she'd kept mum.

Gentle but firm, she pulled away. "I'm really tired, Sean. How about if we call it a night?"

"Okay." She saw disappointment as his eyes searched her face. "Are you all right?"

"Just tired," she repeated, turning her key in the lock.

"I hear you. What if I call you later in the week and we check out a movie?"

"That might be nice," Gemma murmured, pushing open her apartment door. She smiled up at him and thanked him for a lovely evening, happy when Sean planted a small, sweet kiss on her lips and thanked her for the same. But she could tell he was confused.

He wasn't the only one.

CHAPTER

07

His date with Gemma left Sean kicking himself.

He'd been so elated she was willing to give him another chance he'd grabbed at the first thing they seemed
to share: Irish music. O'Toole's sometimes *did* play traditional Irish music—he should have checked the paper
before heading down there. Judging by the music she
played in her store, it wasn't a stretch to think de Valera's
Playground might not be her cup of tea. So he wasn't exactly surprised when she didn't invite him in afterward,
though he was disappointed. But what was with her tepid
response when he suggested a movie later in the week?
Did she really think it would be "nice" to get together
again? Or was she using polite Lady Speak to tell him to
go chase himself? Why did women have to be so damn
hard to read?

Rather than risk screwing up for a third and possibly
final time, Sean decided to consult someone who knew
Gemma well: her cousin Michael. Looking up the Blades
schedule online, he saw they were playing a home game,

and so he took the subway to Met Gar. His own experience
with the FDNY team told him the Blades got there early to
work on their sticks and skates. He told security he was a
friend of Michael's, they checked with the man himself,
and he was in.

The corridors below the arena were brightly lit and
snaking, their concrete walls decorated with blown-up action photos of both past and present players. Sean found
himself checking the sprinkler system on the ceiling, as
well as the strategically placed fire extinguishers along the
corridor. Funny the things you looked for depending on
your point of reference.

He found Michael standing at one of the skate-sharpening
machines, carefully running the blade of his skate back and
forth, throwing off sparks.

"Mike."

"Hey, Sean." Michael put down his skate and drew him
into a fraternal hug. "What's up? You boys need some tickets for tonight's game?"

"I hadn't come for that, but if you've got 'em, what the
hell."

"Sure, I'll set you up. So, why you here?"

"It's about your cousin."

Michael looked amused. "Which one? I've got twenty."

Sean laughed appreciatively. "Gemma."

Concern flashed across Michael's face so fast Sean almost missed it. Was it possible Michael knew about the
night they'd spent together? Had Gemma come crying to
her cousin about what a creep he'd been? If so, then he was
royally screwed. No way would Michael help him out.

"What about Gemma?" Michael asked carefully.

"I really like her. I took her out on Saturday, and it
didn't go too well. I was hoping you might be able to give
me some advice."

"I can try." Michael looked distinctly uneasy as he
began massaging the back of his neck. "Look, before we

go any further, there's some things you should probably know. About Gemma."

"Like what?" Sean could guess where this was heading, but he decided to play dumb. It would be fun watching Michael scramble to describe his cousin.

"Well, she's kinda crunchy, you know?"

"Crunchy?"

"Crunchy as in granola head. She's into herbs and teas and all that shit."

"I'm fine with that."

Michael's eyes darted away evasively. "She's also very spiritual, if you catch my drift. Intuitive. Very into nature."

"Tree hugger?"

"No, nothing like that. She's—"

"A witch?" Sean supplied.

Michael's eyes shot back to his. "*Madonn'*, she told you?"

Sean nodded.

"And it doesn't freak you out?"

Sean shuffled his feet evasively. "I don't really get it, but if it makes her happy . . ."

"My sentiments exactly," said Michael, looking relieved. "Hey, if you can get past the witch stuff, you're already light-years ahead of most guys. I salute you."

Sean frowned. "Don't salute me yet. I brought her to O'Toole's last week."

Michael's mouth fell open. "O'Toole's? Right around the corner?"

Sean nodded again, more forlorn this time.

"What are you, out of your fucking mind?"

"I know, I know," Sean muttered.

"Gemma at O'Toole's is like me rushing Kristie Yamaguchi. What the hell were you thinking?"

"I wanted to take her to see some Irish music."

"Who was playing?"

"DeValera's Playground." Sean sighed.

"They're good. Theresa's thinking of taking them on as clients. But no way are they up Gemma's alley."

"I know that now. She was playing Enya in the store so I just assumed she liked all sorts of Irish music."

Michael pulled a tortured face. "She loves that stuff."

"What stuff?"

"All that mystical Celtic crap. And traditional stuff, too." Michael shook his head despairingly. "I don't want to scare you, but once, when I was in the store, she was playing bagpipe music. What kind of Italian girl listens to freakin' bagpipes? I told her it was giving me a headache and she just ignored me. She marches to the sound of her own drummer."

"Yeah, she does," Sean agreed. *Which is kind of why I like her.* "Do you think she'd like it if I took her to hear traditional music?"

"Yeah, I do."

"Any other suggestions?"

Michael thought. "I think she'd like it if you cooked for her or something like that. She's kind of a homebody, you know? Likes quiet stuff." His hand shot out to clutch Sean's arm. "Don't ever get in a car with her, though. The woman can't drive to save her life."

Sean patted Michael on the shoulder. "Thanks for your help, Mike."

"No problem. I'll have some tickets put aside for you for tonight. Four okay?"

"Four's great. Thanks again," Sean repeated, starting down the hall. An idea was beginning to coalesce in his mind about what he could do to make Gemma feel excited about him again. It was a little offbeat, but so was she.

Besides, what did he have to lose?

"*You were at* O'Toole's? You?"

The incredulity in Frankie's voice made Gemma want

to yank off the hat she'd been wearing to cover her imaginary baldness and wing it to the kitchen floor. Gemma knew she wasn't ultrahip, but she wasn't a total geek, either. At least she didn't think she was.

"Why is that so hard to believe?"

"Because you're—you. You don't go to places like that."

"Yes, and if you'd been there Saturday night, you'd know why."

"Who was playing?" Frankie asked as she tucked in to her pasta.

"The Devil's Schoolyard. Something like that."

Frankie's fork halted in midair. "Do you mean deValera's Playground?"

"That's it."

"Oh my GOD! They're one of the hottest up-and-coming bands in New York! They're right on the verge of breaking out!"

Gemma filled her plate with salad. "That's nice."

"Were they great?"

"Frankie, they were awful. When Sean said we were going to hear Irish music, I expected to hear Irish music. Not screaming electric guitars and bongos."

"They're very eclectic. Big on the Afro-Celt scene. Did they do that rap song, 'Homey's Tipperary Crib'?"

Gemma took a sip of wine. "I think so. I'm not sure."

"Dinner's great," Frankie raved. "Thanks for inviting me." Helping herself to some garlic bread, she continued regarding Gemma with disbelief. "I can't *believe* you didn't like deValera's Playground. You need to expand your musical horizons, *señorita*."

"My horizons are wide enough, thank you very much." Recalling the evening made her melancholy. "Honestly, the night just went from bad to worse. What worries me is Sean thought it was fun."

"The world would be pretty damn boring if everyone liked the same thing, don't you think?"

Gemma paused to consider. "You're right. But"—she shifted uncomfortably in her chair, tucking her right leg beneath her—"what if his idea of fun and mine don't gel? I mean, I'm getting the idea that we move in . . ."

Gemma halted. A keening was coming from the street below.

"What the hell is that?" asked Frankie.

"Got me."

Both paused, listening for more. Gradually the sound began taking shape.

Bagpipes.

Intrigued, they ran to the bank of windows in Gemma's living room looking out on Fifty-ninth Street. There, on the sidewalk below, was Sean. With him were four bagpipers. Gemma recognized their bright red tunics and green-and-blue tartans from every photo she'd ever seen of a New York firefighter's funeral. They had to be members of the FDNY's Pipe and Drum Band.

"Oh my God," Gemma murmured to herself as they continued the lilting tune they were playing. Spotting her, Sean began waving like a lunatic.

Frankie turned to Gemma in alarm. "You know that guy?"

"That's Sean."

Frankie pressed her nose up against the glass for a better look, knocking her hat off her forehead. "He's hot, honey."

"Apparently he's also insane."

"He's motioning for you to open the window."

Gemma opened the window and leaned outside.

"Better than Saturday night, isn't it?" Sean yelled up to her over the din of the pipes.

"You're a madman!" she shouted back down to him, affection creeping into her voice.

"He's adorable," Frankie noted again with envy. "Not to mention creative."

But Gemma wasn't listening. Her mind was a-swirl with questions. How much was this costing him? How did he know she'd be home from work? How did he know she would like this?

Under any other circumstances, the thought of someone publicly serenading her might have embarrassed her. But this was different. This was extraordinary. Gemma closed her eyes, letting the haunting sounds of the pipes wash over her. She pictured herself surrounded by fields of green, golden sun pouring down on her face. And there, standing on a distant hillside beaming at her, was Sean.

"Care to come down?" his voice called up to her.

Gemma opened her eyes and turned to Frankie. "Do you think I should?"

"If you don't, I will. This guy's unbelievable!"

Gemma was inclined to agree. "I'm on my way," she shouted.

By now, a small crowd had gathered around Sean and the pipers, and traffic had slowed. People were hanging out the windows of surrounding apartment buildings, listening. Gemma made her way to Sean. The pipers had launched into "Danny Boy."

Sean's eyes danced with delight as Gemma joined him. "So, what do you think?"

"I think you're out of your mind. How much did this cost you?"

"Not much. A small donation." He pointed to the piper closest to him. "This is my brother-in-law, Tom." Tom gave a small wave. "He was helpful in putting this together." Sean took Gemma's elbow and steered her a few feet away from the four musicians, the better to talk. "There. Now we don't have to yell."

Boyish uncertainty took hold of Sean's face. "I know

you didn't have the best time Saturday night. I wanted to make it up to you."

Tenderness swept through Gemma. "You sure like to do things in a big way, don't you?" She smiled. "Suppose I hated bagpipe music?"

"I happen to know you don't."

"Oh?" Gemma playfully cocked her hip. "And how's that?"

"A certain hockey player told me."

Gemma couldn't hide her surprise. "This was Michael's idea?"

"No, this was my idea. But I thought I'd check first with someone who knew you well to find out your likes and dislikes."

"Uh-oh. What else did Michael say?" She knew what a wise-ass her cousin was. He probably told Sean she howled naked beneath the moon for fun or liked to spend Saturday nights growing mold specimens.

"He said you were kind of a homebody. Quiet. That you would probably like it if we stayed in and I cooked you dinner."

Gemma flushed with pleasure. "True."

"Good. Because here's what I was thinking." He came in closer, and Gemma's heart nearly burst right out of her chest. God, if only she could run her hands all over him right there on the sidewalk.

"Remember I told you I had a buddy in Long Beach who lets me use his apartment sometimes?" Gemma nodded. "Well, he's going away next weekend. And I thought—if it appealed to you, no pressure—we could spend the weekend there. We could take walks on the beach, I could cook for you, we could do other things . . ."

"Other things?" Gemma repeated softly, touching his arm.

"Well, yeah." Sean looked encouraged. "Sound good?"

"Sounds great." The mere thought of getting out of the

city for a few days made Gemma feel happy. "I'll just have to check with my part-timer to make sure she can cover the store." She clasped her hands together excitedly. "I've never stayed at the beach off-season!"

"You'll love it. Especially now that the summer crowds have left."

"I can't wait. We can take my car, if you want."

"No, that's okay," Sean said quickly. "I'll drive."

He said it so fast suspicion gripped Gemma, but she shrugged it off. "Fine with me."

The sound of the bagpipes faded away. Sean's brother-in-law lowered the instrument from his lips. "Need us to play anymore, Sean?"

Sean's gaze lit on Gemma, and held. "No, thanks, Tommy. I think you've done the trick."

Pristine white sand . . . endless blue horizon . . . wind kissing your face . . .

"I can see why you like to come here off-season," Gemma told Sean as they walked along the shoreline.

Sean gave her hand an appreciative squeeze. "After Labor Day weekend, it's like a switch gets thrown. All of a sudden, the crowds are gone, and Long Beach is just the locals and the birds."

Gemma followed his gaze, taking in the wide wooden boardwalk that seemed to go on for miles. A jogger made his way past the line of benches looking out to sea, while the center bike lane boasted an elderly couple cycling at a leisurely pace. A few feet beyond them, a young mother pushed a blond baby in a stroller, the infant blinking helplessly against the sun. Gemma turned her gaze back to the ocean. Lifting binoculars to her eyes, she zeroed in on a brown bird floating serenely on the waves, its bill tilted slightly upward.

"Do you know what kind of bird that is?"

Sean peered through her binoculars. "Common loon."

Gemma looked up into his face, so handsome in profile as he continued to study the sky. "I didn't know you knew so much about birds."

"It comes from goofing off in school," he confessed. "I was always looking out the window when I should have been paying attention. My teacher finally wised up, and had me write a report on all the different kinds of birds I saw. I guess the info stuck."

"Funny what sticks and what doesn't," Gemma mused. "Ask me who attended the First Continental Congress and I couldn't tell you. But ask me about George Clooney and I can rattle off facts faster than a machine gun."

They both laughed. Gemma felt a sweetness filter through her system.

They continued down the shoreline in perfect, contented silence. Gemma pondered the lonesome cry of the gulls as they wheeled overheard, their movements looking almost choreographed. She inhaled deeply; the salt tang in the crisp fall air had a revivifying effect.

"You grew up near here?"

Sean nodded. "About ten minutes away."

"How wonderful, to be able to go to the beach anytime you wanted."

"It was pretty great, I won't lie." His arm stole around her shoulders. "You said you have relatives here on Long Island?"

"My cousin Paul in Commack. Everyone else is still in Brooklyn."

"Yeah, I meant to ask you about that." His expression was curious. "How come you didn't talk to your mom at the christening party?"

Gemma felt a small quickening in her chest. "I'm surprised you noticed."

"I noticed everything about you that day."

"I'm flattered." She felt safe with his arm around her—

safe enough to talk about what was, for her, a very painful subject. "My mom and I don't get along. I'm an only child, and I guess I've failed to live up to her expectations."

"How? You're smart; you run your own business."

"In my mom's eyes I'm just plain weird."

"What did she expect from you?" He sounded indignant.

"A mother-daughter house in Bensonhurst and at least three grandchildren. So far I've failed to deliver."

Sean stopped, drawing her into his arms. "She's crazy," he murmured, pushing her wind-whipped hair from her face. "You're perfect just the way you are."

He lowered his head, lips meeting hers perfectly. His tongue playfully danced along her lips, and then it was inside her mouth, blood pounding in Gemma's ears as Sean crushed her to him. *Thank you for this man,* she thought. *I never thought I could be so lucky.*

"Ever make love on a beach?" Gemma whispered slyly.

Sean drew back. "It's the middle of the day!"

"I'm not talking about now! I'm talking sometime."

He kissed her forehead. "Someday. I promise." He took her hand and they resumed walking along the shore. Then Sean stopped. "Wait—have *you* ever made love on a beach?"

Gemma grinned mischievously. "You really want to go down that road?"

"Nope. Besides, there's no need to. I'm the first and only man you've ever been with. The end."

Gemma laughed and they ambled on in silence for a few minutes more. She loved that they could just be quiet together.

"Do you get along with your folks?" she finally asked.

"Yeah," Sean said without hesitation. "I'm a lot like my dad—a chip off the old adrenaline junkie block."

"Really?"

"Oh, yeah. Most firefighters are adrenaline junkies, not

that they'll admit it. There's a certain feeling you get when
you climb on the truck and head off to a situation where
you don't know exactly what's waiting for you. It's a total
rush."

"And what if what's waiting for you is a life-and-death
situation?"

Sean shrugged. "You deal with it."

"Isn't it scary?"

Sean kicked up a spray of sand. "Sometimes. Usually
there isn't enough time to think about it."

Gemma swallowed nervously. The thought of him rushing into burning buildings—of saying goodbye to him before he left for work and the possibility that he might not
come home again—overwhelmed her. Just picturing it
made her feel queasy. She pushed it from her mind. Far off
in the distance, a gray cloud stole onto the horizon, mar-
ring the azure perfection of the sky. Gemma clutched
Sean's hand and pressed it to her lips. She hoped it wasn't
an omen.

"I have an idea."

Gemma's ears perked up as she watched Sean at the
stove, flipping pancakes. Last night, he'd made her a deli-
cious portobello mushroom quiche and salad, followed by
the most exquisite Scottish shortbread she'd ever tasted.
They'd spent the evening relaxing, reading, and making
love. Gemma thought that if she could fall asleep to the
soothing, steady rhythm of the waves every night, she'd
never suffer insomnia again. Of course, having Sean's
body to spoon with and keep her warm hadn't hurt either.

Wrapping her robe tighter against the ocean chill, she
approached him. "What's that?"

"How about we pop over to my folks' house this afternoon and say hi?"

"Your folks?" *Meet his parents? Now? So soon?*

"Yeah. Sunday's the day my mom makes a big roast and my sisters and their families come over. I think it would be fun."

Gemma didn't quite know what to say. She was flattered Sean thought her "family worthy." It meant he thought their relationship had real potential.

Sean looked bemused as he slid two more perfectly done pancakes on a plate and poured more batter on the grill. "What? Are you nervous?"

"Of course! I want to make a good impression."

He ruffled her hair, kissing the top of her head. "You will."

Gemma's mind went into overdrive. "Is there a florist around here? Should I bring flowers? I can't show up empty-handed."

"Relax! Yes, there's a florist. We'll stop off before we go to my folks." Hope flickered in his eyes. "Is that a yes, then?"

"Yes, yes, yes!" Gemma chirped happily. "I'd love to meet your family."

Sean's family lived two towns over in Oceanside. Gemma was so nervous she couldn't speak on the short drive over. Instead, she contented herself with looking out the window, taking in the scenery, and trying to imagine what it was like for Sean to grow up here.

"This is it," Sean announced after a few minutes, turning onto a leafy cul-de-sac. Gemma watched as Sean waved to a man washing his Lexus in the driveway; the man squinted to recognize Sean, then waved back. Sean slowed in front of a split-level with maroon shutters and white trim. The driveway was filled with three minivans. One had an image of the Twin Towers painted on the rear window, and beneath it the words FDNY FINAL CALL/9-11-01/FOREVER IN OUR HEARTS."

He hustled around to the passenger side and opened the door for Gemma, who could feel her heart beginning to race as they started toward the Kennealy house.

"Nervous?"

"A little," Gemma admitted, grateful for his concern.

"It'll be a cakewalk, I swear." They walked up the front steps. "Just two things," he added, pressing the doorbell.

"What's that?"

"Don't get Tom started on the Jets."

"And—?"

There was the sound of a lock being clicked back.

"Don't say anything about being a witch."

CHAPTER

08

Sitting in the Kennealys' crowded living room, Gemma struggled to keep Sean's family straight. There were his parents, who insisted she call them Mary and Steve. There was Sean's sister Christine and her husband—Joe? Joel? Gemma wasn't sure she'd heard his name correctly, and was too embarrassed to ask him to repeat it.

Christine and Joe/Joel seemed to be the parents of three little girls, the youngest an infant. Or did the baby belong to his sister Pat and her husband, Tom? No, wait: Tom made a crack over dinner about both his *boys* becoming firefighters. That meant Pat and Tom were the parents of the twins. That left Sean's sister Megan and her new boyfriend, Jason. Luckily, Jason seemed as overwhelmed as Gemma, and she was glad he was there. It meant she wouldn't be the only one put under the family microscope at day's end.

"More coffee, Gemma?" Like Stavros, Sean's mom seemed to have the coffeepot permanently welded to her hand.

Gemma held up her mug. "I would love some Mrs. . . . Mary."

"Here you go." She topped Gemma off, moving in a graceful arc around the room, providing refills. Gemma contrasted Mary's easygoing nature with that of her own mother, who would go into full-blown cardiac arrest if anyone dared bring food or drink into her living room. In fact, she cordoned the room off with a velvet rope as if it were a museum.

Don't say anything about being a witch. He couldn't have shocked her more if he'd turned to her and declared he had superpowers. What did he think she was going to do? Pull down her jeans and moon them all with her tattoo? She knew when it was appropriate to be open about it, and when it wasn't! Meeting a boyfriend's family for the first time fell into the latter category.

"Gemma, would you mind helping me with the dishes in the kitchen?"

Gemma smiled affably and rose, following Mrs. Kennealy and Megan. She was pleased to be included, though she knew part of the reason she was being spirited away was so they could quiz her about Sean. How many family secrets and stories had women swapped in the kitchen under the auspices of doing chores?

A system was quickly established: Mrs. Kennealy scraped food off the plates into the garbage. Gemma rinsed them, and Megan loaded them in the dishwasher.

"So," Mrs. Kennealy began, and Gemma held her breath. *Here it comes.* "How long have you known Sean?"

"A few months. We live in the same building."

"And you run your own store in the city, you said?" Sean's mother was looking at Gemma with interest.

Gemma nodded. "Yes. I sell books, candles, incense, that sort of thing."

"Cool," chimed Megan, who at twenty was the baby of the family.

"Sounds interesting," Mrs. Kennealy agreed.

Megan looked up from where she was bent over the lower rack of the dishwasher. "Has he dragged you to a stupid firehouse party yet?"

"Megan." Mrs. Kennealy flashed her a look of warning before smiling warmly at Gemma. "For some reason, my youngest daughter has a problem with firefighters, despite the fact half the men she knows do it for a living."

"Maybe that's why," Megan sniffed derisively. "It's like a cult. Get out now while you can."

Gemma grabbed another plate and ran it under the tap. "What don't you like about it?"

"Megan." Mrs. Kennealy's voice was a warning.

"Ma, she asked me!" Megan whined.

"Fine," said Mrs. Kennealy with a long-suffering sigh. "Give her your little speech."

Megan smirked triumphantly. "'Why I Will Never Go Out with a Fireman,' by Megan Kennealy. One: They drink too much."

Mrs. Kennealy glared with indignation. "That's a stereotype and you know it!"

Megan ignored her. "Two: They work fucked-up hours. Three: For what they do, the pay is absolute shit."

"Nice language," said her mother.

"Four: Over half of all firefighter marriages end in divorce. Why? Because five: Firefighters are about as open with their emotions as the Sphinx. And they drink. And the pay is shit so they have to work lots of overtime or second jobs to make money, so they don't see their families." Her voice dripped with sarcasm. "Oh! Did I forget to mention the pay is shit?"

Mrs. Kennealy's frown returned. "They don't do it for the pay."

"Oh, that's right, they do it to serve, I forgot. Which brings me to six: I don't want to hitch my wagon to any-

one who might die on me when he goes to work." She
smiled at Gemma gaily. "That about covers it."

"Very nice," Mrs. Kennealy said sourly. "I'm sure Sean
will want to thank you for sharing your views with his new
girlfriend—views which are immature, I might add." She
glanced up at Gemma apologetically from the plate she
was scraping. "Megan prides herself on saying outrageous
things just to get a reaction. Don't pay any attention."

"It's all right," Gemma assured her. She winked at
Megan covertly to let her know she wasn't siding with
Sean's mother, but inside, Megan's words had made her
uneasy. "One thing Megan said did interest me," she
timidly admitted aloud.

"What's that?"

"Well, how do you deal with the danger factor?"

Mrs. Kennealy blinked. "You just do."

"But how?" She hoped Mrs. Kennealy didn't think her
too pushy, but this was preying heavily on her mind. If she
and Sean were truly going to be a couple, she was going to
have to deal with the harsh realities of his job.

"Sean's father and I had a rule: Never go to bed mad at
one another. That advice holds whether you're married to
a firefighter or not. Beyond that, the only advice I can give
is if he wants to talk, listen, and if he doesn't, leave him be.
The truth is, some women can't deal with it. The uncertainty drives them crazy."

"So does the macho bullshit," Megan added under her
breath. "And the stress. And—"

Mrs. Kennealy spun angrily to face her daughter. "One
more word out of you and you can find someone else to
pay your college tuition, got that?"

"Fine." Megan sulked.

Their dynamic made Gemma uncomfortable, reminding
her of her own relationship with her mother at that age, the
two of them constantly locking horns. Yet on another level,
it felt completely normal. Dante-esque. She wondered if

they sparred like this in front of everyone. If not, then it had to mean they felt comfortable around her. She felt accepted.

From out in the living room came the sound of roaring laughter. Megan rolled her eyes. "Some stupid firehouse story, I'm sure. They've got a million."

"For once she's not exaggerating," Mrs. Kennealy added with a rueful shake of the head. "They should write a book." Her eyes strayed to the clock above the sink. "I hope Uncle Jack and Aunt Bridie get here soon. I'm dying for a piece of that chocolate cake."

"So, have a piece," Megan urged. "You made it. You've earned the right to nibble."

Mrs. Kennealy frowned with disapproval. "That wouldn't be polite. And we don't want our guests thinking we're shanty, do we?"

Gemma blinked, confused. "Shanty?"

"Shanty Irish, as opposed to lace curtain."

Gemma stared blankly.

Mrs. Kennealy looked surprised. "You've never heard that expression?"

"No."

"It's an old, rude way of saying high-class Irish versus low-class Irish."

"We're definitely low-class," Megan joked.

"Speak for yourself," her mother said. She bit her lip, restive, unable to tear her gaze from the cake sitting on the counter. "Maybe I will have a piece. I'm sure the O'Sheas won't mind."

"*You were kind* of quiet during dessert," said Sean when they got back to the Long Beach apartment.

"I was thinking about some things your sister said to me in the kitchen," Gemma said, unbuttoning her shirt.

Sean didn't respond immediately, choosing instead to

perch on the edge of the bed to remove his socks. When he spoke, his voice had an edge. "Let me guess: She gave you her 'Why Firefighters Suck' speech."

"Yup." Gemma moved to the closet to hang up her blouse. "Why is she so vehement?" she asked over her shoulder.

Sean's eyes followed her. "Well, for one thing, she knows it's going to get up my mother's nose. And if there's one thing Megan enjoys, it's trying to raise Mom's blood pressure."

"Ah, yes, parent baiting," Gemma mused as she slipped out of her yoga pants. "One of the pleasures of being twenty."

Sean chuckled in agreement. "The other reason she's so pissy is that she was dating a probie last year. They met at a St. Patrick's Day Dance at the Knights of Columbus Hall in Mineola, I think it was." Sean looked tired. "Anyway, they were going all hot and heavy and pfftt! One day he just pulls the plug, no explanation, nothing. She's still not over it. Her way of dealing with it is to villify all of us."

"Poor Megan."

"Yeah, it was a pretty raw deal." Sean rose to unzip his jeans. "I think she's pissed my dad wasn't around a lot, too. By the time she came along, he was doing a lot of carpentry work on the side to keep our heads above water."

"I see." So Megan wasn't exaggerating. The uneasiness Gemma felt in the Kennealys' kitchen returned.

"You and my mom seemed to get along okay," Sean observed as he slithered out of his pants, standing there in just his briefs.

"She's nice," Gemma replied with a smile as she unfastened her bra and put it to rest on the dresser. "She made me feel very welcome."

Sean moved to the sliding glass doors looking out on the ocean. "When you were in the bathroom, she asked me what perfume you were wearing. Said it reminded her of the sixties."

Gemma slipped on the oversized T-shirt she intended to sleep in, then joined him at the doors. "Is that good or bad?"

"Good, I think."

"I hope."

Moving behind her, Sean wrapped his arms around her, pulling her close. "Did you have fun today?"

Gemma's eyes drifted shut. "Yes and no."

Sean lifted her hair, pressing his mouth against her right ear. "I'm listening."

"I was a little upset when you told me not to mention being a witch." She turned around in his arms. Some things had to be said face-to-face, though God knows, she wished they could have this entire conversation looking out at the dark ocean.

"Gemma—"

"Let me finish."

Sean dipped his head, acquiescent.

"You made me feel dumb, Sean. Of course I wasn't going to mention it! Not the first time I met them! But it does make me wonder . . ." She hesitated.

Sean pushed a stray lock of hair behind her ear. "What?"

"If it embarrasses you in some way."

"Of course it doesn't," he scoffed.

"Because eventually they're going to find out."

"I know that. But not yet." There was mild panic in his voice.

"When?" she asked softly, running a finger up and down his bare shoulder.

"When it's time." He drew her into a more intimate embrace. "Enough talking." He pressed his lips to hers.

"Trying to hush me up with kisses, huh?" Gemma teased.

"You object?"

Gemma laughed, wrapping her arms around his neck. She assumed Sean was strong, but she wasn't prepared for him to lift her with one arm and throw her over his shoulder like some modern-day caveman.

"What are you doing?" she cried, watching the sliding glass doors recede as he carried her to the bed. As swiftly as he'd picked her up, that's how delicately he put her down, the nubby chenille of the bedspread a soft shock against her skin. Then he was on her, skin sliding against burning skin, lips demanding and hard as he greedily pressed his mouth to her throat. Gemma moaned as the twin torments of heat and desire coiled themselves around the two of them, binding them. She couldn't tell where Sean left and she began. There was only this moment, this outpouring of need that seemed unstoppable.

Sean lifted his head just enough to look into her eyes. "Kiss me," he demanded.

Breathless, Gemma did as she was told, powerless to do anything else. She lifted her head off the bed slightly and, gripping his head in her hands, pulled his face down to hers and held it there, one second, two seconds, three, their lips almost touching but not quite, their heated breath mingling. Unable to take it any longer, Sean gave a guttural groan and pressed his mouth to hers, raw and desperate. The taste of him, Gemma thought dizzily, was like wine, like divinity. She clutched him close, afraid that if she loosened her grip, he would turn to an apparition and disappear into the night without a trace. She wanted every nerve in her body to register that this was a real, solid, flesh-and-blood man who was pressing into her with all his might. A real, solid man who wanted her.

Two pulses were fluttering wildly within her now: the one at the base of her throat, throbbing like a trapped, quivering bird, and the one pounding between her legs. Squirming in desperation beneath him, she hooked her thumbs in the waistband of his briefs and tugged. The motion seemed to inflame Sean: Without a sound he rose up and tore the briefs from his hips before crashing back down onto her, his hard-on burning against her. Gemma wondered if he could tell how badly she wanted him as she pressed herself urgently against him. She would not be complete until he had filled her. She would not rest until they spoke the same blazing language of the soul.

Ravenous. That was the word that sprang to Gemma's mind as Sean's mouth raced over her upper torso, tongue pausing to tease at her nipples through the cotton of her T-shirt. Thought ceased, veering into pure sensation. *Hot, wet, burning, yes*—Gemma's overloaded mind could barely form the words. *Rough, hard, shocking, please.* She knew she should be patient, knew how it all would end and that it would be good, so damn good, but she couldn't help herself. The conflagration burning within her was out of control. She needed relief now.

Sean knew. Gemma sensed he was just waiting for her to give him a signal. And so, too overcome to speak, she dragged her nails across his back. She lapped at him like a cat. Sean reared up and, in a move both unexpected and thrilling, roughly parted her legs, plunging his fingers deep within her. The room reverberated with the sound of Gemma's shocked screams, so loud they drowned out the background music of the surf. His pacing perfect, the thumb of his free hand caressed her sex, coaxing her to delirium while his nimble fingers dipped and played. Trembling, eager, she let herself plunge into the shuddering abyss, knowing that Sean would be there to catch her when she broke free of the bounds of earth. She was tumbling, flying, eternal. She was perfectly, absolutely his.

Weak, she opened her eyes, whispering her thanks. Smiling, Sean kissed her sweating forehead before gently withdrawing his hand. Gemma knew what was going to happen next; she craved it, body already retensing in anticipation. She swooned as his fingers grasped her hips tightly in preparation. And then he was inside her, burning, moving, demanding, each punch of his hips against hers an invitation. *Come . . . with . . . me.* Gemma's heart danced madly in her chest. Come with him? Gladly. Tightening herself around him, she answered his invitation.

He loved that. Loved it. Gemma could tell by the frenzy of his body, his driving need pushing both of them farther and farther up the bed. Reaching up, she curled her fingers around the wooden spindles of the headboard, bracing herself. And then it came: the breaking of the dam as he poured himself into her, breathing her name. *Gemma. Gemma. Gemma.* Was it possible to get drunk on the sound of one's own name? If so, then she was plastered, she was destroyed, she would never, never move again. Above her, Sean's body still quivered in the aftermath of their fierce union. Gemma slowly lowered her hands from the headboard and wrapped them around Sean's back. They were both limp, wrecked.

And more satisfied than words could ever express.

Afterward, lying in Sean's arms, Gemma realized that bed was where they communicated best. It was just the two of them, reading each other perfectly. No crossed wires, no fears on her part about what she might be getting herself into, no fears on his about what she believed. They simply were.

Lifting her head from Sean's chest, she looked at him. "You awake?" she whispered.

"Uh-huh." The arm he had clasped around her tickled her shoulder. "What's up?" he asked drowsily.

"Nothing." She put her head down to rest again on his chest. *Except I'm falling in love with you.*

The realization scared her since she had no idea if he felt the same. He obviously felt something—he'd taken her to meet his family and had just made voracious love to her. But was it *love?* Were men and women speaking of the same emotion when they used that word? A shaft of moonlight dissected the bed with its diagonal glow. Outside, Gemma could hear the wind coming off the ocean, buffeting the sliding glass doors, which trembled slightly in their tracks.

"I think there's going to be a storm," she murmured.

"Mmm." Sean drew her closer. "Go to sleep now."

Gemma snuggled close to him, enjoying every second as their legs twined together beneath the tangle of covers. She sighed, planting a series of tiny kisses on his chest before closing her eyes.

Everything was going to be all right.

CHAPTER
09

"Where were you this weekend?" Michael asked as he strolled through the door of the Golden Bough.

"Away," Gemma answered with a secretive smile, moving over to make room for him behind the counter.

"With Sean?"

"Sean who?" Gemma asked as she put on a Clannad CD.

"I know all about you and Firefighter Joe."

"You told him I liked bagpipes, didn't you?"

Michael's face lit up. "Did I do good?"

"Very good."

"Of course, I could have told him the truth."

"What's that?"

"That your idea of a good time is dissecting old episodes of 'Charmed,' but I held back."

"I appreciate that, Mikey. Truly."

"Anything for my favorite cousin. Did you have a good time?"

"Yes." Gemma slid back onto her stool. "We were in

Long Beach. A friend of Sean's owns an apartment there and he lets Sean use it sometimes."

"Sweet."

"It was."

"You really like this guy?"

"I do, but . . ."

Michael scowled. "But what?"

Gemma stared down at her lap. "I don't know. The whole firefighter thing makes me nervous."

"What, the fact he could burn to a crisp on any given day?"

Gemma jerked her head up, shocked.

"That *is* what's got you spooked, right?"

"Kinda," Gemma mumbled. "That and some other things. I'm not so sure we fit, you know?"

"Gee, why not?" Michael replied sarcastically. "Just because you're an Italian witch who runs an occult shop and he's a fireman who thinks a dive like O'Toole's is a good place for a first date? Sounds like you two have a ton in common to me."

Gemma cocked her head appraisingly. "I'm trying to remember: Were you always an ass, or did you gradually become one over time?"

"Came out of the womb with ASS stamped across my forehead, *cara.* Sorry." He leaned back to turn the music down a notch. "My advice? Just go with the flow and see what happens."

Gemma couldn't resist a smirk. "You mean the way you did with Theresa, Mr. Read My Tarot Cards or I'll Die?"

Michael colored. "That was different. That was fate."

Gemma burst out laughing. "Oh, I see. And this isn't. Michael Dante, the grand vizier of romantic relationships."

"I'm just saying," Michael huffed.

"I know what you're saying, and I appreciate it."

"Is he good to you?"

The way he said it, with the barest hint of a threat as if

he were Gemma's older, protective brother, brought a
smile to her face. "He's wonderful, Michael. Don't worry."

Michael rubbed her back. "You're my favorite cousin,
Gem. Of course I worry."

"Don't. I can take care of myself."

"Yeah, well, I'm not so sure Nonna can." He looked
pained. "That's why I'm here."

Gemma felt a wave of anxiety. "What's going on?"

"A couple of weeks ago, Anthony and Angie took
Nonna to church at her usual time. Angie decided to stay.
She told Ant that ten minutes into Mass, Nonna got up and
started wandering around. At first Angie thought she just
couldn't remember where the bathroom was. But when she
went to get her, Nonna didn't seem to know where she
was, or who Angie was, for that matter."

Gemma tensed.

"Then, on Thursday night, Nonna ran a bath for herself
and left the taps on. The tub overflowed, and water started
dripping through the ceiling."

Gemma wound her fingers together tightly.

"You should see the water damage. When the ceiling
started leaking, Nonna panicked and called me. By the
time I got there, the ceiling was starting to bow. I turned
off the taps, and cut a hole in the kitchen ceiling so that it
wouldn't collapse. You wouldn't believe the friggin' del-
uge. I said, 'Nonna, what the hell were you thinking?' I
swear to God, Gem, she looked like a scared little kid who
was afraid of getting in trouble. 'I don't remember turning
the water on,' she said."

"Shit." A million thoughts ran through Gemma's mind,
none of them positive.

Michael's gaze was quizzical. "Has she seemed forgetful with you? Different? Absentminded?"

"She has seemed forgetful. But it could just be old age."

"It could be," said Michael, not sounding convinced.

A sense of foreboding seemed to swirl through the

store, oppressive and heavy. Gemma could barely look at Michael without her chest beginning to constrict. "You're afraid it's more serious, aren't you?" she asked.

"Yeah." Michael looked up, eyes misty.

Gemma clutched at hope. "It could be a million things, Mikey. Drug interactions. Lots of old people go to different doctors and they don't tell one what the other has prescribed."

"It's not her drugs. I took her to the doctor and I brought the list of her prescriptions with me. None of them interact."

"Maybe we should get her to a specialist?"

"We are." Michael was grim. "Theresa's getting the names and numbers of top gerontologists in the city. Once she does, we'll make some appointments."

"That could take months."

"Not if your husband plays for the Blades and can get the doctor rink-side tickets to a home game," Michael explained matter-of-factly.

Gemma reached out, squeezing Michael's shoulder. "We'll figure this out. You know we will." Her mind continued racing to come up with explanations for her grandmother's memory lapses. Hardening of the arteries. Lack of sleep. Lots of old people had trouble sleeping. Maybe Nonna wasn't sleeping and that's why she was forgetful.

"Depending on what the doctors say, we'll have a family meeting and figure out what to do."

"Who's taking her to the doctor?"

Michael glanced away. "Your mother and Aunt Millie."

"What?" Gemma squawked.

"She's their mother, Gemma."

"One of us should go, too. You or me or Ant or Angie or Theresa. Don't you think?"

Michael looked troubled. "They'll think we think they're incompetent if we suggest it."

"They are incompetent!" Gemma cried. She could just

picture it: her mother tapping her foot impatiently, barely listening to what the doctor said because she was dying to get out of there and make it home in time for *Oprah,* while beside her, Millie the Sicilian chimney twitched with nicotine withdrawal.

"Gem." Michael's voice was gentle. "One of us can always call to speak with the doctor afterwards."

But Gemma was adamant. "I'm going, Michael. To hell with hurting my mother's feelings. This is Nonna we're talking about here. *Nonna.* No way am I going to rely on Heckle and Jeckle to come back and give us a report. You and Theresa call me when the appointment's made and I'll go with my mother and Millie."

"Okay," said Michael, sounding dubious. He checked his watch and stood. "I hate to depress and run, but I've got to get to Met Gar." He rustled Gemma's sleeve. "You gonna be okay, chooch?"

"Yes. You?"

Michael nodded, wrapping his arms around her in a big bear hug. "As soon as Theresa gets an appointment, I'll call you. Meantime, try not to worry."

But that was easier said than done. Gemma decided to visit her grandmother.

Ever since she was little, Gemma loved the smell of Nonna's house. It smelled fresh, as if her grandmother had just finished spring cleaning right before you visited. It wasn't until she was older that Gemma realized the scent permeating Nonna's home was rosemary. Nonna grew it in pots around the house as well as outside in her postage stamp–sized yard. Gemma loved to sit on the front stoop on summer evenings and wait for a passing breeze to help envelop her in its scent. Even now, no matter where she was, the smell of rosemary always brought her straight back to her childhood, and to happy times spent in Bensonhurst with the woman who made her feel special.

Gemma phoned ahead of time to let Nonna know she'd be stopping by the next evening. Even so, Nonna's face creased with surprise as she swung open the front door.

"*Bella!* I wish you'd told me you were coming, I'd have bought some biscotti!"

Gemma's heart sank. "I did tell you, Nonna. Last night. On the phone. Remember?"

"Oh, right, right," Nonna said hastily, ushering Gemma inside. Gemma sensed Nonna knew she was starting to forget things but was trying to cover up.

Gemma held up a paper bag. "I brought the biscotti, so you don't have to worry."

"*Perfetto!*" Nonna clasped her gnarled hands together in delight. "Come, we'll make some espresso, yes?"

"Okay." Gemma wasn't sure her nervous system, only recently introduced to the world of caffeine, would be able to handle Nonna's espresso. The family joke was that it could be used to tar roofs in an emergency. Screw it. One cup of espresso was not going to kill her.

Following her grandmother into the kitchen, she was shocked by the sight of the sagging, water-stained ceiling.

"Have you called Mr. Rosetti yet?" Gemma asked, referring to the sheet rock contractor whom her father had known for years. "You really need to get the ceiling replaced as soon as possible, Nonna."

Nonna glanced up at the ceiling. "I will, I will. Everything in its time." She fluttered her hands at Gemma. "Sit, sit."

Gemma sat, carefully watching her grandmother prepare the espresso. Her movements were as steady and sure as ever. She knew where the coffee was kept, she measured out the right amount, she knew how to turn the machine on. So far, so good.

"So, *bella*," Nonna said as she arranged the biscotti on a plate, "tell me what's new and exciting."

"Nothing. Well, something," Gemma amended. "Someone."

Nonna's eyes lit up. "Yes?"

"His name is Sean Kennealy. He's a firefighter."

Nonna's face fell. "Irish?"

"Yeess," Gemma chastised, half rising from her chair in case Nonna needed help getting into hers. But she was fine.

Nonna sighed. "I guess it's too much to hope for that you would find an Italian boy."

"What's wrong with an Irish boy?"

Nonna's tiny, gnarled fingers curled around a piece of biscotti. "They drink too much."

Gemma frowned, disappointed. "Not true and you know it."

Nonna bit down on her cookie. "I know what I know."

"In this case you're wrong."

"So, this Irish boy." Gemma loved that her grandmother referred to a thirty-five-year-old man as a "boy." "Are you making sex with him?"

"Nonna!" Gemma couldn't believe her grandmother would say such a thing.

"That's all men want, the sex," Nonna groused. "You tell them no, they say yes. Poking, poking, poking until you give way."

Gemma stared at her grandmother in disbelief. Who was this woman sitting across the table from her? She had never heard Nonna talk this way. Never. She knew her grandmother was devilish and irreverent, but this was something different. Correction: This was someone different.

"Nonna," Gemma repeated, her voice gentler this time. "Are you feeling all right?"

"I'm feeling fine," Nonna snapped. "Why?"

"Nothing, you're just talking strange, is all."

"Nothing strange about the truth, *cara*."

Perhaps it was cruel, but Gemma decided to conduct a little test. "What happened to the ceiling, Nonna?"

Ignoring her, Nonna rose from the table to check the espresso machine.

"Nonna?"

"Someone left the water running," Nonna mumbled. "That's what Michael says."

"Someone?"

Nonna was silent.

Gemma rose and put her arms around her grandmother. "You don't remember, do you, Non? You don't remember leaving the taps on."

"No," Nonna whispered. Her expression was desperate. "But don't tell. Don't tell."

"I won't tell," Gemma promised, steering her grandmother back to the table. "Here, you sit. I'll get the espresso."

"I keep forgetting things. But I don't remember forgetting. Maybe I'm *ubatz*. Who knows?"

"You're not crazy."

"Then why else—?"

"I don't know," Gemma said, preparing the espresso. "But we're going to find out." She turned around to check her grandmother's expression, surprised to see the suspicion in her eyes.

"Who's we?" Nonna demanded.

"Me, mom, and Aunt Millie. We're going to take you to a special doctor and we're going to get to the bottom of what's wrong."

"I'll tell you what's wrong," Nonna said, huffing. "Your mother comes creeping around here every day, poking, prying, asking questions. She thinks I don't know she steals my tomatoes, either. She should mind her own business, that one. And Millie! I should have drowned that one at birth. Her and Betty Anne."

Gemma flinched. Some alien had possessed her grandmother. That was all there was to it.

"Don't say things like that," Gemma admonished. "It's not nice."

"I'm old. I don't have to be nice."

Gemma laughed. Now that sounded like her grandmother. Maybe all wasn't lost.

Nonna took a sip of espresso, declaring it splendid. Gemma did the same and almost passed the black sludge through her nose. It was beyond horrible: It was toxic. Her first sip would be her last.

"Do you want to hear more about my boyfriend?" Gemma asked, trying to get off the topic of her mother and her two aunts, who apparently were lucky to have survived infancy.

"Sure," Nonna said eagerly. "I want to hear every blessed detail."

Gemma told her as much as she deemed necessary and flattering.

"Does he know about *La Stregheria?*" Nonna asked.

Gemma nodded.

"And—?"

"He's a little confused by it," Gemma admitted.

"Confused you can work with. Fear you can't." Nonna reached across the table for Gemma's hand. As always, Gemma was shocked by how cold it was. Cold but soft, the sweet scent of Jergen's lotion wafting up to her nostrils. Gemma loved that scent. Almond. It was Nonna's scent.

"This is what I'm going to do," Nonna said, squeezing Gemma's hand. "I'm going to light a candle for you at St. Finbar's on Sunday, and pray to the BVM that all your dreams come true."

Gemma was touched. "Thank you."

"And then," Nonna mumbled, turning away as she rose to get a refill of espresso, "I'm going to say a special prayer to the *querciola* for you."

Gemma leaned forward, straining to hear. "What did you just say?"

Nonna looked confused. "What?"

"Just now. Who did you say you would pray to?"

Nonna looked thoughtful. Then her expression faded into one of blankness. She shook her head slowly. "I don't remember."

Gemma let it go. But the word—*querciola*—stuck in her mind. It sounded familiar, but she couldn't quite place it. She'd have to poke around, do some research when she got home.

"That was Peter Gabriel with 'Shock the Monkey.' Before that, Elvis Costello told us to 'Pump It Up'—Yes, sir!—and we started the set with a classic from AC/DC, 'You Shook Me All Night Long.' Stay tuned, weather coming at ya in just five minutes."

Going to commercial, Frankie whipped off her headphones and stared at Gemma in disbelief. "Excuse me, what did you just say?"

"I think my grandmother might be a witch."

Frankie looked doubtful as she hopped off her chair to load a stack of CDs back in their cases. It was Saturday afternoon, and she was filling in for another jock. It felt odd to Gemma to see her in the studio in the daytime.

"I told her about Sean, right? And in addition to telling me she'd say a prayer to the BVM—"

"Who?"

"It's Catholic shorthand for the Blessed Virgin Mary: BVM."

"Sounds like a terrorist group, but go on."

"She mumbled something about saying a special prayer to the *querciola.* So I looked it up. According to one of my books on Italian witchcraft, the *querciola* are special spirits who look out for lovers."

"Gemma, no way is your grandmother a witch. The woman practically lives at St. Finbar's."

"Maybe she's both."

"Wouldn't that qualify as a 'Pass Go, Proceed Directly to Hell'–type situation?"

"How else would you explain it, then?"

"She's old and she was born in Italy, right?" Frankie trekked across the worn carpet of the studio and began putting CDs away. "It's probably something she heard about when she was a child, some old superstition." Gemma frowned. "C'mon, Gem, think about it. Your grandmother's house has more religious imagery per square inch than the Vatican."

"True." She shrugged. "I just thought it was interesting, that's all."

Her eyes followed Frankie as she hustled back to the control board, pressing a button that launched into another commercial. She loved watching Frankie at work—she had impeccable timing honed after years of practice, not to mention between-song patter she made look effortless. Frankie was in her element in the studio.

"I see you're not wearing your hat," said Gemma.

"Nope."

"The baldness has cleared up, then?"

"Scoff all you want," Frankie said heatedly, "but my hairline is receding. Just not as badly as I thought."

"And the sunglasses? Are you hung over?"

"No."

"What's the deal, then?"

"I think I'm developing cataracts." She slipped her headphones back on. Gemma held still while the ON AIR sign above the studio door lit up. "It's fifty-five degrees and sunny in Midtown Manhattan on this glorious Saturday afternoon. Don't know about you, but I can't think of a better way to celebrate the day than with a little taste o' the Fabs." Frankie hit a button and the opening chords of

"Good Day Sunshine" filled the studio. She turned to Gemma. "Go ahead and laugh. Accuse me of being a hypochondriac."

"I didn't say anything!"

"You didn't have to." Frankie lowered the sunglasses, squinting. "Bright lights hurt my eyes. That's one of the symptoms."

"You know, God forbid you ever do have anything seriously wrong with you. No one will believe you."

Frankie stuck out her tongue before pushing the glasses back up her nose and turning to a nearby computer. "What did your grandmother have to say about Sean?" she asked, typing.

"What do you think? She's disappointed he's not Italian."

"Have you met his firefighting buddies yet?"

"No."

"I'm surprised. I always thought firefighters thought of their comrades as their second family."

The observation pricked at Gemma. She'd met his flesh-and-blood family. Didn't that count?

"*You* still haven't met Sean."

"Correction: Sean hasn't met *me*. Let's not get confused over who's more important here."

Gemma chuckled. "True." She took a sip of the tea she'd brought with her in a thermos. "Think I should say something? About meeting his friends?"

"Absolutely." Frankie turned to her. "And find out if he has any single friends while you're at it."

"You serious?"

"I wouldn't mind putting an end to my dating drought."

"Hhmm." In all honesty, Gemma couldn't imagine Frankie with a firefighter. She tended to be attracted to more flamboyant types: musicians, foreign jugglers, performance artists who smeared their body with crude oil to protest foreign cartels, that type of thing. The more offbeat the man, the more intrigued Frankie was. And that's when it hit her.

"I think I might know someone!"

Frankie's eyes lit up. "Who?"

"The guy I've been giving tarot lessons to. Uther."

"The one you said looks like a refugee from ZZ Top?"

"Yes, but he's really nice, Frankie. Really smart. He has a photographic memory. And"—she wasn't sure if this would be an enticement, but it was worth a try—"he makes a boatload of money."

Frankie grunted. "Huh. I'll think about it. In the meantime you need to think about meeting Sean's friends."

"*What are you* doing still up?"

Gemma sat curled on Sean's couch, sipping peppermint tea. It was 6 A.M. Sunday morning, and Sean was just returning from covering another firefighter's shift. There was more than surprise in his eyes when he saw her. There was dismay.

Gemma's gaze danced away. "I couldn't sleep."

"Oh, honey." Sean sat beside her and wrapped an arm around her. "You've got to do something about this. This is crazy."

They'd been together two months now, and rather than getting used to his being a firefighter, her anxiety seemed to be getting worse. She did protection spells, but nothing seemed to quell her nerves. She was okay when she was at the store, because work gave her something to focus on. But the rest of the time, she was haunted by the sound of sirens. When a fire truck roared down the street, her heart stopped as she worried about where the men inside it were going, if they had families, if they'd all return safely. Night shifts, like the one Sean had just pulled, were the worst. She would lie awake staring at the ceiling, wondering if the kiss he'd given her before he'd walked out the door would be the last one they'd ever share.

"Did you get any sleep at all?"

Embarassed, Gemma shook her head. He was near enough that she could catch his scent: fresh lemon. That meant he'd showered at the firehouse. Showering at the firehouse meant he'd gone out to a fire. Maybe more than one.

"How was work?" she asked quietly, knowing she'd get the same answer she always did. Sean didn't know it, but his tendency toward being tight lipped contributed to her anxiety as well. She was a Dante, for God's sake. She was used to dealing with people who called each other up to announce they'd just blown their nose.

Sean yawned, seeming to consider her question. "It was okay. Slow."

"Any calls?"

Sean rubbed his eyes. "Yeah. One." His bloodshot eyes met hers. "It was pretty bad. I really don't want to talk about it, okay?"

Gemma bit at her cuticle anxiously. "Can't you tell me just a little? I worry so much."

"It was a suicide," Sean said quietly. "Let's leave it at that."

"Okay." Morbid curiosity roiled inside her but she refrained from asking him anything more. The things he saw in the line of duty were a dual-edged sword. She wanted to know, but at the same time, she didn't. Better to keep it light.

"Did the guys like your brownies?"

"Yeah, they were gone in five seconds flat. They inhaled them. Then Ojeda's face swelled up. He's allergic to walnuts but he scarfed down a bunch anyway."

"Is he okay?"

"He's fine. Leary ran him over to the emergency room at Lenox Hill. They gave him a shot and sent him on his merry way." Sean shook his head. "What kind of an idiot forgets he's allergic to walnuts?"

"A hungry one?"

"I'll leave 'em out next time."

"Am I ever going to meet any of these guys? She touched Sean's hand lightly. "They seem to mean a lot to you."

"They do."

"So, let's do something with them and their wives. Or girlfriends. Isn't it about time I met your 'second' family?"

Sean's expression was tentative. "I guess we can figure something out."

"Is everything okay between us?" Gemma asked quietly.

"Why do you ask that?"

"It's just . . ." She paused to find the right words. "We've been dating for two months and I haven't met your friends. Sometimes I get the feeling that you're afraid—"

"You want to meet some of the guys?" Sean cut in, rising from the couch. "Consider it done."

CHAPTER

10

"How do I look?"

Sean looked up from the latest issue of *Firehouse* magazine to see Gemma standing before him in a purple sari, gold bangles ringing her left arm from wrist to elbow. They were going to meet Mike Leary and his wife Ronnie, as well Ted Delaney and his girlfriend Danielle, for dinner at Dante's. At least, that had been the plan. Now Sean wasn't so sure.

"Um . . ."

Gemma twirled for him. "Don't you love it? My friend Kai brought it back for me from India."

Sean scratched his cheek. "It's very—Indian."

Gemma's smile slowly faded. "You don't like it."

"No, no, you look great." She did. She looked exotic, gorgeous, and delectable. To him.

"So—?"

Sean clasped his hands between his knees. "It's a little"—he paused—"it's a little over the top."

"You think so?"

"Yeah, kinda."

Gemma looked surprised. "Oh, well. Guess I'll go change."

Watching her walk back into her bedroom, Sean was wracked with guilt. Who was he to tell her what to wear? The answer came swiftly: the guy who was gonna catch major shit if he showed up at a Brooklyn spaghetti house with Indira Gandhi on his arm. Quirky was one thing. Out-and-out eccentric was another. He wanted his friends to like her, not laugh at her.

"How's this?"

She reappeared in the living room in billowing black pants, beaded Chinese slippers, and a purple velvet tunic with a paisley scarf tossed over one shoulder. Funky but stylish.

"Great," said Sean, meaning it. He crossed to her and took her in his arms, burying his face in her hair. "Aren't you going to wear that perfume I love?"

"I thought it might be over the top."

Their eyes met and Sean saw the imp in hers.

"You busting on me?" he asked, pinching her butt.

"Maybe."

"Wear it," he urged, lightly kissing her temple. "Please."

"Do you think your friends will like me?"

"Of course they will," he assured her—and himself. "What's not to like?"

"Willkommen. Bienvenue. Welcome."

Gemma shot Michael a look as she and Sean walked through the door of Dante's. Maybe coming here wasn't such a great idea. Knowing Michael, he'd be unable to resist swinging by the table repeatedly under the guise of "Making sure everything was all right." As for Anthony, God only knew what could happen. If he was good Anthony, he'd hide in the kitchen and cook. But if he was bad Anthony . . .

The look, mildly withering as intended, appeared to freeze Michael in his tracks. "What?" he asked defensively.

Gemma leaned close to him. "No hovering," she whispered.

Michael put a hand over his heart. "I swear to God, you won't see hide nor hair of me tonight. I'll pretend you don't exist. However, we do need to talk soon."

"About?"

"Nonna."

"Not good?"

Michael frowned. "Not good."

"Call me," Gemma said sadly.

"Will do." He pointed to a large table toward the back where four people already sat chatting. "The other parties have arrived."

"Thanks, Mike," said Sean.

Gemma's hand tightened around Sean's as they walked toward the table. She was so nervous she felt nauseous. She wanted these people to like her. She wanted to like them.

"Do I look okay?" she murmured to Sean.

"Yeah, now that no one's in danger of mistaking you as a Bollywood extra."

"Ass," Gemma whispered affectionately.

Sean squeezed her hand. "Just be yourself and you'll be fine."

"Okay."

"Everyone: This is Gemma."

Four pair of eyes simultaneously swiveled to look at her. "Hi," Gemma said to the party in general as Sean pulled out a chair for her. "It's nice to meet you all."

"You, too," said Mike Leary, previously known as Mustache. His poker face told Gemma he wasn't going to mention meeting her previously, which was fine. "I'm Mike

Leary," he said, then turned to a small, freckled brunette at
his side, "and this is my wife, Ronnie."

"Hi," said Ronnie, her eyes doing a sweep of Gemma
from head to toe.

The other man at the table, blond, plump, and younger
than both Sean and Mike Leary, extended a hand to
Gemma. "Hi, I'm Ted Delaney."

"He's a probie," Sean explained.

"He'll be serving us our dinner tonight and mopping up
in the kitchen later," Leary joked. All three men laughed.
Gemma smiled graciously.

The woman at Delaney's side, also plump and blond,
extended a hand to Gemma. "I'm Ted's girlfriend,
Danielle. Nice to meet you."

"You, too."

Leary leaned over to Sean. "You know who that is
greeting people at the door? *Michael Dante.*" His voice
rang with a reverence that made Gemma want to giggle.

Sean turned to Gemma. "Should I tell them, or do you
want to do the honors?"

"I'll do it. Michael is my cousin," she told them.

"No shit!" Leary looked impressed.

"He is *hot,*" Danielle said dreamily.

"He is," Ronnie Leary agreed. She looked to her husband. "Who is he again?"

"He plays for the New York Blades," Leary explained
patiently. "He's one of the toughest SOBs in the NHL."

"He's really a pussycat," Gemma confided. The others
all turned to gaze at Michael. Gemma could tell they enjoyed being privy to this piece of private information.

"Hot," Danielle said again.

"Very," Ronnie agreed.

Gemma relaxed a little; Sean's friends seemed nice. The
evening would go well. She was sure of it. Then Anthony
came bounding out of the kitchen, making a beeline for
their table. "*Willkommen. Bienvenue.* Welcome!"

"Mikey already said that."

Anthony scowled. "He did?"

Gemma nodded.

"The little bastard stole my lines!"

"You two know each other?" asked Ronnie Leary.

"He's my cousin, too. In fact, he's Michael's brother. Anthony, say hello to the nice people."

Anthony bowed deeply.

"Good evening, one and all. I'm Anthony Dante, and I'll be your chef this evening. Allow me to tell you of our two specials: We have grilled T-bone steak Florentine style, as well as pan-roasted lamb with juniper berries. Aldo will be by shortly to take your orders." He looked at Gemma. "What should I get you? A tofu dog?"

"Very funny."

Anthony took another bow and disappeared back into the kitchen.

"Tofu dog?" asked Danielle.

"I'm a vegetarian," Gemma explained. "Anthony likes to tease me about it." She saw Ronnie Leary roll her eyes to her husband.

"What made you decide to not eat meat?" Danielle asked.

Beneath the table, Gemma felt Sean's hand squeeze her knee. Gemma squeezed back. "Health reasons."

The waiter swung by with menus, and for a few minutes, the talk was of food. But once drinks were served and dinner ordered, Gemma could feel a certain sense of awkwardness.

"So, Gemma, what do you do?" Ronnie Leary asked.

"I own a shop in Greenwich Village."

"Oohh, la di da," sang Mike Leary.

Gemma shot Sean a quick, quizzical look. Was this guy teasing? Making fun of her? Putting her down? Which? Sean seemed oblivious.

"What kind of shop?" Danielle wanted to know.

Another squeeze from Sean. Unfolding her napkin, Gemma pushed his hand away.

"I sell books, candles, crystals, that kind of thing."

Mike Leary laughed loudly. "People really buy enough of that shit for you to make a living?"

Gemma colored slightly. "Yes."

He nudged Sean in the ribs. "There's one born every minute, huh?" To Gemma's surprise, Sean chuckled his agreement.

"What do you do?" Gemma asked Ronnie Leary.

"I'm a nurse."

"That must be hard work."

"It's hard on the feet, that's for sure."

Gemma brightened, seeing a way to connect. "You know what's good for that? Peppermint oil. Mix a little into some hot water and then soak your feet in it. Works like a charm."

Ronnie looked uncertain. "Um . . . okay."

"I'm not so sure I want a wife with tootsies that smell like candy canes," Mike Leary joshed.

"Like you ever go anywhere near the lower half of my body," Ronnie drawled. Leary turned red and unfurled his napkin with a snap.

Gemma looked away uneasily. She hated couples who aired their dirty laundry in public. Thankfully, the Learys weren't the only ones there. She turned to Danielle. "What do you do?"

"I'm a haircutter." She was eyeing Gemma's tresses with interest.

Mike Leary patted the top of his bald head. "Haven't seen one of those in a while."

Everyone laughed.

"I could fix that, you know," Danielle continued.

Gemma was confused. "Fix what?"

"Your hair. If you let me thin it and shape it—"

"No, thank you," Gemma said politely. Again her eyes

sought Sean's, wondering if he noticed Danielle had just insulted her, though Danielle was clearly unaware of having done so. And again Sean seemed to be just rolling along, listening to conversation.

"So," said Mike Leary, "you all catch 'King of Queens' the other night? It was hilarious."

Spirited discussion ensued and Gemma had no idea what they were talking about. Ted Delaney noticed and asked, "Not a Kevin James fan?"

Gemma smiled apologetically. "I don't know who that is. I don't watch a lot of television."

Conversation died hard, if only for a moment. Gemma felt herself sinking. *They hate me,* she thought miserably. *They think I'm a snobby weirdo who's obsessed with peppermint oil.* The moment was rescued by Sean. "Gemma doesn't watch much TV because she's so busy taking pictures." He beamed at her. "Gemma takes great photos."

"Oh yeah?" Ted Delaney's interest was piqued. "I always wanted to do that, but I could never figure out the f-stops and all that stuff. I'm strictly a point-and-click man now."

"That's why God invented autofocus," said Gemma, happy to be part of the loop.

Then conversation turned to the firehouse and some baseball player named John Franco and she was lost again, reduced to Sean's smiling, silent companion. It didn't help her nerves that Michael appeared every fifteen minutes like clockwork and Anthony could be seen periodically peering out at them from a crack between the swinging doors.

"How we all doing?" Michael asked on what had to be his fifth visit to the table.

Gemma looked up at him imploringly. "We're doing great, Mikey, except for a certain chef who keeps popping his head out the kitchen door to stare at us. Maybe you can fix that?"

"I'll see what I can do," Michael soothed, striding force-fully toward the kitchen and slamming through the swinging doors, where he could be heard bellowing, "Stop staring at Gemma and her boyfriend, you oversized moron!" at the top of his lungs. Naturally, Anthony returned fire.

"Some pussycat," Ronnie Leary noted above the din of pots clattering to the floor.

"Italians are like that," Danielle said knowingly. "Very emotional people."

"Are you Italian?" Gemma asked. Perhaps they'd be able to commiserate about crazy families.

"No, Irish. But I've heard stories. And I watch the *Sopranos*." She looked at Gemma with newfound curiosity. "Do you know anyone in the Mafia?"

"I'm not sure your friends liked me," Gemma said un-certainly as she and Sean drove back to Manhattan.

"They liked you fine."

"Then why did Danielle insult my hair? And what was with Mike Leary's 'la di da' when I said I owned my own business?"

"Ah, neither of them meant anything by it," Sean said good-naturedly, reaching across to squeeze her knee. Which reminded Gemma . . .

"Why did you keep squeezing my knee? What did you think I was going to say?"

Sean shrugged. " I don't know. I just thought it was a good idea to keep it light, you know?"

Gemma glanced out the window. "I guess."

"Did you like them?"

"They were nice," Gemma replied carefully.

"Not exactly a ringing endorsement," Sean noted dryly.

"I don't watch TV, Sean. I don't care about baseball. I don't know anyone in the firehouse. I don't know anyone in the Mafia."

"Just relax," said Sean testily. "It'll come."

"What if it doesn't?"

Sean turned his head to look at her. "What does that mean?"

"Nothing. I'm tired. Just forget it."

"How's Peppermint Pattie?"

Sean glanced up from the sports pages of the *Daily News* to see Mike Leary standing over him, stroking his mustache. Dinner was done, the dishwasher was churning away, and most of the guys were gathered around the TV set in the ready room watching a *Sopranos* rerun. It had been a pretty dead shift so far: one false alarm and one trash can fire set by a homeless man up the street.

Sean folded up the paper. "Don't talk about my girlfriend like that."

"Ooh, girlfriend. Owns her own business, too. Seany's got himself a sugar mama, huh?"

"Putting aside the fact that you and your pinky-sized dick are obviously threatened by an independent woman, what did you think of her?"

Leary bit his lip, thoughtful. "Cute. Hair's gotta go, though. They could probably find the Lindbergh baby in there."

"You're such an asshole."

Leary slapped him affectionately on the back. "Ah, I'm just raggin' on ya, you know that. Sometimes—"

He was cut off by the shrill sound of the alarm horn as it blasted through the firehouse.

LADDER TWENTY-NINE, ENGINE THIRTY-ONE, FIRE RE-PORTED AT BROWNSTONE AT 334 EAST SEVENTY-NINTH OFF LEXINGTON AVENUE.

Jumping to his feet, Sean, with Leary right behind him, ran down to the apparatus floor to put on his turnout gear. Sean wondered if the quiet night was about to change.

Adrenaline rushed through him, hot and fast. It didn't matter how long he'd been doing this or how many times he got called out during a shift: It was always a rush, the potential for facing down and conquering unknown danger the most amazing high he knew. Grabbing his tank and helmet, he swung up onto the ladder truck and into the back cabin, lights flashing and siren blaring as they sped out of the engine bay.

Racing to a fire always made him think of Moses and his little trick with the Red Sea: Traffic parted for them as the city flew by the outside window in a blur. In his mind Sean reviewed who'd be doing what. As the Irons Man, Sean would be going interior with Lieutenant Carrey to conduct the primary search. They'd bring Delaney with them, too, for experience's sake. Mike Leary would be handling outside ventilation. Joe Jefferson, the chauffeur, would remain with the truck. "Socrates" Campbell would take care of the roof, cutting a hole for ventilation. Twenty-nine Ladder was a good crew: fast, strong, and competent. Even the battalion chief said so, and he wasn't a man given to high praise.

Sean could smell the smoke as they turned onto East Seventy-ninth. If someone asked him to describe it, he wouldn't be able to, though another firefighter would understand exactly how he could so accurately pinpoint the mixed aromas of burning wood, chemicals, and plaster. By the time they reached the brownstone and he caught sight of the thick black smoke billowing out the second- and third-floor windows of the brownstone, his heart sank. It was gonna be a real job. He hoped to Christ no one was in there.

Jumping off the truck, he waited for instructions from Lieutenant Carrey. As he suspected, he, Carrey, and Delaney were being sent inside to do the primary search. On the sidewalk, a small crowd of neighbors had gathered, their expressions anxious as they watched the guys from Thirty-one Engine unfurl their hoses and charge the lines. A woman in a pink silk dressing gown told Lieutenant Carrey she was pretty sure a child lived in the brownstone. Just a child? Carrey pressed. Two adults and a child, the woman amended. Sean filed the info away as he fixed his mask's face piece to his head and turned on his bottled air. He ran up the front steps and broke down the door with his rabbit tool. Then, bracing himself for his inevitable plunge into the smoky maw, he went inside, following closely behind Carrey.

He was hit immediately with a rolling wall of smoke. The fire, wherever it was, had to be "going good." Dropping to his knees, Sean crawled forward. The heat roiling through the house was intense. With Delaney right behind him, Sean crawled into what he thought was the dining room. Once or twice he stopped, backing up when he didn't feel Delaney's hand on his air tank. The last thing he needed was to lose a probie in smoke as dense as this was.

Sweeping his ax handle in front of him in a slow, back-and-forth motion, Sean gave two quick prayers. One was they wouldn't find anyone in the house. The other that if they did, they'd be able to save them. No one in the dining room, living room, or kitchen. Sean paused as his radio crackled and Carrey's voice came through.

"Battalion Six, this is Ladder Twenty-nine Carrey. Main floor appears to be clear. I'm going up to search the parlor floor with Kennealy and Delaney k."

Sean could barely hear the battalion chief's response on his radio as a deafening crack exploded above him, sending sparks showering down the stairwell. "Ladder Twenty-nine, proceed to parlor floor."

Sean turned around to Delaney. "You doin' okay?" he yelled.

"Great," Delaney yelled back.

Slowly, Sean followed Carrey up the stairs on his hands and knees. The higher they rose, the more intense the heat. Sweat was pouring off his forehead, down the back of his head, rolling down his carefully protected neck. One crack in his protective gear and he had no doubt his neck would be scalded. Black smoke clogged his vision, making progress slow.

The parlor floor clear, Sean waited as Lieutenant Carrey radioed back down to the incident commander that they were going up to the third floor, where most of the bedrooms were. Remembering back to his own days as a probie, Sean was impressed by Ted Delaney's coolness— at his own first major fire, he'd been breathing so hard and heavy he went through his oxygen in fifteen minutes.

They tackled yet another set of steps on all fours. It was like crawling through hell, Sean decided as he slowly edged forward onto the landing. Dark. Like crawling into oblivion. Suddenly Carrey turned to him, speaking through the radio.

"Kennealy, you go search the two front bedrooms and meet me back here at the steps. I'll take Delaney and search the back bedrooms."

"Gotcha."

Crawling down the hallway, Sean felt along the wall until he came to a door frame. Reaching up, he felt for the doorknob and pushed the door open. The room was black as dead of night. Amazing, how there were degrees of darkness, degrees of black. Search clockwise, he reminded himself. Clockwise, clockwise. Where was the goddamn fire? Fourth floor? Where was the kid? His parents? Anyone? Was anyone in the house?

Crawling into the room, Sean felt along the outer wall, hoping to find a window. The wall was hot to the touch; maybe the bastard was within the walls and the ceiling. Moving forward into the deathly darkness, he met resistance. Sean pushed; the obstacle was large and solid, some kind of chifforobe blocking the window. Fuck! He'd have to feel around further, see if there were any other windows in the room he might be able to use for a possible escape.

Fear whispered in his ear, but he pushed the distraction aside as he concentrated on continuing his search of the room, though he knew it could light up at any minute. He crawled forward three steps, his axe handle hitting what appeared to be the leg of a bed. Anxious, he reached up and patted the top. Empty. Did the same thing on the other side of the bed. Still nothing. He checked under the bed: clear. Rising up on his knees, he rolled the mattress back so it was folded in half lengthwise. If any firefighter came in after him, he'd know the room had been searched.

He continued his circuit around the room, encountering a bookshelf and a dresser. At least that's what they felt like. Checked the closet. No one there. Out beyond the door of the bedroom, he heard crackling. Fire had erupted in the hallway. Having completed his circuit of the first bedroom, he crawled forward into the hallway. Flames danced on the ceiling above him, creating an eerie, otherworldly glow in the darkness. Grabbing his can, Sean doused the flames just enough to enable himself to get to the next bedroom. The fire was too big for him to put out. For now, containing it this way would have to do. Besides, he had to look for this kid. *Find the kid.*

The heat was close to unbearable now, visibility a memory. Sean inched forward on his hands and knees, feeling the wall until he came to another door frame. This time the door was open and he crawled right across the threshold. Turning left, Sean immediately made out the shape of a bed. On top of the bed? Nothing. Under the bed? Nothing. He rolled back the mattress and continued on, feeling his way through the darkness. Dresser. Chair. Closet. Ladies dresses. *No kid. No one.* He glanced up: Fire was scorching the bedroom ceiling. As quickly as he could, he crawled back out into the hallway, meeting Lieutenant Carrey and probie Delaney by the stairwell as instructed.

"Both bedrooms are clear," he said. Carrey nodded, getting on his radio.

"Ladder Twenty-nine to Battalion Six. Primary search of the third floor completed. We're going to head on up to four k."

"Battalion Six to Ladder Twenty-nine, this is Murphy. Carrey, I want you and your men to back out now. The fourth floor is about to collapse. Repeat: The fourth floor is about to collapse. Back out NOW."

Shit, Sean thought, looking up from where he crouched on the floor on all fours. Flames were dripping down from the ceiling now like icicles. Any minute, the walls were going to go up. As fast as he could, Sean followed Carrey, and Delaney down. They had just reached the bottom of the steps when a portion of the fourth floor collapsed, sending burning wood and plaster crashing down, a flaming beam missing Sean by mere inches as he, Carrey, and Delaney made it back out through the front door to safety.

Whipping off his breathing apparatus and helmet, he gasped at the fresh air, more out of release than need. A chill shuddered through him as the steaming sweat rising off his body collided with the cool night air. A second later came a roar that sounded as if it had come from the depths of hell itself.

Sean forced his eyes back to the brownstone, watching as the house was consumed with flames. What the hell could have started it? Faulty wiring, a dropped cigarette? He doubted it was arson in a neighborhood like this. Sean checked his watch. They'd been at the scene for less than fifteen minutes.

"Shit."

The fire had been knocked down, and the brownstone had been cleared of smoke. Sean and the rest of the ladder company were doing salvage now, covering intact furniture with tarps to protect it from water and debris, dragging burned items into the street to soak them with water. Hearing Sal Ojeda's exclamation, Sean walked from where he was covering a dresser to see Ojeda standing by a hope chest. The lid was open.

"What?" Sean asked, his heart beginning to punch in his chest.

Ojeda just shook his head and backed away. Sean reached the chest and looked inside.

There, curled up on top of a brightly colored patchwork quilt, was a little boy. A thin layer of soot coated his small body. There was soot around his nose, and the ring of it circling his mouth reminded Sean of a child's sloppily eaten ice cream cone. His blond hair fell across his forehead in wisps, and his hands were clasped together as if in prayer. He looked as though he were sleeping.

"Oh, Christ," Sean whispered. Revulsion at himself bubbled up his throat.

"Sean."

He jerked Ojeda's hand off his shoulder just in time to crouch low as the first wave of vomit spilled from his mouth. *How did I miss the fucking hope chest? Jesus Christ. I let him die. I let that kid die.*

"Wait! I think he's breathin'!"

Sean lifted his head to see Ojeda gingerly lift the boy from the chest and lay him on the ground. Wiping his mouth, he elbowed Ojeda out of the way. Tilting the boy's head back, he put his hand in the boy's mouth to make sure all was clear. Then he pinched his nostrils and began administering CPR.

"Breathe!" Sean yelled as he switched from breathing into the boy's mouth to compressing his chest with the heel of one hand. He gave five small pumps. "Don't you fuckin' die on me, kid! C'mon!"

His mouth returned to the boy's. Breathe. Pump five. Breathe. Pump five. Breathe.

"Sean!"

Sean looked up to see an EMT frantically racing toward him.

"Let me take over!"

"Sean, come on." It was Captain McCloskey. "Devlin can take it from here. There's an ambulance on the way. Go back and wait in the truck. We're almost done here."

Heart hammering in his chest, Sean did as he was told.

Back at the firehouse, Sean's shift was ending and he was getting ready to leave. Even though Carrey had done a quick diffusing at the scene, there was still going to be a debriefing at the firehouse the next day. Everyone at the fire scene would be asked to talk about what they did and how they felt about what happened. Self-loathing seized Sean just thinking about it. *I fucked up. How the hell do you think I feel about it?* he imagined himself sneering at the facilitating firefighter, who would be brought in from another house.

"Kennealy, come here a minute," said Carrey.

Obeying his lieutenant's wishes, Sean approached Carrey where he sat on the shiny chrome bumper of the engine truck. "What's up?"

"Look, I know what you're thinking right now. You're thinking you're a fuckup. You're beating yourself up for missing that hope chest."

"Pretty much."

"Well, I'm here to tell you it could have happened to any one of us. It has nothing to do with your skill as a firefighter."

Yeah, right.

"Shit like this happens, Sean. Just be grateful the kid's still alive."

"He at Lenox Hill?"

Carrey nodded.

"I might head over there tomorrow. See if he's okay."

"Good idea. It might make you feel better. Just try not to dwell on this or it'll make you nuts. You know you can talk to me if you need to, right?"

"Yeah."

"You know there's a mental health unit, too, and—"

"I'm fine," Sean cut in. "No offense, but I'm fine."

"Okay." Sean could tell Carrey didn't believe him, but he wasn't going to pursue the point any further. He clapped Sean on the shoulder. "Go home and try to get some rest. It's been one long fuckin' night."

"You got that right," Sean muttered.

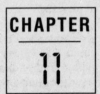

CHAPTER 11

"His friend actually said 'La di da' when you told him you owned a store?"

"Yup."

"Sounds like a jerk."

Gemma didn't disagree as she followed Frankie to the next street vendor, this one selling colorful handwoven sweaters from Guatemala. They were at the Park Avenue South Autumn Fair, waiting for Sean to show. Though a dinner date had been set the following week for Sean to meet her friends, she wanted him to meet Frankie alone first. It was important to Gemma that her best friend and her boyfriend get along.

"Did you at least have fun?"

"I don't know if 'fun' is the word I'd use." Gemma lifted the arm of a sweater, rubbing the material between her fingers. "It was . . . illuminating." The sleeve felt scratchy. She let it drop.

"Illuminating. Haven't heard that one in a while." Frankie strolled on to the next booth, where a squat, unsmiling couple in matching blue polyester sat selling paintings done on black velvet. She pointed to a large rectangular portrait of John Wayne beaming down from heaven on a circling wagon train. "What do you think?"

Gemma watched as Frankie casually forked over forty dollars, tucking the painting under her arm. "They were really nice people—apart from insulting me about my hair and the store, of course." Thinking about it, Gemma's heart sank a little. "This is going to cause problems. It *is* causing problems. They were talking about TV shows and someone named John Franco and I was totally lost. I mean, I couldn't contribute *anything*. I think they thought I was kind of weird."

"You are. But in a good way."

Gemma frowned. "That's not helpful. I don't think 'weirdness' is high on Sean's list of qualities he's looking for in a girlfriend."

They were about to walk on when Gemma heard her name called. She turned. Uther was strolling toward her, a big smile on his pale face. *Perfect,* she thought.

"Hey, you." Gemma motioned him over. "Uther, I want you to meet my best friend, Frankie Hoffmann. Frankie, this is Uther Abramowitz. I'm teaching him tarot."

Uther's smile was pleasant as he shook Frankie's hand. "Nice surprise to see you here," he said to Gemma.

"We're waiting for her boyfriend," Frankie explained.

Uther's face fell slightly. "Oh."

"Uther's that student of mine I was telling you about," Gemma said quickly, fumbling to salvage the moment. "You know, with the photographic memory?"

Frankie nodded. "Yes, I remember. Very cool. Computers, right?"

Uther narrowed his eyes, intrigued. "And you're—?"

"A DJ," Frankie replied in her Lady Midnight voice. "WROX, the city's best rock."

Gemma suppressed a laugh. She'd seen Frankie per-
form this trick a hundred times, and it always had the same
effect: Men went weak in the knees. Uther was no exception. Blood flooded his face and, Gemma imagined, other
parts of his body she didn't want to think of.

"Your voice is like the song of the nightingale," Uther
said rapturously. "I listen to you all the time!"

"Of course you do." Frankie gestured to the black plastic bag in Uther's hand. "Whatcha got there?"

Uther opened the bag, pulling out a chain mail tunic.
Gemma and Frankie just stared.

"I'm a medieval reenactor in my spare time. We're stag-
ing the Battle of Hastings in Central Park next Sunday."
His eyes brushed Frankie's. "You should come."

"Maybe I will," Frankie purred.

Gemma's heart gave a small leap of glee. A medieval
reenactor! This was eccentric enough to be right up
Frankie's alley. She had no doubt she could bring the two
together. She tugged Frankie's sleeve.

"We should get going." She smiled at Uther. "Tuesday?"

"As ever, madam." He bowed deeply before Frankie.
"Charmed to have made your acquaintance, m'lady." With
that he shimmied off.

"What did you think?"

Frankie pursed her lips thoughtfully. "Kinda cute in a
Renaissance Fair kind of way, you know?"

"So I can give him your number if he asks?"

Frankie shrugged. "Why not? There are worse things in
life than dating a guy who dresses up and pretends he's
William the Conqueror." She glanced down at her watch.
"Honey, your man is L-A-T-E. He was supposed to meet
us twenty minutes ago."

"I know." Gemma fought rising embarrassment as they
strolled along to the next vendor. It wasn't like Sean to be
late. He must have encountered heavy traffic. Or maybe he

forgot to set his alarm. She hadn't talked to him since he'd left for his shift the night before.

As they strolled past a booth selling chunky turquoise belts and rings, Gemma's eye was drawn to a newspaper tossed on an empty chair: FIRE RIPS THROUGH UPPER EAST SIDE BROWNSTONE, the headline read. ONE INJURED.

"Oh, God." Gemma approached the vendor, who was showing a potential customer a necklace. "Can I see your paper? Please?"

The vendor nodded and Gemma rushed into the booth to retrieve the paper. Hands trembling, she opened to the story. A black-and-white photo of the brownstone's charred remains jumped out at her, sending her stomach plummeting to her feet. *Sean.* Mouth dry, she quickly skimmed the text. As soon as she saw the words *Ladder Twenty-nine*, she stopped.

"I have to go."

"What?" Frankie looked confused as Gemma handed her the paper and began anxiously pacing in place like some caged animal. Frankie read fast. "You're sure it was Sean's firehouse who handled this fire?"

Gemma nodded, blinking back tears. "Yes. What if something's happened to him?"

"Calm down. You're making yourself crazy over nothing. The article said it was a kid who was hospitalized, not a firefighter."

"So? That doesn't mean anything!"

"Maybe he's just delayed. " Frankie looked genuinely concerned. "Gemma, you have to calm down. You're acting nuts."

"I feel nuts." Gemma stopped pacing and folded her arms tightly across her chest. "Every time he walks out the door, I get this scared, sick feeling: what if, what if. I can't take it."

"Clearly." Frankie pulled her aside so they were out of

the way of foot traffic. "What do you want to do?" she
asked, wrapping an arm around Gemma's shoulder.

"Call him. I don't know."

"How about this: Why don't we wait another half hour
or so, and if he doesn't show up, then you call him, or go
home, or whatever. Does that sound good?"

"Okay."

"I can't believe he stood me up on our first date,"
Frankie joked with a smile, trying to lighten things up.

Gemma tried returning the gesture, but her smile
wouldn't come.

*Wake up. Wake up so I can see you with your eyes open
and believe you're really alive. Wake up.*

Sitting alongside the hospital bed of the little boy who'd
hidden in the chest, Sean tried to will him awake. The boy
had a name, Jason Duffy, and according to the nurses, he'd
suffered severe smoke inhalation but otherwise appeared
to be "fine," meaning no brain damage from lack of oxygen as far as the doctors could tell. Unlike the staff at
O'Toole's, the nurses had Lenox Hill had a soft spot for
firefighters; all Sean had to do was tell them who he was
and they let him in, no questions asked, despite the fact it
was nowhere near visiting hours. Of course, he felt like a
fraud telling them he'd saved the boy's life. It was his fault
the kid was here, but he'd deal with his self-loathing later.
For now, it was crucial he see the child alive.

He moved his chair an inch closer to the bed, the better
to watch the rise and fall of the boy's chest. The room was
eerily quiet, TV on but sound off, the silent image of Big
Bird flickering across the small screen mounted up near
the ceiling. In the next bed lay another little boy who'd un-
dergone an appendectomy. Every time he groaned, "It
hurts . . . it hurts," Sean's guts twisted. There was nothing
worse than kids in pain.

He'd gone right home after his shift, but was unable to sleep. His mind kept insisting he revisit the brownstone fire. How could he have missed the chest during the primary search? It was so basic it was embarrassing. He was haunted by the image of the boy lying curled up inside. Had Ojeda waited two more minutes to crack it open, the kid would be dead. Eventually he had put his clothes back on and headed over to Lenox Hill. He had to see with his own eyes that his negligence hadn't killed the child.

And now here he was, keeping silent vigil. From what he'd been able to gather from his lieutenant, the boy's parents had been out at a party when the fire started. The babysitter called 911 and then fled the house, leaving the little boy inside. The source of the fire had yet to be determined.

Things like this happen, Lieu had said, referring to Sean's fuck-up. *Just be grateful the kid's alive.* Sean was grateful. Of course he was. But he was also deeply ashamed and shaken. He'd never messed up this badly before. Ever. Yeah, shit happens, but this was major, this was inexcusable. Telling him not to beat himself up was a joke. How could he not? Staring into Jason Duffy's sleeping face, all he could think was: *I almost killed him.* Not "Thank God we found him in time," but "I almost killed him." How was he supposed to live with that?

The boy stirred. *Please wake up. Please.* But he was only shifting position in his sleep. Sean sat beside him another half hour. Then he made himself go. Were it up to him, he'd sit here all day and night. He'd stay until the boy was discharged. Crazy, but he couldn't help it. He felt responsible for the boy's condition. He was responsible.

It wasn't until he was back outside in the sunshine that he remembered he was supposed to meet Gemma and her friend at the street fair. He checked his watch. He was over an hour late. They'd probably left by now, so he headed for home. Now that he'd seen the boy with his own eyes, maybe he'd be able to catch some sleep. Maybe. Gemma would just have to understand.

At the sound of locks being clicked back, Gemma flew off the couch. She and Sean had given each other keys to one another's apartment, and Gemma took advantage of the privilege, using her key to let herself into Sean's place to wait for him. An anguished cry slipped from her lips at the sight of him walking through the doorway, weary but clearly all right. Running to him, she crushed him to her, hugging him, kissing him, frantic, grateful.

"Hey." Troubled, Sean gently disentangled himself from her grasp and looked down into her eyes. "What's going on?"

Gemma began to cry. "That brownstone fire—you were there, weren't you? And when you didn't show at the fair . . ."

"Sshh, come here." He took her in his arms. "I'm sorry I missed the fair. I had to go visit someone in the hospital."

Gemma swiped at her eyes. "Who?"

Sean swallowed. "A little boy."

"The little boy from the fire?"

"Yeah." He drifted from her embrace and sank down on the couch. "I'm exhausted."

"Is the little boy okay?"

"He's fine."

Gemma approached the couch. "Are you okay?"

"I'm fine."

Gemma wrung her hands helplessly. "I was so worried."

"You always are." There was annoyance in his blood-shot eyes. "You know, if you're gonna freak out every time I get called to a fire—"

"I can't help it," Gemma interrupted quietly. "I care about you."

Sean rubbed his eyes vigorously with the heels of his palms. "I know you do, Gem, but it makes me feel pressured. I've got enough shit to worry about without worrying that you're losing it every time I go to work."

"I'm sorry."

She knew Sean was right, but his testiness still hurt.

"I'm sorry, too." He held his hand out to her, and Gemma joined him on the couch. "Does your friend hate me?"

"Of course not. You'll just meet her next Saturday night, that's all."

Sean's face was a blank.

"Dinner? My apartment? With my friends?" Gemma prompted.

"Right, right." He let his head drop back, staring up at the ceiling. "That's next week?"

"Yes." Gemma tensed slightly. "It's not a problem, is it? I thought we agreed—"

"It's fine. I'm just tired and my sense of time is off."

"Are you sure you're okay?' Gemma asked, smoothing his brow. She knew she was pushing. She could feel it. But she couldn't help it. Maybe it was in Sean's mother's nature to let things go. But she was a Dante. She couldn't. If her man was in pain, she wanted to know. She wanted to help.

Sean slowly lifted his head from the back of the couch to look at her. "I could have sworn I already answered that question."

Gemma backed off. "You did. I'm sorry."

Sean rose with a heavy sigh. "I'm sorry, babe, but I have to crash. Now."

"I understand." Gemma slid off the couch. "Want me to tuck you in?"

Sean shook his head. "Nah, you go on downstairs. I'll call you when I wake up, okay?"

Gemma stood on tiptoes to kiss his cheek. "I'm very proud of you, Sean."

"What do you mean?"

"Proud of what you do. And that you're the kind of man who goes to visit kids in the hospital. He wouldn't be alive if it wasn't for you."

Pain cracked behind Sean's eyes. "Right. I'm a real hero."

Without another word, he kissed her forehead and went into the bedroom, closing the door behind him.

CHAPTER

12

Urging himself down the one flight of stairs to Gemma's apartment, Sean was in no mood to socialize; hadn't been all week. Part of it was insomnia: Every time he closed his eyes, he was back at the brownstone, and if there was one thing that made him ornery, it was lack of sleep. But mostly, he just had an overwhelming urge to withdraw—from people, from places, from all the vicissitudes of daily life.

Simply put, he wanted to be left the hell alone.

Still, he knew it was important to Gemma that he meet her friends. He was determined to push himself through the evening, the same way he was pushing himself through life these days. He knocked on the door. The sight of Gemma, radiant in her purple sari, made him smile. He was pleased to note he could still feel. He leaned in for a quick kiss.

"Am I late?"

"Perfect timing," she murmured, leading him by the hand into the living room. The quiet buzz of conversation slowly faded as a tall, gangly blonde with a patch over her left eye; a slight, platinum-haired man clad all in black; and a handsome young man who looked like a Hispanic Errol Flynn all watched him approach.

"Everyone, I want you to meet Sean." There was excitement in Gemma's voice as she led him to the blond woman, who looked like Heidi turned pirate. "This is Frankie."

Sean extended a hand, flashing his most charming smile. "Nice to meet you."

"You, too." Frankie tapped the eye patch. "Scratched cornea. David Crosby threw a paper airplane at me in the studio."

"Does this mean your cataracts have cleared up?" Gemma inquired sweetly.

Frankie flashed Gemma a scowl.

Sean thought it was pretty cool that Frankie got to rub elbows with rock stars. He made a mental note to ask her about it later.

Still holding his hand, Gemma led him next to the man in black. Sean toyed with making a Johnny Cash joke, then thought better of it. This guy didn't seem like someone you could rib.

"Sean, this is Theo."

"Tay—oh," he corrected crossly.

Gemma put an apologetic hand over her heart. "Sorry, I mean Tay-oh. I can't keep track of your ever-changing names. Theo's a performance artist."

"Nice to meet you," Sean said again, reaching out to shake Tay-oh's hand. He couldn't wait to get this guy's story.

"Last but not least, this is Miguel. He's the fashion editor at *Verve*."

"*Enchanté,*" Miguel purred, dark eyes flashing. "You're the fireman, right?" Sean nodded. "Mmm, I love a man in uniform."

"Behave," Gemma chastised affectionately. She squeezed Sean's hand. "What can I get you to drink?"

"A Guinness would be great." He settled down on the couch beside Frankie.

"Oh." Gemma seemed at a loss. "Sweetie, I forgot to get beer."

"No problem." *You know that's the only alcohol I drink, but hey, that's okay.* "I'll drink what everyone else is drinking."

"You won't regret it," Miguel assured him. "Gemma's mixed up the most divine margaritas."

"A margarita sounds great."

Gemma flashed him a happy smile as she scurried into the kitchen, leaving Sean to wonder whose responsibility it was to pick up the conversational ball. He decided to take the bull by the horns.

"I know you and Gemma have been friends since you were kids," he said to Frankie. He turned to the two men. "But how do you guys know her?"

Theo sighed. "We met many, many moons ago when we were in the same coven."

"Really." *Just what I wanted to hear. File that under "Info never to be repeated."*

"Yes, but it wasn't her cup of tea, though we all adored her. She's clearly a solitary."

Sean nodded. "And are you still—er—"

"Pagan? Dear God, no. That was just a step in my evolution as an artist." Miguel snickered and Theo turned to him furiously. "Up your hole with a Mello roll."

Miguel rolled his eyes dramatically. "Theo's very touchy about his art."

"I'd like to hear about it," said Sean, trying to sound friendly and encouraging. He was having a hard time getting a handle on these guys. *Are they a couple? Did they used to be a couple?* Gemma hadn't said. His fingers itched for a drink.

Theo's expression was earnest. "My performances explore the oppression of man in an increasingly gynocentric society."

Sean's brows knit together so hard it hurt. "Excuse me?"

Miguel chuckled meanly. "He wishes he had a hoo-hoo."

Before Sean could respond—not that he was sure there was a response to that—Gemma swept back into the room and handed him his margarita, saving him. "Here you go."

"Thanks." He held his cocktail glass aloft. "To friends."

"To friends," everyone echoed.

"What did I miss?" Gemma asked brightly as she cozied up to Sean.

"I was just getting the lowdown on how everyone knows you," Sean explained. "It's Miguel's turn."

Miguel peered at Gemma quizzically. "Sister woman, how did we meet? Do you remember?"

"Yes. We both wanted that royal blue boa at Screaming Mimi's. We nearly came to blows over it."

"Thaaat's right. I won, if I recall correctly."

"Only because I let you."

"So generous." He blew Gemma an air kiss. *Pretentious twit,* thought Sean.

"Screw boas, I want to hear about firefighting!" Frankie exclaimed.

Sean instinctively stiffened. "What about it?"

"It must be interesting."

"It is." *But please don't ask me if I've ever saved anyone's life.*

Miguel flicked a piece of lint off his trousers. "You must get dirty a lot."

"Yup."

Miguel pursed his lips. "I don't think I'd like that very much."

Theo snorted. "Oh, puh-lease. You go into cardiac arrest if you're within ten feet of dirt."

Miguel shuddered. "That's why I hate the country."

Sean concentrated on his drink. What the hell did you say to something like that? You could challenge the guy, sure, but where would it lead? To some bitchy witticism that would leave him feeling like a schmuck. Not worth it.

Putting down her drink, Gemma reached forward to grab the tray of crudités and hummus from the coffee table and started passing them around. "Did I tell you guys Sean was on Wall Street before he was a firefighter?"

Theo looked bored. "About a hundred times."

Sean shot Gemma a questioning look. *What, being a firefighter isn't good enough?* He reached for a carrot and, swiping it in the hummus, popped it in his mouth. "Great hummus, babe."

"I love when men call women 'babe,'" Miguel sighed. "It's so Neil Diamond."

"Neil Diamond wears so much cologne he could choke a train car," cracked Frankie.

Finally, a line of conversation Sean could get interested in. "You've met Neil Diamond?"

"She's met 'em all, honey." Miguel smirked.

"Yeah?" Sean turned to Frankie. "Mick Jagger?"

"Swears by Elizabeth Arden."

"Steven Tyler?"

"Borrowed my favorite scarf and never gave it back."

"Bruce?"

Frankie groaned. "What is it with firefighters and Bruce? They all love Bruce."

"He sings their pain," mocked Theo.

Sean felt a rush of anger but he beat it back. "Tell me about Bruce," he urged Frankie, consciously ignoring Theo.

"Bruce is really nice, really down to earth."

"He needs a makeover," Miguel opined. "I mean, *hello,* men over fifty in tight black jeans? Pa—the—tique. And that cross he sometimes wears around his neck? So 2003."

Time to tune out, Sean told himself, practically chug-
ging his margarita. He stayed that way for most of the
evening, dinner included, which was vegetarian, of course.
It was the best way for him to cope with conversation
about designers he'd never heard of and defacing Tampon
ads and calling it art. He did tune back in once in a while
to hear what Frankie had to say about radio and the music
business. She was the only one of Gemma's three friends
who seemed genuinely interested in him. A little weird—
what's with the eye patch?—but friendly and clearly de-
voted to Gemma. The other two? Stuck-up, self-absorbed
assholes. As he watched Gemma laugh and chat with them
over the course of the evening, his guts churned a little.
*Who is she? What is she doing being friendly with them?
And what is she doing with me?*

"*You were quiet* tonight," Gemma observed as she put
the last of the leftovers into the fridge.

Sean shrugged. "I guess." He handed her the glass he
was drying, glad the cleanup hadn't taken too long. He was
exhausted. What little energy he'd started the evening with
was completely drained by having to feign cordiality toward Tay-oh the A-ho and Miguel.

Gemma touched his arm. "You okay?"

"Why do you keep asking me that?"

Gemma looked stung. "I don't."

"You do. Constantly. Is there something I'm saying or
doing that would lead you to think I'm not okay?"

Gemma paused. "You've been a little off this week."

" 'Off'? What does that mean?"

"Moody. Quiet. Uncommunicative."

"Maybe I'm just a moody, quiet, uncommunicative guy."

"Maybe." Gemma sounded uncertain as she moved to
put some more glasses away. "You and Frankie seemed to
get along well."

"Yeah, I liked Frankie," said Sean, taking over so Gemma wouldn't have drag out her step stool.

"She seemed to like you. I'm sure she'll give me the full report on the phone tomorrow."

Sean chuckled.

"I think Miguel and Theo liked you, too," Gemma said tentatively.

"Hard to tell, since all they did was talk about themselves." Sean could feel the last ounce of patience drain from his body.

Gemma sighed. "I know. They were a bit over the top tonight."

"You mean they're not always like that?" Sean asked.

"God, no. Be thankful: At least they spared you their dueling Liza Minnelli impersonations."

Sean looked stricken.

"That was a joke, honey. Relax. I think they were deliberately trying to scare you off."

"Why's that?"

"They don't like to share me. I'm going to call both of them tomorrow and tell them they were very naughty boys."

"Good. Because I have to tell you, my initial impression was that Miguel's a nasty queen and Tay-oh is a pretentious ass. I was having a tough time understanding why you're friends with them."

Gemma looked taken aback. "They weren't *that* bad."

Sean snorted. "That's debatable."

"At least they're interesting," Gemma blurted defensively.

"And my friends aren't?" Sean felt his blood pressure surge when Gemma looked away guiltily. "I don't believe you! At least my friends are down to earth!"

"So? That doesn't mean they're interesting!" Gemma slammed the cabinet door shut.

"Oh, excuse me. I guess being a firefighter and saving

people's lives is boring. I guess being a nurse is boring, too. And a haircutter. At least my friends are doing something meaningful with their lives! At least they contribute!"

"Why are you being so critical?"

"I'm not being critical, I'm being honest. They're jerks, Gemma."

"Well, your friends watch stupid, mind-numbing shows on TV and baseball and think it's funny to insult someone who runs their own business!" Gemma countered hotly.

Sean chuckled softly. "That says it all."

"I think your friends are nice," was Gemma's lame comeback. "I just—"

Sean held up a hand. "Never mind. Let's just drop it, all right? I'm too damn tired." He took the plate Gemma passed him and stacked it in the cabinet. "One thing, though: Why did you make such a big deal of my being a stockbroker before I was a firefighter?"

"I didn't make a big deal of it. I just thought it was interesting, that's all."

"Yeah?"

Gemma looked at him warily. "What are you getting at?"

"You sure you didn't tell them I used to be on Wall Street because you didn't want them to think I was a plain, dumb firefighter who listens to Bruce and drinks beer?"

Gemma looked on the verge of tears. "Does that really sound like something I would do?"

The plaintiveness in her voice cut him. He knew he was being a prick. "I don't know."

"Well, I wouldn't. And if you think I would, then you don't know me at all." She put the last of the dishes away.

Sean wished he could open a window and let the tension just waft away. Or better yet, turn back the clock a few minutes and lie politely, telling her he thought the evening went well. But he couldn't. His eye caught Gemma's; she was feeling it, too, the estrangement, the sense of dislocation.

"So, now what?" he offered glumly.

Gemma covered a yawn with her hand. "I'm exhausted. Let's go to bed."

"Actually," said Sean, "I'm going to sleep at my own place tonight, if you don't mind."

"Oh."

How, Sean wondered, could such a little word ring with both surprise and pain?

"Don't worry, nothing's wrong," he assured her, drawing her into an embrace. "I just haven't been sleeping well and I do better in my own bed. You know that."

"No problem." Gemma gently cupped his face with her hand. "Why aren't you sleeping?"

Sean broke away. "Stuff. You know."

"Sean—"

"Gemma. " His voice rang with warning. "Let it go, baby, okay?" He twined his fingers through hers, pressing his lips tenderly to her forehead. "I'll give you a call tomorrow after my shift. Maybe we'll drive out to the beach."

"That would be nice," Gemma replied in a thoroughly noncommittal voice—the same voice she'd used after their disastrous date at O'Toole's.

Another kiss and he was out the door, back upstairs to his own place. *Thank God that's over with,* he thought to himself, reflecting back on dinner. Stripping off, he slid between the sheets and closed his eyes, expecting sleep to hit him like a prizefighter throwing the final victorious punch. Instead, he was back at the brownstone, and when he wasn't there, his mind was chasing itself thinking about Gemma. Sleep never came.

Sean didn't call the next day. Or the next. Uneasy, Gemma left him a message—just one—though she knew he might accuse her of worrying over trifles. When another day passed and he didn't call back, she called an emergency meeting at the diner with Frankie.

"I have to tell you, I don't think it looks good." Frankie sounded like a doctor delivering bad news to a patient. "First he tells you not to tell his folks you're a witch, then he doesn't like your friends—except me, of course"—she added happily—"and to top it all off, he passes up an opportunity for sex?" Frankie shook her head. "Not good."

"He hasn't been himself since that brownstone fire. Not that I can get him to talk about it."

"This goes beyond the brownstone fire."

"I know, I know." Gemma picked listlessly at the English muffin on her plate. "What do you think I should do?"

"That's obvious: Knock on his door and find out what the hell is going on."

"You don't think that's too pushy?"

"Pushy? Gemma, this is your boyfriend we're talking about here. If my boyfriend went AWOL for three days and didn't return my calls, you can bet your butt I'd be pounding on his door. You deserve an explanation."

"I know. I'm just not sure I want to hear what it is."

"Hang on."

Sean's voice through the closed door sounded put-upon. Gemma tensed, not knowing what to expect. The knuckles of her right hand were throbbing. Two more minutes and she would have called the fire department to break in. Talk about irony.

The door swung open, and there stood Sean. He looked like he hadn't slept in days.

"Come on in," he said in a flat voice. Apprehensive, Gemma followed him inside, surprised to see Pete and Roger's cages covered in the middle of the day. Usually, when Sean was up, the birds were, too.

"I've been worried," she told him.

"I know." He sounded weary. "I've been meaning to call you back, I just . . ." He licked his lips, looking lost. "Have a seat."

Gemma sat down, unable to take her eyes off him. "What's going on, Sean?"

"I'm not feeling too well."

"Flu?"

He laughed bitterly. "I wish."

He flopped down in a chair opposite her. She couldn't believe how awful he looked. His lively blue eyes were shockingly lackluster, ringed with dark circles. Three days' worth of stubble grizzled his face and neck. He looked more than sick; he looked tormented.

"Talk to me, Sean."

"About what?"

Gemma worked to keep her voice gentle. "Why haven't you returned my calls?"

"I told you: I haven't been feeling too hot."

"Physically or mentally?"

His eyes slowly rose to hers. "Both, actually."

Gemma knit her hands together. "Does this have anything to do with that brownstone fire?"

"Does what have to do with it?"

"You're not feeling well," Gemma said carefully.

Sean leaned back in his chair, sighing. "No."

She studied his face: the haunted eyes, the pale skin. "You're lying."

"You're right. I am."

"Oh, Sean." She wanted to go to him but his expression—remote, inaccessible—stopped her.

"I don't want to talk about it, Gemma."

"Sean." Her voice bordered on a plea. "There's no need to suffer alone. I'm here for you, I'll listen."

"I just said I don't want to talk about it."

"You might feel better if you do."

"How would you know?" Sean sneered. He gave a short, staccato laugh. "I mean, what the fuck do you know about searching a house, thinking you did a good job, then finding out later you almost left a kid to burn?"

Gemma flinched. *So that's what happened.* "I don't." Her eyes began filling with tears. "But I'm here for you. Please, let me help you."

"There's nothing you can do," Sean said woodenly.

"I can hold you. I can listen."

"I'm fine," Sean insisted through clenched teeth.

"Cutting yourself off from people is not 'fine.'" She twisted her hands helplessly. "Have you been calling in sick to work?"

"What?" He frowned. "No. I pulled a forty-eight-hour shift, so now I'm off for seven days."

"When do you go back?"

"Sunday."

"And what are you going to do until then? Hide in here and play it over and over again in your mind?"

"Maybe," Sean mused bitterly, looking away. When he looked back at her, Gemma got the sense that, right now, the simplest human interaction took tremendous emotional effort for him. He could barely meet her eyes. "Look, I'm not sure this is working for me right now."

Alarm shot through Gemma. "'This'?"

"Us. I don't like your friends and you don't like mine. You can't deal with the facts of my job and frankly, if we're being honest here, your being a witch is just a little too weird for me. Face it, Gemma: The only place we work is in bed."

Tears threatened but Gemma held them back. "That's not true," she said quietly.

"Yeah, babe, it is."

"So, what are you saying?" Gemma struggled to keep her voice from getting shrill or desperate. "You want to split up?"

Sean looked pained. "For now, yeah, maybe."

"For now?" Gemma couldn't believe what she was hearing. "What, I'm supposed to be at your beck and call when and if you change your mind?"

"No."

"Then what?"

"I don't know," Sean groaned, clutching his head. "I can't even think straight right now."

"Well, think about this: Either we're together, or we're apart. You choose."

Sean hung his head. "I think you better go."

Shaking, Gemma slowly stood. "You're sure about this?"

"I just told you I can't even think straight right now!" Sean snapped. His face was a map of misery. "Look, just do whatever the hell you want, okay?"

Gemma moved toward the door, taking back the key to her apartment that lay on a small side table. She was determined to at least hold her tears until she was back at her place. She thought of slamming the door, or just leaving without a word, but that wasn't who she was, and she didn't wish to leave things that way. Instead, she made herself turn back to face him.

"Take care of yourself, Sean. Please." She returned his key.

Sean jerked his head in an approximation of a nod, refusing to look at her.

She slipped through the door without a word more.

CHAPTER

13

He hadn't planned to tell her he wanted to take a break.

He'd been pissed off yesterday when he'd first heard her knocking at the door, but he knew he owed her an explanation, however lame. He just wasn't prepared for how raw he felt, how resentful, at being asked to talk about the brownstone fire; at being asked to talk, period. He knew she meant well, and she was simply reacting to the sight of him in pain. But it angered him rather than making him feel appreciative. It felt like intrusion. Then the words slipped out, a by-product of his bottled-up anger and confusion. But now that she'd granted his wish—permanently, he guessed—he wondered if it had been the right thing to do.

Forcing himself up and out of bed, he went to the kitchen to make some coffee and feed his birds. He had to face the outside world today: There was a retirement party for one of the guys at 49 Engine, and if he didn't show, he'd never hear the end of it. He'd go, have a beer, offer his congrats, then crawl back into his cave.

Anything was endurable for half an hour.

"No offense, but you look like shit."

"Nice to see you, too," Sean replied to Mike Leary as he walked into the Huntington Elks Club. The place was packed with firefighters and their families. The man of the hour, Dennis McNab, was holding court at a long table in the front of the room with some of the guys from his company. Raucous laughter was the soundtrack of the day, making Sean feel even worse for being such a sad sack.

"Where's Rapunzel?"

Sean frowned. "You're friggin' relentless, you know that?" In no mood to tell Leary about the breakup, he thought fast. It was Saturday afternoon. "She's at her store. Couldn't get anyone to fill in for her."

"What's the name of the store again? I'd love to check it out."

Sean pretended he didn't hear as he drifted away. That was the last thing he needed: Mike Leary checking out the Golden Bough, scoping out all the weird stuff Gemma sold. He could just imagine the tales Leary would tell back at the firehouse.

He made his way to one of the coolers and pulled out a Guinness. Scanning the room, he spotted JJ Roper sitting alone off in a corner. JJ, one of the handful of women in the FDNY, entered the fire academy the same time as Sean. But unlike Sean, she had yet to be truly accepted by the guys in her house. Sean had heard more than one firefighter express relief there wasn't a woman at their house. It would change the whole dynamic, some guys claimed. We'd have to watch our mouths and take the porn out of the bathroom, others pointed out. A few even doubted women could pull their weight on the job, despite evidence to the contrary. Sean figured guys were threatened by JJ. She was strong as a horse and totally competent, but she was also drop-dead gorgeous, with legs up to her neck and cascading blond hair she usually wore back in a braid. If she heard half the sexual innuendo she generated, the department would find itself with a major harassment suit. He felt bad seeing her sitting there alone, her outsider status obviously still intact. He decided to join her.

"Hey."

"Hey." JJ's smile was grateful as Sean sat down beside her. "I didn't expect to see you here."

"What, are you kidding me? Miss Nabby's retirement? Not for the world."

JJ looked to the front of the room at the man in question. "What's he going to do now, I wonder?"

"His brother's a contractor. Nabby's been working for him on the side for years. I think he's gonna work with him full-time now."

"And how does Mrs. Nabby feel about that, I wonder?"

"Mr. and Mrs. Nabby split up about seven month ago, I believe."

"Really? A divorced firefighter? That's hard to believe." Her laugh was hard as she drained her drink.

Her bitterness caught Sean's attention. "Trouble at home?" His eyes did a quick scan of the room. "Where's Chris?"

Chris was JJ's husband. In addition to being a prick of world renown, he was also a cop. Lots of cops secretly longed to be firefighters, and the animosity between the two professions was strong. The annual hockey game between the two departments' teams was always a bloodbath. It wasn't uncommon for JJ to bring Chris to firefighter functions and the evening to end in fisticuffs.

"He's on duty, making the world safe for democracy."

"Am I detecting a little sarcasm here?"

"A little."

"What's up?"

JJ held up a hand as if to say, "Wait a minute," and jogged off to refill her drink. "You sure you want to hear this?" she asked Sean when she returned.

"Sure, as long as it's not X-rated."

"It's not." She sipped from her plastic cup. "I want a baby and Chris doesn't. And he wants me to quit the department. Says it's too dangerous."

Sean shook his head, guffawing loudly. "Jesus. I wonder if he's related to my gi—ex-girlfriend." *Ex-girlfriend.* It felt odd even saying it to himself.

JJ looked at him with newfound interest. "I didn't know you had a girlfriend."

"I did, until yesterday."

"What happened?"

Sean shrugged, not exactly eager to talk about it. "She couldn't handle my being a firefighter, among other things." He glanced away. "We just didn't work as a couple, you know? It's hard to explain."

"That's too bad."

"Yeah, it is."

Her expression changed to one of concern. "You look really awful, you know."

"Thanks. You're the second person in less than ten minutes to tell me that."

"Aren't you sleeping?"

"Not much."

There was a split second of hesitation before she asked, "Does this have to do with the brownstone fire?"

Sean slumped against the wall miserably. "Maybe. What have you heard?"

JJ looked uncomfortable. "You know. The kid. The chest."

Sean glanced at her sharply. "So word's gotten around I'm a fuckup."

JJ peered down into her drink. "It could have happened to anyone, Sean."

"Then why is everyone talking about it?"

"Firefighters are gossiping old biddies. You know that." She put a hand on his shoulder. "Look, I'm sorry I even brought it up."

"Yeah, me too. Thanks for ruining my day." Sean tilted his head back and drank.

JJ, stung by Sean's response, started to get up to leave. Sean, feeling even worse now, reached out for her elbow. "I'm sorry. That was totally unnecessary. Sit back down. Please." He made himself look at her. " Do I really look that bad?"

"Yeah."

"Great."

"When was the last time you took a few days off, Sean? Got away on your own?"

"I don't know. Months ago."

"Maybe you should go away for a long weekend or something. It might help." JJ sighed. "I would love to get away on my own for a few days. Just to think."

"Why don't you?"

"Can't afford it. We're mortgaged up to the eyeballs on the house. Plus, Chris would probably squawk."

"So let him squawk." Out of the corner of his eye he saw Leary motioning to him. "Can you excuse me a minute?"

JJ nodded and Sean went to rejoin his friend. "What's up?"

"You hittin' on her?" Leary asked excitedly.

"What are you, out of your mind?"

"Why not? She's hot."

"She's also married. To a prick who carries a gun. Remember?"

"Oh, yeah, New York's finest. Forgot about that."

Sean poked him hard on the shoulder. "Here's an idea:

Why don't you mind your own business instead about worrying about everyone else's?"

Leary's mouth fell open. "What wild hair is up your ass today?"

"Nothing. Look, I gotta go. Give my best wishes to Nabby." He gave Leary a light, playful punch in the arm. "I'll catch you on the rebound, okay?"

He strode away. Everyone was getting on his nerves. Everything. JJ was right. He needed to get away.

"Kiss her again and she'll get a complex."

Gemma looked up from cuddling baby Domenica to see Michael and Theresa coming through the front door. Only twenty minutes earlier, they'd left to go out to dinner alone for the first time since their daughter was born. Now they were back, Theresa hurrying toward the couch with outstretched arms. Michael sounded like he was teasing but he looked alarmed.

"Is everything okay?" Gemma asked, surrendering the baby.

"You tell me." Michael sighed, regarding his wife affectionately. "Mama Bear couldn't relax. As soon as she ordered, she was convinced there'd been some catastrophe and we had to rush home."

Gemma eyed Theresa. "Thanks for the vote of confidence."

"It's not you," Theresa swore, kissing her daughter's plump fists. "It's some weird maternal thing. I couldn't bear to be away from her."

"You're away from her when you're at work," Michael pointed out.

"Only because I have to be. This is different."

"I can't wait 'til she goes away to college and you want to be her roommate," Michael teased.

"She's not going away to college. She's living at home and getting her degree online."

Crouching down, Michael put his mouth to his daughter's ear. "Your mama's *ubatz,* Domenica. The sooner you know it, the better."

Touched as she was by this domestic scene, Gemma felt out of place. "I guess my services aren't needed tonight."

"Don't go," Michael said. "We haven't had dinner yet." He gave Theresa a look. "We're going to order Chinese. Stay."

"You sure?"

"Stay," Theresa echoed. "I want to hear all about you and Sean."

"Actually," Gemma said, working hard to sound nonchalant, "Sean and I broke up."

Storm clouds brewed in Michael's eyes. "What happened?"

"It was mutual, Mikey. No need to spear him with your hockey stick."

"If you say so," Michael grumbled, heading toward the kitchen. "What do you people want to eat?"

"Eggplant in garlic sauce," Gemma called out.

"Moo shu pork," Theresa said. She turned to Gemma. "It was mutual?" she repeated, sounding unconvinced. Off in the kitchen, they could hear Michael opening and closing drawers, looking for the takeout menu.

"Kind of. I don't know."

As Theresa held her daughter on her lap, she and Domenica looked like a modern-day Madonna and Child. Both of them glowed with contentment, making Gemma painfully aware of the void in her own life. Gemma wanted what Theresa had: a husband, a baby, and a quiet Saturday night at home eating Chinese takeout and watching videos. Was that too much to ask?

"What happened?" Theresa demanded in a low voice tinged with urgency. Gemma took this as a sign they should have this discussion quickly, since Michael was now on the phone ordering their food.

"It just wasn't working," Gemma confessed sadly. "I was a wreck every time he went to work, which annoyed him, and my being a witch was a little too far off the beaten track for him. It was all sorts of things."

"What about the sex?" Theresa mouthed, as if the baby she now jostled on her knee might hear and understand.

Gemma blushed. "It was great. But he was involved in this bad fire a couple of weeks ago, and ever since then, it's been like talking to a brick wall."

"Maybe he was afraid that if he talked to you about it, you'd really freak out."

"Maybe."

It was possible Theresa had something there. Still, Sean's silence felt more symptomatic of a lack of trust, a failure to connect. Thinking about him, Gemma was overcome with remorse and self-doubt. Maybe she should have left him alone rather than prodding him to open up? But keeping your thoughts and feelings to yourself was so alien. Her family wore their hearts on their sleeves. She and Frankie talked everything to death. Communication was the yardstick by which you measured relationships: how intimately people knew each other's business. Now she wondered: Were there other ways of being intimate?

Michael reappeared in the living room. "Ten minutes on the chow. Which really means twenty." He settled down on the couch between his wife and cousin, transferring the baby onto his lap. "So, what did I miss?"

"Nothing," Theresa said.

He looked at Gemma, who detected sympathy in his eyes. "I can set you up with another of the guys on the team, if you want," he offered.

"I'll think about it." She held out her arms. "Give that baby back to me. You guys get to hold her all the time. I've got to steal time with her when I can."

Michael willingly obliged, handing Domenica over to Gemma. She was such an easygoing baby, affectionate, with a big, gummy smile for everyone. Holding her reminded Gemma of fiddling with a camera lens: It brought everything into sharp focus, including her own behavior. She should have cut Sean some slack. She should have waited for Sean to call her. He would have eventually; she knew that. She hated the way they parted, him snarling and angry, her just withdrawing. It felt wrong. She loved him. She wanted him. She would fight for him. If he needed some space, she'd give it to him. But there was no way she was going to give up on him, or let him give up on himself.

She waited until the next morning to pay Sean a visit. She had toyed with the idea of stopping by as soon as she got back from Michael and Theresa's, but it was late, and she had no idea of his schedule that week. Besides, she didn't want to look desperate. Or crazy.

It wasn't much of a peace offering, but Gemma had run out to battle the typical Sunday morning crowd to get coffee and some of the chocolate chip muffins Sean loved. Walking back to their building, she rehearsed what she'd say. *I come bearing muffins.* Too geeky. *Can we talk?* Better, more her style: simple, direct. Once he smelled the coffee and muffins, still warm in her hand, how could he resist? She wasn't feeling nervous, exactly. More anticipatory.

By the time she reached Sean's door, her heart was beating double time. She went to knock then hesitated, convinced she heard shouting coming from inside his apartment. Glancing around to make sure no one was looking, she quickly pressed her ear to the door. Definitely shouting, though it was muffled. Sounded like just one voice. Unsure of what to do, she stopped eavesdropping. If he was asleep and having a nightmare, ringing the bell would wake him. If he was on the phone having an argument, she would interrupt him. *What to do?*

She bit her lip. The raised voice seemed to have gone quiet, at least momentarily. Meanwhile, the coffee in her hand was getting cold.

"To hell with it," she said out loud and rang the bell.

Immediately, Pete and Roger went crazy in their cages, their excited squawking louder than Gemma could have imagined. She cringed, praying Sean came to the door before his neighbors up and down the hall got angry. Ten-thirty on a Sunday morning might be too early for some people.

From within the apartment, footsteps pounded across the floor, and Gemma felt hope spring inside her. In just a few seconds, the door was going to open, and they'd be face-to-face. He'd smell the coffee and muffins, and break into that rugged smile that she loved, beckoning her inside. By the time the morning was through, everything would be worked out and they'd be back in each other's arms.

One lock clicked back. Gemma's stomach did a somersault.

Two more sprang back. Gemma held her breath.

Then the door opened, and everything fell apart.

Standing there wrapped in Sean's robe, her long blond hair shimmering wet from the shower, was a woman. She had a cell phone in her hand and a scowl stretched across her gorgeous face.

"Yes?" she asked impatiently. Behind her, the birds' squawking was deafening. "Shut the fuck up!" she yelled before her face seemed to collapse in on itself, from stress or annoyance, Gemma couldn't tell which.

"Um . . ."

"Sean's not here," the woman said curtly. From her clenched hand came the tinny sound of someone's voice shouting on the cell phone. "I'm sorry, I can't talk now."

She closed the door.

Gemma stood there, stunned. Who was that—? Were they—?

Gemma moved away from the door. *Sean and another woman.* She felt as though a giant invisible hand had plunged into her chest and torn her heart right out, leaving it hanging there, bruised and bloody. What a sap she'd been. Numb, she trudged back to the elevator. The sight of her own hallway drew tears as she remembered it strewn with stuffed animals, its emptiness now taunting her. How enchanted she'd been, willing to take a risk. Why had her intuition failed her?

Back in her own apartment, she made a beeline for the kitchen, throwing the coffee and muffins into the trash with gusto. She could still hear footsteps above—*boom! boom! boom!*—as the blond continued her fight with whomever was on the phone. Maybe it was Sean and they were having a lover's quarrel. *Good.* She hated her pettiness, but there it was. She didn't want to hate him, but she did. She hated them both. She slid into a kitchen chair, head in hands. Now what? The urge to wail, to just let it rip, was strong. Never, she vowed. Never again would she give her heart away so fast. If her faith had taught her anything, it was that things always happened for a reason, though the reason might not become clear for some time. There was a lesson in this, Gemma knew.

She just wished she knew what it was.

CHAPTER
14

After two days at the Blackfriar Inn, Sean had had enough. Walking through the woods, reveling in the scent of pine as shifting rays of sunshine dappled through the branches of the bare trees, his mind had returned again and again to the fire scene. He couldn't escape the boy in the hope chest. As he headed out for a final amble through the woods before going home, his thoughts turned to JJ. He'd called once to thank her for agreeing to bird-sit. It had been the perfect barter: JJ got a weekend away free of charge, and he got to go away without freaking out Roger and Pete.

He inhaled deeply, letting the crisp air fill his lungs. At least the weekend gave him space to think about Gemma. Their timing had been off from the beginning. Then there were her friends. And the witchcraft. Part of him envied her freedom to be completely who she was, convention be damned, open to the world. But that wasn't who he was. A fantasy flashed through his mind. He was apologizing to her for the way things had ended. "I hope we can still be friends," he heard himself saying. He burst into bitter laughter, the sound booming through the still woods, scattering a flock of starlings. He remembered a woman saying that to him and thinking, "Fuck you! You just wrecked my life and you have the gall to think I want to keep you as a friend? Screw you!"

But he did want Gemma to remain his friend.

Being with her was like opening a new book by your favorite author: You weren't quite sure what was in store, but you knew you'd like it. She was full of mystery and surprise, as sweet as she was iconoclastic. But he was toxic. As much as he yearned to maintain some kind of contact, he knew he shouldn't. Gemma deserved better than being dragged down with him into his black hole. He walked on, dead leaves crunching beneath his feet. Her last words to him had been unselfish, asking him to please take care of himself. He closed his eyes, sending a message to her. *I'm trying, Gemma, in the only way I know how. Please forgive me.*

He couldn't blame her if she didn't. He couldn't blame her for anything.

Turning the corner onto his street, Sean tensed as it dawned on him he might run into Gemma—if not today, then some other time. The thought made him sad, mainly because he could so vividly picture his own inept reaction to such an encounter: shuffling feet, muttered phrases. He sucked at post-relationship stuff.

Approaching his building, he noticed what looked like a bulging, fractured rainbow wrapped in plastic. Coming closer, he saw it was the menagerie of stuffed animals he'd bought for Gemma. She had put them out in the garbage, a clear message. He tore open the bag, rescuing the hot pink wildebeest. He wasn't sure why, only that it disturbed him to see that particular item carelessly tossed away. He'd give it to one of his nieces the next time he was out on Long Island.

Deflated, he entered the lobby and went up to his apartment. This was not how he'd wanted his day to begin.

Letting himself in, he noticed immediately that things were pretty much the way he'd left them—only cleaner. The rug was shampooed and vacuumed, windows denuded of grime, and nary a speck of dust could be seen on any surface.

"Merry Maids were here, I see," Sean teased, throwing his bag down and closing the door behind him. JJ's smile was friendly. At least someone was glad to see him.

"I couldn't help myself," JJ confessed, eyes momentarily straying to the TV, where she appeared to be watching some kind of canine competition on *Animal Planet*. "I get some of my best thinking done with a dust rag in my hand. How 'bout you? How was your weekend away?"

"I'm back early. What does that tell you?"

Pete and Roger were going nuts at the sight of him. Crossing the room, he released them from their cages, watching as they joyously winged around the room, reveling in their freedom. Most women screamed when he freed his birds, but JJ seemed unfazed. *How would Gemma have reacted?* he caught himself wondering. He shook his head, clearing his mind.

"So, what did you do for fun?" he asked.

"Went shopping. Cleaned. Mainly relaxed and did some thinking." Her eyes finally caught sight of the stuffed animal sitting by the doorway, and she looked at Sean questioningly.

"It's for one of my nieces. Go on: What else did you do?"

"That's it, really. You?"

"Hiked. Ate. Thought. Didn't sleep."

"We're quite a pair." Pointing the remote at the TV, she turned it off. "I can't tell you how grateful I am to you for letting me use your apartment this weekend, Sean. It really helped me clear my head."

"Hey, I got a free bird-sitter out of the deal, so we both benefited." He knew it was impolite, but he found himself hoping she'd leave soon. He wanted to be alone.

JJ rose from the couch, yawning. "I guess I should get going."

Thank you, Lord.

"Here, I'll walk you downstairs."

Throwing his jacket back on, he picked up her suitcase, quiet as she followed him out to the elevator.

"You know, anytime you want to talk—or anything— I'm here," JJ stuttered awkwardly.

"You, too," Sean managed.

"You're a good friend, Sean. I hate to see you feeling so sad."

Sean could feel his left temple pulsing. "You're a good friend, too, JJ. But I'm fine."

Isn't this better than sitting in your apartment crying? Gemma asked herself as she pedaled home from a bike ride around Central Park. It had been less than twenty-four hours since she'd knocked on Sean's door and had been kicked in the teeth, and she was still feeling pretty low. But Mother Nature's amazing restorative powers helped, and for that she was grateful.

Unlike some New Yorkers, Gemma didn't stash her bike away when the weather turned cold. She enjoyed riding in the fall and winter. There was something invigorating about bundling up on a cold morning and feeling the wind slap you awake. Gliding onto her street, she was brought up short: There, beneath the awning of her building, stood Sean and the willowy blond she'd seen in his bathrobe. She hit the breaks, squealing to a complete stop. They were talking animatedly, a smile lighting Sean's face as he turned back to say something to Tommy, the door-man. She kept watching, unable to help herself. Sean hailed a cab. And before the woman slipped inside, Sean drew her into an embrace.

Gemma froze, all feelings of well-being gone.

Here she'd had a lovely morning, had done something nice for herself, and how had the Goddess rewarded her? By smacking her upside the head with a vision from her own personal hell! Feeling sick, she turned her bike around and quickly pedaled off in the other direction. She would go to Frankie's.

"Are you pulling my pistol? He's screwing someone who looks like Malibu Barbie?"

Gemma nodded.

"That's pretty fast if you ask me. He must have been nobbing her all along."

Gemma grimaced, hating Frankie's penchant for brutal truth. Phrased that way, it made her relationship with Sean sound insignificant, a mere blip on the radar screen of his life. She watched as Frankie tried to bluff her way through making some grilled cheese sandwiches. Many of the tasks of daily living seemed to elude Frankie, including food prep. Gemma had no doubt her friend would subsist completely on Diet Coke, cigarettes, and Balance bars if she could get away with it.

Frankie awkwardly turned the sandwiches in the frying pan. "Shit—why is the butter smoking?"

"Turn down the heat."

"Here, you cook it."

They switched places, Gemma relieving Frankie of her spatula. "Maybe I should move," Gemma muttered.

"What are you, nuts? You're living in a great apartment in a great building and you're paying peanuts for it!"

"Yeah, but—"

" 'I don't know if I can handle running into them,' "
Frankie mimicked, knowing exactly what Gemma was
going to say.

"Bingo."

"Screw him," Frankie railed. "Don't let him drive you
out! Don't let him win."

"It's not a war, Frankie."

"Well, it should be! Goddamn asshole hurts my best
friend? He deserves death." She sidled up to Gemma at the
stove. "Can't you put a spell on him? Make sure that every
cab he hails for the rest of his life passes him by or something?"

"I would never do that." She pressed down on one of
the sandwiches with the spatula. "Though it is tempting."

"So, what happens now?"

"Business as usual, I guess, with the added bonus of
hoping I don't run into them. And worrying about my
grandmother."

"Yeah, what's up with that?"

"Michael's working on getting her an appointment with
one of the top geriatricians in the city. She's forgetful,
moody . . ."

"Maybe it's PMS," Frankie joked.

"I wish."

"Keep me posted, okay?"

Gemma nodded, while Frankie went to the fridge.
"Know what I think you should do about Sean?" she
asked, pulling out a carton of milk.

"What?"

"Kill him."

Gemma laughed.

"No, seriously. Hire a hit man. I bet you anything your
cousin Anthony knows some people who know some people. Take him out. Smoke him. Arrange for him to sleep
with the fishes. Put a cap in his ass."

"You're nuts, you know that?"

"Yeah, but I made you laugh, didn't I?"

"True."

"So, any movement on the Uther front?" Frankie asked casually as she took a slug of milk directly from the carton, then put it back.

"I'll do it this week, I promise. It'll give me something happy to focus on." Gemma mulled this over as she slid the crisp, golden sandwiches onto two waiting plates. Playing Cupid's assistant always made her feel better. It would help take her mind off things. "What do you want me to do if he says he's not interested?"

"He won't," Lady Midnight replied.

"*I never got* to ask you: How did your Battle of Hastings reenactment go?"

Gemma handed Uther a cup of chamomile tea, sliding back onto the stool beside his. Half an hour into tarot lessons she always took a brief ten-minute break, having learned over the years that most people's attention span couldn't last a solid hour. Uther was the exhausting exception, but she took the break anyway. Her goal was to slip Frankie's phone number into his hand by the time the ten minutes were up.

Uther looked so pleased to be asked about his reenactment it almost broke Gemma's heart. "It was fantastic," he raved. "I was part of King Harold's shield wall. I had to pretend to get hit in the eye with an arrow."

"Wow. That must have been . . . painful."

"Painful but rewarding." Uther sipped his tea. "We might tackle the Battle of Agincourt this summer."

"Sounds great."

"You should come to a meeting sometime." He gave a small pause. "You and your friend."

Gemma smiled slyly. "You liked her, didn't you?"

"Lady Midnight? Ho ho, I should say so."

"Her name is Frankie. Lady Midnight is her on-air personality." *Confuse the two and you're doomed.* "She thought you were cute." *In a Renaissance Fair kind of way.*

"Really." Uther puffed up with pride. "I found the damsel rather alluring myself."

You should see her with her eye patch on, thought Gemma. How perfect were these two for each other, Frankie with her patch, Uther running around the park in chain mail pretending to be hit in the eye with an arrow?

"Would you like her phone number?"

Uther turned guarded. "Phone number?"

"Yes. To call her. So the two of you can get together?" *I know you'd prefer writing her a note on parchment and putting it in a raven's beak, but this is the twenty-first century, Uth.*

"Are you giving it to me of your own volition or did she say you could give it to me?"

"She said I could give it to you," said Gemma, feeling like she'd taken a time machine back to seventh grade. What next? Would he ask her to ask Frankie to meet him by his locker after necromancy practice?

"I'll take it, then. Are you sure you're all right with this?"

Gemma did a double take. "Why wouldn't I be?"

"I feel you and I have a connection that seems to go beyond this world, sweet lady, and I wouldn't want to upset you," said Uther as he attempted to peer at her seductively over the rim of his mug.

"Uther, I have a boyfriend," Gemma lied. There was no way she was going to let him know she was available. Not when he was talking about otherworldly connections, whatever that meant.

"Oh yes, him." Uther looked displeased. "You mentioned him at the street fair. What is his trade?"

Her temptation was to answer, "None of your business," but since she was trying to grease the wheels of romance for Frankie, she felt she had no choice but to be chatty and amiable.

"He's a firefighter, but he used to be a stockbroker."

As soon as the words were out, Gemma thought: *Sean's right. Why do I do that? Use his past profession as some sort of qualifier, as if what he does now might not be enough?*

Uther looked impressed. "A very noble profession indeed. When you think about it, he's a dragon slayer of sorts."

"Yes." Time to steer the conversation away from Sean. "Here, I'll write Frankie's number for you." She grabbed one of her business cards from the seashell by the register and jotted her friend's number down on the back. "As you already know"—she flashed him a smile—"Frankie is on the air from midnight to six during the week. The best time to call her is usually after two in the afternoon."

"Thank you, sweet lady. I shall call her anon—or not anon exactly, but on the morrow." He looked at the card before slipping it into his pocket. "One quick question: Is she Pagan?"

"She's undecided. She believes in the trinity, but in her case it's Aerosmith, the Beatles, and Led Zeppelin."

Uther seemed amused by this, and smiled. "Fascinating."

"I agree. Let's get back to our tarot, shall we?"

CHAPTER

15

"I'm trying to decide which I hate you for more," Gemma told Michael as they met up in Dante's parking lot and began strolling toward the restaurant. "Setting me up with another crazy hockey player, or not calling me when you got the geriatrician appointment for Nonna."

"I didn't call because there was no way you could have come," Michael said, holding the door open for her. "It was in the middle of the day in the middle of the week."

"Plus my mother didn't want me there, right?"

Michael was silent.

"I knew it."

"As for Boris," Michael continued, changing the subject, "I asked if you wanted me to set you up with another nice guy on the team, and you said yes."

"He took out his teeth over dessert, Michael. Said he felt comfortable with me."

Michael cringed. "But he was nice, right?"

"I don't know! Maybe! I was focused on trying not to stare at his gums."

Michael looked surprised. "What happened to my sweet, open-minded cousin who feels love and compassion for all God's creatures?"

"She got burned by a firefighter. Next question, please."

Entering the banquet room where the rest of the extended family were gathered, Gemma detected a wave of tension ripple through the room. She'd been a witch for years; you'd think they would get over it by now. But no: All she had to do was show up and some of her family acted as if Satan had materialized. It was disheartening, not to mention tiresome.

All morning, as a way to cope, Gemma had changed the words of a song from *The Sound of Music* and had been singing, "How do we solve a problem like Nonna Maria?" Nonna was the reason everyone was here: She'd been diagnosed with middle-stage Alzheimer's disease. Living alone was no longer an option.

"I hope this isn't too awful," Michael confided as they sat down at the long, extended table with the rest of the family.

Gemma took in the sea of familiar faces surrounding her. Everyone she expected to be present was there: her own mother, her Aunt Millie, Theresa, Anthony and his wife Angie, assorted cousins and their spouses. Her eye caught her mother's, and for a split second, it almost seemed as if her mother might acknowledge her, maybe even smile. But the moment passed as Gemma's mother pointedly turned her body to talk to Aunt Millie. Gemma had become a pro at shaking off such blatant rejection, but deep down, it still hurt. She turned to Anthony, seated to her left.

"Where's Aunt Betty Anne?"

"Home taking care of Nonna," he answered glumly before squeezing her arm. "Glad you came, Gem. Ignore the *faccia brutas* who won't give you the time of day."

Gemma smiled, touched, since it wasn't too long ago Anthony was among them himself. "Thanks, Ant."

"All right, everybody, let's get down to business," Michael said, clapping his hands briskly to get everyone's attention. Gemma stole a sidelong glance at Anthony; he was rolling his eyes, his lifelong annoyance at Michael's tendency to take control evident. Amazing how some things never changed. The two of them would be in their nineties and they would still be rubbing each other the wrong way.

"As you know," Michael began, "last week Theresa, along with Aunt Connie and Aunt Millie, took Nonna to a geriatrician. After giving her a bunch of tests, the doctor determined it was Alzheimer's."

"What kind of tests?" asked cousin Paulie, who'd come in all the way from Commack.

Michael looked to Theresa.

"Memory tests, language tests, you name it. There's something called the seven-minute screen that doctors use to check for Alzheimer's, since there's no one test for the disease, *per se*. Nonna didn't do very well."

"Tell 'em straight," Aunt Millie croaked, sucking on her Winston. "She couldn't tell a friggin' banana from an orange. Didn't know what year it was. The doctor told her to draw a clock with hands pointed at quarter to three and she couldn't do it. It was awful."

Paulie thrust his head forward, squinting with disbelief. "They ask you to draw fruit and that's how they tell if you're senile?"

"Senility is different than Alzheimer's," Theresa said patiently. "Believe me, Paulie, this doctor knows what he's doing. He's one of the top geriatricians in the city. If he says Nonna has Alzheimer's, Nonna has Alzheimer's."

"Shit," Paulie muttered. "Poor Nonna."

"So, what do we do?" Anthony demanded.

Theresa sighed. "Well, they want to put her on drugs

to help slow the progress of it, so that's one good thing." She looked distraught. "But there's no cure for Alzheimer's. It just gets worse and worse. In the meantime, Nonna's reached the stage where it's dangerous to leave her alone."

Leaden silence followed as the family contemplated this. Then Anthony's wife Angie spoke up.

"I guess we gotta put her in a home."

Anthony groaned, a dead giveaway that his wife had put her foot in her mouth. Closing her eyes, Gemma quickly envisioned a protective blue light around Angie. She was going to need it. Gemma opened her eyes just in time to see her own mother glaring at Angie from across the table.

"Did you just say what I think you said?" Connie Dante asked.

"Ma," Gemma warned.

"You keep out of this," her mother commanded sharply. Her eyes flicked back to Angie contemptuously. "Did you, who weren't even born into this family, suggest putting my mother away like she was a piece of furniture going to a warehouse?"

Gemma's heart went out to Angie as she struggled to put things right. "I didn't mean to suggest—"

"Where you from, hon?" Aunt Millie cut in.

Angie blinked in confusion, her face turning red. "I don't—"

"She means where are your people from," Gemma's mother clarified as she drummed her pointy purple fingernails on the tabletop.

"Oh. Como."

Gemma's mother and Aunt exchanged knowing glances, as if geography determined behavior. Her mother's voice was patronizing as she addressed Angie. "We're Sicilian, hon. Maybe in the North families throw out the elderly like an old pair of boots, but not in the South. Sicilians care for their elderly."

"North, south, what is this, the friggin' Civil War here?" Anthony asked plaintively. "Let's focus on what we're gonna do." He put a protective arm around Angie's shoulder. Gemma was glad to see it.

"Well, we're sure as shit not putting her in a nursing home," cousin Paulie declared, looking around the room nervously to make sure he wasn't doing something radical, like expressing his own opinion.

"Then what are we going to do?" Theresa demanded. "Angie's suggestion wasn't out of line."

Aunt Millie shook her head disgustedly as she stubbed out her cigarette. "Another one with the nursing home."

"I'm not saying we should put her in a nursing home," Theresa said sharply. "I'm asking what the alternative is."

"Taking care of her at home," Michael said as if it were the most obvious thing in the world.

"Who, Mikey?" Gemma prodded gently. "Are we hiring home health aides? What?"

Cousin Paulie looked horrified. "I can't afford to chip in for some nurse. I'm barely making ends meet as it is."

"Maybe if you stopped buying a new car every freaking year, you'd save money," Anthony observed.

Paulie half rose out of his seat. *"Vaffancul!"*

"Whoa, everyone, come on, settle down," Michael pleaded. "This is a serious problem here. We need to take care of it."

"You're just jealous," Paulie jeered at Anthony.

"Yeah, right, I wish I could buy a guineamobile—"

"Cut the shit, Anthony!" Michael snapped. Anthony and Paulie settled back in their chairs, glowering at each other.

"I don't want some stranger taking care of my mother," Gemma's mother declared.

"Amen," Aunt Millie agreed, lighting up as she turned

to regard her sister. "Remember Mrs. DiNuova, used to live on Seventh Avenue?"

Gemma's mother nodded fearfully.

"Well, her mother got sick and they hired some Dominican nurse to take care of her. By the time the old lady died, all the Hummel figures were gone from the house."

"I hear there's a huge market for Hummels in the Dominican Republic," Michael said drily.

"Don't make fun," Aunt Millie rasped, shaking a finger at him across the table. "It's true."

"So, if neither of you want 'some stranger' to take care of your mother, does that mean you're going to do it?" Gemma asked.

The family looked at her mother and Aunt Millie expectantly. Gemma almost felt sorry for them: They looked like two aging deer trapped in headlights.

"I'll do it part of the time," Gemma's mother conceded reluctantly.

"Me, too," said Aunt Millie, blowing smoke out of the side of her mouth. "And so will Betty Anne."

"Let's nail this down," Michael insisted. "Because if we're going to do this, we have to start right away. Today."

Gemma's mother heaved a world-weary sigh. "I can watch her during the day on Monday, Tuesday, and Wednesday."

"I'll do Thursday and Friday," Aunt Millie offered.

"What about weekends?"

The room went silent.

Gemma ran through her own schedule in her head. "I can do Sundays," she offered tentatively.

"I don't think that's a very good idea," a voice piped up. It belonged to her cousin Sharmaine, Paulie's sister. Gemma and Sharmaine had never gotten along. Once Gemma revealed she was a witch, she became *persona non grata* to the holier-than-thou Sharmaine, who, ironically, was rumored to be banging her parish priest on a regular basis.

"What's your beef?" Michael asked politely.

"You know what my beef is," Sharmaine sniffed, staring disdainfully at Gemma. "I don't think it's a very good idea for her to spend too much time around Nonna. That witch crap might upset her."

Gemma went to open her mouth but a quick look from Michael told her that, as family facilitator, he preferred to handle it. That was fine with Gemma.

"Are you saying you'll watch Nonna on Sundays, Sharmaine?" Michael asked.

"I can't," Sharmaine said coolly. "I'm busy."

"Doing what?" Anthony chortled. "Letting Father Flynn slip you his special communion wafer?"

"Bite my ass, Anthony," Sharmaine snapped.

"Just one bite?" Anthony lobbed back. "Two or three might help make it smaller."

"You sonofa—"

"Stop!" Gemma shouted. Sometimes she wondered why she still gave a damn about being accepted in her family, especially when they behaved like sniping, backbiting lunatics. She knew it happened in lots of families, but hers seemed to have elevated it to an art. "Can we please stop tearing each other to pieces and focus on the problem at hand?" Her family's gaze bordered on the mutinous, but she'd made her point. She turned to Michael. "You were saying?"

"You sure you can be at Nonna's on Sundays?"

Gemma nodded. "Yes. I can do all day Sunday and Sunday night, and probably Monday and Wednesday nights as well. I just need to check with my part-timer."

Michael looked around the room, his gaze pointedly resting on Sharmaine. "Can anyone else help out?"

Sharmaine suddenly became fascinated by her own feet.

"If Connie does some, I do some, and Gemma does some, Betty Anne can do the rest," Aunt Millie said. "She doesn't have a job."

"She'll kill you if it means missing bingo," Gemma's mother pointed out.

"Let her try," Millie growled.

Gemma thought the matter settled, but Michael's uneasy expression said otherwise. "Are you sure about this?" he asked her again. "With the exception of Paulie, everyone here lives in Brooklyn. You sure you don't mind jackassing out from the city?"

"It's not a problem," Gemma assured him. "Besides," she added with a hint of self-deprecation, "I have no life anyway."

"Plus broomsticks are faster than public transportation," Anthony kidded her under his breath, winking as he nudged her in the ribs.

"You're an idiot, you know that?" Gemma murmured back.

"An idiot who gives you free cannolis all the time, so watch it."

"That settles it, then," Michael said. "Nonna will be watched at home by Aunt Connie, Aunt Millie, Aunt Betty Anne, and Gemma."

"Depending upon what shifts I'm working, I can be a backup person," Angie offered.

"Me, too," Theresa put in.

"We've got it covered then," Michael said, looking relieved. "Meeting over. Everyone *mangia*."

Moving toward the buffet table where Anthony had set up steaming trays of lasagna, Gemma was suddenly hit with a profound sense of exhaustion. Though the family meeting had lasted less than an hour, the emotional pitch had left her drained. Or maybe she was feeling drained by the prospect of shuttling back and forth between Manhattan and Bensonhurst? She didn't doubt she could help to take care of her grandmother while still running her store, nor was she having second thoughts. She *was* a little worried about where all her energy would come from.

She had just scooped out a helping of lasagna when she felt a light tap on her shoulder. She turned. Her mother was there.

"Hi, Ma," she said, instinctively tensing. Her reaction to her mother had become Pavlovian by now, her body bracing for rejection and stress. "What's up?"

"Thank you for offering to help take care of your grandmother," she said stiffly.

"I love Nonna. You know that."

"Yes, well, it's very nice of you," her mother continued, not quite looking at her. With nothing more to say, she moved to join Aunt Millie at a nearby table. Gemma stared after her, touched. Her mother had never been one for compliments, even before they were estranged. For her to say something nice was monumental. Elated, Gemma turned back to the buffet table. Perhaps something positive would come out of Nonna's illness. She certainly hoped so.

"*Let me just* say one thing: You're out of your fucking mind."

Frankie's voice was so loud that Gemma sank down in her seat as the other patrons in the diner turned to look at them. It was bad enough Frankie had come strolling through the door with a neck brace on, drawing attention to herself. Did she have to bellow on top of it?

"Keep it down, will you, please?"

"How on earth are you going to run your store *and* help take care of your grandmother?"

"I can do it."

"How? No wait, let me guess: Your magickal powers enable you to practice bilocation."

"I wish."

"Seriously, Gem, how are you going to manage this? You'll be so exhausted you won't have time for a life."

"What life do I have now?"

"That's not the point," Frankie insisted. "You and I both know why you offered to do this."

Gemma shifted uneasily. "Oh? Why's that?"

"Because you want to get back in your mother's good graces."

Gemma took a sip of coffee. "That's part of it." There was no denying it: She had come to the same realization a few days before, sitting at her kitchen table loading her new insane schedule on to her Palm Pilot, envisioning months, maybe even years, of sheer bloody exhaustion. Then it hit her: Part of her reason for doing it was because maybe—just maybe—it would somehow help redeem her in the eyes of her family, especially her mother.

"You don't understand. My mother came up to me after the meeting and actually thanked me for offering to help. That's major, Frankie."

"No, it's sad. I hate seeing you scraping and bowing when Queen Connie decides to throw you a few crumbs."

"Better crumbs than nothing." She appreciated Frankie's protectiveness toward her, but in this case, Frankie was missing the point. Her mother had to start somewhere. One crumb, however miniscule, was a step in the right direction.

Frankie frowned. "I still think you're nuts to take this on."

"I love my grandmother, Frankie," Gemma replied softly. "I want to spend as much time with her as possible before"—she began choking up—"she doesn't know who I am anymore."

"Oh, Gem." Digging into the Beatles lunchbox she used

as a purse, Frankie pulled out a minipack of tissues, handing them across the table. "That's really sweet."

"I guess." Gemma dabbed at her eyes.

"No, it is. Nonna's lucky to have you. Really."

"Please shut up before you make me sob," Gemma joked, but she wasn't kidding. One more tender word about how nice she was being to her Nonna and the waterworks would commence in full. That would really endear them to the surrounding diners.

Since Frankie rarely beat around the bush, Gemma thought she'd return the favor. "What happened to your neck?"

"I think I ruptured a disk."

"How?"

"Playing frisbee with Alice Cooper."

"Why don't you go to a doctor and find out for sure?"

Frankie mumbled something about insurance, and Gemma let it go. How did people at the radio station, people who might not know and love Frankie the way she did, react to this never-ending parade of afflictions and illnesses? "Don't you worry about being perceived as sickly by your bosses?" Gemma asked. "Isn't it a liability?"

"It's not my fault my immune system is suppressed and I'm unlucky," Frankie replied indignantly. "Besides, I rarely ever miss work. Ever. As long as Lady Midnight sounds great behind the mike, who cares if her body is falling apart?"

But it's not. You just think it is. Or want it to be. Or something.

"Speaking of Lady Midnight, did you ever hear from Uther?" Gemma asked.

She couldn't believe it: Frankie, who'd probably spent the night with more rock stars than Pamela des Barres, looked almost bashful. "I did."

"And—?"

"We're going out for a goblet of mead on Saturday night."

"That's great!" She was happy for Frankie. For Uther, too. Maybe this would help Frankie get over her loser ex-husband. "Your neck should be okay by then, right?"

"I hope so." Unable to move just her head because of the brace, Frankie craned her entire torso around, looking for Stavros. "Where's the man with the coffeepot when you need him?"

"I'm sure he'll be along in a minute."

"Speaking of men," Frankie said as she stiffly turned back to face Gemma, "have you run into Sean?"

"No, thank God. I'm sure he and Barbie have been holed up in his apartment having fun."

"Torturing ourselves again, are we?"

"Not torture," Gemma replied calmly. "Just fact."

She was grateful when Stavros interrupted them, making a big fuss out of Frankie's injury and giving them a blow-by-blow account of his recent hernia operation. Sean Kennealy wasn't a subject on which she wanted to dwell.

This time, Sean thought, crawling on his hands and knees through smoke so thick he couldn't make out his own hand in front of him, *I am not going to leave anyone behind.* Having already checked one bedroom and finding no one, he'd moved on to the next, and the next, always with the same feverish tape loop running through his brain: *Check the closet. Check under the bed. Check the furniture. Check everywhere you have to.*

Swinging his ax in front of him, he hit something solid, and felt for it. Bed. Raising himself up on his knees, he patted the top of the mattress. Empty. Move on.

Feeling his way, he came to another door, and felt for the handle. It seemed stuck. Jostling it, he heard the piercing warning bell go off on his breathing pack. He had five minutes of air left and then he'd have to get the hell out. Shit. He gave the door handle one good turn, and it seemed to do the trick. Proud of his determination, he flung the door open wide.

The boy stood smiling at him, glowing green in the jungle of his mother's wardrobe. "Why didn't you find me last time?" he asked Sean. Sean scooped him up into his arms and started crawling toward the bedroom door. But just as he reached it, the door slammed shut in his face. Then he woke up.

"Sean?"

Sean looked up from his dad's La-Z-Boy to see his mother shuffling into the living room. She'd been complaining about not seeing enough of him, so he'd decided to go home to Oceanside for the weekend. "You okay?" she asked.

"I'm fine. Go back to bed. It's the middle of the night."

"I could say the same to you," she pointed out. "What's going on? I heard you rattling around in the kitchen before."

"I was just getting some milk. I'm sorry. I didn't mean to wake you."

"I was awake anyway," his mother yawned, gathering the folds of her bathrobe around her as she sat down on the couch.

"Oh, yeah?" Sean found it amusing they were both up treading the boards at 3 A.M. He'd forgotten his mother was an insomniac. He had strong childhood memories of waking up to pee in the middle of the night and there she'd be in the living room, staring into the flickering blue light of the TV screen. "What's eating you?"

"Life," his mother replied.

Sean chuckled. "You and me both."

"Everything okay with you and Gemma?"

"Great," Sean lied. He didn't want to have this discussion with his mother at three in the morning.

"I like her," his mother said thoughtfully. "She's very genuine, down to earth. Pretty, too."

Sean forced himself to smile. "I'll tell her you said so."

His mother reached out, putting a hand on his knee. "You sure you're all right? You forget: I'm a mother, which means I've got a built-in bullshit detector. What's going on?"

Sean shrugged. "Just, you know"—he coughed nervously as the feeling of his throat closing up suddenly seized him, and he realized he might cry—"work stuff. Bad dreams about work."

His mother reached out to touch his cheek. "Talk to me, honey. C'mon."

"Uh, no, I really can't."

"Sean—"

"I almost let a kid die, Mom," he blurted out, unable to hold it in any longer. "There was a fire and I fucked up and I almost let a kid die." He felt haunted as he stared into his mother's eyes. "Ever since then I can't stop thinking about him. I see him everywhere."

"Oh, Seany." His mother gathered him up into her arms as if he were still her little boy. "It's okay."

"It's not okay!" Sean replied hoarsely. "Part of my job is to be thorough and I failed, I failed that little boy—" He broke off, sobs shaking his shoulders as he covered his face with his hands. "Oh, Christ."

It felt good to cry. What was the word? *Cathartic.* Though a rogue thought kept appearing as his mother soothed him and held him tight: *I wish it was Gemma I was talking to. I wish it was Gemma holding me tight. Fuck, I miss her.*

Eventually, he pulled himself together and pulled away.

"Sorry about that," he said gruffly, embarrassed at having lost control.

"Don't be ridiculous. What you're experiencing is very, very common. Your father used to react the same way."

"Yeah?" It made him feel a little better to hear that.

"Absolutely."

He pressed his fingertips against his eye sockets. "I'm so tired. But I'm afraid if I go back to sleep . . ."

"I think you might need to talk to someone about this," his mother suggested, sounding like she was walking on eggshells.

"Yeah, I know," Sean admitted miserably. "But it's not my way, you know, talking things to death."

"But this is affecting your life, Sean."

"I know." Guilt descended on him as his mind flashed back to the last time he'd seen Gemma. She'd said the same thing, and he'd cut her off at the knees. Now he saw that she wasn't pushing, wasn't prying, wasn't trying to make him into something he wasn't. Like his mother, she simply saw someone she loved in pain and wanted to do whatever she could to alleviate it. What a clueless jerk he was.

"They have therapists at the fire department now," his mother continued carefully. "Maybe you should check it out."

"I might, Ma. Thanks."

Much to his chagrin, he found himself still dogged by embarrassment. The guys at the house kept their mouths shut when they needed help. Was he being weak because he was unable to suck it up and take it "like a man"? Then he asked himself, where had that attitude gotten his father? He remembered the awful, stomach-churning feeling of coming home from school not knowing what mood his father would be in, and he knew he had to talk this out no matter how uncomfortable it made him. Exhaustion suddenly swallowed him up, making him feel muzzy-headed.

He hadn't been exaggerating when he'd told his mother he had qualms about going back to sleep. But now that he'd spilled his guts, maybe sleep would come, and he could rest. He appreciated that she'd listened to him and hadn't passed judgment. She was a good mother; he told her so and saw the pleasure in her eyes.

But he wished he'd been comforted by Gemma.

CHAPTER

16

The last time Gemma had slept over at her grandmother's house, she'd been twenty, seeking solace after a particularly bad fight with her mother. They'd stayed up late into the night talking, Gemma wishing Nonna were her mother. When she was small, she used to sleep over all the time, the sound of Nonna's snoring up the hall a comfort to her. Gemma smiled, remembering the pure joy of sitting at the kitchen table, legs swinging, while Nonna made ricotta pancakes. Afterward they'd go to church, and Gemma would be entranced by the multicolored shafts of sunlight filtering through the stained glass windows. Nonna said sunbeams were God's fingers reaching down to touch the earth. Gemma found that a comfort, too.

Now, pulling up in front of Nonna's house on a Sunday morning, she was surprised she felt nervous about the day and night ahead. Gemma knew she must be conscious of not behaving differently toward her grandmother, unless she needed to for Nonna's own safety. Yes, a definite diagnosis of Alzheimer's had been made, but Nonna was still the same person, and deserved to be treated with the same love and respect, not like a child or some doddering old woman. She prayed everyone else in the family was on the same page.

The door was opened by her cousin Anthony, who had insisted on continuing his tradition of taking Nonna to early Mass at St. Finbar's.

"How ya' doin?" he asked, leaning in for a quick peck to the cheek. "Traffic okay?"

"At this hour, it was a breeze." Shrugging off her cape, Gemma shivered. "It's like an icebox in here."

"Nonna says she's hot."

"Where is she?"

"In the kitchen having her traditional post-Mass snack: espresso and *sfogliatelle*." Anthony reached for his coat, draped over the back of the easy chair. "She did good in church: knew where she was, didn't want to get up and wander around." He chuckled. "She didn't know who Father Clementine was, though. She leans over to me and says really loud, 'Who's that fat bastard?'"

Gemma laughed appreciatively. "I'm sorry I missed that."

"Bella?"

"In here, Nonna, talking to Anthony," Gemma called in the direction of the kitchen. "I'll be in in a minute."

"You need anything?" Anthony asked, turning up his collar.

"I'm fine."

"Okay, then, I'm gonna take off. I'll be at the restaurant around noon if you need me. Ange is on duty today. Mikey's in Pittsburgh, but I think Theresa's home if you need help or anything. Just give a shout."

"Maybe I'll give Sharmaine a call," Gemma joked.

"Putan'," Anthony growled under his breath. "I never liked that one."

"You and me both. Take care, Ant," she said as she

watched him plod down Nonna's steps and up the street. Michael was a bounder, Anthony a plodder. What was she?

"Bella, I'm so happy you decided to visit." Nonna's face flushed with pleasure as she looked up from the kitchen table. "Can you stay for lunch?"

"Lunch, dinner, the whole shebang!"

No sooner had the words slipped out of her mouth than Nonna's visage darkened. "In, out, in, out, all these people trooping through my house. What the hell is going on? Can't an old woman live in peace?"

Same old Nonna. Speak the truth. "You don't have a choice, Non," Gemma explained gently. "Remember when you went to see the doctor with Mom and Aunt Millie?"

Nonna looked suspicious.

"Well, the doctor said you shouldn't be alone anymore. That's why we've all been here. We're keeping you company, making sure you don't get hurt."

"I can take care of myself," Nonna muttered fiercely.

"I know you can. We're just here to help."

This seemed to pacify her. "All right."

Gemma slid into a chair next to her. "What would you like to do today?"

"I'd like to get out of my church clothes, for a start."

"Okay." Gemma hesitated. Should she let her grandmother go upstairs on her own to change, or should she go with her? One option courted the potential for injury, the other for insult. Gemma decided to be straightforward. "Would you like some help?"

"The company would be nice."

Gemma waited until her grandmother had finished her coffee, then followed her upstairs. She couldn't remember the last time she'd actually been in her grandmother's bedroom. It had to be when she was a very small child. She was shocked but not surprised to see nothing had changed.

The sagging double bed with the faded chenille bedspread was still there, and the walls were still adorned by pictures of saints, their beatific smiles rendered all the more mysterious by the glow of the votive candles atop Nonna's dresser that never seemed to go out or need replacing.

Those might have to go.

Her eye caught the set of rosary beads draped over one corner of the dresser mirror, and a cross made of palm fronds stuck into the corner of the other. As a little girl, she'd been frightened by the religious accoutrements of her grandmother's room, convinced the eyes of all the paintings were following her. But now she found comfort in their immutability, appreciating their value as symbols of a life richly lived in faith.

Sinking down on the bed, Nonna took off her shoes. She peeled off her stockings next before moving to her dresser to remove her jewelry.

"Want these?" she said to Gemma, holding up her earrings.

Gemma scrunched up her nose. "What?"

"Take them," Nonna urged. "I'd rather see you enjoy them while I'm still alive."

"Thank you." Gemma took the marcasite teardrops and slipped them into her pocket. She had no intention of keeping them, knowing that some members of her family would accuse her of starting to clean out Nonna's house while she was still alive. Besides, Nonna might not be fully aware of what she was doing. Tomorrow she might want to wear those very same earrings, and then what?

Sighing heavily, Nonna grabbed the hem of her skirt to pull her dress over her head. Gemma was initially shocked by the lumpy terrain of her grandmother's bare legs, the sagging flesh crosshatched with a network of varicose and spider veins. *This'll be me someday,* she thought, and her heart filled with tenderness. *This will be all of us.*

The dress was up around Nonna's neck now, covering her face.

"Help!" Nonna cried out, her voice muffled through the material. "I'm caught on something."

Alarmed, Gemma went to her aid. The crocheted neckline of Nonna's dress was snagged on a chain she wore around her neck. As delicately as she could, Gemma worked to untangle the two. That's when she saw it: The charm hanging from Nonna's necklace was the *cimaruta,* an ancient Pagan charm traditionally used to ward off the evil eye. She stared at it. In Italy, it was called "the witch charm." Its three main branches symbolized the goddess Diana in her three aspects as maiden, mother, and crone. Hanging from each branch were other symbols: a fish, a hand, a key, a crescent moon—each having a specific meaning.

"Nonna," Gemma asked as she helped her off with her dress, "where did you get the *cimaruta?*"

"Ah," said Nonna, fingering the beautiful silver charm. "You like it?"

"Where did you get it?" Gemma asked again. "How long have you had it?"

Nonna turned away, an almost imperceptible smile playing across her lips. "That's my secret."

Gemma's eyes were glued to her as she went to her closet to pull out a pair of slacks and a blouse. *She's a witch. I know it. I feel it!* The thought excited her. It meant the ancient ways were part of her birthright. She wasn't an oddball at all; this was in her blood! What would her mother have to say about that?

Nonna, meanwhile, had slipped into her slacks. But as her fingers went to the neck of her blouse, they hesitated, rubbing the button there. Gemma watched and waited. Maybe Nonna wanted to wear something else? Nonna looked down at the open blouse, then at Gemma, her face contorted with bafflement.

Oh, God. She can't remember how to do the buttons.

"Here, let me," Gemma said softly. Slowly, with great care, she buttoned the front of her grandmother's blouse. "Better?"

"Better," Nonna repeated, her relief obvious. She glanced at Gemma shyly. "Would you mind brushing my hair?"

"I would love to."

Steering Nonna to sit at her vanity, Gemma loosened the silver braid of her hair. Picking up the stiff horsehair brush Nonna had had for as long as she could remember, she began brushing. Nonna closed her eyes, seeming to lose herself in the luxurious sensation. When she opened them, her eyes met Gemma's in the vanity mirror.

"You and me," Nonna said. "We're a lot alike."

Gemma leaned over, lovingly pressing her own cheek against her grandmother's older, more papery version. "I know," Gemma whispered.

Sean hadn't been sure what to expect. He was pleasantly surprised to find the counseling unit looked like any other office, with out-of-date magazines littering the low coffee table in the waiting room, and furniture that had seen better days. He had an appointment to talk to Lieutenant Dan Murray, who had put in his twenty years of active service with the department and was now working as a full-time counselor. Sean liked him on sight: Bow-legged, pot-bellied, with a big, white handlebar mustache, he brought to mind a friendly, talking walrus.

Murray's tone was friendly but concerned. "What can I do for you, Sean?"

As briefly as he could, Sean explained what he'd been going through since the brownstone fire. Murray listened intently, giving the occasional encouraging nod. He seemed neither surprised nor shocked by what Sean told him, even when Sean related the details of how, walking down the street, he'd felt like he couldn't breathe after seeing a hope chest in the window of a furniture store.

"That's called a trigger," Murray explained. "Extremely common after a traumatic incident. Something visual, a certain smell, a sound—anything can bring you back to the fire scene and with it comes all those attendant feelings: guilt, pain, fear, you name it."

"Yeah, but what can I do about it?"

"Exactly what you're doing. Talk about it." Murray leaned back in his chair. "You know, after you called yesterday, I ran a check on you. You've got a great record, Sean. But I know what you're going through: one fuckup cancels out years of hearing 'Great job, buddy.' Right?"

Sean nodded, relieved that Murray knew exactly how he was feeling. He couldn't have said it better if he tried.

"Well, I'm gonna try to help you with that. You've taken the all-important first step, which is getting your ass in here and opening your mouth. The rest is gravy, relatively speaking."

"I'm having trouble sleeping," Sean confessed.

"That's common, too. Don't worry: I won't let you walk out of here without some coping techniques. You familiar with deep breathing? Visualization? Meditation?"

Sean laughed.

"What's so funny?"

"Nothing, it's just that I used to date this girl who was into all that stuff, and I gave her a hard time about it, that's all."

"Well, she was on to something," said Murray, "but the key will be finding what works for you. Every guy in the department for any length of time has gone through what you're going through right now at one time or another. Anyone who says otherwise is a liar. Now, why don't you tell me about the fire."

•   •   •

The next morning, Gemma was eager to get to work so she could do some research on the *cimaruta*. How long had Nonna been wearing it, hidden under her clothes? She already knew each of the charms hanging from the three branches of the tree had a specific meaning—she just couldn't remember what they were. Now, fired up by the possibility that the beloved matriarch of the family might turn out to be a keeper of the "old ways," Gemma wanted to learn everything she could about the two-sided medallion. She felt like a soldier loading up on ammunition; the next time her mother decided to get on her case about being a witch, Gemma would be able to turn to her and say, "So's your own mother, and here's proof."

Spending twenty-four hours with Nonna had been more exhausting than Gemma had anticipated. Sometimes Nonna was her old devilish self, and they laughed. Other times the simplest task—like remembering how to hold a fork—overwhelmed her and she became irascible. At 3 A.M., Gemma heard her rooting around in the kitchen and got downstairs just in time to stop Nonna from going out the back door into the freezing night with nothing on but her nightgown. To keep a better eye on her, Gemma spent the rest of the night in the other half of the ancient, lumpy bed. She didn't get much sleep; Nonna seemed to be more agitated at night. Luckily, by the time Gemma's mother arrived to relieve her, Nonna had exhausted her stores of energy and was sleeping soundly.

So Gemma was tired but in good spirits as she turned onto Thompson Street. But her mood changed when she saw Uther and three other men in medieval garb standing outside her store. Uther was wearing his chain mail and a pewter helmet that looked like an inverted soup bowl, his his left hand gripping a tall halberd. The other men were in burgundy tights and leather jerkins. One had on a metal skull cap; the other two wore felt caps with long trailing feathers. Each of Uther's chums boasted a quiver of arrows on his shoulder. Gemma contemplated turning around and running but it was too late: Uther had spotted her and was waving madly.

Plus she had a business to run.

"To what do I owe this pleasure?" she said mildly, regretting her phrasing immediately. She *should* have said, "What's up?" Now Uther was bound to address her as if they were starring in *Camelot*.

"I wanted you to meet some of my reenacting companions, good lady. They are eager to meet you, as I've told them great tales of your tarot prowess. But I thought if you could see us in our Agincourt garb, you might be tempted to come to our next meeting. We're in sore need of damsels to rescue—"

"Or camp followers," added the man in the skull cap, leering.

Gemma had no idea what a "camp follower" was, but deduced it couldn't be good, if the deadly look Uther cast his way meant anything. She nodded, trying to be polite. "Do you have any literature I could take? That would be helpful."

Uther tapped the side of his head. "It's all here."

Great, Gemma thought, putting the key in the lock. "Well, I'll think about it. Thanks for stopping by. Bye now."

She pushed open the door, expecting them to disperse. Instead, they followed her inside.

"Uther, what are you doing?"

"I want them to see the store."

Gemma pinched the bridge of her nose. "That's fine, but if you guys are going to browse, I suggest you put your weapons behind the counter."

"Why?"

"Because they might scare the customers."

"Oh."

Uther and his friends dutifully followed Gemma to the

counter, stashing their arms for safekeeping. Gemma was beginning to wonder if Uther had a screw loose. As his friends fanned out across the aisles, talking to each other in a way that set Gemma's teeth on edge ("Methinks I see a book on fairie lore!" "Forsooth, a soft chair to set my botty upon!"), Gemma tugged lightly on Uther's chain mail, holding him back.

"How was your date with Frankie?" She hadn't had a chance to speak with Frankie yet.

"A gentleman doesn't kiss and tell."

"You can tell a little. Did you have fun? Are you seeing each other again?"

"Aye," Uther revealed, looking pleased.

Gemma's heart lightened. "I'm glad," she said, giving his arm a little squeeze as he walked off to join his friends.

She didn't mind them being in the store, but when one potential customer entered and left, then another, then a third, she knew she was going to have to ask them to leave. The buying public apparently was not entranced by chain mail, skullcaps, and jerkins. It did make her wonder: As weird as those fleeing the Golden Bough perceived Uther and his friends to be, was that how her mother perceived her?

She had felt the first hint of the worst headache of her life minutes after letting Uther and his friends into the Golden Bough, but had thought it would go away when they did. She was wrong. By the time her part-timer, Julie, came in to work at five, Gemma knew she was going to have to hit the nearest Duane Reade and get herself some aspirin. She hated putting anything like that in her body, but this headache was *bad.* How on earth did Theresa deal with migraines? The relentless hammering on Gemma's temples gave her newfound respect for Michael's wife.

Exhausted, in pain, she pushed open the heavy glass

door of Duane Reade. The lighting was harsh and artificial, the narrow aisles crowded with shoppers. Directed to the pain relief aisle by a sullen teen whose baggy pants looked on the verge of falling off, she found herself confronted with rows and rows of similar-looking boxes, all promising to soothe this ache or relieve that spasm. Didn't anyone take plain aspirin anymore? It took a while, but she finally found it, on the shelf nearest the floor.

Clutching her precious booty, she made for the front of the store, dismayed to see only one cashier behind the register. Taking her place in line, she closed her eyes. *Please, Goddess, don't let this take too long. I just want to take my drugs and crawl in bed.*

She opened her eyes, resigned to spending the next fifteen minutes in the crowded, overwarm store. Desperate to pass the time, she studied her surroundings. That's when she saw it: the FDNY Calendar for 2006. With Christmas right around the corner, all the calendars for the upcoming year were out and on display.

Telling herself it was nothing more than curiosity, she plucked the nearest one from the rack and began thumbing through it. The firefighter selected for the month of February was cute enough; blond and buff, he was the "can man" for an engine company on the Upper East Side. The April guy didn't do it for her, though. He was too sculpted, too perfect, a Ken doll come to life. She flipped through May, June, July, and then, shockingly, she hit August. Her heart jolted: The firefighter featured was Sean.

Heat swam to her face as she studied the image of the man who had wooed her so vigorously, only to give up at the first hint of difficulty. The photo didn't do justice to the piercing quality of his blue eyes. Nor did it adequately capture his crooked, boyish grin. But that was his body, all right. The very same one that had embraced her so tight and moved so fluently inside her. Choking back tears, Gemma abruptly closed the calendar.

"Can I see that?" the woman on line behind her piped up. "That guy was hot."

Gemma handed over the calendar and turned back to face the front of the store.

Once upon a time, she would have viewed stumbling across Sean's image in the calendar as an omen. But she no longer believed in omens or coincidences or even fate. It wasn't that she didn't want to; she couldn't afford to.

It hurt too much.

CHAPTER

17

"No offense, but what are you doing?"

Sean slowly opened his eyes to find JJ standing in front of him, staring worriedly. He was sitting alone at the table in the firehouse kitchen. JJ had stopped by at the end of his shift so they could grab a bite to eat.

He unclasped his hands, smiling up at his friend. "Deep breathing. Relaxing." Just as Dan Murray had recommended, when he was feeling stressed, Sean now closed his eyes and concentrated on his breathing. Miraculously, it seemed to be helping. He could actually feel his heartbeat slowing down, the tension in his shoulders fading. Gemma hadn't been kidding: Alternative stuff really *worked.*

"Jesus Christ, you look like you died sitting up. Since when did you aspire to swamidom?"

"Since I went to talk to the counseling unit about the brownstone fire."

"You did?" There was no mistaking the relief in her voice as she waited for him to rise and put on his leather jacket. "Do you think it helped?"

Sean picked his words carefully. "It seemed to." He wasn't yet ready to say so definitively. But Dan was right about one thing: Talking about it helped. The Kennealy household might have functioned a helluva lot more smoothly if there'd been a counseling unit back when his father was still dragging hose.

"Where we going?" JJ asked, following Sean out the door.

"I need to stop by my apartment to check on Pete and Roger. Is that okay?"

"Sure."

"What are you in the mood for?"

JJ looked hopeful. "Italian?"

He shrugged. "No problem."

"That's what I love about you. You're so easygoing."

The irony of JJ's words struck him a few minutes later as they stepped off the elevator in his building's lobby and ran smack into Gemma. He felt tongue-tied and awkward. Concerned, too: She looked exhausted; her soft brown eyes were ringed with circles, the airy bounce in her step conspicuously absent. Was he the cause? Guilt engulfed him.

"Hi," he said, straining to keep his tone light and casual.

"Hi." Gemma's placid face was all politeness. Her eyes flicked to his friend. "Hello."

JJ nodded, smiling. "Hello."

Sean turned to her awkwardly. "Would you mind giving me a minute?"

"Sure." JJ threw him an odd look before smiling again at Gemma. "Nice meeting you."

Gemma's eyes were downcast. "You, too."

As JJ walked to the front door, Sean felt sick. He wanted to spill his guts, here, now, tell Gemma everything he'd learned from talking to the counselor; apologize, beg her to give him another chance, make her laugh till her eyes lit up again and there was color in her cheeks. Instead he stood there paralyzed, watching as she moved toward the elevator.

"Gemma?"

Her expression was wary as she turned back to him.

"Are you all right? You look a little pale."

"I'm fine. I just have a bad headache, is all."

"There must be an herb for that. Or something."

It was the right thing to say. Her mouth almost curled into a smile. Almost.

"There is. Feverfew."

"Is that what's in the bag?"

He knew he sounded like an idiot, but he didn't care. He wanted to keep the conversation going. He wanted to keep her here until he figured out how to say what needed to be said.

Gemma rattled the bag. "Aspirin."

He nodded. What could he say to that? How much? What kind? Ah, aspirin, yes, that always works for me? She was looking at him a bit oddly now. Could he blame her? It was none of his business what was in her bag.

He nervously licked his lips. "Well, um, I hope you feel better."

"Me, too." She turned to the elevator.

Well, that's that, Sean thought glumly. *Opportunity blown, over and out.* Then she abruptly turned back to him.

"I'm sorry. I didn't ask how you were."

"Fine, fine." Sean nodded vigorously. Nothing like a good lie to get the heart racing. *Keep nodding, keep smiling.*

"I'm glad," Gemma said quietly.

Maybe it was the headache, but Sean thought she looked distinctly pained as she stepped into the elevator, though she was doing her best to hide it.

"Have a nice night, Sean."

"You, too," he said as the elevator doors snapped closed in his face.

And . . . cut! That's a wrap. Frowning, Sean zipped up his jacket and went outside to meet JJ. He knew women; she'd want to know "what that was all about." JJ would probably tell him he was an idiot not to seize the moment. Sadly, he agreed with her.

"Do you think I'm a jerk?" Sean asked abruptly.

He and JJ had just given their order to a waiter named Dodge. As predicted, JJ wanted to know all about the woman they'd run into in the lobby. As Sean filled her in on all the facts, JJ listened attentively and a battle raged inside his head over whether or not he was a fool not to have made better use of the encounter. A larger question ate at him as well: If he missed her so much, why didn't he apologize and try to get back together with her? That's when he had blurted out his question.

JJ smiled politely at the waiter as he placed their salads before them. "Can I get Sir or Madam anything else before I depart?" he asked, clasping his hands behind his back.

"This is fine, thanks," Sean said, watching him go.

"Why would a mother saddle a child with the name 'Dodge'?"

"You think that's his real name?" Sean said with disbelief. "Get a grip. He's probably an actor."

"No one trying to break into show biz is going to take the name 'Dodge,' believe me." She reached for the pepper. "Now, what was your question again? Do I think you're a jerk?"

"Yeah."

"In general, or does this have to do with a specific situation?"

"Specific. Specifically Gemma."

JJ looked uneasy. "I thought so. You've been distracted ever since we ran into her."

Sean poked at his salad. "I miss her."

JJ swallowed nervously. "Sean, I have to tell you something, and you have to promise not to get pissed."

"Okay."

"That woman—Gemma? Your ex-girlfriend? She, um, stopped by your apartment that weekend I was bird-sitting."

Sean felt the bottom drop out of his stomach. "She did?"

"Yeah. I forgot to tell you."

"And—?"

"This is the 'Don't get pissed' part."

Sean's fingers tightened around his napkin. "Okay."

JJ's words tumbled out in a rush. "She came to the door and I opened it and I was wearing your robe and she asked for you and I was on the phone fighting with Chris and I just said 'He's not here right now' and I closed the door and forgot all about it until now. I'm sorry."

Sean made a sound like a dying moose and covered his face with his hands. "Oh, shit."

Eventually he uncovered his face, staring in disbelief at JJ. She sank down lower in her seat.

"I really wish you'd told me sooner, JJ."

"I know. I'm so, so sorry, Sean."

Sean sighed. "It's not your fault. Well, it is, but there's nothing I can do about it now." His fist hit the table, making JJ flinch. "Shit!"

"There is something you can do about it," she said tentatively. "Go talk to her. Tell her you miss her. Beg her forgiveness and ask her to go out with you again."

"I can't."

"Why not?"

"Because the woman clearly hates me. She could hardly stand talking to me. Now I know why."

"I thought you said she asked how you were?"

"She did."

"Women don't ask how you are if they wish you were dead."

"You don't know Gemma. She's nice to everyone. Bin Laden could step into the elevator beside her and she'd try to talk him out of jihad. That's the kind of person she is."

"I don't know what to say. You cut her loose, and now you want her back. There's only one way to make that happen: Apologize."

"Yeah, but—"

"But what?" JJ asked softly. "It's not rocket science, for God's sake."

"No, but it is complicated." He grimaced. "I don't know if you could tell by seeing her for those few seconds, but Gemma's not exactly a typical firefighter's girlfriend, you know?"

JJ looked appalled. "What the hell does that mean?"

"I told you about that night we went out with some guys from my house. It was a disaster."

JJ put down her fork. "Okay, let me make sure I'm getting this straight. You miss Gemma, but you're hesitant to get back with her because a few of the boneheads you work with think she's a little offbeat?"

"I guess," Sean muttered.

"Then you *are* an idiot."

"Gee, thanks."

"You wanted to know what I think; there it is. No offense, but who the hell cares what those guys think of Gemma? It's what you think that matters."

"They'll give me shit, JJ. They already have."

"Then give it back to them! We all give each other shit about everything anyway! If it's not Gemma, it'll be something else. This is ridiculous, Sean. Are Leary and those other yahoos the ones you're going to come home to after a long day's work? Are they going to give you a family?

Grow old with you? I know you worked hard to get them to accept you, but you succeeded, Sean. Any hell you catch from here on in is just bluster. And if it's not, then I think you need to get yourself some new friends. Life's too short to screw around with this stuff," she concluded in a choking voice.

Sean thought her food had gone down the wrong pipe. Then he realized: She was starting to cry.

"Hey." His hand snaked across the table to hers. "You okay?"

"Ignore me," she sniffled, waving him away. "It's PMS."

"Bull."

"Okay, it's not. It's me and Chris. If Gemma makes you happy, go after her."

"I don't know if I can give her what she wants. Not right now, anyway."

"Then offer what you can and see what she says. If she tells you to get lost, at least you'll know you gave it your best shot." Swiping at her eyes, she glanced frantically around the restaurant. "Now where's Dodge? I need a glass of water."

"Excuse me, Janucz?"

Sean tried not to feel embarrassed for the building super as he jerked awake at the sound of Sean's voice. Janucz had been snoring so loudly Sean had been able to hear him all the way down the hall. He wasn't surprised, therefore, when he arrived at the super's tiny basement office to find him with his feet up on the desk and his head lolling on his chest.

"Sean, Sean, how are you?" The burly Pole motioned for Sean to come through the doorway. "What can I do for you?"

"A favor. A big one."

"For you? Anything."

Sean smiled at the compliment. The staff and the other tenants in his building loved that a firefighter lived under the same roof. They thought it somehow made them safer. Sean had never traded on his status, but there was a first time for everything.

"I need you to go into 5B when the tenant isn't home and put this inside." He reached outside the doorway and grabbed a large, wrapped box.

"What is this?" Janucz asked suspiciously.

"A present."

"And you want Janucz to place it in 5B? Falconetti?"

"It's not Falconetti anymore, but yeah."

"Why for?"

To his surprise, Sean felt mildly embarrassed even discussing it. "It's a surprise. For the woman who's living there now."

"Yeah?" Janucz wriggled his eyebrows suggestively. "That little redhead in 5B? She is your special friend?"

Sean feigned a wolfish grin he knew would communicate better to Janucz than words. "She was. I want her to be again. That's why I need you to put this in her apartment. I want to surprise her."

"Hhmm." Janucz folded his hands across his soft belly, and tilted back in his old office chair. "This is illegal, you know, just going into someone's apartment for no reason. Janucz could get in trouble."

"I know." Sean felt badly, compromising this kind soul. "But it's for a good cause. And I could pay you," he added.

"You pay nothing," Janucz shot back, sounding insulted. "You are a great hero of this city."

Yeah, right, Sean thought. But to Janucz he simply said, "Thank you."

Janucz looked up at him with earnest, narrowed eyes. "If I do this for you, do you swear to tell no one, not even you own mother?"

Sean crossed his heart. "I swear."

"You swear on the grave of you father?"

Exasperated, Sean bit the inside of his cheek. "My father's still alive, Janucz. But yes, I swear."

"All right." Pitching himself out of the chair, Janucz leaned forward and, picking up the box, put it on his desk. "Let me see . . . 5B, 5B, 5B," he muttered to himself. Then: "Oh, shit."

"What?"

"You know who live on that floor? Croppy." He shook his head sadly. "Sorry, Sean. Too dangerous."

"Croppy won't be a problem," he assured Janucz.

"What? Are you crazy? Croppy's always problem. Her late husband? Beelzebub, I'm telling you. He's the only one who would have her."

"Listen," Sean said patiently. "It's none of her business why you're going into Gemma's apartment with a gift box. For all she knows, Gemma asked you to bring it up for her."

"Hhmm." Janucz rubbed his pocked chin. "You are right, Sean. But if Croppy sees me, she will bust my balls. You know this. But I will do this for you anyway."

"Thank you." Sean couldn't express his gratitude enough. "Gemma usually leaves for work at around eight, and is home between six-thirty and seven. Can you do it tomorrow?"

"I can do it. No sweating," Janucz said proudly.

Sean patted Janucz's shoulder. "I really appreciate this."

"No sweating," Janucz repeated. "You are a great hero of this city."

A day later the encounter with Sean still had Gemma rattled. It was too much, seeing his image on the calendar and then running into him in the lobby minutes later with his new girlfriend in tow. It felt like a cruel sensory overload. Despite looking tired, he was still handsome in that rugged, heart-stopping way of his, with his unkempt hair hinting at wildness and the faintest hint of his cologne teasing her through the weave of his faded denim shirt. Malibu Barbie was a lucky woman.

Unlocking her front door, she found herself face-to-face with a large, wrapped box.

Her first thought was panic: *What on earth is this? Someone's been in my apartment!*

Nervous, she looked around to see if anything had been moved or changed. Nothing had. Then it hit her. *Sean.* It had to be. Didn't it? Before her galloping pulse got the better of her, she forced herself to focus and listen to the still, small voice inside, the one that told her things, true things, about herself and others. *You want this gift to be from Sean. But is it?* Yes.

She tore off her cape and sank to the floor, tearing at the wrapping paper and carefully lifting the top flap of the box. A flash of hot pink hit her eye and she gasped in delight as she pulled it free, knowing just what it was: a hot pink wildebeest. Where Sean had managed to find another one, she couldn't imagine. Nor did she care. All her focus and attention was on the beautiful, fuzzy, unwieldy beast, its beaded eyes staring at her in supplication. There was an envelope pinned to its chest, and just for a moment, Gemma remembered the last time he'd used the wildebeest as a messenger: *Back killing me. Went back to my own rock hard mattress.* But that was then and this was now. She tore open the envelope.

Gemma,
Can you meet me at the Starbucks around the
corner tomorrow night at eight? I really need to
talk to you.
Sean

Gemma pressed the note to her chest, breathing hard. *Oh, God. Maybe he wants to apologize? Maybe he wants to get back together?* Barely able to think, she got up off the floor and rushed to the phone, punching in Sean's number.

That's when she remembered.

Nonna.

Shoot.

She hung up. Tomorrow was Wednesday, one of her nights to watch Nonna. There was no way out of it, unless she switched nights with her mother or one of her aunts. She could already hear her mother: *You've only watched her once and already you're changing things around, making it a big pain in the ass for everyone, blah blah blah.* But this was Sean she was talking about here. Sean. The man whose eyes had appeared to her in the first love spell she'd ever cast for herself. The man who loved his family, and walking the beach in winter.

The man she loved.

Bracing herself, she dialed her mother's number. Her mother picked up on the third ring, her voice tired.

"Hello?"

"Mom, it's Gemma."

Silence ensued.

"Mom?"

"I'm here."

"I—I need to ask a favor of you."

More silence. Deeper, resentful. Gemma held her breath.

"What would that be?"

"I need to know if you can watch Nonna tomorrow night."

"Why's that?"

Gemma hesitated. Should she tell her the truth? Why not?

"I have a date."

"With who? A warlock?"

"A firefighter," Gemma said, ignoring the dig. "I was hoping you could watch Nonna for me tomorrow night and then I'd watch her for you Thursday. We'd switch."

"I have my widows' group tomorrow night."

Gemma dug her nails into her arm. "It's just one night, Mom. I promise."

Judging from the drama of her mother's sigh, Gemma felt as though she were asking her to bring peace to the Middle East. *We're talking about watching your* own *mother for* one *night!* Gemma longed to yell. She bided her time and waited.

"I suppose I could do it," her mother eventually said. "Or I could get Millie or Betty Anne."

"Thank you so much, Mom."

Gemma heard a grunt of acknowledgment. Then: "You know, I hope you're not going to make a habit of this, Gemma. Because it's not right, especially on such short notice. You're not the only one with a life."

"I know that, Mom." Gemma swallowed her annoyance. "And I appreciate it. These are extenuating circumstances."

"Oh, yeah?" Her mother's tone was caustic. "Why's that?"

"Because firefighters work such odd hours. If I don't see him tomorrow, it could be weeks before we can find time again when we're both free."

"Huh." Her mother seemed to be considering this. "You sure you want to go out with a fireman?"

"Why not?"

"Because they can die on the job. Like Daddy did."

Gemma jolted. She'd never made the connection between her father's death while working on a construction site and her all-consuming fear for Sean. "I know they risk their lives, Mom. It's a chance I'm willing to take."

"Well, I hope you know what you're doing."

"I do."

"All right, then, you're covered."

Gemma released her nails from her arm. *Ask me how I'm doing,* she thought longingly. *Talk to me.* But her mother remained silent.

"Great." Gemma stared at the crescent moons she'd dug into her flesh. "I'll talk to you soon, Mom. And thanks again."

"You're welcome," her mother said, hanging up.

Gemma pulled the phone from her ear and stared at it, as if she couldn't quite believe she was sitting there listening to the buzz of the dial tone. But she was. Her conversation with her mother was over. It had been painful, but she'd gotten what she'd wanted.

There was just one thing left to do. She called Sean.

CHAPTER

18

One more hour until I talk to Gemma. This was the only thought Sean could keep in his head while he helped two probies clean the firehouse kitchen. Technically, he wasn't obliged to help, but he had so much anticipatory energy he felt he'd split his skin if he didn't do something.

It had been such a relief to come home from a visit to his folks to find the red light blinking on his answering machine. And then to hear Gemma's voice on tape . . . *Hi, Sean, it's Gemma. I got your note. I would love to meet you at Starbucks, say, at eight? If I don't hear from you, I'll assume that's okay. Okay, so, um . . . see you then. Bye.*

He'd allowed himself to feel self-congratulatory for approximately five seconds before doubt began creeping in. Had her voice sounded a little cold and detached? He played the tape. No, it was fine. Five minutes passed. Wait: Had she said *if I hear from you,* I'll assume we're on, or *if I don't hear from you*? He played the tape again. *If I don't hear from you.* Ah. He knew it was nuts, but he rewound the tape and played it once more, noting every pause, every nuance in her voice just for good measure.

"Yo, where's Birdman?"

Hearing Sal Ojeda asking for him, Sean strolled out of the kitchen onto the apparatus floor.

"Hey, Sal, what's up?"

"Gotta ask a mega favor of you, my man."

"Shoot."

"You up for pulling a twenty-four and covering for me tonight? I was supposed to cover for Hanratty on the five to nine but now I can't. Something came up."

Sean rubbed his chin thoughtfully, staring down at the cement floor. These were not words he wanted to hear. Normally, he'd have no problems switching with Sal or anyone else, no questions asked. But this involved rescheduling Gemma. Sean looked up.

"What's going on?"

"It's Janine." Janine was Sal's wife. "Today is our one-year anniversary, and of course, I forgot. She brought me breakfast in bed this morning along with this mushy card. I almost croaked. I covered by saying I had something special planned for tonight. I need to hustle down to the diamond district and pick something up, then take her out for a nice candlelight dinner or my ass is grass, my friend. Can you cover for me?"

Sean took a deep breath and blew out. "Sure." He had no choice. It was part of the code: When someone asked you to cover for him with good reason, you accommodated him, especially if you were single and had more flexibility. Christ knows Sal had covered for him on short notice a few times. He had to reschedule with Gemma.

"Gemma?"

"No, this is Julie." The young female voice on the other end of the phone sounded suspicious. "Can I help you?"

"Julie, my name is Sean Kennealy. I'm a friend of Gemma's. We're supposed to meet for coffee, but I'm stuck at work and won't be able to make it. Gemma's not listed in the book and I don't have her home number on me. Would you mind giving it to me, please?"

"I can't give out my boss's home phone number," Julie scoffed.

Sean's left hand slowly curled into a fist. "Then, would you mind calling Gemma's home number and leaving a message for me?" There was no answer. "Julie?"

"Hold on, I have a customer."

Sean twitched with irritation as Julie, who obviously ran the Golden Bough for Gemma at night, smashed the phone down on the counter. Just his luck to miss Gemma. Just his luck for her not to be listed in the goddamn phone book, either. He could just make out the muffled voice of Julie telling someone where the books on candle magick were. A second later Julie was back on the line, her voice blasting Sean out of the reverie playing in his own head, which went like this: *Please please please say yes.*

"Sorry 'bout that. You were saying?"

"Can you leave a message for Gemma on her home machine for me?"

Julie hesitated. "I can leave a message for her here that you called. But I'm really not comfortable leaving a message for her at home when I don't know you from Adam."

Sean closed his eyes, gently pounding his forehead against the concrete wall three times before getting back on the line. "This is an emergency, okay?"

"I'm sorry, but I can't help you." Julie was curt. "The best I can do is leave a message for her here that she'll get tomorrow."

"Fine," Sean snapped. "Tell her Sean called and he needs to reschedule our coffee date because he has to pull a double shift at work. Tell her I'll call her as soon as I can."

"Do you want to leave a number?"

"She's got my number. I just wish I had hers."

He slammed the phone down. The reverie in his head changed its tune. It now went like this: *fuck fuck fuck fuck fuck.*

Now what?

Starbucks. He'd call Starbucks and leave a message.

He lunged for the phone book, heart sinking as he scanned what seemed like hundreds of listings for Starbucks within Manhattan. Finally he found the one he was looking for and called. No one answered.

"Pick up the phone, you lazy cappuccino-sucking bastards!" he yelled just as the Cap walked by.

McCloskey threw him a puzzled look. "Everything okay, Sean?"

"Peachy," Sean muttered, hanging up the phone. His captain stood there. "I'm having a hard time getting ahold of someone I need to talk to," Sean explained lamely.

The Cap nodded and moved on. Sean waited until he was out of earshot and dialed the number for Starbucks again. Again there was no answer. But this time he didn't have time to throw a conniption. The bell sounded and he, along with everyone else on the shift, went running to the apparatus floor to put his turnout gear on. Time to go to work.

Gemma could forgive someone for being fifteen minutes late. After all, you never knew if a subway was delayed or a bus trapped in traffic. Even half an hour could be excused if the circumstances were extenuating. But forty-five minutes? Peering down into her chai latte, Gemma wondered if she qualified as totally pathetic for having waited this long for Sean.

The universe answered resoundingly: yes.

She drained her cup and threw it in the trash, making

her way outside. Had she ever been stood up before? She combed her memory. No . . . wait . . . .yes. Sophomore year of college, New Year's Eve, right here in Manhattan. Zev Greenberg, NYU film student who made her heart go pit-a-pat, had promised to call her to finalize plans to meet in Times Square and kiss her passionately as the ball came down. He never called. Gemma rang in the New Year by throwing herself across Frankie's bed and crying her heart out.

Men.

Of course, it was feasible that something had come up. But if that was the case, why didn't he call? Maybe he had; maybe she'd come home to a message from him? It was beginning to dawn on her it might indeed be time to join the twenty-first century and get a cell phone. She'd resisted up until now: The idea of anyone being able to get ahold of her at any time horrified her. But she was beginning to see there were some advantages to cellular technology. For example: It could save you the humiliation of sitting in a Starbucks staring into space for forty-five minutes.

Despite swearing off omens, at least where Sean was concerned, Gemma's gut told her she'd be a stone idiot not to take his failure to show as a divine sign that this wasn't meant to be. What she wanted and what the universe knew to be best for her were clearly two different things. How else to explain the continual failure of expectation and reality to meet?

She approached her building with dread. Any other woman who'd been stood up had the luxury of slipping into their apartment unnoticed to nurse their wounds in private. But not Gemma. She always ran the risk of running into Sean.

Gloomy, Gemma hustled inside and up to her apartment, fully expecting to find a message from Sean. There wasn't one. However, there was a message from her Aunt

Millie, panicked because she couldn't find Nonna's med-
ication. Gemma called her back and in the end wound up
going out to Brooklyn herself for the night. Why not? She
had no life anyway.

The next morning at work, she found a note from Julie.
"Sean called. Something came up at work, he needs to
reschedule coffee. He'll call."

Sure he will, Gemma thought ruefully. *And Nonna will
get better and Mom will embrace me for who I am and
Frankie will stop succumbing to imaginary ailments.*
Something was wrong with her, something she'd never
really experienced before. She felt despairing and out of
sorts. Poise and equanimity were retreating, replaced by an
overwhelming sense of exhaustion and futility. Some people would say she was sliding into depression. But Gemma
saw it differently.

What she was experiencing was a complete and utter
lack of faith.

And she hated it.

Dialing Gemma's home number and getting her answering machine—again—Sean hung up the phone, cradling
his head in his hands. She was deliberately screening his
calls. How else to explain not being able to get ahold of her
all Thursday night? All day Sunday? All Sunday night?
The woman was a self-proclaimed homebody, was she
not? That had to mean she was home, but didn't want to
talk to him.

He knew he could leave a long, drawn-out message for
her, explaining all about Sal and pulling a twenty-four, but
he hated people who babbled away endlessly on answering
machines. He'd been keeping his messages short and to the
point, simply asking her to call him back so they could

reschedule coffee. He'd left three. He wasn't going to leave another. Three messages was pathetic enough as it was.

Maybe I should take the hint and leave her alone.

Or . . .

Sean threw on his coat. It was time for another visit to the Golden Bough.

Arriving at the store, Sean was dismayed to find not Gemma behind the counter, but a young woman in her mid-twenties with jet-black hair, her slim, bare arms covered in snaking tattoos. The unhelpful Julie, no doubt. How she wasn't freezing her ass off wearing a tank top in the middle of winter was beyond him. Perhaps the hipper you were, the less you felt the cold.

"Hi," Sean said, friendly. "Is Gemma around?"

The kohl-rimmed eyes regarded him suspiciously. "You are—?"

"Sean. I called last week, remember? The guy you wouldn't give Gemma's home number to?"

"Riiiight."

"Is she here?"

"She's in the stockroom. Hang on a minute, I'll see if she wants to talk to you."

Sean managed a polite smile. "Thanks."

Who was this girl, Gemma's bodyguard? *I'll see if she wants to talk to you, my foot. Go get your boss, kid, and be quick about it.*

A few seconds later, Gemma emerged from the back. It wasn't until that moment that Sean realized he'd been hoping she would break into a big smile when she saw him. When she didn't, he wondered whether he hadn't acted too impulsively in coming.

"Hello," Gemma said.

"Hi." Sean was immediately struck by how tired she

looked. There were bags forming beneath her wary eyes, and her color wasn't good. He was tempted to ask if she was feeling okay, but he didn't want to risk getting off on the wrong foot and insulting her. He held his tongue.

"What's up?" Gemma asked.

"I've left you a couple of phone messages." Sean craned his neck past her, checking to make sure he wasn't going to be interrupted by her sullen henchwoman. Luck was with him; it seemed Elvira would be remaining in the back. "I don't know if you got them."

"I haven't been home much."

"No?" A homebody who wasn't home much; that got his attention. "Where have you been?" The words were no sooner out of his mouth than he regretted speaking them, especially when he saw the hardness that came to Gemma's eyes. "I know," he said hastily. "It's none of my business."

"Not really. But it's nothing mysterious," she volunteered. "My grandmother in Brooklyn is sick and I've been helping to take care of her. That's why I haven't been around."

"Oh. Is she starting to feel better?"

"No." Gemma looked distraught. "She has Alzheimer's. She's not going to get better."

"Geez, I'm sorry to hear that," Sean said, feeling at a loss for words. Gemma just shrugged.

"I wanted to apologize for having to cancel our coffee last week. One of the guys at the house asked me to cover for him, and I couldn't say no."

Gemma looked baffled. "Why not?"

"Because you can't do that. When someone asks you to cover for them, you cover for them, unless you absolutely can't."

Gemma's expression remained confused. "Why couldn't he have asked someone else? You had plans."

"You don't understand." Sean could feel his back knotting with tension. "There's a code—"

"I know all about your code," Gemma said irritably. "I experienced it firsthand, remember?"

Sean blinked, bewildered. "What's the problem here, Gemma?"

She looked hurt. "You stood me up."

Sean grit his teeth. "I left a message for you here. I would have left a message for you at home but your assistant"—he tossed a disgusted look toward the back of the store—"wouldn't give me your number, and you're not listed in the book. What was I supposed to do? I even called Starbucks. The putzes wouldn't pick up the phone."

"Hhmm." This seemed to mollify her somewhat.

Sean hunched his shoulders. "You didn't wait long, did you?"

"About forty-five minutes."

Sean's face fell. "Shit. I'm so sorry, Gem."

Gemma acknowledged his apology with a small nod. "So, getting back to Starbucks. What was it you wanted to talk about, anyway?"

As always when confronted with the moment of truth, Sean found his capacity for words suddenly diminished. Digging his hands deep in the back pockets of his jeans, he rocked on his heels. "Can we make another date to talk about this over coffee?"

Gemma shook her head. "I don't have time, Sean."

He could see she was telling the truth—or part of it, anyway. But her eyes gave her away. They were guarded, full of mistrust. *She doesn't believe I won't stand her up again.*

"So that's it? I'm dismissed?"

Gemma smiled sadly. "I'm just trying to save us both a lot of time and pain. Clearly, your priority is the fire department. I understand that. But that doesn't mean I like it. Let's be honest here: I don't fit the image of a firefighter's girlfriend. They're probably never going to accept me, and neither are you. Not really."

Frustration burbled up in his throat. "Look, you don't understand—"

"No, I don't. And I'm not sure I want to. All I know is we made a date to meet, and you bailed out on me because work came first—work you couldn't even talk to me about when we were together."

Sean glanced away, embarrassed. "I'm working on that."

"I'm glad."

He made himself meet her eyes. The sadness he saw there wounded him. "I apologize if I hurt you, Gemma. Obviously I wasn't emotionally available to you in the way you needed me to be. I'm working on all this stuff, believe me."

"That's really good, Sean." Her voice was genuinely encouraging, but he still knew he was being dismissed.

"So maybe—"

"Maybe," Gemma interjected softly. "But not now. Besides, what about your girlfriend?"

"My—? No, wait, that's something else we need to straighten out, I—"

The front bell tinkled, and a gaggle of young women stumbled into the store, laughing.

"I have to see to my customers." Gemma slipped past him. She looked glad to be ending their conversation.

"It's not what you think," Sean called after her, his voice strident. The girls fell silent, staring at him.

"Never mind," Sean muttered to himself. He zipped up his coat. She'd never believe him anyway.

"*Today you are* the late one, eh?"

Gemma met Stavros's comment with a curt look and hurried toward the booth where Frankie sat waiting patiently. Ever since taking on the responsibility of helping to care for her grandmother three months ago, it seemed she was always running, and worse, running behind, time a commodity that seemed always to be in short supply. Thankfully, Frankie wasn't one of those watch tappers who would take her to task. Gemma was pleased to note Frankie's neck brace was gone, and hadn't yet been replaced by a sling, hearing aid, or crutch.

"Sorry I'm late," she said breathlessly as she shrugged off her jacket and slid into the booth opposite her friend.

"No problem." Frankie closed the *Post.* "Jesus, you look like—"

"Don't even say it."

Stavros sidled up to the table, wordlessly handing Gemma a cup of coffee. He didn't even ask anymore whether she wanted any of the "bullsheet hippie tea" she used to sip so demurely. Those days were gone. Nowadays Gemma couldn't conceive of surviving without caffeine.

"I'm sorry," Frankie apologized. "I didn't mean to insult you. You just look really, really tired."

"Frankie, I am really, really tired. Between Nonna and the store, I feel like one of those gerbils on a wheel."

"I told you this was going to drive you into the ground," Frankie sang under her breath.

"Yes, you did," Gemma snapped. "Would you like an award?"

Frankie went wide-eyed. "Yo, foxy, this is me you're talking to, your best friend?"

"I know." The numbing sameness of her days, coupled with the sense of always being one step behind, had made her tense and irritable. "I'm sorry."

"You know it's going to be a good day when we've both apologized within the space of two minutes," Frankie joked. They smiled at each other sheepishly.

"It's good to see you," Gemma murmured.

"You, too. It's been—what?—ten years?"

"Feels like." Gemma sipped her coffee. "What's new?"

"Not much."

"Things going well with Uther?"

"Yes and no." *Oh, no,* Gemma thought. *Please don't let her tell me he's sending love notes on the tip of a flaming arrow.*

"He's a really interesting guy," Frankie said carefully. "But the medieval talk is kind of getting to me. Plus, he's always asking me questions about you."

"Me?"

"Yeah. It's weird. It's like, no matter what we talk about, he always manages to bring the subject back to you."

"Maybe he's nervous and he knows I'm one thing you share in common," Gemma suggested, hoping herself that was the case.

"Maybe. It's getting on my nerves a little, though. That and his constantly asking me to speak in my Lady Midnight voice."

"Tell him to stop."

"I have. He doesn't listen very well."

"Bend him to your will," Gemma suggested.

"I'm trying. Enough about me. What about you?"

"Work, Nonna, sleep. That's my life."

"No close encounters of the firefighter kind?"

"No." She hadn't seen Sean since the day he'd shown up at her store after standing her up, and for that she was grateful. Nor had she run into him with his girlfriend, though Gemma thought she once heard her voice behind the closed door of the elevator.

Frankie looked sympathetic. "I'm sorry that didn't work out, sweetie. Seriously."

"If it was meant to be, it would have been." She smiled sadly. "In my next life, maybe."

Frankie cupped her chin in her palm and sighed. "In my next life, I want to be attracted to gorgeous, stable men with lots of money who are always great in bed."

"Good luck." Gemma drained her coffee cup and stood up.

Frankie peered at her in alarm. "Where are you going?"

"If I don't leave now, I'll be late getting to Brooklyn." She slipped her jacket back on.

"Jesus, Gemma. You weren't kidding when you said you could only give me half an hour tops."

"No, I wasn't." Gemma looked glum. "Call me, okay?"

"Sure. I'll give you a ring tomorrow."

"Sounds good." Gemma hurried out the door.

She was halfway to Brooklyn before she realized she'd neglected to pay for her coffee.

Arriving at Nonna's, Gemma was surprised to walk in and find her mother in the kitchen, helping Nonna eat her cereal. Usually it was her Aunt Millie who took care of Nonna on Saturday nights, the house reeking of Winstons by the time Gemma got there.

Nonna looked up and smiled. "Benedetta!"

"THAT'S GEMMA, YOUR GRANDDAUGHTER," Gemma's mother shouted. "Benedetta is your sister. She's been dead for ten years," she added under her breath in an annoyed voice.

Gemma put the bag of groceries she was carrying down on the counter and tapped her mother on the shoulder, motioning her into a corner.

"She's not deaf, you know," Gemma pointed out quietly. "A loud voice isn't going to make her understand any better."

"I think it does."

"Fine. Whatever, Ma." Her eyes traveled to her grandmother. "How did she do last night?"

Gemma's mother shook her head. "Up practically the whole goddamn night. I hardly got any sleep."

"I'm sorry."

"She kept raving about Coca-Cola or something, I don't know what the hell she was talking about."

Gemma's pulse looped. *"Querciola?"*

"That's the word!" Her mother looked at her suspiciously. "You know what that is?"

Gemma held back a smile. "Yeah, I do."

"What?"

"It's nothing."

Her mother's hand shot out, gripping her arm like a vise. "Tell me."

Gemma unclenched her mother's fingers from her forearm. "They're the spirits in *La Stregheria* who aid lovers."

Gemma's mother's face fell. *"La Stregheria?* Have you been filling her poor addled head with your witch crap?"

"No!" Gemma was offended.

"Then how else would she know about these fairies or whatever the hell they are?"

"Maybe she's a witch herself," Gemma suggested, going to sit beside her grandmother.

"Let me tell you something, Miss Smarty Pants." Her mother's expression was indignant as she approached the kitchen table. "My mother is a good, obedient Catholic!"

"Who has her spiritual roots in Paganism."

"N. O."

"Maybe I inherited it from her. Maybe it's in the blood."

"What's in the blood?" Nonna asked innocently.

"Being a *stregh,*" said Gemma.

"Don't say that in front of her!" her mother hollered. *"Madonn',* what are you trying to do, confuse her *further?"*

Gemma put down the spoon she was about to lift to her grandmother's mouth. "Why are you so threatened by this?"

"My daughter worships the devil and now she's trying to suggest my own mother is a devil worshipper, too!"

"I've told you a million times, it's got nothing to do with the devil."

"You listen here. I know what I know. My mother lives by the cross, period. You understand?"

"Sure. That's why she wears a *cimaruta*."

Gemma's mother narrowed her eyes. "A cima wha?"

"*Cimaruta.*"

"What, that ugly necklace with the branches? She got that from her own mother. It's an heirloom from the old country."

"It sure is."

"I don't like what you're inferring."

"What? That my being a *stregh* really is in the blood?"

She checked her grandmother's face to see if she was comprehending any of this. If she was, it didn't show. Instead, she was smacking her lips impatiently like a baby bird waiting for food. It broke Gemma's heart.

"There's leftover ziti in the fridge if you don't feel like cooking," her mother said briskly, completely changing the subject. She slipped on her coat as she made ready to leave.

"Anything else I need to know?" Gemma asked.

"You know it all already," her mother replied sarcastically.

Gemma sighed.

"She's bad at night, like I said. But you already know that. I spoke with Anthony: no Mass today. She's getting too agitated and it's getting too hard keeping her in the pew. Don't forget her medicine."

"I won't."

Frowning, Gemma's mother kissed Nonna on the forehead. "YOU BE GOOD FOR GEMMA, MAMA, YOU HEAR ME?" Gemma waited for her mother to kiss her, too. The kiss never came.

Nonna turned to Gemma after her mother left. "Why does she keep yelling at me?"

"It's just who she is," Gemma explained gently, biting back her own pain. "She doesn't mean any harm."

I can't do this much longer. I love her, but I feel like I'm the one losing my mind.

Trudging through the door of her apartment building on Monday morning, Gemma fantasized about collapsing on one of the couches in the lobby. That's how exhausted she was.

She'd passed a horrible day and night at her grandmother's. Nonna's lucidity was slipping; more and more she was in her own world. Her habit of repeating the same questions over and over made Gemma want to scream. She knew her grandmother couldn't help it. But she herself couldn't help the rising frustration and exhaustion overtaking her life. Frankie had been right: She'd been nuts to take this on while trying to run her business at the same time. Thank God she'd had the presence of mind to have Julie open the store this morning. Gemma would come in after lunch, after she'd had a chance to shower, change, and maybe even close her eyes for a little while.

Walking past Mrs. Croppy's door, Gemma heard her whisper, "Slut."

"I wish," Gemma replied, laughing to herself. No doubt the old busybody thought she was trudging home in the early morning after a night of debauchery. If only she knew.

Opening the door of her apartment, she was greeted by the sight of the red light blinking on her answering machine. *Sean.* Then: *Why on earth would you immediately assume that?*

She took her time hanging up her coat, kicking off her shoes, and putting away the few groceries she'd picked up. Then she went to the machine. It was Frankie.

"Gem, hi, look, it's me. Not only is there a suspicious mole on my shin, but—"

Gemma hit "Delete." She couldn't take it anymore: not Frankie's self-obsessed hypochondria, not her mother's coldness, not Nonna's deterioration, none of it. She needed to escape. She called Julie at the Golden Bough and told her she'd be in at 6 P.M., not noon as planned. Then she unplugged her phone, took a few drops of valerian, and slid between the sheets, praying for the oblivion of deep, unbroken sleep. For the first time in a long while, her prayers were answered.

CHAPTER

19

When Frankie failed to show up for their diner date four days later, even stretched as she was to the limit, Gemma knew something was wrong. Phone messages left for her at WROX and on her home machine yielded nothing. Gemma knew she was going to have track Frankie down in person to get to the bottom of her sudden disappearance.

Leaving the store to Julie in the middle of the day, she trekked over to Frankie's. She knew her friend was there: Frankie had been on the air overnight and had to be sleeping. It was just a matter of waking her up, then annoying her enough to get her out of bed to let her in. To achieve this, Gemma leaned on the intercom buzzer relentlessly. After what felt like forever, the intercom crackled and Frankie's cranky voice could be heard loud and clear.

"Yeah?"

"It's Gemma."

She pulled at the door, assuming she'd be buzzed in immediately. Instead there was silence. *What the hell was going on here?* She spoke into the intercom. "Frankie?"

"Yeah, okay, come on up. I guess."

You guess? *Not good. Not good at all.* Gemma slipped inside and headed for the elevator.

She arrived to find Frankie's door open a crack, a clear indication to let herself in. The apartment was shrouded in darkness, a necessity for someone who slept during the day. She could hear Frankie bustling in the bedroom, and took off her cape, taking the liberty of turning on the living room lights. She kept the shades down.

Frankie finally emerged, looking like what she was: someone who'd just been woken up. Her flannel pajamas were crumpled and her hair hung in thin, unruly sheets. There was no mistaking the unhappiness on her face as she stood in her bedroom doorway, regarding Gemma warily with her arms folded across her chest.

"Yes?"

Gemma looked at her like she was nuts. "What do you mean, 'yes'? I've been calling you for days and you haven't called me back. You also stood me up at the diner. What's going on?"

"You tell me," Frankie said tersely.

Gemma scowled. "What?"

"Didn't you get my phone message?"

"What, about the mole?" Gemma asked cautiously.

"The mole and Uther. You never called me back about that."

Gemma looked away from her friend. Painful as it was, she knew she had to tell Frankie the truth. "I didn't listen to your whole message," she confessed quietly. "I thought you were being your usual hypochondriac self."

Frankie appeared stunned. "Oh."

"I'm so sorry."

Frankie looked mortified. "Am I really that bad?"

"Honey, you know you are. Admit it."

Frankie hung her head. "I know. I'm sorry."

Gemma went to her. "No, I'm sorry. I was wrong, I

should have listened to the whole message. What's up with Uther?"

Frankie sank down on the couch with a heavy sigh. "I'm not sure you're going to want to hear this. God knows I didn't."

Gemma braced. "What?"

"Well, things were getting a little hot and heavy, you know? We were rolling around and I thought, 'What the hell, I'll sleep with him.' I haven't had sex in so long I'm getting cobwebs between my legs. So I asked him if he wanted to spend the night, and he said yes, but then he tells me"—Frankie pressed her lips together—"that he prefers to do it with his helmet on."

Gemma recoiled. "That pewter soup bowl thing?"

"You got it. Which is fine. I've dealt with much kinkier things than that."

"You have?"

"Oh yeah. Remember that guy in college who wanted me to pretend to be Eleanor Roosevelt?"

"I must have blocked that out. Go on."

"So he put the soup bowl on his head and we rolled around some more and then guess what happened?"

"He insisted on pinning you to the headboard with two arrows from his quiver?"

Frankie frowned. "I wish. No, in the heat of passion he called me 'Gemma.' "

Gemma sank down onto the couch feeling dizzy and nauseous all at once. It was if someone had knocked the wind out of her. "That's awful."

"Yeah, tell me about it. Needless to say, I told him to put on his jerkin and with a hey nonny nonny to get the hell out of here. I don't think I'll be seeing him again."

Gemma nervously raised her eyes to her friend's. "Frankie, I'm so sorry."

"Don't worry about it."

Gemma could see she was trying to brush it off, but it had to hurt.

"Are you sure you're okay?"

"Yeah. I mean—was it a blow to my ego? I'll say. But it's not like I imagined this relationship really going anywhere. I just wanted you to know so you can be on your guard. Seems Robin Hood wants you to be his Maid Marion."

Gemma groaned. "This is the last thing I need."

Frankie smiled sadly. "Guess it's back to me and Russell Crowe." Russell Crowe was Frankie's pet name for her vibrator.

Gemma laughed. "Who needs men anyway?" She relaxed a bit. Then she noticed Frankie, who'd been chuckling with her a moment before, was now staring at her worriedly.

"Gemma, no offense, but have you taken a look at yourself in the mirror lately?"

Gripping her shoulders, Frankie steered Gemma into the bathroom, turning on the light. Gemma gazed at her reflection: Her complexion was sallow, there were dark circles ringing her eyes, and her hair was dull as weak tea.

"It's the light in here," she told Frankie.

The look Frankie flashed her clearly indicated she thought Gemma was delusional. Gemma looked again. It had nothing to do with the light, and everything to do with trying to do it all.

Gemma turned away. "Take me away, spirit, I've seen enough."

"You have to take care of yourself, Gem."

"Look who's talking." She followed Frankie out of the bathroom. "I should let you get back to sleep."

"Forget it. I'm up now. I'll go put some coffee on. Go sit down."

Doing as her friend requested, Gemma sat back down on the battered couch. She felt awful about deleting Frankie's phone message before it was done. She was her oldest and best friend, and the fact that she didn't even have the patience to listen to it in its entirety spoke volumes about the life she was leading—or wasn't, depending on how you chose to view these things. She knew Frankie's hypochondria made her partly culpable, but still . . . *I should have been able to tell by her voice that something was up. I should have had the patience and consideration to play her entire message.*

But she hadn't. *What is happening to me?*

It was crazy to be here, Sean knew, as he walked through the door of the Golden Bough. She had told him she didn't have time for him. She had made it clear she didn't understand firefighter culture, nor did she care to. She'd intimated to his face that she thought he was emotionally stunted.

So why did he care so much that Gemma be clear about his relationship with JJ?

The issue had been haunting him ever since he'd visited the Golden Bough last time and she'd asked him about "his girlfriend." He wasn't here because he thought he could talk Gemma into giving him another chance. He was here because, when all was said and done, it was important to him that Gemma be clear on what kind of man he was: the honorable kind. JJ had stayed at his apartment right after he and Gemma broke up. He didn't want Gemma thinking he'd been fooling around behind her back. He wanted to set the record straight. He wanted her to know he didn't have a girlfriend.

The store smelled vaguely of cinnamon, while the haunting lilt of a tin whistle keened from the sound system. A smile twitched at the edge of Sean's lips as he recalled their disastrous first date going to see deValera's Playground. He could almost hear Gemma's voice in his head: *That wasn't Irish music.* This *is Irish music.*

He was dismayed when he saw it was Goth Girl Julie behind the counter, not Gemma. Julie looked about as thrilled to see him as he did her.

"Gemma's not here," she announced before Sean even got the chance to ask.

"At her grandmother's?"

"Where else?"

"Is everything okay?"

"How should I know?" Julie sniffed, scratching the two-headed snake tattoo on her left forearm. "I just work here. I thought you were her friend. Don't you know?"

"Actually, I don't. We're kind of running on opposite schedules right now."

Julie smirked. "I could tell."

Sean ignored her. "Could you do me a favor? Could you tell her I stopped by?"

"No prob," Julie said, surprising Sean. "Anything else?"

"Nope," Sean said, heading back in the direction of the door. "Have a good one."

"Yeah, right," Julie muttered gloomily, cranking up the music.

Sean fought the disappointment growing within him as he emerged back into the bright sunlight. He'd missed her. They were always missing each other in one way or another, weren't they? Perhaps it was a sign. *Why should it matter that she knows you're not a bad guy? It's over between you anyway.*

Even so . . .

He'd nearly reached the corner when he recognized a blond, skinny-bearded guy he'd seen hanging out at Gemma's store. He was barreling down the street at a furious pace, his normally hang-dog expression now a scowl. He wondered what the guy was so pissed about and if it had anything to do with Gemma. Sean hoped not. The woman had enough on her plate already.

•   •   •

"Mayhap I can try the Celtic Cross spread?"

There was no way Uther was ready to read such a complicated tarot spread, but Gemma told him to go ahead and try it anyway—anything to help diffuse the subcurrent of tension between them. She'd heard from Julie that Uther had come looking for her the day before, and that he'd seemed very agitated. When he arrived for his lesson today, he immediately wanted to talk about Frankie, but Gemma put him off, telling him they'd talk during their ten-minute break. She watched as he stared down at the ten cards spread before him. He looked befuddled.

"What's puzzling you?"

He pointed to the sixth card. "I can't remember what it signifies."

"Influences in the future," Gemma prompted.

"Right, right." His eyes traveled the circuit of the cards again. Now he looked pained.

"What?"

"I really need to speak my piece now," he pleaded. "Until I do, my brain is but a sieve."

"Can you please speak like a normal human being?" Gemma asked irritably.

Uther looked cowed. "I need to talk to you."

"That's better." Gemma scooped the cards back into a pile. "I'm all ears."

"I'm sure that vixen told you what happened."

"What 'vixen'?"

"Francis," he spat. "Frankie. Lady Midnight. The trollop! The camp follower who should get herself to a nunnery hence!"

"Hey!" Gemma pointed at him. "That's my best friend you're talking about! You watch your language."

"Yes, m'lady."

"Go on."

"I'm sure she told you of her foul seduction."

"Language!"

"Did she tell you?"

"Yes," Gemma replied, growing increasingly uncomfortable.

Uther looked at her with moist eyes. "Then you know the reason for my accursed state is that I'm in love with you."

Shit. "Uther, I'm very flattered—"

"Nay, say not 'flattered.'" His bony hand reached out to cover hers. "You know we're meant to be together. Surely you must feel it."

Gemma politely slid her hand out from under his. "Look, I'm flattered, I really am, but I already have a boyfriend."

Uther flashed a knowing smirk. "Liar."

Gemma blinked. "Excuse me, what did you just call me?"

"Okay, fibber, you're a fibber," Uther hastily amended. "Frankie told me all about you and the firefighter, and how it's over now."

Double shit. It never even crossed Gemma's mind that Frankie might casually discuss her relationship with Sean. She'd never told her not to.

"Well, it is over now," Gemma admitted, trying to recover from her fumble, "but we only broke up very recently. I'm not ready for another relationship."

Uther's eyes shone with either lunacy or unrequited love, Gemma wasn't sure which. "Madam, what I'm talking about goes beyond the bounds of relationship. We're soul mates, you and I."

"I don't think so."

"Stop playing the saucy minx and succumb to thy destiny."

Lunging at her, he tried to plant a kiss on her mouth. Gemma jerked away, horrified. "How dare you!"

"I want you, Lady Faire!" He lunged at her again. "And I won't live without you!"

"Better learn!" Gemma snapped, scurrying to the other side of the counter. "Because we are done here." Shaken, she took his cards and stuffed them into his leather satchel.

"What dark dealing is this?" Uther cried.

"I just told you: We're done here. You've made me very uncomfortable with both your words and your actions, and I don't want to be your teacher anymore. Not only that, but if what you say is true"—she could hardly bring herself to say it—"that you care for me, then you were using my friend, and that's despicable. There are lots of good tarot teachers in the city. I'm sure you'll hook up with one." She slid his cash for that day's lesson toward him. "Goodbye, Uther."

Uther stared back at her in disbelief. Then he started to yell.

"You trollop! You and your friend—trollops both! You think I can't do better than you, you base, dissembling harlot? You think you can send me packing just like that? You—"

"I'll give you ten seconds to get out of here," Gemma said calmly as she picked up the phone. "Then I'm calling the cops."

"I SHALL NOT BE BESTED THIS WAY, LADY!" he railed as he stormed to the front of the store. "YOU HAVE AROUSED MY WARRIOR SPIRIT!"

"Oh, sweet God in heaven, please get out of here, you raving lunatic," Gemma moaned to herself as he finally slammed the door, leaving her in blessed silence. Sighing, she put the phone back in its cradle.

CHAPTER

20

"We go to Mass." Nonna sounded peevish as she peered down from the edge of her sagging bed at Gemma, sitting cross-legged on the floor. She was gingerly trying to trim her grandmother's yellowing toenails.

"No Mass. I'm doing your toenails. Now sit still."

"We go to Mass!"

"No." Taking a deep breath, Gemma gently grabbed Nonna's left foot with her left hand and tried to trim her big toe with the right. But it was no use: Whether deliberate or not, Nonna kicked at her, hitting Gemma squarely in the chest with the heel of her foot.

"SON OF A GODDAMN BITCH!" Gemma yelled, throwing the clipper across the room, where it landed on the wooden floor with a thud. Shamed, she glanced up at her grandmother, who looked on the verge of tears. But it was Gemma who began to cry, covering her face with her hands.

"I'm sorry," she sobbed through the screen of her fingers. "I didn't mean to yell at you. I'm sorry." But inside she thought: *Yes, I did mean to yell. It was either that or pop you one. I did mean to yell because you're driving me nuts. I know you can't help it, but my nerves are shot. I'm tired, I'm overworked, I'm alone . . .*

She was beginning to understand what drove caregivers to elder abuse. It was desperation. Frustration. Anyone who claimed they could "never do anything like that" was, in Gemma's all-too-expert opinion, lying through their holier-than-thou teeth. Either that or they'd never taken care of someone with Alzheimer's.

"Cara?" Nonna's voice was nervous, like that of a recently scolded child.

Gemma lowered her hands from her face. "Yes?"

"We go to Mass?" she asked eagerly.

"Oh, God." Snot was streaming from Gemma's nose. She wiped it onto the arm of her sweatshirt before reaching up to take Nonna's cold, little hands in her own. "It's nighttime, honey. There is no Mass. Plus it's Wednesday, not Sunday. *Capisce?"*

Nonna nodded, smiling, but Gemma could see from the confusion clouding her eyes that she may as well have been speaking Swahili. "Can I finish your nails, please?"

Nonna nodded again. Crawling across the floor, Gemma retrieved the clipper and resumed the task at hand. She didn't mind doing it, though judging by the length of Nonna's nails, she seemed to be the only one willing.

Nonna snorted disgustedly. "I should be doing this myself."

"It's okay. I don't mind." Gemma shook her head, mystified. There it was, the old lucidity, the old proudness. It seemed to come and go without any rhyme or reason. Gemma loved when the Nonna she knew and loved suddenly appeared, fully present and conversant. It felt like a gift.

"There. All done." The last of the toenails clipped, Gemma gathered them up and threw them in the nearby trash can.

"What are you doing?" Nonna screeched, shuffling to the garbage can. Picking it up, she dumped it out on her bed. "You don't throw nails out! You want your enemies to be able to put a spell on you? Burn or bury, burn or bury! What's the matter with you?"

Gemma watched in fascination as her grandmother began picking through the wadded-up tissues and candy wrappers, searching for her nails.

"Nonna," she asked quietly, "are you a witch?"

Nonna muttered something and continued collecting the nails from among the refuse.

"Nonna, are you?" Gemma asked again, louder this time. "*La Stregheria?* You? *Sì?*"

Her grandmother turned to her.

"*Sì,*" she whispered.

"I knew it!" Joining her grandmother at the bed, she began helping her retrieve the nails. "Why didn't you tell me? Why have you kept it hidden?"

Nonna cast her a knowing, sidelong glance. "You knew. I didn't have to tell you." She chucked Gemma's chin. "*Stregheria,* we know one another, yes?"

"Yes. But why did you keep it hidden? And why do you go to church?"

"Because I love God. One is the old way; one is the new way. When I came to this country, I took up the new way, but didn't forget the old. Who says you have to worship in only one way? Besides, my boyfriend doesn't mind the old way."

Gemma froze. "Your boyfriend?" Nonna was obviously sailing off into the outer dimensions of her own mind again.

"Him." Nonna pointed to the picture of Christ hanging above her dresser, one with dewy eyes that followed you wherever you went. It had always given Gemma the creeps.

"That's your boyfriend, huh?"

"I love him and he loves me. Here." She held out the collected toenails to Gemma. "You'll burn these, yes?"

Gemma took a fresh tissue from the nightstand and wrapped the nails in them before pocketing them. "Yes."

"One more thing." Nonna fumbled at the neckline of her shirt, pulling out the *cimaruta*. "I want you to have this."

"What?"

"Go on, *cara,* take it. It belonged to my mother." Her eyes twinkled wickedly. "She was one of us, too. It will protect you."

Speechless, Gemma helped her grandmother remove the amulet from around her neck and put it on her own. "How does it look?"

"Beautiful. *Buon compleanno!*"

Happy Birthday.

"Thank you," Gemma whispered, hugging Nonna as she slipped away again. It was nowhere near her birthday.

Nonna looked into Gemma's face happily. "Now. We go to Mass?"

When her mother, not Aunt Millie, showed up the next morning to relieve her, Gemma sensed immediately that things weren't right. For one thing, her mother never took care of Nonna if she didn't have to. For another, her mother was cordial. After running through the preliminaries ("How did she sleep? How much did she eat? Did she recognize you?"), she actually asked Gemma how Frankie was, and how business was at the store. Gemma answered, then waited for her mother to lower the boom.

"Listen, your aunts and I have to ask you a favor."

"What's that?" Gemma asked, trying to quell the rising resentment hissing through her.

"Your Aunt Millie was toodling around online and found a great two-night package deal to Atlantic City. We were wondering if you wouldn't mind bringing Nonna into the city with you for a few days."

Gemma stared at her mother. "Mom, I do run a business, you know." Her voice was strained.

Her mother's lips set in a hard line. "I know that, Gemma, but this is a special request."

"Can't Angie do it? Or Theresa? Mikey?"

To Gemma's surprise, her mother's expression softened slightly. "She loves you best. You know that. Last time Theresa was here, Nonna just cried and cried. She was afraid of her."

"Jesus." Just picturing it broke Gemma's heart. How awful it must have been for Theresa. And Nonna. "Why couldn't I watch her here?"

"Because if we can get her out of the house for a few days, we can finally get the ceiling in the kitchen properly fixed. You know how she'll react if workmen come here while she's home. She'll go gaga."

"Mom, Alzheimer's patients can become very agitated if they're put in unfamiliar surroundings. You know that."

"But she'll be with you," her mother insisted.

"Why is this so important?"

"It's for Betty Anne. She's going to be sixty-five and she doesn't have a pot to piss in. All she's ever wanted her whole damn life was to go to Atlantic City. So Millie and I want to surprise her and take her there."

Gemma was touched. "That's so sweet, Mom."

"Can you help us, *Gattina?*"

Gattina. Pussycat. Her mother hadn't called her that since she was a little girl. It was one of the "before" words: Before her father died and her mother turned bitter. Before she told her mother she was a witch and her mother cut her off. Was her mother trying to manipulate

her, or had the nickname slipped out in a moment of un-
guarded affection?

"When would this be?" Gemma asked cautiously.

"Next month sometime." Her mother looked defensive.
"Don't worry, I'm not asking you to do it for us tomorrow."

"No, no, I know that." Gemma wracked her brains, trying to figure out how to make this work. She supposed she
could take off two days in a row, leave the running of the
store to Julie. It would be a pain in the neck, bundling
Nonna up and taking her into the city, but anything was endurable for two days, right? And it was for a good cause.
Two good causes.

"All right. I'll do it."

Her mother's face creased with a rare smile. "We knew
we could count on you."

Gemma snorted derisively. "Yeah, because I'm a total
patsy."

"No, because"—her mother broke eye contact and
looked at her own hands, seeming almost reluctant to continue—"you have a good heart."

"Even though I'm a witch?" Gemma said, unable to resist.

"Even the devil used to be one of God's angels."

Instinctively, Gemma fingered the chain of the
cimaruta hanging from her neck, the amulet hidden inside
her shirt. Shouldn't she tell her mother she had it? It was a
family heirloom of sorts, after all. She didn't want to be the
potential cause of acrimony between her mother and her
sisters, nor did she want to be accused of perhaps taking it
without permission when Nonna wasn't in her right mind.
Feeling it was the right thing to do, she pulled the necklace
out from beneath her shirt.

"Mom, Nonna gave me this this morning."

Her mother, who was now at the kitchen table thumbing through the *Daily News,* barely glanced up. "That's nice."

"Are you sure you don't mind?" Gemma came closer to the table. "It's an antique. It belonged to your grandmother."

"I don't want it." Her mother seemed repelled by the idea.

"What about Aunt Millie or Betty Anne?"

"They're not going to want it either, believe me."

"Are you sure?" Gemma asked uncertainly.

Her mother peered up from the paper. "Why are you so concerned about me and my sisters and the locket? What, did you steal it from her?"

"No!"

"Then what?"

"Geez, Mom. I'm trying to be nice. I thought it might have some sentimental value."

"None." Licking the index finger of her left hand, Gemma's mother turned a page of the paper. "But feel free to tell my mother that if she doesn't want that antique bureau in the spare bedroom, I'd be glad to take that off her hands."

Gemma marveled at her mother's crassness and put the *cimaruta* back under her shirt, where it nestled comfortably between her breasts. "Do you know what the necklace means?"

Her mother's eyes remained fixed to the paper. "What are you talking about, 'means'? It's some superstitious old medal from Italy. Ugly to boot."

"It's Pagan," Gemma corrected softly. "It has to do with *La Stregheria.* Nonna is a witch. So was your grandmother."

A bitter laugh burbled up from the back of her mother's throat. "She told you that?"

"Yes."

"Gemma, Nonna is demented now. You know that."

"She still has moments of lucidity!"

Exasperated, her mother pushed the newspaper away. "Fine, my mother is a witch. What do you want me to say?"

"Say it's okay."

"It's not okay. It's evil. Period. God forbid this ever got out at St. Finbar's. Father Clementine would have her excommunicated."

"She calls Jesus her boyfriend," Gemma revealed tenderly. "Isn't that sweet?"

Her mother slapped a palm to her own forehead. "She's nutty as a goddamn fruitcake and so are you. No wonder you two get along so well."

Gemma frowned. "That's a nice thing to say. How about 'Thank you, Gemma, for offering to watch your grandmother for two whole days'?"

"Thank you," her mother muttered begrudgingly.

"You're welcome."

Her mother rose and went to the stove to begin making coffee. "Anything else before you go?" she asked, glancing over her shoulder at Gemma.

Gemma swallowed. "Did you mean it when you called me *'Gattina'*?"

Her mother turned back to the stove. "I haven't called you that since you small. You must have imagined it."

"Nonna? Are you comfortable?"

Gemma's question fell on deaf ears as Nonna's eyes remained glued to the television set, all her concentration focused on *The Wiggles*. Ten months ago, Nonna would have waved a dismissive hand and muttered *"Feh!"* at the idea of wasting her time in front of the TV. But that was before the plaque clogging her brain became her master. Now, the children's show, with its quick skits and lively songs, was one of the few things that could completely absorb her attention. Though she felt guilty about it, Gemma found herself sticking Nonna in front of the set more and more, especially when Nonna became anxious. It provided respite for both of them.

Bringing Nonna from Brooklyn to Manhattan the previous day had been harrowing. Despite repeatedly explaining to her grandmother that she was going to be taking a trip in the car, when the time came to bundle her up into the decrepit VW, she put up a fuss. Desperate to assuage her, Gemma lied and told her they were going to Mass. She sang songs in the car to calm her as they bumped their way back to Manhattan, courtesy of killer potholes and constant roadwork. It all seemed to work until they arrived at Gemma's apartment. Then it fell apart.

The tentative grip Nonna had maintained on normalcy disappeared completely, replaced by violent agitation that took Gemma hours to quell. Nonna cried. She screamed. She demanded to be taken home immediately. No matter what Gemma did or said, there was no soothing her.

Then, just as suddenly as they had begun, the tantrums inexplicably stopped. Whether from sheer nervous exhaustion or a brief flash of cognizance, Gemma wasn't sure. But she accepted the reprieve gratefully.

That night, Nonna barely slept, and neither did Gemma. Gemma kept reminding herself she had to endure only one more full day and night with Nonna at her place, and then she'd be able to take her back to Brooklyn. Besides, she was doing a good deed. At that moment her mother and aunts were probably chowing down at the breakfast buffet at their Atlantic City hotel, fortifying themselves for a day of serious gambling ahead.

"Can I have some water?"

"Of course," Gemma told Nonna, going to the kitchen to get it. The plaintive quality of her grandmother's voice made Gemma feel tender toward her, in addition to causing a twinge of remorse over the months of frustration. The Alzheimer's wasn't Nonna's fault. Gemma had to remind herself of that, and try always to keep her mind fixed on one thing: compassion.

"Here you go."

Gemma handed Nonna the glass, smiling. Nonna smiled back, looking at the glass in puzzlement. A few seconds later she looked back up at Gemma in mute confusion. Gemma's heart was seized with sadness. *She doesn't know what to do. She doesn't remember how to drink.*

"Here, let me help you." Gemma gently uncurled her grandmother's fingers from around the glass and began helping her to drink. That's when the phone rang. Setting the glass on the mantel where it couldn't spill, Gemma reached for the phone.

"Hello?"

"Is this Gemma Dante?"

"Yes," Gemma replied cautiously to the male voice she didn't recognize. "Can I help you?"

"Ma'am, my name is Captain James Eisen and I'm with NYPD's Emergency Services Unit. I need you to come down to your store right away. We've got a hostage situation."

Gemma blanched. "What?"

"Some guy named Uther is here, saying he's not going to release your employee unless you come down here and talk to him in person."

"Officer, I know Uther. He's harmless."

"Ma'am, he's got a weapon on him."

That idiot. "Does it look like a blade on a long pike?"

"Yes, it does. And he's threatening to use it on your employee if you don't get down to the store."

"He would never do that," Gemma said.

"Ma'am, we need you down here," Eisen repeated. "I don't want to have to send in the SWAT Team."

SWAT Team? Gemma blinked hard as nausea shot up the back of her throat. Then, in a voice of completely manufactured calm, she addressed Captain Eisen. "I'll be there as soon as I can, Officer."

"There's a car on its way to pick you up right now, ma'am," said Eisen flatly as he hung up.

Goddess, why? Gemma anguished as she shakily hung up the phone. *Why this? Why now? What did I* do? She began twisting and untwisting a lock of her hair. She had to think. Clearly. Rationally. Think clear thoughts and execute them. Rational thought number one: *Nonna.* Someone had to come over and watch her.

Brooklyn came to mind first. Theresa, Michael, Anthony. Then rationality returned. It would take her Brooklyn relatives too long to get here. That left someone closer. Someone in the city. *Frankie.* Gemma knew she was sleeping but her hand shot out for the phone anyway. Desperation surged through Gemma as Frankie's machine picked up, instructing callers to leave a message. Gemma did as instructed, shouting her message into the mouthpiece of the phone in hopes of rousing Frankie. She frightened Nonna, who began, not surprisingly, to cry. Gemma longed to join her.

"It's okay, *cara*," Gemma soothed distractedly, stroking Nonna's thick, white hair. Then, back into the phone: "PICK UP PICK UP PICK UP I'M BEGGING YOU PICK—"

"Cool your damn jets." Frankie sounded pissed.

"I'm sorry but it's an emergency," Gemma began babbling. "Uther is holding Julie hostage at the store! I need you to come here and keep an eye on Nonna for a little while. *Please*, Frankie, *please*."

"Slow down, honey." Frankie paused. "I think I might have heard wrong. Did you just say Uther was holding Julie hostage at the store?"

"Yes!"

Frankie yawned. "How come all the fun stuff happens to you?"

"This isn't funny! The cops just called me and they're going to send in a SWAT team if I don't get down there and talk to him! I need you to come over as soon as possible. I won't be long, I swear!"

"No problem. Just let me throw on some clothes and I'll grab a cab."

"I'll tell the doorman to let you right up. You're a lifesaver, Frankie, I swear to God."

"I try."

Ten minutes passed. Fifteen. No Frankie. In the interim, the police car arrived downstairs and Captain Eisen had called twice, claiming the situation was becoming increasingly more urgent. He did little to hide his impatience at having to wait for Gemma to arrive. Gemma kept picturing her own head bursting open from pressure, brain matter showering down like confetti. She glanced at her grandmother, who was dozing peacefully on the sofa, her soft chin resting on her chest. Gemma was torn. If she left now, before Frankie arrived, and Nonna should wake up . . . but if she didn't leave now . . .

A decision had to be made, and fast. As she had always done, Gemma took a deep breath and tried to quiet her mind, but it was no use. Since no clear instruction came swimming up from her subconscious, she grabbed on to the next thought that came twirling by.

Go to the store. Now.

Throwing on her coat, Gemma left her sleeping grand-mother alone in the unlocked apartment, and prayed for the best.

CHAPTER

21

Slouching in the back of the police cruiser, Gemma searched for the positive. Uther was distraught, not dangerous. All she had to do was treat him with respect, and he would come to his senses and let Julie go. That belief lasted until the cruiser turned the corner onto Thompson Street and she saw that *Dog Day Afternoon* was being reenacted outside her store.

"Oh my God!" she burst out. "This is *completely* unnecessary!"

"Ma'am?" The officer in the driver's seat turned around to look at her as the car coasted to a stop. "I hope to hell you're right."

Swallowing, Gemma lurched out of the squad car. Police cars clogged the streets. A large, white Emergency Services Unit truck was parked outside the store. Guys in black jackets with SWAT written across the back stood around talking. Two men with SWAT jackets and rifles were on the roof of the opposite building.

"Where's Captain Eisen?" she asked as the two cops who had fetched her brought her toward the white truck.

"Right here." A lanky police officer with a kind smile and a scar dividing his right cheek politely extended his hand. "Captain James Eisen."

"Gemma Dante." She caught the officer sizing her up, and immediately felt ashamed. She'd left the house without so much as running a brush through her tangled hair, in sweats, and in her slippers.

"I understand this must be very upsetting for you," Captain Eisen said.

Gemma looked around at the cops, the flashing lights, the flak jackets, the guns. "Officer, Uther isn't dangerous. Believe me." She began heading toward the store when Eisen pulled her back.

"Whoa! What do you think you're doing?"

"I'm going to talk to him. Isn't that why you brought me here?"

Eisen looked at her like she was nuts. "You can't go in there. We've set up a telephone line into the store. You can talk to him on that."

"Oh—okay," Gemma said. Her head was spinning. It all felt surreal, like she was dreaming, or in some prime-time TV show. She barely registered it when Eisen put the phone in her hand.

"Say anything you need to say to get him out here. Anything. Lie if you have to. People's lives, including his, are at stake. If he won't listen to reason, we have a hostage negotiator standing by." He slipped on a headset and gave her the signal to go.

Gemma nodded; inside she was filling with panic. Had Frankie arrived at her apartment yet? And if not, what had happened? Was Nonna screaming, crying, frightened, out of control? Would Uther listen to reason?

The line picked up and Uther answered. "Yes?"

"Uther, it's Gemma. I'm right outside the store."

"Stand where I can see you, Lady Love."

Gemma covered the mouthpiece. "He wants me to stand where he can see me," she whispered to Eisen.

Eisen motioned for her to stand in front of the store window, and Gemma obeyed. "I'm right here in front of the window, Uther."

A few seconds later, she could see Uther inside the store. The damn fool was in his chain mail and soup bowl helmet, halberd in hand. He peered out at her, then disappeared back into the bowels of the store. The cops had to think he was a freak.

She heard him pick up the phone. "Uther, do you see me?"

"I do, lambkin, I do."

"Talk to me. What's going on?"

"You wounded me to the core of my mortal being, sweetness."

"I—I'm sorry. I thought a lot about it after you left."

"Thought what?" Uther's voice was a tightly wound coil.

"About my folly. I was o'erhasty, was I not?"

"You were." Uther gave a satisfied chuckle. "Speak on."

"My mettle ran so hot I acted rashly. I acted the flibbertigibbet. It was wrong of me to cast you out as my student."

"Wrong to reject the proclamation of my heart, too."

Gemma closed her eyes. Eisen *said* to lie if she had to. "Yes. I realize now that thou wert right; the stars hath decreed we should be together. My blindness was my folly. I see that now."

Eisen shot her a severe "What the fuck?" glance.

Gemma returned a "Believe me, I know what I'm doing" scowl.

She could sense Uther beginning to relax as she spoke to him in a language he felt comfortable with. "Canst thou forgive me?" she asked humbly.

"I must think on it." There was a long silence. "How do I know this isn't some infernal trick to get me to surrender to mine rancorous enemy?"

Gemma covered the mouthpiece of the phone. "He means you," she whispered.

"I don't care if he means the Dalai freakin' Lama," Eisen whispered back fiercely. "Just keep doing what you're doing. I think it's working."

"I'm a lady of honor, Uther." Her voice dropped. "Not only that, but you're a Pagan, or have you forgotten? Pagans eschew violence. All violence. If you're truly a bard of the old ways, you'll let Julie go and come out peacefully."

She heard Uther sigh. "'Tis true. In my haste to plead my case, I forgot to honor the old ways."

"You can honor them by letting Julie go. Now."

"I release the fair maiden to your care."

Gemma and the surrounding police all held their breath. Seconds crawled like decades. Finally Julie emerged, pale but unharmed. Seeing Gemma, she ran to her and burst into tears.

"That was awful!" she cried.

Eisen motioned for her to be quiet and signaled Gemma to get back on the phone.

"The maiden is here beside me, Uther. You are a fair and generous fellow."

"You doth inspire me."

Gemma swallowed. "True inspiration requires you to come forth as well."

"Without his weapon," Eisen whispered urgently.

"Will you do that?" Gemma coaxed. "Will you come to me plain, no weapon in thy hand?"

Uther's voice was pathetic. "Will you love me true?"

Gemma blinked back tears. "I will. Hang on one moment." She again covered the mouthpiece and turned to Captain Eisen. "You're not going to shoot him, are you?

Promise me if he walks out that door peacefully, nothing will happen to him!"

"I promise," said Eisen.

Gemma got back on the phone, her voice cracking. "I await you with loving and open arms, my liege."

The tension was unbearable. Gemma closed her eyes. *Please, Uther, do as I asked and walk out without your weapon. Please.*

There was total stasis, everyone holding their breath, the air itself unnaturally still. Then, blinking against the bright morning sun, Uther emerged. Before Gemma could go to him, two cops sprang from either side of the door, clamped Uther's arms behind him, put him in handcuffs, and quickly carried him toward a waiting cruiser.

"Wait!" Gemma shouted, throwing down the phone. Reaching Uther, a tear trickled down her cheek. "I'm so sorry, Uther. But what you did . . ." She shook her head, unable to continue. Uther smiled at her sadly and let the cops guide him into the back of the squad car. The lights on the roof began flashing and then they were off.

"Where are they taking him?" Gemma asked a nearby cop.

"To the precinct to process him. Then to the psych ward." The officer laughed.

Pained, she turned away. Poor Uther; she never would have guessed his eccentricity would spin this far out of control. She walked back to Eisen.

"Good job," he said, clapping her on the back.

Gemma barely heard him. "Can I go in my store now? I need to make a phone call."

Eisen looked apologetic. "You'll have to wait a few minutes, I'm afraid. It's a crime scene. The bomb squad needs to go in and make sure your friend didn't leave any gifts behind."

"He didn't," Gemma said, "but you do what you have to do."

Remembering her recently purchased cell phone, she rooted frantically in her purse, stepping away from the action for some privacy. If she'd left it at home, she'd walk in front of the next cab that came barreling down the street, so help her God she would. Her fingers finally touched upon it, and she dredged it up from the depths of her bag. Turning it on, she dialed her own number. *Frankie, I'm sorry this is taking so long . . .* She was dumbfounded when her machine picked up. She disconnected and tried again. The results were the same. *Frankie, where are you? Please be there! Please just be too busy with Nonna to pick up. Please let there be nothing majorly wrong . . .*

Shoving the phone back in her shoulder bag, she returned to where Julie stood with Eisen and three other officers. She wrapped a protective arm around Julie's hunched shoulders. "I'm so sorry you had to deal with this, sweetie. I'm leaving, why don't you go home too?"

Eisen's expression was grim. "She can't. Detective Purcell here needs to speak with her. You, too—"

"But officer, you don't understand, I have a situation at home—"

"It'll only be a few questions, Miss Dante. I promise."

A few questions turned out to be many. How long had she owned the store? How long has she known Uther? What exactly was the nature of their relationship? What had she done to upset him? Had he ever threatened her before? Did she notice him acting in any unusual or suspicious way in the past few weeks?

By the time Detective Purcell was done, Gemma was beside herself with worry. This was too long to be gone from Nonna. And why didn't Frankie answer the phone?

"That should do it," Purcell said, snapping his reporter's notepad shut. He was a small man, serious, with a slightly crooked nose and a chest like a barrel.

Gemma's mind was spinning. "Can I go now?"

Purcell looked at her kindly. "Free to go. Thank you for your cooperation."

Gemma made herself smile. "You're welcome."

Purcell slipped her his card. "If anything else comes to mind, anything you think might be helpful in our investigation, don't hesitate to call me. You, too," he added, passing another card to Julie.

"Now what?" Julie asked forlornly as the cops took their leave.

"Go home. Rest."

"Aren't we going to open today?"

"No, we are not. I believe this qualifies as a mental health day."

Julie nodded gratefully. "What are you going to do?"

"I have to get back to my grandmother."

Julie kicked anxiously at the sidewalk with the steel toe of her Doc Marten. "So, am I still opening tomorrow?"

"If you can handle it." *If you can't, I'll just be closed tomorrow, too, while I bring Nonna back to Brooklyn. Screw it.*

"No problem."

"You sure you're going to be okay?"

"Fine." She peered at Gemma anxiously. "You?"

"I'm fine," Gemma lied.

"So, um, okay, then." Julie picked up her backpack from where it rested against the side of the building and swung it up onto her shoulder. "See you, Gem."

"I'll call you later to make sure you're okay."

"You don't have to."

"I want to."

"Okay." Julie shrugged. "See you," she repeated.

She set off down the block, then abruptly stopped, turning back to Gemma with a panicked look on her face.

"I just remembered something."

"What?"

"About three weeks ago, that guy stopped by looking for you."

"What guy?" Gemma asked patiently.

"Whatsisname, the fireman guy—"

"Sean?"

"That's it. He just said to tell you he stopped by." Julie looked sheepish. "I'm sorry I forgot, Gem, but things have been so nuts at the store with the constantly shifting hours—"

"Don't worry about it," Gemma said.

Reassured, Julie walked away. Exhausted, Gemma looked at her store—the scene of a hostage crisis!—one final time before hailing a taxi. Her mind drifted as she watched the world outside scroll by the window of the cab.

She didn't want to think about what she'd come home to.

"What are you making again?"

Sean shot Sal Ojeda a disbelieving look. Along with the rest of the ladder company, they were on their way back to the firehouse after a trip to D'Agostino's to pick up the ingredients for that day's lunch. Ojeda had asked the same question when they pulled out of the firehouse, and again as he trailed Sean down the produce aisle. Either Sal was extremely distracted, or his brain was leaking intelligence like a slowly deflating tire.

"Steak, grilled peppers and onions, garlic mashed potatoes," Sean repeated for the third time that day.

Ojeda blinked. "Oh. Right."

Sean leaned over, tapping him lightly on the side of his head. "Hello? Anyone home?"

The action returned Ojeda back to full consciousness, and he shrugged. "Sorry. Spring fever, I guess."

Sean understood completely. It was a sunny, early spring morning, freakish in its warmth. White clouds cod-

dled the skyscrapers, while the breeze was steady enough
to playfully rustle the skirts of women as they hurried
down the sidewalks, teasing the imagination. It was one of
those days Sean felt acutely aware of being alive.

He peered out the window, watching people as they
watched the truck go by. There was something about the
sight of the sleek, red vehicle in motion that seemed to in-
trigue the public. Ditto firefighters themselves: Whether
they were sitting outside the firehouse or grocery shopping, folks always came over to say hello. Sean was proud
of their approachability.

"So, whatever happened with you and that New Age-y
chick?" Ojeda casually asked, cracking the window open
farther. It was getting stuffy in the back of the truck.

Sean turned to him, puzzled. He couldn't remember
telling Ojeda about it. Ojeda caught the expression on his
face and laughed, pointing a finger at Leary.

"He told me."

"Figures." *Firefighters: the biggest friggin' gossips in
the world.* "It just didn't work out."

"Too freaky?"

"Nah," Sean said evasively. "The timing was all wrong,
you know? Plus, she's got a lot of other stuff going on."

Ojeda nodded sympathetically. "I hear that."

I wish I did. Sean knew it was stupid, but it still both-
ered him that he'd never heard back from Gemma after
stopping by the store. He knew she was dealing with a lot,
but a simple acknowledgment would have been nice. Then
again, silence could be its own answer.

Not one for excessive self-reflection, he nevertheless
found himself thinking about how much he'd changed
over the past few months. Part of it, he knew, was his willingness to go for help after the brownstone fire. But much
of it was simply the passage of time, and the gift of hind-
sight. He'd been shallow to worry about her "not fitting in"
with his world. Opposites attracted all the time. If his head

hadn't been so far up his ass, they could have made it work. All it would have taken was compromise and an open mind. And another thing, too: He'd been wrong not to talk to her about things, wrong to feel annoyed with her worries for his safety. At the time, he couldn't see how one fed the other, how silence and worry chased each other in a never-ending spiral that could only lead to failure. Now he could. He would not make the same mistake again.

They had traveled less than a block when a young woman, standing on the nearest corner clutching a small chihuahua under her arm, frantically waved them down. Obliging, Joe Jefferson eased the ladder truck over to the curb. They all rolled down their windows.

"I think there's a fire around the corner on East Fifty-ninth," she said breathlessly. "My dog was doing his business, and I looked up and saw smoke coming from the window of an apartment."

"You got an address?" Captain McCloskey asked her.

The girl nodded. "One fifty-seven."

"We're on it," he told her as Jefferson switched on the siren and they sped away.

"Did she say one fifty-seven?" Sean called up front. Jefferson nodded. "Holy shit, that's my building."

Gemma, Janucz, Tony the doorman, his birds—names and images bombarded him. There were a million different things that could cause a fire. He just prayed it was a small one, and that no one he cared about was anywhere near it.

The truck had barely rolled to a halt before Sean jumped out.

"This is it!"

Peering skyward, he tensed: Whorls of black smoke were tumbling out of Gemma's partially opened living room window. "Fuck."

"What?" Captain McCloskey demanded. They were all

out on the sidewalk now, hurriedly slipping into their turnout gear.

"I know the woman who lives in that apartment," Sean said, trying to keep his emotions in check. "I gotta go—"

"Whoa, hold up a minute." McCloskey adjusted the air pack on his back. "What's the exact location of the apartment?"

"Fifth floor, second door on the left."

"Okay. Kennealy, you and Ojeda take your cans to the fifth floor and scope things out. Do not enter the apartment in question, you hear me? Leary and I will go up to six. Delaney, you and Campbell stay put for now." He turned to Joe Jefferson. "Radio back to the house for the engine and backup." Putting on his helmet, he looked at Sean curiously. "You say you live here?"

"Yeah. Sixth floor—right above the apartment in question, in fact." He picked up his can. "Can I go now?"

"We're all gonna go now," the captain said. "Just remember what I said."

"*Looks like there's* a fire. You want me to drop you here?"

Gemma, who'd been daydreaming as best she could, tore her eyes from the window and stared at the back of the cabbie's balding head.

"Excuse me?"

He impatiently directed her gaze to the fire truck parked in the middle of the street, its flashing light a warning. "Drop you here?"

Gemma nodded, dread filling her as she paid the cabbie and made her way out to the sidewalk. Invisible cables of steel were tightening around her chest, crushing her ribcage, making it hard to breathe. Hurrying, she hustled as fast as she could up the street. The fire truck was parked directly in front of her building. Absolute panic choked her as she looked up: Smoke was billowing from the window of her apartment.

She broke into a run. "My grandmother's in there!"

"Gemma! Gem!"

Hearing her name, Gemma halted abruptly and turned. There was Frankie, waving her arms madly amid the small crowd of bystanders and wide-eyed, terrified tenants. Unthinking, Gemma pushed her way through the crowd to join her.

"What are you doing out *here?*" she cried. "You're supposed to be with my grandmother!"

"There was a traffic accident on Third Avenue. I was stuck in the cab for forty minutes! By the time I got here, the fire department was already here! They're not letting anyone into the building. I tried calling you, but your cell phone was off."

Gemma's eyes flashed with doubt as she shoved her hand deep into her pocketbook, pulling her cell phone out. Frankie was right: She'd turned the damn thing off. Gemma looked around wildly, thrusting the useless instrument back in her purse. "Does anyone know anything about this fire?" she asked loudly. "Anyone?"

"They think it's just in 5B right now, but they're not sure," said a freckled woman holding a small orange cat on her shoulder as if it were an infant. She was petting it ferociously.

Gemma crumbled. "Nonna," she sobbed. "I should never have left her alone! This is all my fault!"

"That's ridiculous!" Frankie grabbed Gemma's shoulders firmly. "You have to calm down. You have to." She marched her over to the nearest firefighter. "Tell him! Tell him about your grandmother!"

Gemma cleared her throat, trying to get ahold of herself. "M-my grandmother is in 5B."

The firefighter immediately got on his radio. "Ladder Twenty-nine Chauffeur to Ladder Twenty-nine, we have a report of a person still in 5B k." He turned to Gemma. "We'll do what we can. Please step back."

Reluctantly, Gemma let her friend lead her away. Her frightened eyes met Frankie's. "Nonna's in there," she repeated, sounding completely lost and bewildered as tears poured down her face.

"I know, baby." Frankie's voice cracked as she folded Gemma into a fierce embrace. "But the fire department is doing all they can. You have to have faith."

CHAPTER

22

Adrenaline pounding, Sean flew up the stairs and carefully opened the door to the fifth floor, Ojeda right behind him. A smoky haze clung from floor to ceiling, while up and down the corridor, the piercing sound of individual smoke detectors going off created a skull-rattling cacophony. Sean marched up to the door of the nearest apartment and started pounding.

"Fire department! Please evacuate the building!"

They repeated the procedure up and down the length of the hallway. Thankfully, no one seemed to be home except the dreaded Mrs. Croppy, who, despite the noise and the smoke, peered suspiciously at Sean as she opened the door a crack.

"Ma'am, I have to ask you to evacuate the premises immediately." The woman simply stared at him, her milky blue eyes distrustful. "Ma'am?"

"It's that whore across the hall, isn't it? With her incense and her—"

"Ma'am, I don't know, but you have to *leave the build-*

ing right now." Taking hold of the doorknob, he pushed the
door open enough to gently grab the woman's elbow and
pull her out into the hall, closing the door behind him. He
began steering her toward the stairs at the end of the hall.
"Can you make it down the steps on your own? Or do
you—"

The woman jerked her arm out of Sean's grasp and
pushed the door to the stairwell open with the other. "I
don't need your G-D help," she growled, gnarled fingers
latching on to the banister as she started off down the
stairs.

"Suit yourself." Under his breath Sean muttered, "You
nasty old cow." How Gemma could stand living on the
same floor with that old biddy was beyond him.
Gemma . . .

He met Ojeda outside Gemma's apartment. Smoke was
steadily seeping out from beneath the door, its aroma acrid.
Sean put his hand to the door. Hot to the touch. Without
further thought, he started putting his mask on.

"What the hell are you doing?"

"I'm going in," Sean said, tightening the straps on either side of his neck.

"You wanna get your ass kicked? Cap said not to."

"Cap doesn't know the woman who lives here." *He
doesn't have feelings for her, either.* He didn't want to tell
Ojeda he had a "feeling" someone was in there. It would
sound too airy-fairy, not to mention unprofessional. But it
was true. A renegade thought invaded his mind: Gemma
would be proud of him for listening to his gut. His inner
voice. He laughed out loud.

"You losin' it or what?" Ojeda asked worriedly.

"I'm going in," Sean repeated. "You stay here and hold
the fire at the door."

Sean gripped the door handle, surprised to find it unlocked. Ojeda radioed downstairs: "Ladder Twenty-nine
Chauffeur, this is Ladder Twenty-nine, we're holding the

fire at the apartment door." Bracing himself for the worst, Sean opened the door slowly: A wave of heat and black smoke drove him down to his knees. It was worse, far worse, than he'd imagined. The shriek of the smoke detector—thank God she'd gotten a new one like he'd asked—was like a jackhammer to his brain. Can in hand, he crawled forward toward flame, an unconscious mantra beating through his brain: *Gemma, don't be here, Gemma, don't be here, Gemma, don't be here.* The heat was becoming more intense, but he'd known worse. Finally, after what felt like an eternity, he was in close enough to hit the fire and he let the can rip. The fire darkened down. For a split second, Sean allowed himself the luxury of relief.

Still on his hands and knees, he continued scanning the floor, not surprised when his radio crackled. "Ladder Twenty-nine Chauffeur to Ladder Twenty-nine, we have a report of a person still in the apartment k."

"This is Ladder Twenty-nine to Ladder Twenty-nine Chauffeur, I'm in the apartment right now conducting a search," Sean radioed back down to the street. *Damn.* His intuition had been right. Someone was in here. But the front door had been unlocked. Could Gemma, or whomever it was, have run out when the fire started? Not an assumption he dare make.

With renewed determination, he pushed himself farther into the heat and darkness. That's when he heard it. Distinct, almost chilling: halting coughs and gasps interspersed with what sounded like mumbling from behind Gemma's bedroom door. Sean pulled out his radio.

"This is Ladder Twenty-nine. We've definitely got a viable rescue in 5B," he reported.

Grateful he knew the layout of the place, he crawled in the direction of Gemma's bedroom, reaching up for the doorknob. *Fuck.* Gemma or whomever it was had locked themselves in. Rising up on his knees, he started hammering on the door.

"Fire department! Open the door! We're gonna get you outta here!"

He waited, then tried the door again. Still locked. A lump formed in his throat as he realized the cries behind the door had faded away to silence. Behind him, the fire had flared up again, roaring its intention to devour everything in its wake. As quickly as he could, Sean pulled out his rabbit tool and popped the lock. Just as he pushed the door open, the fire rolled over the living room. If ever time was of the essence, it was now: Flashover was imminent.

Dropping back down to his knees, Sean crawled forward, kicking the bedroom door shut behind him. Dark smoke poisoned the room. He soon found himself at the nighttable closest to the window. He reached up, patting the bed. Nothing.

He continued his clockwise search, crawling around to the other side of Gemma's bed. He found an old woman curled up in a ball on the floor, her white hair spread across the lower half of her face like a veil. Gemma's grandmother. At first Sean thought she was dead. But closer examination revealed she was still breathing, albeit shallowly. "Don't worry," Sean shouted. "I'm gonna get you out of here." There was no response.

Grasping her firmly beneath the armpits, Sean began dragging her toward the door, stunned by how light she was. She was shrunken and small, almost child sized. He had almost reached the door when his radio once again crackled to life.

"Ladder Twenty-nine to Ladder Twenty-nine Chauffeur, I'm backing out. It's too hot to hold off k." It was Sal Ojeda.

"Battalion Six to Ladder Twenty-nine, back out," came the return message. Sean recognized Battalion Chief Murphy's voice. "Engine Thirty-one has arrived. Repeat: Engine Thirty-one has arrived."

Sean got on the radio. "Ladder Twenty-nine to Ladder Twenty-nine Chauffeur. Position the ladder at the fifth-floor window. We will be bringing the victim out k."

"Got it," Joe Jefferson said. "I'm bringing the stick to the window."

Sean hurriedly crawled in the direction of murky sunlight, rising up to break out the window with his ax. Then he dropped back down, quickly crawling back to the tiny form he'd left resting on the floor. As gingerly as he could, he gathered the fragile, withered body up in his arms.

"Hang in there," he urged, as much to himself as to her, as he climbed over the window sill and out onto the ladder. His eyes quickly swept the scene below: The engine truck had arrived, and backup from another house was just pulling onto the street. Mindful of who it was he was carrying, he began his careful descent.

"Gemma, look!" Frankie shouted. "Look!"

Gemma looked skyward. There, crawling out of her bedroom window, was a firefighter. She squinted until she could just make out BIRDMAN across the back of his jacket. In his arms Sean carried a small, inert bundle which he carefully sheltered with his body. Nonna! Gemma shot forward, only to find herself running smack into the barriers the fire department had erected to keep civilians at bay.

"Please!" Gemma shouted in a desperate voice. "Please!"

Sean was on the ground now, easing Nonna onto a waiting stretcher near the base of the ladder. Gemma's guts twisted as an EMT immediately clamped an oxygen mask on her grandmother's face, while the other began checking vitals.

"SEAN! SEAN!"

He turned, whipping off his face mask as he approached

her. "She's still alive," were the first panting words out of his mouth.

Gemma gasped. "Oh thank God."

Sean pushed aside one of the barriers, motioning for her to come through. "Come on, go with her in the ambulance."

Gemma turned to Frankie. "Will you come?"

Frankie looked to Sean. "If I can," she said uncertainly.

"Not a problem," Sean said.

"Sean," Gemma said again, as unrestrained emotion avalanched through her. "I don't know how to thank you—if you hadn't saved her—I swear to God I—I just don't know—"

"Sshh." He patted her shoulder. "We'll talk later, okay? I'll stop by the hospital." He seemed preoccupied, his breath still coming hard. "Right now I gotta go get checked out."

Before Gemma could answer, he strode away, joining a cluster of firefighters. The EMTs had already loaded Nonna inside the nearest ambulance and were about to swing the doors shut when Mrs. Croppy pushed her way to the front of the crowd, straining against the barrier as she pointed at Sean.

"That fireman manhandled me!" she shouted to a nearby fire chief. "That fireman dislocated my elbow!"

"Too bad he didn't dislocate your jaw," Frankie muttered.

Gemma shook her head sadly and began climbing into the back of the ambulance with Frankie.

"That's my grandmother," Gemma explained to the female EMT, looking down at Nonna. "We're coming with you."

"You're both family?" the EMT asked.

Gemma grabbed Frankie's hand and squeezed hard. "Yes. We're family."

•   •   •

Despite Uther proving to be far from sane, and her apartment no doubt reduced to cinders, Gemma was still grateful. Whether this was a sign of faith or her own insanity, she didn't know. But Nonna had clung tenaciously to life, and right here, right now, that was all that mattered. Sitting beside her grandmother's bed in the hospital room, she watched the old woman's breath rise and fall, the endotracheal tube in her throat ensuring enough oxygen could pass through her swollen airways. *Lucky* is the word the doctor had used. "She's very, very lucky. Most elderly people don't survive smoke inhalation like this."

Most elderly people aren't my Nonna.

His words had shocked Gemma, because Nonna sure didn't look lucky. Her face was swollen to twice its normal size, and soot clogged her nostrils. Blistering burns ringed her nose and mouth. Red, crusty splotches marred her face. There was no telling how long she would remain in the hospital. The doctor seemed to think at least a week, though given Nonna's frailty and "mental condition"—a nice euphemism for Alzheimer's—it was possible she could be there up to a month.

Exhausted, Gemma checked her watch. Ten P.M. Frankie had long since left, needing to catch at least a few hour's sleep before her air shift. Anthony and Angie had come and gone, too, as had Michael and Theresa, who graciously offered to let her live with them while her—correction, Theresa's—apartment was rebuilt. No one blamed her for what happened, not when they heard about the hostage situation. Yes, they all agreed, leaving an Alzheimer's patient alone was foolish, but what else could she have done, given the circumstances? It wasn't her fault Frankie was delayed. Their understanding gave Gemma something else to be grateful for.

The only people yet to show up were her mother and her aunts. Gemma had no intention of leaving the hospital until they did. She'd called them in Atlantic City hours ago, relieved to get her Aunt Millie on the phone and not her mother. "We'll be back as soon as we can, doll," Millie had croaked in her smoker's voice. "You sit tight." Gemma felt awful about interrupting Aunt Betty Anne's dream weekend, but what was she supposed to do? Wait to tell them their mother had almost died in a fire? She'd agonized, but in the end even Frankie agreed it was better to call than to wait. "Either way, you're the loser," Frankie noted matter-of-factly. She was right.

Still, Gemma wondered what was keeping them. She knew it was a bit of a drive, but it wasn't that long. New worries beset her: What if something had happened to "Mo, Larry, and Curly" as Anthony facetiously referred to them?

As if on cue, her mother and aunts appeared in the doorway. Gemma wearily rose to greet them, and was met by a slap across the face from her mother. "*Idiota!* How could you be so stupid as to leave her alone?! HOW?"

"Jesus, Connie!" Aunt Millie looked mortified as she dragged her sister out into the hall. "What the hell kind of greeting is that?"

Stunned, Gemma raised a hand to her stinging cheek. She was tempted to leave without a word. She needed this kind of abuse like she needed a hole in her head.

"*Cara,*" Aunt Millie coaxed from the hallway, "please come out here. I promise I won't let this madwoman lay another finger on you!"

Dazed, Gemma did as her aunt requested. She deliberately stood a distance from her mother, whose eyes burned with unchecked fury.

"What the hell happened?" her mother railed. "We let you take her out of the house for one day AND SHE WINDS UP IN THE HOSPITAL?"

"Connie, let the girl talk, for Chrissakes!" Aunt Millie barked. "And try to remember where you are, please! This is a hospital, not Giants Stadium. Keep your voice down!"

Huffing and puffing, Gemma's mother made an effort to calm down. In the meantime, Gemma closed the door to Nonna's room. The last thing she wanted was for Nonna to stir to consciousness and find her lunatic family yelling at one another. Assuming she'd even recognize them.

Gemma's eyes traced all three women. "Where have you been?"

"Traffic was a nightmare," Millie said. "Then this nutcase here"—she jerked her thumb in the direction of Gemma's mother—"insisted we go home to Brooklyn first and drop off our stuff. Believe me, if it were up to me, we would have been here hours ago."

"Listen to Miss Eagle Scout," Gemma's mother jeered. "Stick it up your ass, Millie."

"Can we stop this, please?" Gemma pleaded. "It's not very productive." She approached her Aunt Betty Anne, who'd been silent up until now. "I'm sorry I ruined your weekend, Aunt Betty Anne. I know how important it was to you."

Betty Anne just nodded as tears filled her eyes. "We can always go back."

"Not if Ma's a vegetable!" Gemma's mother exclaimed dramatically.

Gemma glared at her. "She's not a vegetable. She suffered severe smoke inhalation. It might take a while, but the doctor said she's going to be fine."

"Sweetie, what caused the fire?" Aunt Millie asked kindly, shaking a cigarette out of the pack she always kept in her coat pocket. She put it in her mouth and was striking the match to light it when she suddenly remembered where she was. Shamefaced, she hurriedly put them away.

"I don't know," Gemma replied, distraught. "Nonna could have turned the oven on, or tried to cook something. I just don't know."

"She doesn't know!" Her mother threw two imploring

hands up to heaven. "Her own grandmother almost burns to death and she doesn't know!"

"Mom, I want you to listen to me." Gemma's voice was unnaturally calm. "Nonna wasn't supposed to be alone. Frankie was supposed to be there. A traffic accident delayed her."

"YOU SHOULD NEVER HAVE LEFT HER ALONE FOR ONE MINUTE!" her mother shouted. "NEVER!"

"YOU THINK I DON'T KNOW THAT?" Gemma shouted back. "You think I don't feel like complete and UTTER SHIT about what happened? A loony was holding my part-timer hostage! I had to get to the store to HELP!"

Her mother looked confused. "Wha? A loony wha?"

"A tarot card student was upset that I wanted to stop teaching him, and he held my part-timer hostage. It was a big deal, with the police and a SWAT team and everything."

"This doesn't surprise me one bit." Her mother snorted. "You're loony yourself. It stands to reason you'd attract other loonies."

"*Cara,* I'm so sorry," Aunt Millie said, ignoring her sister. Her eyes searched Gemma's. "Is your part-timer all right?"

"She's fine. No one was hurt."

"Except your grandmother," her mother muttered.

"Ma, did you hear one word I said?" Gemma said sharply, voice rising. "There was a *hostage situation in my store.* My apartment burned down. You're not helping with your snide comments!"

"Amen," Aunt Millie said.

"And if it wasn't for me telling the firefighters she was in there, Nonna might well have died."

"What, so now you're the hero?" her mother shot back.

That was it. Last straw. "I'm done here." Quietly opening the door to her grandmother's room, Gemma stepped back inside to fetch her things. "The doctor who treated

Nonna was named Dr. Kaiser," she said to no one in particular as she reentered the hall. "The head nurse on duty is named Molly. Have a good night."

"Gemma, don't leave this way," Aunt Millie called after her as she strode down the hall.

But Gemma refused to look back.

CHAPTER

23

"Gemma!"

"Sean?"

They were in the hospital lobby: Gemma on her way out, Sean on his way in.

Gemma looked up at him, bewildered. "What are you doing here?"

"I told you I'd stop by to see how your grandmother was doing."

Gemma blinked. "But—how did you know I'd still be here?"

"Wild guess." He looked around. "I'm sure the coffee shop's closed, but there's a Starbucks up the street."

"Sounds good."

She followed him through the sliding glass doors, out into the spring night. The temperature had dropped considerably, but there was still something in the air—a tang, a feeling—that promised warmer days to come.

"How is she?" Sean asked.

"Severe smoke inhalation, but the doctor thinks she's going to be fine. She's tough as nails, my grandmother."

"Yeah, no kidding." He paused. "I want you to know I got to her as soon as I could."

Gemma was taken aback. "I know that, Sean. Please. We can't thank you enough."

He waved away her praise. "All part of the job. Thank God no one else was hurt."

Now at Starbucks, he held open the door for her. Taking in his faded jeans and crisp blue Oxford shirt, Gemma was reminded of how grubby she must look in comparison. She'd been in the same sweats all day. And she was still in her slippers. Maybe Sean wouldn't notice.

"Why don't you go grab a table and I'll order? What do you want?"

"Chai, please. Grande." Sean nodded and went to order while Gemma slid into a small table for two near the front window. The place was filled with student types, most of them tapping away on laptops. Gemma felt old.

"Cookie?"

She looked up to see Sean at the counter, holding up a giant chocolate chip cookie. Gemma nodded yes. Apart from a cup of coffee from a hospital vending machine, she hadn't put anything in her stomach all day, mostly because the thought of food made her sick. Now she was ravenous.

Settling back in her chair, she felt a wave of exhaustion roll over her. All she wanted to do was curl up in a ball and sleep. That, and turn back time. If she could restart the day, waiting for Frankie to arrive before she went down to the store . . . Inevitably, her gaze drifted to Sean. He looked as tired as she did, the faintest hint of stubble beginning on his face. *So handsome.*

"Here you are."

He handed her a cookie and a chai.

"Didn't want to share, huh?" Gemma said, noticing

he'd bought a cookie for himself as he sat down opposite her.

"Nope."

"Thank you, Sean."

"Don't mention it." He tore the plastic wrapping off the cookie with his teeth. "You look tired," he observed gently.

"So do you."

"Long day." He took a sip of coffee, not quite meeting her eyes. "We did salvage and overhaul on your apartment, Gemma."

"What's that, exactly?"

"It's where we go in and try to salvage any furniture we can, board up broken windows, rip open the floors and walls that still feel warm and douse them with water. It's also where we try to figure out what started the fire."

"Any ideas?" she asked quietly.

"As far as we can tell, it looks like wind might have blown your living room drapes into the flame of a candle sitting on the windowsill. They went right up. That started everything."

"You're sure it's a candle that did it?"

Sean nodded. "Pretty much." His thumb traced the edge of his coffee mug. "I remember you had a lot of candles in there."

"But none of them were lit." Her throat went tight. "My grandmother must have done it." She put her hand to her forehead, closing her eyes. *Candles.* How could she have left an Alzheimer's patient alone in a room full of candles? *What an idiot, what a—*

Warmth suddenly blanketed her free hand. She opened her eyes: Sean's big hand was covering hers, his blue eyes—eyes she once drowned in, eyes she could drown in still, if she let herself—studying her with concern.

"Don't beat yourself up, Gemma. Stuff like this happens all the time."

"Not to me it doesn't."

"What does that mean?"

"I'm the responsible one," Gemma said wearily. "Good old responsible Gemma." Her voice caught. "Well, not this time. God, did I screw up."

Sean squeezed her hand. "It's okay."

"It's not," Gemma whispered, blinking back tears. She would not cry. She had cried enough today, cried so much she got on her own bloody nerves, and there was no way she was going to lose it now. She clamped her jaw down tight, pain radiating all the way up to her earlobes. Then, like a beam of bright light cutting through fog, she became increasingly aware of sensation in another part of her body. It was Sean. He was caressing the top of her hand with his thumb.

"What happened?" he asked.

"It's a long story."

Sean smiled that crooked grin of his. "I'm not going anywhere."

"I'll give you the condensed version. I got a call from the police department. You know Julie, the girl who works for me?"

"Tattoo queen?"

Gemma laughed, surprising herself. "Yes. She was being held hostage by an ex–tarot student of mine."

Sean looked shocked. "Get outta here."

"I'm not kidding. Anyway, I called Frankie to come over and watch my grandmother. I know it was dumb to leave her, but she was sleeping, and I thought, even if she did wake up, it would only be a few minutes until Frankie arrived. Wrong. Frankie's cab got stuck behind an accident on Third Avenue. By the time she got to my apartment, you guys were already there."

"Jesus, Gemma." Sean sounded horrified.

"Not my best day," Gemma agreed.

She tore open the cookie wrapper and popped a giant piece in her mouth, washing it down with a shot of chai.

A year ago she would never have let these kinds of toxins into her body. Now she reveled in them. *Sugar? Fat? Bring 'em on, wake me up. Life's too short.* She took another huge bite. As she devoured the last of the cookie, she noticed Sean was watching her with an amused expression on his face. Embarrassed, Gemma halted midchew.

"What?"

"You haven't eaten all day, have you?"

Gemma blushed. "Does vending machine coffee count?"

"No way." He pushed his cookie toward her. "Finish it. I had dinner."

"Are you sure?" She hoped he wasn't just being polite. She wanted that cookie badly.

"Completely. It's yours."

"Thank you." She ducked her head self-consciously. "I seem to be saying that to you a lot."

"Better stop," said Sean, sipping his coffee. "I might get a swelled head."

I wouldn't mind. She was shocked she could even come up with such a filthy pun in her current state. It only proved what she'd known deep down for months: She'd never stopped being attracted to him. It would be nice if he felt the same way about her. Maybe some small part of him did? His hand still rested atop hers, though his thumb had ceased its comforting caress. More than likely he was just being kind. Even so, the weight of his hand on hers, the remembered brush of his fingertips across her knuckles from just a few moments before . . . lovely.

"Tell me about the store."

"Well, like I said, an ex-student of mine was annoyed I cut him loose, and he decided to make a statement by holding Julie hostage."

" 'Annoyed'? That's a nice way of putting it. Sounds like the guy's deranged."

"He's not," Gemma sighed, dabbing cookie crumbs from her mouth. "He just kind of lost it for a minute there, is all. He's sad, really."

An odd expression stole across Sean's face.

"What?"

"Is he skinny? With a long beard?"

"Yes," Gemma said cautiously.

"I saw him heading toward your store a couple of weeks ago. He looked fit to be tied."

A couple of weeks ago . . . that had to be the visit Julie was referring to, the one she forgot to mention. Gemma peered down at the paper napkin in her lap for a moment. "I just found out this morning that you stopped by the store that day, Sean. Julie forgot about it. If I'd known earlier, I certainly would have gotten in touch with you."

Shyness snuck into his eyes. "I was wondering why I hadn't heard from you."

"It's because I didn't know." He was making her feel shy, too. "Why did you stop by?"

"I wanted to set the record straight about JJ."

Gemma's heart plummeted. "Your girlfriend."

"*Not* my girlfriend," Sean corrected. "JJ was bird-sitting for me while I went upstate for the weekend to try to get my head screwed back on. She's a firefighter, too. She was looking to get away so it seemed like the perfect swap: She got to use my apartment for free, and I got a bird-sitter out of the deal. End of story." His eyes held hers. "She's my friend, Gemma. Nothing more."

Gemma could feel her heart beginning to climb back to its rightful place, beating a little faster. "I'm glad you told me that. Because I thought—"

"I know what you thought, which is why I wanted to set the record straight."

"Again," Gemma said humbly, "I thank you."

Sean looked relieved. Leaning over, he chastely kissed her cheek. "You're welcome."

Before Gemma had time to react, she caught sight of the barrista behind the counter staring at them imploringly. She looked around. Everyone else had left.

"I think he wants to close up."

Sean twisted around in his chair, told the kid to give them a minute, and turned back to chug his coffee.

"Where are you staying while they rebuild the apartment?"

"Michael and Theresa's."

"I'll give you a lift."

"It's in Brooklyn, Sean. Really, you've done enough already."

"Take me twenty minutes. C'mon."

"All right. Just let me . . ." Suddenly tears filled her eyes.

"What's wrong?" Sean asked, alarmed.

"I was going to say, 'Just let me stop by my apartment' to get a change of clothes, but I've got no apartment and so"—her jaw began throbbing—"I've got no change of clothes."

"You do have some clothes. We got some out during salvage. They don't smell too good, though. Smoky." He gulped the last of his coffee. "Got your altar out, too," he added.

Gemma was shocked. "You did?"

"Yup. But don't thank me again, or I might have to throw up."

Gemma laughed, wiping a tear from her eye as discreetly as she could. "Was your apartment okay? The birds?"

"Birds are fine, and the apartment is okay save for a little smoke damage that wafted up through your ceiling. Better than that incense you burn." He winked at her before moving around the table to pull out her chair for her. "Shall we?"

●   ●   ●

"Yo, if it's not the man of the hour."

It wasn't unusual for Sal to greet Sean like this when he walked into the firehouse. This time, though, he was waving a newspaper at him.

"That's me," Sean deadpanned, hanging up his denim jacket.

"You better believe it is." Ojeda stopped waving the paper and held it still for Sean to see. There, on the front cover of the *Sentinel,* was a picture of him carrying Gemma's grandmother down the ladder. Beneath it the headline declared: FIREFIGHTERS RESCUE ELDERLY WOMAN FROM DEADLY APARTMENT FIRE.

"I didn't know the press were there," Sean said, pouring himself some coffee.

"The press are everywhere," Ojeda said ominously. He studied the paper a moment. "This is good PR for us. Maybe Mayor Jackass will think twice about some of those budget cuts."

"Doubt it."

"I don't know, bud. I think it might help. It's certainly gonna help you: You might be the first firefighter at this house to get a commendation and a reprimand at the same time."

Sean laughed. "We'll see."

Captain McCloskey had already reprimanded him at the fire scene for disobeying his order and entering Gemma's apartment, but as Ojeda said, it was quickly followed by a slap on the back and a "Job well done" after he'd rescued Gemma's grandmother. Whether Sean received a formal commendation remained to be seen. Ultimately, it really didn't matter. What was important was he'd made the rescue, saved someone's life, and restored his faith in himself and how he performed his job.

Ojeda passed him the paper, and he skimmed the article. In general, he hated reading about fires he'd been involved with, mainly because the reporter inevitably got some small fact wrong and it set his teeth on edge. But seeing his picture on the cover made him think of Gemma.

He'd heard of people having bad days before, but hers had been "a doozy," as his mother liked to say. Yet there she'd been last night, still upright, still smiling, still able to laugh. A lesser soul would have been driven down to their knees from sheer despair. But not Gemma. It impressed him to no end.

She impressed him to no end.

He continued thumbing through the paper, eyes scanning page after page to see if there was any mention of the hostage situation at her store. He finally found a small, one-paragraph piece on it on page forty-nine, next to an article about how popular Buffalo chicken wings were in Manhattan. Sean clucked his tongue. He'd love to know how these editors decided what was newsworthy and what wasn't.

"Where's Leary?" he asked, folding up the paper.

"Weight room, I think." Ojeda's eyes were glued to the kitchen TV. He was watching *Live with Regis and Kelly*. "Why?"

"The bastard owes me twenty-five bucks, that's why. In case you didn't notice, the Blades won yesterday. They're gonna make the Playoffs."

"Good luck collecting," Ojeda said distractedly. "He's so tight you could bounce a quarter off his ass."

Sean chuckled to himself and went off to find Mike Leary.

Gemma awoke the next morning to the news that a family meeting was going to be held later that day at Michael and Theresa's. "Not a big one," Michael was quick to assure her. "Just me and Ter, Ant and Angie, you, your ma, Millie, Betty Anne—the people in the family who've actually been taking care of Nonna." Gemma didn't relish another round in the ring with her mother, but she supposed it was inevitable. Something had to be done.

She'd passed a comfortable night in Michael and Theresa's spare bedroom, an old jersey of Michael's serving as her nightgown. Sean had been right about her clothing smelling awful: Leaving Starbucks, they'd gone back to their building so she could see if there was anything she could salvage. There wasn't: Everything smelled acrid, sooty—there was no way she could wear any of her clothing without a trip to the dry cleaner first. Sean offered to take them to a dry cleaner the firefighters used. Now, sitting in Michael and Theresa's living room in a pair of Theresa's sweats and a shirt of Michael's whose sleeves she'd had to roll up repeatedly, she felt like a Victorian urchin. As soon as the family meeting was done, she was going shopping. That's what credit cards were for, after all.

Anthony and Angie arrived first, bearing cannolis and Miraglia Brothers coffee, the only brand Anthony would drink. Gemma caught the annoyance on Michael's face as he went to put up the pot, but he kept his mouth shut. Anthony and Michael: They'd fight over whether the sun was coming up the next morning if they could. Sometimes Gemma was glad to be an only child.

"How ya doin', toots?" Anthony's bear-sized hands massaged Gemma's shoulders, their brute strength an interesting contrast to the gentleness in his voice.

"I'm okay."

"Mikey told me about the store. Let me tell ya: If someone called me and said there was a hostage situation at Dante's, I would have left my own mother to fry, believe you me." Gemma winced. "No one blames you for anything, hon."

"Except my mother."

"She needs a swift kick in the ass, that one," Anthony replied, echoing one of Nonna's favorite expressions. With a final squeeze to Gemma's shoulders, he rejoined his wife

on Michael and Theresa's sleek black leather sofa. A fuss
was raised when Theresa entered the room with Domenica,
who was promptly passed from relative to relative for individual doses of adoration. All she was missing was a tiny
tiara.

The baby was a wonderful diversion, keeping everyone's blood from boiling over the fact that, as usual,
Gemma's mother and her sisters were late. When they arrived, Gemma shifted seats, making certain to sit as far
from her mother as possible.

"Did anyone call the hospital this morning to check on
my mother?" Gemma's mother asked, helping herself to a
cannoli from the platter on the coffee table before she even
had her coat off.

"'Anyone'?" Aunt Millie echoed sarcastically. "What,
your fingers are broken?"

"I called," Theresa informed them. "They're not allowed to give out information on the phone. All they'd say
was that she was resting comfortably. Michael and I are
going over there later this afternoon."

"What are we going to do about Nonna?" Michael
asked, getting right to the point. Gemma knew Michael:
He was in no mood for bickering, backbiting, or inter-
Dante politics.

Gemma's mother looked confused. "What do you
mean? Assuming she gets out of the hospital, I say we just
go back to the same routine."

"No." Gemma's voice was firm without being sharp,
and it drew all eyes to her. "I can't do it. I live in the city,
I work in the city, and this going back and forth to Brooklyn trying to take care of Nonna while trying to run my
store at the same time has practically killed me. I was nuts
to think I could do both. I can't."

Aunt Betty Anne looked distressed. "So, what do we
do?"

"Simple," Theresa said, passing Domenica to Aunt Millie, who was motioning vigorously for her turn with the little *principessa*. "Either we get a home health aide for a number of hours a week, or—"

"Don't say it," Gemma's mother cut in dramatically. "Don't even think it."

Gemma and Michael exchanged glances. "We're going to have to face the reality of it sometime," Michael told his aunt.

"Not yet," Aunt Millie insisted with a shudder, agreeing, for once, with her sister. She began bouncing the baby on her knee. "As long as we can keep her in her own house, I think that's what we should do."

"How are we going to do that without Gemma?" Gemma's mother asked plaintively. Her tone surprised Gemma; it seemed genuine, without rancor or accusation.

"Home health aide," Theresa repeated to no one in particular.

Aunt Betty Anne began nibbling on the cuticle of her left index finger. "That costs a lot of money."

"Not as much as you think," Michael said. "Medicare will take care of part of it. Between the rest of us, I'm sure we can cover the difference."

Aunt Millie stopped bouncing the baby and frowned. "Speak for yourself, Mr. Hotsy Totsy Hockey Star. Some of us are on a fixed income."

"That's right," Anthony snorted. "You're living on cat food in an SRO hotel. How could I forget?"

"Jesus Christ." Michael sighed his dismay. "For once can this family have a conversation without someone sticking in the knife and twisting it?"

"What knife?" Anthony implored. "What twist?"

"I'm sure I can kick in some money," Gemma said, though she wasn't really sure at all. "I just need to figure out things with the apartment . . . insurance things . . ."

"We'll kick in money," Theresa said.

"And us," Angie added.

"Sounds like the problem's solved," Michael said. "I'll look into how much it'll cost and get back to everyone." He reached for a cannoli. "Let's eat. At least that way our mouths will be full and we won't be able to attack each other."

"Wanna bet?" Anthony garbled as he bit into a cannoli. Everyone laughed.

Later, in the kitchen, Gemma was refilling her coffee cup when Michael sidled up to her.

"Can we talk?"

"Always."

"No way in hell are you chipping in for Nonna's home health aide," Michael informed her quietly. "You've got enough shit to worry about right now. Whatever your share is, I'll cover it."

"Michael—"

"No Michaels. Not only that, but you're living here rent-free until your apartment is rebuilt. Theresa and I have discussed this. You are forbidden to say no."

Gemma flushed. "I don't know what to say."

Michael put an arm around her shoulder. "You don't have to say anything. That's what family is for." He kissed the top of her head. "One more thing."

"There's more?" Gemma joked, trying to keep the tone light. One more act of generosity on Michael and Theresa's part and she'd start bawling.

"When's the last time you had a vacation?"

"About two years ago. When I went on safari in Kenya. Why?"

"Theresa and I were thinking. Why don't you take some time at our house on the shore? It's quiet, off-season . . . you could stay as long as you wanted. You deserve it, Gem. Seriously."

"What about the store, Michael?"

"You can't get away for a long weekend?"

Gemma crinkled her nose. "I suppose I could, but I feel bad springing it on Julie like that. She's been filling in for me left and right."

"Here's a novel idea, then: Give Julie a break, too. Take a week off and close the store completely. People do, you know."

"I know, I just . . ." Gemma looked down, overwhelmed by her cousin's care and concern. When she looked up, her mother was standing in the doorway.

"Gattina," she murmured uncertainly. "Can I talk to you?"

CHAPTER

24

Amazing, Gemma thought, how people can conduct entire conversations with their eyes. Hearing his aunt's request, Michael looked up from preparing himself a cup of coffee, locking gazes with Gemma. *We can tell her we're busy right now, or I can leave you alone with her. Your call.* Gemma stared back, half smiling her appreciation. *You can go. I'll be okay.*

Michael nodded, finished preparing his coffee, and ducked out of the kitchen.

Alone now with her mother, Gemma felt an immediate shift in atmosphere. It was as if Michael's presence had acted as a buffer. Now that he was gone, unresolved business hung heavily in the air. "What's up, Ma?" Gemma asked. This time, she was determined not to let the invocation of her childhood nickname through her off balance. Little *Gattina* was on guard.

Her mother looked down at her hands. "I wanted to tell you I'm sorry for slapping you last night. I was crazy with worry and I just didn't think."

Gemma's immediate impulse was to say, "It's okay," but she suppressed it. What her mother had done was *not* okay, and remembering the slap was like experiencing it all over again. She felt queasy inside, hot in the face. "That was really humiliating."

"I can imagine." Her mother looked up with sorrowful eyes. "I'm so, so sorry, *Gattina.* Forgive me."

"Please stop calling me *Gattina.* The last time you called me that you denied afterward ever saying it."

Her mother looked ashamed. "I'm not a very nice person sometimes."

"Tell me about it."

"But you forgive me?" her mother asked uneasily.

Gemma rolled her eyes. "Of course I forgive you."

Relief settled over her mother's features, a sentiment Gemma didn't dare share as she waited for the other shoe to drop. But maybe that wasn't going to happen this time? Her mother was actually looking at her with a repentant expression she wasn't sure she'd ever seen before.

"I was doing some thinking last night."

"About?"

"You."

"Yes?" Gemma tried hard not to sound defensive or skeptical. Her mother was really trying, really struggling to connect. The least Gemma could do was hear her out.

"I was thinking"—her mother coughed nervously— "that I've always been very hard on you. Even when you were a little girl, I expected you to be perfect."

Gemma waited, listening.

"I think it's because you were an only child. All my dreams were pinned on you, and what you did reflected back on me. That's the way I thought." She knit her hands together. "So, when you turned out to be different—different than I imagined you would be—different than I wanted you to be—two things came to my mind. One was 'What will people think of me?' The other was, 'God, how can I protect her?'" She raised her eyes to her daughter's. "Because you and I both know that people who march to the beat of their own drum have a hard time, Gemma."

This was extraordinary. Yes, that was the word. Extraordinary. Gemma took a second to savor it. She wanted to hear more—needed to hear more.

"I've known for years Nonna was a *stregh.*" Her mother laughed mirthlessly. "That was another thing that stuck in my craw: that you were more like her than me."

"But that's ridiculous!" Gemma blurted. "I mean, you're my mother, for God's sake. No one could replace you. Not even Nonna."

"How was I supposed to know that?" Her mother shrugged. "I was a stupid, frightened woman. Plus, it's not like you and I ever got along. At least not since you were a teenager."

"Ma—"

"Let me finish, Gemma." She paused at length. When she resumed, there was a quiver in her voice Gemma hadn't heard since her father died. "When I saw your grandmother in that hospital bed last night, I realized how close I came to losing her. My own mother. That hit me hard.

"But it also got me thinking. Did I really want to be someone with no mother and no daughter? And the answer is no." She reached up, cupping in her hand the very cheek she had slapped the night before. "This is hard for me, *cara.* Very hard. You know your mama isn't very good at talking about her feelings. But if I want you back, I realize I have to learn to talk to you. To listen to you. To see you. And I have to be willing to tell you what I really think."

Gemma swallowed. "What's that, Ma?"

"That you're a good girl. A good person, and that's what matters, not that you're a-a—"

"Witch?"

Her mother nodded, frowning. "Witch. Right. It doesn't

matter that you're a witch, or that you don't dress like other people, or that you believe in things I think are kooky, or any of that stuff. What matters is what's in your heart. And judging from all you've done for your Nonna, you have a very good heart, *Gattina*. And that makes me proud."

"Ma," Gemma whispered, laying her hand over her mother's.

"It's been hard on me all these years without your father. I've had to learn to do for myself. But you"—her eyes lit up with admiration—"you've been doing for yourself since the beginning. You were always so smart, so independent." She tugged affectionately on a lock of Gemma's hair. "My little girl."

Gemma's breath caught. "I love you, Mom."

"I love you, too." She wrapped her arms around Gemma. "Maybe we could try to get along better."

"Maybe," Gemma agreed cautiously. "I don't know if it will work."

"It has to work." Her mother squeezed her tight. "We can't afford to lose any more time."

"*Michael spiked your* coffee and you hallucinated the whole thing." Frankie held out her coffee mug for the ever-bustling Stavros to refill. "Either that or your mother's an alien pod."

"Cross my heart and hope to die," Gemma practically sang. "It's all true."

"Lordy," Frankie groused. "What the hell is the world coming to? You didn't hold hands afterward and sing 'We Are the World' or anything like that, did you?"

"I hate you," Gemma mouthed across the table.

"No, you don't," Frankie mouthed back. "Guess what I did yesterday?" she asked aloud.

"Got fitted for a prosthetic limb you don't need?"

"Gemma Dante, you're a one-woman laugh riot. No, I went to see Uther in the hospital."

"You did?"

Frankie nodded.

"And—?"

"Well, he's heavily medicated, so it's hard to tell what's really going on. But I'm pleased to tell you that our conversation, short though it was, was spoken entirely in modern English."

Gemma clapped. "Bravo!"

"Did you know his real name is Wendell?"

"No wonder he used his Craft name." Her appreciation of Frankie, always high, rose considerably. "That was a really nice thing you did."

Frankie shrugged dismissively. "I felt bad for the guy. Plus, he was the first man to ever make love to me wearing medieval combat gear. That has to count for something, right?"

"I suppose."

"So, I'm leaving New York," she abruptly declared.

Gemma steadied herself. "Fleeing the law?"

"Fleeing WROX. You know how sick I am of the nepotism. I interviewed for the program director's job at an adult alternative station up in Churchill, New York, and I think they're going to offer it to me."

"That's great," Gemma fibbed, feigning enthusiasm. No, wait. It was great if that's what Frankie wanted. It just didn't happen to be what Gemma wanted.

Frankie snorted. "Don't pretend you're happy. You look like I just snotted in your coffee."

"Metaphorically speaking, you did."

"It's only three hours from the city, Gem. We can see each other all the time."

"That's true." She peered at her best friend inquisitively. "You're sure about this? You sure this is what you want to do?"

Frankie bit into her bagel. "Sure as I'll ever be."

"What's in Churchill beside this radio station?"

"Two colleges where I can ogle hot, young undergrads, a food co-op, a Birkenstock store, a farmers' market, and lots of artistic types. Beyond that, I'm not sure."

"Sounds like the type of place I'd fit in."

"So, come visit," Frankie urged. "A lot."

"Program director," Gemma murmured aloud, trying to picture Frankie as a honcho. "I thought you loved being on the air?"

Excitement sprang into Frankie's eyes. "I'll still have an air shift—and it won't be overnight! I can join the land of the living and keep normal hours!"

"It's not Manhattan," Gemma warned. "You won't be able to order Chinese food in the middle of the night if you feel like it."

"I'll live."

"You won't be able to see the Blades play for free because of my connections."

"I'll live."

"You won't—"

"If it doesn't work out, I'll come straight back to New York, I promise." Frankie winked. "I'll just crash with you until I get another radio gig."

"I live with Michael and Theresa, remember?"

"Not forever. How's that going, by the way?"

"They think I need a vacation."

"They're right."

"Really?"

"Gemma, you've been through a shitload of stuff the past few weeks! Take some time off to recharge your batteries."

Gemma brightened. "I know: I'll help you move!"

"Ixnay," Frankie replied promptly. "Though I appreciate the offer, helping me move is not a *vacation.*"

"Fine. Make me go to the Jersey shore to relax."

"Sounds horrible."

"It is," Gemma smiled. "But before I go, there are a couple of things I need to take care of."

Gemma had never been inside a firehouse before. This struck her as odd, considering she'd lived in or near the city most of her life. Most life-long city dwellers had been taken on school tours as children—or at the very least felt compelled to stop by and offer thanks and a word of condolence after 9/11. But Gemma couldn't bring herself to do it; she didn't think she could bear to see the pain of these men up close. She'd made a donation to the New York Police and Fire Widows and Childrens' Benefit Fund, and left it at that.

Now, walking into Sean's firehouse carrying two bags full of pastry boxes loaded with Anthony's cannolis, she finally understood the impulse to go in person to thank the firefighters for their bravery. Were it not for them, her grandmother might well be dead, along with countless other tenants in her building. She knew the pastries were a small offering compared to the degree of gratitude she felt, but she also knew they'd like them. Sean had once told her food, especially desserts, were always welcome at the firehouse.

Walking into the open engine bay, she was immediately flagged down by a squat, muscular firefighter sitting in a small room off to the side, his feet up on a battered wooden desk. "Help you, ma'am?"

"Yes. I was wondering if Sean Kennealy was here? He rescued my grandmother the other day and I wanted to say thanks. Not just to him, but to everyone," she added nervously.

"He's here." The firefighter eagerly eyed the boxes. "What you got there?"

"Cannolis. Want one?"

"That would be great. Sean's in the kitchen with the rest of 'C' shift having lunch," he told her as Gemma extracted a cannoli from the top box and handed it to him. "The kitchen is through that door on the right. Go up the hall a bit and it's the first door on the left."

"Thank you."

"No—thank *you*." The fireman bit into a cannoli. "Sweet God, I've died and gone to heaven."

Gemma chuckled and started toward the kitchen, butterflies tumbling in her stomach. She knew why: It was not only the prospect of seeing Sean in his work environment, but the environment itself. The red brick walls decorated with awards, photos, and memorials, the gleaming red engines parked in their place, the rows of coats and boots neatly lined up, just waiting to be donned at a moment's notice—there was an unspoken vitality here. A sense that there was a place for everything and that everything was in its place. She supposed it had to be that way. Disorganization could waste precious time.

Raucous laughter and animated discussion floated down the corridor as she tentatively approached the kitchen. There was a smell of spice in the air, too. Curry? Cardamom? Very intriguing.

Arriving at the kitchen door, Gemma was prepared for the men inside to be surprised by her presence. What she was not prepared for was conversation to stop dead, eleven pairs of male eyes training on her simultaneously.

"Um . . ." Flummoxed, her gaze instinctually sought out Sean, the one person in the room she knew well. "I just wanted to stop by to thank you guys for saving my grandmother's life."

Sean stood. "Everyone, this is Gemma Dante. Hers was the apartment that burned last week—"

"The old lady candle fire?" someone asked.

Sean nodded. "Yeah."

"Close one," muttered a small man shoveling curry onto his plate as if it were his last meal.

Gemma held up the bags. "I brought you guys some cannolis to say thanks."

Mike Leary squinted at her. "Real cannolis or fake cannolis?"

"What the fuck, fake cannolis?" another firefighter chastised. "A cannoli is a cannoli is a cannoli." Tension blanketed the table. The firefighter looked around him, then slumped down in his seat. "Sorry about the language," he apologized to Gemma.

"There are real cannolis and fake cannolis," Leary insisted.

"These are real," Gemma said. "They're from Dante's in Brooklyn. Made fresh this morning."

Ten pairs of eyes lit up in recognition.

"You related to Michael Dante?" asked a firefighter who looked to be about eleven years old.

"He's my cousin."

"Frickin' Einstein over here," Leary cracked, smacking him affectionately on the back of the head. All the other firefighters laughed.

Ted the probie (for the life of her, Gemma couldn't remember his last name) held up a plate. "Want some lunch? It's good. Chicken curry."

"It'll clear your sinuses, that's for damn sure," said an older, graying firefighter with a cross pinned to his lapel.

"Clear your intestines, too," a growly voice muttered from the stove.

Gemma shook her head. "No, thank you. I really have to take off." She handed the bags of cannolis to Sean. "Thanks again for everything you did for my grandmother."

"She doin' okay?" Leary asked.

"Much better. She'll probably be out of the hospital in a week or two."

"That's good to hear," Sean said. He motioned toward the door. "Here, I'll walk you out."

"Bye," Gemma called over her shoulder.

"Bye now," they all called back, some of them waving. "Thank you!"

Well, that was weird." Gemma stood with Sean outside the firehouse. Maybe she was imagining it, but it seemed like every woman who walked by was checking him out. She was surprised to find herself bristling.

"What was weird?" Sean wanted to know.

"The way the room went completely silent when I walked in."

Sean rotated his palms upward. "What did you expect? You were a stranger. They lightened up once they heard who you were, didn't they?"

"True."

"So, how are you doing?" Sean asked, hands thrust deep in the front pockets of his pants. Gemma had never really noticed before, but he looked very handsome in his work "blues." In the past she'd been so preoccupied with worry for him she'd failed to appreciate what a dashing figure he could be—solid, formidable, striking.

"I'm okay."

"Is the loony safely locked up?"

"Don't call him that. It's not nice. He's being treated at Bellevue."

Sean rocked on his heels. "That's good."

Gemma's urge to wrap up the conversation was strong. It was so hard, standing here on the pavement with him, chatting away like good friends, when deep down inside, she still got a fluttery feeling every time she looked at him, followed swiftly by regret over their abysmal inability to meet each other halfway. It was time she faced the truth: She would probably never feel his mouth conquer hers again, or experience the utter tranquility of lying in his arms. And that hurt.

"I really should get going," she murmured.

"I guess."

"Thanks again for all you've done."

"No problem." Sean bunched his shoulders. "I guess I'll see you around."

"Actually, I'm going away for a week."

Sean looked interested. "Yeah?"

"A week at Michael's summer house on the Jersey shore."

Sean nodded appreciatively. "Nice. When you leaving?"

"Friday."

"Have a good time."

Gemma smiled. "I'll try."

"*What took you* so long?" Mike Leary called out as Sean reentered the kitchen. "She give you some special herbs to sprinkle on the cannolis?"

Bill Donnelly's eyes popped. "That's the New Age whackjob?"

"That's her," Sal Ojeda confirmed. "Too bad she couldn't read some tea leaves, see Grandma was in danger, and teleport herself over to rescue the old broad herself, huh?"

The guys laughed.

"Maybe she knows what crystals to use to get the freakin' LIRR to run on time," Joe Jefferson chimed in.

Disgusted, Sean peered around the table. "You guys are pricks, you know that?"

"What are you, on the rag?" Leary sniffed derisively. "We're just having some fun."

"She comes down here to thank us in person, she brings fresh-baked cannolis, and what do you do the minute she leaves? Start tearing her to shreds. Real nice."

"We tear everyone to shreds," Leary pointed out. "It's the American way."

"If people knew how we talked when we were alone, they'd think we were assholes, not heroes."

Leary looked amused. "Gather 'round, boys, young Kennealy here is developing a conscience. Let's watch it grow."

"Fuck you, Mike."

"No, fuck you, Sean. This is the way things are around here and you know it. No one's immune. Unless, of course, you still like her."

"What if I do?"

Leary's expression changed immediately from one of belligerence to support. "Well, in that case, we'll all back off, no ifs, ands, or buts. 'Cause no one—but no one—rags on a firefighter's woman. Right, boys?"

"That's right," rang an assortment of voices around the table.

"Okay, then," Sean declared with a defiant lift of the chin. "I still like her."

Leary cleared his throat as if preparing to make an important announcement. "In that case, gentlemen, Miss Gemma Dante is now off-limits as an object of derision, since young Sean here still has feelings about her." He turned to Sean. "Which prompts me to ask: Whatcha gonna do about it, bro?"

CHAPTER
25

If I were rich, Gemma mused as she strolled the moon-lit beach, *I would buy a little house here on the shore just like Michael and Theresa. I'd pay for full-time care for Nonna. I'd expand the store. And I'd get a really nice hybrid bike.*

She stopped, closing her eyes to better enjoy the night breeze as it gently caressed her face. *You are rich,* she reminded herself, breathing in the briny scent of the sea. Tough times made that hard to remember, but it was true. That's why she'd come outside tonight: to remind herself of all her blessings, to sit peacefully under the stars and take stock of her life, and most important of all, to relax.

Eyes still closed, she delighted in the absence of noise, so much a part of life in the city. She heard nothing but the wind, the tranquil lapping of waves, and her own slow, steady breathing. She opened her eyes, noticing the beach was deserted, which amazed her. It was a clear, beautiful night. Why weren't people out, delighting in the sand squishing between their toes, or reading the stars? Then she remembered: It was off-season. No wonder the only beach house with light coming from it was Michael's.

Feeling more relaxed that she had in weeks, she strolled a few more yards, walking right up to the edge of the shoreline. Water rushed over her bare feet, cold and invigorating. The full moon beamed down on her, its gentle rays of light stippling the surface of the water. Taking it all in, Gemma's heart swelled with appreciation. *Thank you for this beautiful, natural world.*

She backed up, out of the reach of the waves, heading toward a flat expanse of sand. Unclasping her cloak, she removed it and put it down before setting up eight wind-proof, glass-encased candles she'd brought with her in a small bag. She lit each candle carefully and set them in a wide, wide circle. They flickered tenaciously, their dancing brightness against the night sky hypnotic. Taking a deep, cleansing breath, she sat down in the center of the circle.

She thought about her family, and how lucky she was to have them, despite all the craziness. A warm feeling spread throughout her body as she recalled the sensation of finally being hugged by her mother, the soft skin of baby Domenica, and the rice paper thinness of her grandmother's hand.

She thought about her closest friends, and how much they enriched her life: Frankie, Theo, Miguel. Especially Frankie. Her best friend's freckled face popped into her mind, and Gemma smiled. Michael and Theresa came to mind as well. Yes, they were family, but they were also her friends. Good friends who were sheltering her, taking care of her. Just thinking about all of them made her feel tranquil.

Drawing her knees up, she wrapped her arms around them, rocking a little as she thought about poor Uther, and how troubled he was. She hoped he got the help he needed, and that he eventually found the right woman. There was someone for everyone. She firmly believed that. Somewhere out there in the big, wide world, there was a damsel who longed for a lover with a Norman helmet, a woman who dreamed of meeting her knight in shining armor at a reenactment. Gemma prayed Uther found her.

Thoughts of Uther inevitably led to thoughts of the Golden Bough. Now that she had a little distance, she could see how serious the hostage situation had truly been. She was glad nothing had happened to Julie. Julie: a little moody, but a hard worker. Without her uncomplaining flexibility, Gemma doubted she would ever have been able to manage juggling Nonna and the store all these months. Julie was getting a raise.

Finally, with a sweet twinge of melancholy, she thought about Sean. How handsome he was. How kind, sexy, romantic. How, if she were given the chance to do it all over again, she wouldn't worry so much about what he did for a living, nor would she fret so much about whether they fit into each other's worlds. If you loved someone, you made it work. You took chances, expanded your horizons. Compromised. You accepted them as they were.

"Is this a private party, or can anyone join?"

Gemma froze. Someone had been watching her! Serenity went on hold as she peered anxiously into the darkness.

"Who's there?"

She heard someone scrambling through the beach grass. Then, stepping out of the shadows, she saw him.

Sean.

He halted at the ring of candles, which were still blazing strong.

"What are you doing here?" Gemma asked, not unkindly, curling and uncurling her toes in the sand.

"I wanted to talk to you." His expression, illuminated in the flickering candlelight, was uneasy, almost pained. "Is that okay?"

"Of course it's okay." She tried to regain the feeling of

relaxation, but her heart had started fluttering. "Just let me blow these out and we can walk back—"

"Don't blow them out." Sean stepped into the circle. "Let's talk here. This is really nice."

"Okay." Gemma's heartbeat picked up even more momentum. "I'll get us something to sit on." She hurried out of the circle, returning with her cloak. She spread it on the ground like a blanket. "Here." Sitting down, she patted the ground beside her, doing her best to mask her nervousness. "Is this all right?"

He sat down right next to her, so close their shoulders practically touched. "This is great."

Gemma looked out at the ocean, his nearness unnerving her. "So," she began, shuddering involuntarily, "let's talk."

"Are you cold?" Without waiting for her answer, he shucked off his leather jacket, draping it over her shoulders.

"Thank you." Again Gemma drew her knees up to her chest and wrapped her arms around them tightly, this time waiting.

"Michael told me how to get here."

"I figured." Gemma glanced sideways, catching a quick glimpse of his profile in the candlelight. As had always been the case, she liked what she saw: the patrician curve of his nose, the strong solid jawline, tousled curls . . . "What did you tell him, if you don't mind me asking?"

"That I knew you were here and we needed to talk."

"And he didn't grill you? Or make you sign a slip of paper vowing you would never cause me undue pain and anguish?"

Sean chuckled. "He did sound kind of suspicious, but I could hear Theresa in the background shouting, 'Give him the damn directions,' so I assume, if he had any reservations about it, she more or less put the kibosh on them."

"That sounds like them." *Thank God for Theresa. Michael is so clueless sometimes!*

"So here you are."

"Here I am." His gaze turned toward the sea.

It was impossible not to contemplate the ocean while sitting on a beach, or at the very least to use it as a distraction while formulating exactly what you wanted to say. Gemma assumed that was what Sean was doing now, his blue eyes fixed on some invisible point on the dark horizon. She rocked a little, keeping warm, keeping faith. She knew Sean: When he was ready to talk, he'd talk.

Eventually, his gaze left the far distance and sought hers. "I want to apologize to you."

"For?"

Sean's laugh was self-deprecating. "Where do I even begin?"

"At the beginning?"

"There's a thought." He swallowed hard. "I'm sorry I asked you to hide your faith from my folks. And that I didn't really give your friends a chance. That was wrong of me."

"I'm sorry, too," Gemma said, dropping her eyes while her finger shyly traced a line back and forth in the sand.

"For what?" Sean sounded genuinely baffled.

Gemma looked back at him. "For turning into a basket case every time you walked out the door to work. That only added to your stress. I can see that now. I also feel badly that I was so pushy, trying to get you to talk about things you didn't want to talk about."

He cleared his throat. "People in a relationship share things. Good and bad. Obviously, given what I do, I would never want to give you the gory details of some of the stuff I have to deal with, but I could have given you more than I did. Shared more than I did."

Gemma's gaze turned sympathetic. "I hear that's not unusual in your line of work."

Sean grimaced. "No, it's not. But it's slowly changing. It has to. It doesn't do any of us any good to hold this shit inside, thinking we're not real men or real heroes if we let things get to us.

"When that kid almost died in the brownstone fire because of me, not only did I doubt myself, but I worried about you doubting me."

Gemma was puzzled. "What do you mean?"

"I didn't want you to think I was a failure, Gemma. Which is what I felt like. It was easier just to withdraw."

"Oh, Sean." Her heart traveled to his, wanting to heal it, ease his pain. "I could never think you were a failure."

Sean's mouth twisted into a rueful smile. "No, but you could think I was a taciturn jackass, hate what I do for a living, and make it clear that you didn't think much of my friends."

Gemma faced him head-on. "I won't lie: I do hate what you do for a living. It scares me. As for your friends," she continued tentatively, "I really don't know them well enough to judge them, and that's what I did. I'm sorry. I was wrong."

Sean shook his head. "It's okay. Look, I know they're not perfect. They can be a bunch of immature pricks: stubborn, opinionated, close-minded. But they're good people with big hearts." His voice rang with emotion. "Any one of them would give me the shirt off his back if I asked. We watch out and care for one another, not only because we have to, but because we want to. Our lives are in each other's hands."

Gemma was genuinely moved. "I never thought about it that way."

"It's the truth." His eyes searched hers, and the intensity she saw there had Gemma fighting for breath. Those blue, blue eyes, asking silent questions of her in the moonlight. The eyes she saw that night when casting her love spell. She broke eye contact.

"You okay?"

Gemma's voice was faint. "Fine."

"You sure?" Sean asked, wrapping a protective arm around her shoulders.

Gemma nodded. She felt she was losing her grip. How else to explain her belief that she could feel the heat of his hand through the leather jacket draped over her shoulders? Safe in the crook of his arm, his arm gripping her shoulders possessively, she felt herself weakening with desire. Was he feeling the same way?

"So now that we've both apologized, there's something else I wanted to say."

Perhaps he was.

"Yes?" Gemma managed, her heart reverberating in her chest like a drum.

His hand gently caressed her shoulder. "I know our timing has really been off. And I know you have a lot to deal with right now, what with the fire and your grandmother." His hand stopped, moving instead to tilt her chin up so she was looking directly into his eyes. "But I'd love it if you could see your way to giving me another chance, Gemma. Because I think we could make each other really happy."

Gemma closed her eyes a moment, letting the words sink in.

"I—I think so, too," she whispered haltingly. Joy had tied her tongue.

"You do?" Sean laughed in surprise. "I was ready to have to talk you into it."

Gemma opened her eyes. "Let me explain something to you." Taking his hand, she wove her fingers through his, holding on tight. "That fire was a wakeup call for me."

"How so?"

"It made me realize you can't put things off, because you never know what's going to happen. Until the fire, I thought: After things get settled with Nonna, then I'll start living my life. That's when I'll have time for a relationship, or be able to spend more time with friends, or take a class. But there's only now. Now and now and now and now." The urgency in her own voice made her look at him apprehensively. "Does that make sense? Or do I sound like some New Age, airy-fairy wacko?"

Lifting their twined hands, Sean brushed her knuckles against his lips with the lightest touch. "Darlin', you are some New Age, airy-fairy wacko. You are who you are, and make no apologies. I love that."

" 'You are who you are'; 'Now is now is now is now'—you and me, Kennealy, we're very deep thinkers. Ever notice that?"

Sean nodded solemnly, but there was playfulness in his eyes. "I have noticed. Very deep, very deep indeed. What should we do about it?"

"Hhmm, let me think." Gemma feigned the pose of *The Thinker*, putting her fist to her forehead in an outward display of profound thought. "I've got it." Smiling, she brought her lips to his, kissing him so lightly their mouths barely touched. "How was that?"

"Hhmm." Sean mulled this over. "Good, but I think I might be able to do better. Here, let me see if I can come up with a kiss worthy of two modern-day philosophers."

Bending his head, he took her mouth, gently at first, then more urgently. Gemma tasted desire, sweet as honey, pass between them. Her mind fogged as his strong arms snaked around her, pulling her to him, hard.

"I want you," he murmured as his mouth moved to the soft terrain of her throat.

"I want you, too," Gemma whispered, all surrender. The sky and sand seemed to be throbbing, every living thing pulsing with vitality as Sean pulled the leather jacket down from around her shoulders. His hands moved over her with the energy of a man who could not get enough. One moment his fingertips were grazing her spine; the next moment he was running his hand through her hair. Gemma didn't mind being the recipient of this random desire. It titillated her, making her ache with wonder as she tried to

figure out where, exactly, he would touch her next. The
only constant was his mouth: Hungry, possessive, it remained crushed against hers for the duration, the need for
words long passed, the submission to ardor the sole driving force.

Sean.

Had she just said his name out loud, or sighed it silently
to herself? Did it matter? They were falling in slow motion
now, limbs entwined as they stretched out on her cloak,
guided by the light of the stars and a hunger that could not,
would not, be denied. He buried his face in her neck, fingers fumbling wildly for the buttons of her blouse. When
the last three proved troublesome, he simply tore, sending
Gemma's heart racing. He could tear her clothing to shreds
if he wanted. She'd submit to anything, as long as it held
the promise of his body against her, inside her.

Nature got in on the act, tantalizing her as it sent a cool
breeze sailing across her heated flesh, making her shiver in
delight. Her breathing, so sure and deep while she took
stock of her life earlier, came now in excited, staccato
bursts as Sean lifted his head and with hungry eyes pushed
her lacy bra up over the top of her breasts. Then . . . nothing. Gemma lifted her head to be greeted by a devilish
smile. Relief seeped through her. He was only playing,
playing well as his mouth clamped down on the rosy crest
of her right nipple and he began to suckle. Gemma gasped,
feeling herself stiffen beneath his lips. He sucked . . . and
bit. Sucked . . . and bit, his teasing driving her to the edge
of madness as he played with pace. Fire spread between
her legs and she arched into the desire to open herself to
him like a flower. And still Sean kept torturing her, shifting his tantalizing ministrations to her left breast. Gemma
closed her eyes, dizzy. When she opened them, the sky was
reeling.

She was panting now, perhaps even moaning softly. She
wasn't sure. All she knew was that moon, sea, and stars

were bearing witness to this, the rebirth of their love. Clutching his head in her hands, she dragged him up her body, and with fevered lips devoured his mouth. Sean groaned, pressing his hips against hers. Gemma could feel his hard-on straining against his jeans, its pulse beating against her inner thigh, hot and insistent.

"Make love to me," Gemma whispered. "Now and now and now and now."

Sean laughed, lust and desire giving the sound an animal tinge. With an assuredness she found entrancing, his hands moved to her jeans, quickly unzipping them. Gemma lifted slightly to help him tug them, and her panties, down around her ankles, her impatience growing. She kicked free of her garments, waiting for Sean to strip quickly and plunge inside her. But he did nothing of the sort.

Instead, he slid down onto his stomach, and with a wicked gleam in his eye as he propped himself up on his elbows, gently parted her thighs. Then, with an animal growl, he put his mouth to her heat.

Gemma bucked as fire climbed through her, devouring reserve. Lap after lazy lap of his tongue against her had her screaming. Frenzied flicking had her twisting in delirium. The ocean roared its approval, but the crashing waves were no match for the pleasured screams escaping her own throat as wave after wave of velvet delight shook her, rendering her momentarily senseless. Now and now and now and now. Oh, Sean . . .

Clearly pleased with the results of his attention, Sean rose up, sitting back on his heels. Gemma felt desire stir anew as he stripped his T-shirt off over his head and threw it clear of their bodies, revealing the muscled torso beneath. Her gaze dropped lower; he was unfastening his belt now, unzipping his fly. Then he stood up, sloughing off the last of his clothing.

Adonis in moonlight. That's all Gemma could think as

she gazed upon every inch of his well-sculpted, perfectly proportioned, aroused form. Startling in its virility, it almost felt to Gemma as if she were seeing him for the first time. Her eyes raked his body appreciatively as she held out a languid hand to him.

Sean took it, dropping down between her thighs. His eyes burned with a need so deep it was almost startling in its intensity. Gemma tensed, waiting, and taking him into her hand, pulled him toward her. She wanted her legs wrapped around those velvet ribs. Wanted to feel him beating out his own pulse from deep within her.

"Open wider," Sean whispered. His voice was ragged, his blinding want clear. Gemma obeyed, guiding him toward her center. But Sean Kennealy was a man who needed no guiding. Barely slipping inside her, he sank into her by degrees, the sensation both maddening and intoxicating. Gemma tightened herself around him, game for a wanton ride. Sean withdrew slowly, then plunged back in hard, burying himself in her as deeply as he could. He did it again. And again. And again, until Gemma thought she would break apart. Then, just when she thought she couldn't take much more, he quickened the tempo, and drove her completely over the edge to madness.

Rhythm laid waste to her senses. Every thought, every dream, every desire she had was reduced to this, Sean's body joined to hers, the heat building and rolling over her in fearsome waves until finally it burst free, hurtling Gemma through space with an ecstatic scream that tore the veil of night. Sean had no choice but to respond in kind: Hips pumping wildly, he brought himself to a juddering climax, spilling himself into her with a fierceness and purity that left her speechless.

"I love you," he whispered as he sank down upon her. Then he wrapped her in his arms, buffering her from the breeze.

•   •   •

Seconds, minutes, hours passed. Gemma had lost all sense of time. All she knew was that the two of them were as closely entwined as two bodies could be, listening to each other's hearts beat back to normal. The temperature had dropped and the wind had picked up, but Gemma didn't care. In Sean's arms she felt neither heat nor cold. Only joy.

"Gemma?"

"Mmm?"

"Have you ever made love outside before this?"

"Does making out in the Poconos with Peregrine Phillips in ninth grade count?"

"No." Sean lifted his head. "Peregrine? You slipped tongue to a guy named Peregrine?"

Gemma playfully pinched his arm and he settled back down, head resting on the cradle of her breast.

"Gemma?"

"Mmm?"

"I've got sand in cracks and crevices I didn't even know I had."

Gemma laughed loudly. "Me, too. Maybe we should go back to Michael's and shower."

"Sounds good to me," he agreed, planting a kiss on the tip of her nose.

"Sean, I have to tell you something." She wasn't sure why, but the spell she'd cast so long ago felt like a secret between them, one it was time to divulge.

"What's that?" he asked, nibbling her fingertips.

"Right before I met you, I cast a love spell."

Sean stopped nibbling.

"In it, I saw a man's eyes quite clearly. They were yours, Sean. I swear it."

Sean considered this. "I believe you," he finally said. "I believe in fate."

"Good, because you're mine."

He smiled at her, that slow, boyish grin that had caused

her heart to seize up in her chest the first time she saw him
do it. "I know."

Slowly, almost reluctantly, they rose, putting their
clothing back on. Donning her cape, Gemma walked
around the wide circle, extinguishing the candles one by
one. The moon would see them home.

"Shall we?" Sean asked, holding out his hand to her.

Gemma nodded, taking his hand. Together they started
up the beach, walking toward their future.

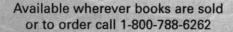

BODY CHECK

Deirdre Martin

0-515-13489-9

She's going to
need a power play
to win this hockey
star's heart.

"Deirdre Martin
aims for the net
and scores."
—*Romance Reader*
(4 Hearts)